CAP TYLER

C.J. PETIT

TABLE OF CONTENTS

Printed in the United States of America

First Printing, 2021

ISBN: 9798729322824

PROLOGUE

September 10, 1877
Fifty-Four Miles Southwest of Bismarck
Dakota Territory

Heinrich burst into the sod house, grabbed his rifle from the wall and in his native German, he shouted, “Take the children to the shelter! Now!”

Erna had been darning a hole in her husband’s sock when he flew through the door and immediately dropped her work. Without saying a word, she took Gustav and Elsa’s hands and rushed to the back of the room and pulled open the trap door.

Gustav shouted, “What’s wrong, Mama?”

Erna simply said, “You and Elsa must be quiet,” then after Gustav had dropped into the hole, she lowered little Elsa into her six-year-old brother’s arms. She knew she had little time, so she hurriedly began gathering things that she knew she’d need.

She first lowered the axe and the shovel to Gustav then hurriedly walked to the shelf and began pulling down clothes and blankets then dumping them into the small shelter. After giving the wooden bucket to her son, she slowly lowered the large cauldron into the hole. Finally, she gathered enough preserves for at least a day and after handing them to Gustav, she carefully lowered herself into the hole and closed the wooden cover over them.

She hugged her children close as Elsa began to weep. As long as she didn't wail, Erna let her cry. She was grateful for the darkness that hid her own terror from her youngsters. She was so rushed to get her children to safety that she'd neglected to put the locking bar in place. Each time they'd practiced for this eventuality, her husband had told her to drop the heavy wooden bar into the iron holders but never had her actually do it. Now it meant that if the Sioux got past her husband, they'd be able to enter the house by just opening the door.

Wilhelm had been out near the creek gathering wood from the small forest when he'd heard gunfire in the distance. He'd turned to the east and spotted a large cloud of smoke billowing from the Hartmann farm about five miles away. He had no doubt of the cause for either the shooting or the smoke. The Sioux who had set the fire would soon be heading his way. He had dropped the bucket and quickly mounted his mule and raced back to the house.

After grabbing his rifle and ammunition, he closed the door and set up for their arrival. He saw the large war party coming just five minutes after warning Erna. The attack wasn't as big a surprise as it normally would have been. Yesterday, he'd seen a company of cavalry from Fort Lincoln riding past his farm on the other side of Buck Creek. They had ridden west, and Wilhelm assumed that they learned of another Indian raid.

Now he had to face his own attack. He had counted the war party and knew he had to make every shot count. If there had only been five or six, he could afford to waste a shot, but there were twelve coming from the Hartmann farm. The distant gunfire had stopped shortly after it had begun, so he didn't know if any of the large family had survived. The Hartmanns had more rifles and shooters, so it was possible that the Sioux had just set the fires before they had been driven off. He knew he wasn't going to be that fortunate.

When he'd started tilling his land more than four years ago, the Northern Pacific had reached Bismarck, and everyone expected the railroad would already be across the Dakota-Montana border by now.

Then the Great Panic descended on the world and stopped everything. Not one mile of track had been laid since then and his wheat crops had to be taken by wagon to Bismarck. It limited how much he could grow and if his adopted country and the rest of the world weren't in worse shape, he would have believed that God was punishing him.

He had explained to Erna that if the Sioux attacked, she was to take the children into their tiny sanctuary and remain there no matter what happened. He knew that their sod house couldn't burn, but the Lakota would set his crop and wagon ablaze then steal their two mules. If they did manage to break down the door despite the locking bar, he prayed that they wouldn't find his wife and children.

Wilhelm knew his only chance to survive was if the Indians didn't all have rifles. But soon after spotting the war party, he realized that each of the warriors had an army-issued Sharps carbine.

By the time Wilhelm realized that he was heavily outgunned, he knew he was going to die but couldn't show fear in the face of the attacking Sioux. He cocked his rifle and stood his ground as the Lakota screamed their war cries.

———

Erna hugged her children tightly in the darkness as she heard the sound of the Indian war cries mixed with the sharp cracks of rifle fire. The volume of gunfire told her that Wilhelm wasn't going to survive. It was when the front door burst open that she realized her mistake. As she heard them loudly ransacking the house above her head, she only hoped that they didn't stay long enough to find her sanctuary.

CHAPTER 1

September 14, 1877
Sixty-Eight Miles Southwest of Bismarck
Dakota Territory

Cap pulled Joe to a stop and stared at the carnage before him. He'd seen the mass of buzzards circling overhead an hour earlier and their sheer number told him what to expect. It still almost caused him to wretch but what bothered him even more than the sight of the dozens of bodies strewn across the prairie was what he didn't see. It looked like an entire company of soldiers, but there were no weapons on the ground nor were there any horses wandering nearby. He estimated that the engagement, if one could call it that, had happened less than a week ago. The army should have dispatched more men to find their missing company by now. But depending on the massacred company's mission, they might not even be missed yet. After the Custer disaster last summer, Fort Abraham Lincoln was probably still well undermanned.

He decided he'd head to the fort to let them know of their loss in men and weapons. But the possibility of running into a large band of heavily armed and angry Lakota would make it a dangerous journey. He was beyond well-armed himself but if a band of forty Sioux carrying rifles decided that he was worth the risk, he wouldn't last long.

Cap nudged Joe into a trot and angled him well to the south of the killing ground. He had Buck Creek just to the north as he left the horrific sight behind him.

He had been a surveyor on one of the lead crews when the Northern Pacific ceased operations in '73. The army had effectively deserted them, and less than a week later, most of his crew had been killed by a large Blackfoot war party north of the Yellowstone River in Montana Territory. He was one of only three survivors and the only one who hadn't been wounded. He was able to bring the other two to Fort Sarpy but was without a job and on his own in the middle of nowhere. The only advantage to being the only functional survivor of that attack was that he left Fort Sarpy with four rifles and six pistols. Since then, his arsenal had shrunk but had been improved by trading and circumstance. He had become a bounty hunter of sorts. A bounty hunter who was never paid.

He now wore two Remington pistols and had two Colt Model 1873s in his first pack mule's panniers. The mule also carried two Winchester 73s. He had kept the pistols because they all used the same ammunition as the Winchesters. On his left scabbard, he had a Sharps rifle with a thirty-four-inch barrel. It had been brought to the Great Plains by an amateur buffalo hunter from Chicago two years ago. They had run afoul of the Sioux and were in dire shape when Cap attacked the Lakota from behind, driving them away. The man was so grateful he had given the powerful rifle to Cap along with four boxes of the massive .45-100 cartridges. He rarely used the big gun as the cartridges were almost impossible to come by.

But one of those rare times he had used it had providentially provided him with the Winchester '76 Joe carried on his right scabbard. In April, as Cap headed to the Black Hills, he had been spotted by a Cheyenne hunting party who must have wanted his weapons. They all had Winchesters and believed that they had an advantage. Cap had set up with the Sharps and when they were more than three hundred yards out, he'd blown one of them off his horse. They suddenly realized that it was the lone white man who had the advantage. But the others were startled by his long-range shot, and as they decided whether to continue the attack, he'd reloaded and shot another warrior. There were only four left and they quickly rode back to their village for reinforcements. After they'd gone, Cap had recovered their Winchesters and was stunned to find that one of them had an almost new Winchester '76. It hadn't found any of the .45-75 Winchester ammunition until he reached Deadwood, but he was pleased to have the added punch and range.

Over the past four years, he had many confrontations with those tribes who would rather fight than trade. His ability to win those confrontations while not suffering a single shot or knife wound had gained him a reputation. He was called 'Mule Killer' by most of the warrior tribes. The Mule Killer nickname was well earned as he always rode his mule, Joe, and for the first year, just had one pack mule, Jasper. As he accumulated more gear, he bought a second pack mule he christened Jed. Jed was much different than Joe or Jasper. While he would have preferred a more subtle coat among his mules, Jed was easily spotted. But Cap still bought him because he was a good animal.

He stuck with the J names but refused to call one Jack because they were already jacks. He preferred mules because they were usually more durable than most horses and needed less water. They were every bit as fast as most horses as well. Other than their rather homely appearance, he never understood why they were so disparaged by most men. He never noticed any amount of stubbornness in any of them, either.

The reason he had decided to head for Deadwood in the Black Hills wasn't the same as most men. He wasn't about to prospect for gold. He simply needed more supplies and thought he might add to his cash reserves by playing some poker. By the time he left a week ago, he had taken advantage of those who had found their gold by enjoying a long stretch of good fortune at the poker table. He had significantly added to his purse and his gun collection before he left the lawless town of Deadwood while he still was able to draw a breath.

In August, when he was preparing to leave Deadwood anyway, he'd heard that the Northern Pacific was coming out of bankruptcy and would soon be laying track again. He planned to go to Bismarck and talk to the man in charge about being rehired as a surveyor. He didn't really need the money but after being on his own for so long and then spending those few months with the unruly Deadwood crowd, Cap wanted to enjoy the company of normal men.

———

After he'd ridden east for another hour and ten minutes, he spotted the burnt fields of a small farm on the horizon. The small sod house was still standing and there was a pile of ash nearby that must have been a wagon in its past life. He was sure that no one was alive and wasn't about to search the house to discover more mutilated bodies.

Thirty minutes later, he approached the sod house and suddenly pulled Joe to a stop when he noticed a recently dug grave. Initially, he suspected that the army had visited the farm and buried the bodies in one grave before they left. But as he examined the ground surrounding the mound of dirt, he didn't see any shod hoofprints anywhere. Besides, the timing wasn't right. If that massacred cavalry company had been dispatched because of this raid, the grave wouldn't have been so fresh.

Then Cap believed that there must have been survivors of the attack and after burying the victims, they had gone to either a neighboring farm or to Bismarck. He was about to tap Joe's flanks to get him moving again when he heard what sounded like a child's muffled cry. He turned to the house and continued to listen. He knew the sound wasn't made by any of the critters that called the Great Plains home. Maybe someone has survived the attack after all.

After another minute he heard it again, so he stepped down and walked toward the open front door. He didn't enter but was surprised to see that the house had a wooden floor which was a rarity for sod houses and huts. The furniture had been destroyed, but he noticed that the wood was stacked in the corner near the fireplace. Then he spotted a cauldron nearby and other kitchen utensils. They were items that the Sioux would never leave behind. But the final confirmation that someone had survived were the two buckets of water on the floor near the cauldron.

He loudly said, "My name is Cap Tyler and it's safe to come out now."

When Erna had seen the rider appear on the western horizon, she believed that he might be coming to finish what the Indians had started and had quickly returned to their hidden shelter with her children. Even when she heard him call, she wasn't sure if he intended to help them. But she and her children were horribly hungry. Despite rationing the food she'd saved, it had only lasted two days. If she didn't take the risk of leaving the protection of their shelter, she would have to hope that the army might arrive before they starved.

As Cap watched, a wooden square about three feet wide slowly opened and a blonde head with fearful blue eyes rose from the small shelter. The woman lifted a little girl onto the floor then hoisted an older, but still young boy out of the hole before she clambered out and took her children's hands.

She didn't approach him but asked, "Hast du etwas zu essen?"

Cap hadn't spoken German in more than fifteen years and had never mastered the difficult tongue even then.

So, he asked, "Do you speak English, ma'am?"

Erna shrugged then said, "Little."

Cap smiled then said, "My German's a bit rusty, but I probably didn't need to figure out what you were asking even if you were speaking Chinese."

He hadn't expected her to understand his attempt at humor. It was just a nudge to make his smile appear more genuine.

Then, in his sorry German, he slowly said, "I have more than enough to share. If you'll bring your children along, I'll give you whatever you need."

He then turned and walked to Jasper to take down one of his two food panniers.

Erna led her children across the wooden floor then stepped onto the ground in front of her house before she stopped and watched the stranger. She looked at his three mules and was troubled by the number of guns she saw. He was wearing two pistols and she counted four rifles. If he hadn't smiled at her and spoken a barely understandable

German, she would have run back inside and thrown the locking bar in place.

Cap unstrapped the pannier from Jasper and lowered it to the ground.

Erna continued to stare and evaluate the man as he removed two tin plates, set them on the ground and placed smoked meat onto each one. She tightly held her children's hands as she began walking closer to the pack mule.

Cap set a spoon on each plate then removed a tin of beans. He was using his pocket knife to open it but left the plates on the ground when he noticed the woman and her children step closer.

He stopped opening the tin and said, "Ma'am, I only have two plates, so you can let your children eat the meat with their hands while I finish opening the tins."

Erna smiled at his mangled German but understood what he meant, so she told Gustave and Elsa to take a piece of meat. Her children quickly snatched a chunk of the smoked venison and began to rip at the meat. If they'd eaten that way on any other day, she would have scolded them. But she was so incredibly relieved that they wouldn't starve that she didn't even take any meat for herself as she watched them devour their bounty.

Cap noticed that she wasn't eating and didn't understand why, but soon finished opening the can of beans and emptied half onto each plate.

He set the empty tin aside and said, "Ma'am, you can eat now."

Erna pulled her eyes away from her children then said, "Thank you," before she bent over and picked up one of the plates.

She took the spoon and slowly began to take bites of the beans. She would have preferred to eat the venison but didn't want to appear to be uncivilized and have to use her teeth to pull apart the large piece of smoked meat.

Cap had been surprised when she had not only skipped the tastier and more nutritious meat but was eating the beans so slowly. He knew she had to be famished and assumed that she would probably prefer using a fork and knife.

He then dropped to his heels and rummaged through the pannier until he found one of his two forks. While he didn't have any knives that would pass for cutlery, he did have several much larger and sharper knives that would serve the purpose. With the fork in his left hand, he walked around Jasper and opened another pannier. He lifted one of the smaller knives from the pack then slid it out of its sheath before walking back to the woman. He smiled and wordlessly handed her the fork and knife.

Erna was surprised but grateful when she accepted them but had to sit on the ground to be able to cut her meat. By then, Gustave had eaten all of his venison and Elsa was almost finished. He then picked up the other plate of beans and began sharing it with his little sister.

As Cap watched them eat, he was already thinking about what she would expect of him. He hoped she had family in the area but would be surprised if she had. She and her husband had probably emigrated from Germany with their young children in search of a better life. Before the depression had driven the Northern Pacific and many other railroads, banks and other businesses into bankruptcy, the Northern Pacific had agents in Germany and Scandinavia offering land at rock bottom prices. They needed the money to continue laying track but just as the company's rails reached the Missouri River at Bismarck, even that income hadn't been enough to keep them solvent.

The town had been called Missouri Crossing before the Northern Pacific arrived in '73. The company had changed the name to Bismarck to honor the German statesman and to inspire more Germans to buy the land the government had given them in exchange for building the railroad. The railroad's agents were salesmen and probably painted a picture of paradise. He wondered how many had left their homeland not knowing the dangers that awaited them.

This German family had probably been offered the land along the railroad's surveyed route at an even lower price than the acreage along the operating tracks east of Bismarck. They had also been sold the land at the southern end of the railroad's land grant. He knew the tracks would be laid just north of the Heart River and it was more than five miles north of their farm. Hopefully, they were able to purchase the land cheaply.

They must have begun plowing the plains near Buck Creek expecting the trains would soon arrive and offer them a method of transporting their grain. With the railroad's failure, they were limited in their ability to plant and harvest but had no other options available to them. Now the Sioux had removed their ability to farm at all, much less wait for the railroad to arrive. This year's harvest had been turned to ash and with it the seed grain for next year's planting.

Cap had no personal animosity toward the Lakota or any other tribe. The Lakota had taken this land from the Cheyenne, who didn't simply thank them and leave. He didn't know which earlier tribe the Cheyenne had pushed off the Plains. The Cheyenne he'd met implied that they had been the most powerful tribe until the Lakota arrived, but even they admitted that the Blackfeet were more ferocious. The Sioux were just more numerous and never seemed to be satisfied with the vast lands their different tribes occupied. Cap considered the tribes to be no different than the Europeans or any other collected group of people in the world. They just used different weapons and tactics than the European or American armies.

But he did take offense when they attacked folks who weren't a threat. He understood their anger at the railroad and the army sent to protect the men who were surveying the land and laying the rails. While they may have viewed the settlers as a harbinger of what was to come, Cap felt should have understood that farming a quarter section of land wouldn't affect them at all.

Erna had finished her smoked venison and half of the beans before she began spooning the rest of the beans to Elsa. She knew that the man was watching her and was already hoping that he'd stay. The Hartmann family were their only neighbors within ten miles. She'd seen smoke still drifting into the sky from their farm when she'd finally emerged from the safety of their shelter. But after a day without any of them coming to see if their neighbors were still alive, she suspected that they were all dead. She wasn't about to take her children to their farm and let them witness the horror. It had been bad enough when she'd found Wilhelm.

Adolphe and Berta Hartmann had two adult sons who had already married and two teenaged girls. They had bought four quarter sections, so it was a much larger farm. They had more guns to protect them as well. But she had been in their houses and knew that they didn't have wooden floors. Nor did any of them have hidden shelters. They had depended on their number of men and guns instead. They were probably lying dead on their farm, so she and her children were alone. The man who had saved them was now her only chance to keep her children alive.

After Elsa had taken her last bite, Erna set the spoon on the plate then took Gustave's empty plate from his hands and approached the man to begin a conversation in her native tongue.

She handed them to Cap and said, "Thank you."

He set the plates down on the ground then asked, "Did the Sioux kill your husband?"

Erna nodded then pointed to the grave and said, "I buried him but not very deep."

"Do you have family?"

"No. No one. We have nothing."

Cap then said, "I can take you to Bismarck. A church charity will take care of you and your children."

Erna flared as she shouted, "This is my land now! I will stay here! I am not leaving to accept charity!"

Cap was startled by her harsh refusal and was only able to intercept and interpret about half of her rushed German.

As much as he wanted to help, Cap couldn't avoid feeling as if he'd been caught in a trap. He'd lived on his own for so long now that he found it difficult to conceive of being responsible for anyone else. But if he was going to help her and her children, he had to set that awkward sensation aside.

He finally said, "I think I understand. You wish to stay. But you are unprotected now. I can take you to Bismarck where you can find a new husband then return to your farm."

Erna stared at him. *Did he really just say that he'd take her to Bismarck where he would become her new husband? She had just buried Wilhelm and he was already planning to take his place?* If she hadn't been in such desperate straits, she would have slapped him for even making such a suggestion. But he had all those guns to keep her and her children safe and could provide for them as well.

Cap assumed that she was thinking about his suggestion. She was still a young, pretty woman, so she shouldn't have trouble finding a German-speaking husband in Bismarck. Maybe she'd find one who would convince her to stay in town rather than return to her burned out farm. He didn't realize that she was evaluating him as a prospective mate.

Erna looked at her children who were both touching his saddled mule's nose then turned and said, "You must wait for me to mourn for Wilhelm. Until October."

Cap shook his head as he said, "I can't wait that long. I want to go to Bismarck to join a survey crew."

He knew that he'd probably butchered the words for survey, but hoped she'd understand why he had to leave.

Erna understood something very different than what he'd meant. She correctly interpreted the part about not wanting to wait and going to Bismarck, but thought he'd finished by saying he wanted to join with her. She may have been desperate, but this was going too far.

She stopped short of slapping him again, but glared as she exclaimed, "I am a good woman and cannot do such a thing!"

Cap was startled for a second time but at least understood what she'd said. Yet he hadn't realized which part of their miscommunication that had driven her angry response. It was just apparent to him that she wasn't about to leave the farm. Now he was facing a dilemma. He couldn't stay nor could he leave her and her children without food or protection.

He displayed his palms and using the simplest German words possible, he said, "I am sure you are a good woman. I will give you food and guns. Then I will leave."

Erna was far from placated after his insult but if he left, she'd still be in danger. The Indians had taken her husband's heavy rifle and she had never fired it anyway. Even if he showed her how to use one of his pistols, it wouldn't provide enough protection. If he left her all of his food, it might last a month, or maybe two if she scrimped. Then the cold weather would descend on them and she knew they'd never survive to see the new year.

She glanced at her children who were now staring at her and knew she had no choice. As she made her decision, she felt as if she'd already been violated.

"No. You must stay to help me and my children. I will be your wife."

Cap stared at her and wondered how she had arrived at that notion. After her almost violent refusal of his offer to take her to Bismarck, he expected her to demand that he leave. Now he began to suspect that he might have improperly used his seldom used German vocabulary. He had to correct the confusion quickly.

He slowly said, "I didn't speak well. I am not a farmer. I asked if you wished to go to Bismarck to find a German farmer husband."

Erna flushed when she realized their failed communication. While she no longer was ashamed for having to offer herself, she still had no intention of leaving her farm. But she was actually pleased that the man offered to take her to Bismarck to find a husband. It made her feel safer.

She replied, "No. I will not leave. The men in Bismarck do not interest me."

Cap wasn't sure he understood what she meant after she said that she wasn't going to leave. Between his poor German and her almost complete lack of English, they weren't communicating well. He'd had more productive dialogues with the tribes using sign language. He decided to start the entire conversation over.

He pointed to himself and said, “I am Cap Tyler.”

Erna didn’t know why he had decided to introduce himself, but said, “I am Erna Braun. My son is Gustave, and my daughter is Elsa.”

Cap smiled at the children and in English, he said, “Hello, Gustave. Hello, Elsa.”

They smiled and said, “Hello.”

After the introductions, he smiled at Erna and offered his hand as he said, “Hello, Erna.”

Erna didn’t smile, but shook his hand and replied, “Hello.”

“I will stay to help. But we must learn to talk better.”

Erna nodded then said, “Yes. You can teach me and my children English.”

“I will help while I remain here. I need to clear my mules now.”

Erna didn’t say anything more as she took Gustave and Elsa’s hands and returned to her house.

Cap still planned to go to Bismarck and see if he could be hired as a surveyor again but knew that they probably wouldn't even begin operations until next spring. By then, he might have found Erna Braun a husband. If he could teach her enough English by the time he left, he might not have to find a German speaker for her, either. He would have to be a farmer because he didn't believe Mrs. Braun would ever leave the land she and her husband had purchased in Germany.

Erna walked with her children to the middle of the room then sat on the floor with her children. She explained that Mister Tyler would be staying to help them and teach them English, too.

Six-year-old Gustave asked, "Is he going to be our new papa?"

"I don't know. For now, we just need thank God for sending Mister Tyler to us."

Four-year-old Elsa whispered, "I miss papa."

Erna kissed her on her forehead before she said, "So, do I. But we need Mister Tyler. You both need to know that I will do anything for you. Do you understand?"

They both nodded, but Erna didn't believe they understood what she meant at all. She wasn't about to provide details of the lengths she would go to keep her children safe and healthy.

Before he began clearing Joe of his tack, Cap removed his large tarp from Jed and spread it on the ground. He laid his Winchesters and Sharps onto the tarp then began unsaddling Joe.

When Joe was naked, he began taking the packs from Jasper. As he dropped them to the ground, he calculated how long his food would last now that he had four mouths to feed. He always kept enough to last him at least a month, but with two adults and two growing children, he doubted if it would last two weeks. He'd have to make a trip to Bismarck or Fort Lincoln for enough supplies to get them through the winter. Nearby Buck Creek attracted enough game to provide meat, but the unpredictable nature of hunting made the long ride to Bismarck or the fort a necessity.

At least he wouldn't have to rely on buffalo chips for fuel. There were a reasonable number of trees along Buck Creek. He understood why the family wouldn't have used them to build a log cabin, at least not when they first arrived. A sod house is actually much faster to build and if the Sioux arrived, they wouldn't be able to burn it down.

He imagined that Mister Braun had planned to build a proper house when the Northern Pacific tracks arrived, and lumber could be shipped in from the east. The rails would be laid on the other side of the Heart River, but that was still a lot closer than Bismarck. Cap knew that the railroad would be building watering stations along the river every fifty miles or so, and Bismarck was just about that distance away. If Mister Braun understood that, then he had selected a good location. It was a tragedy that he'd never get to build the nicer home for his family.

Once the packs from both mules were on the ground, Cap left his tent, saddlebags and his personal panniers then began lugging the more domestic canvas sacks into the house.

Erna and the children didn't stand when he entered but just watched as he dropped the first one on the floor next to the doorway,

He said, "This one has food," then turned and left the house to retrieve the next one.

When he dropped the second one on the floor, he said, "There are things for your home in this one and more food."

Erna nodded then stood with her children. As Cap left the house, she began emptying the panniers.

Cap made three more trips carrying in the packs with anything that he thought she needed. He still had four more panniers outside that were for his use as he wasn't about to stay in her house. On his last trip, he carried his two bedrolls from Jed and set them on the floor.

He said, "They are softer than the hard floor," then left to start setting up his own sleeping arrangements.

It was getting close to sunset when he dragged his packs to the east side of the house as the winds predominately came from the northwest. There was enough grass and unburned stalks of wheat for his mules, and they would be able to walk to the river when they needed to drink. He wasn't worried that they might wander away. If he needed them to return, he'd just whistle. They were smart critters.

While he was pitching his larger tent, Erna had finished emptying the last of the panniers and smiled at her children.

"We have a lot of food now. What would you like for supper?"

Gustave looked at his sister and waited for her to make her request. He was very fond of Elsa.

Elsa quickly asked, "Is that mettwurst, Mama?"

Erna picked up the sausages and replied, "I don't know, Elsa. But they smell good, so we'll have that and boiled potatoes. Alright?"

Elsa grinned as she nodded then turned her smile back to her brother. They hadn't had sausage in more than a year.

Cap's large tent was up, so he began moving things inside. He would use his mules' saddle blankets in lieu of one of his bedrolls. They might be a bit pungent, but he wasn't smelling very good either. He'd remedy that when he could. He moved all of his guns and ammunition into the tent but still covered them with a small tarp. He wasn't sure how long he'd be staying. He hoped that the army would send a patrol to check on settlers.

It usually worked out that way. The army was there to protect them, but it was more common for them to arrive after the Lakota had struck. It wasn't their fault. Like Custer, they were still using Civil War tactics. Those methods might have worked when the Indians were using bows and arrows, but he hoped the generals learned their lesson after the aggressive Custer's crushing defeat. He believed that it would still take a while for them to shake off their old style of warfare.

He had to leave his mules' tack outside but covered it with the large tarp. It took him almost an hour to finish. It wasn't chilly yet, but he knew it would be soon. He'd sleep in his heavy coat and use his lighter, buckskin jacket as a pillow.

Inside the house, Erna took the cauldron of boiling water from the hook over the fire and set it on the flat stones nearby. She wasn't about to waste the water. She used her large wooden spoon to scoop out the potatoes and put them in the large tin bowl that Mister Tyler had given them. While the spuds cooled, she dipped a towel into the scalding hot water and then washed her children's faces before cleaning her own. She wished she could take a bath because she'd found two bars of white soap in the panniers. She'd figure out how to do that later, but now she needed to feed Gustave and Elsa.

With only two tin plates, she set a sausage and potato on each of them, then cut both of the boiled potatoes. She chopped the steaming potatoes and the sausages into pieces then handed Gustave a fork and sat down with Elsa to help her eat. Her daughter was getting better with utensils, but Erna didn't want her to drop any of her food.

Gustave stared at his mother but didn't start eating yet. He wasn't sure if he was supposed to say grace now that he was the man of the house. Maybe she would, or maybe they were supposed to wait for Mister Tyler.

Erna had never said grace before. After the attack, she hadn't felt as if she should be thankful for anything. Now, she was ashamed for doubting God and needed to thank Him for providing the food and Mister Tyler. She then realized that she hadn't heard or seen him since he'd left the panniers and bedrolls. She panicked when she thought that he might have simply dropped off the packs of food and then ridden to Bismarck as he said he would.

She set the plate and fork on Elsa's lap then stood and walked quickly to the doorway. In the low light of late evening, her worst fears were confirmed. There was no sign of Mister Tyler or his mules. He'd deserted them.

Erna wasn't sure if she should be disgusted with the man or blame herself for reacting as she had. Now she had failed her children and except for having enough food to last a month, their situation hadn't improved.

She slowly walked out of the house and turned to the east to see if she could spot Mister Tyler on the horizon. It had been more than an hour since she'd seen him last, so he could be staying in one of the Hartmann houses by now.

She stepped across the front of her house while still staring to the east. When she reached the southeastern corner of the house, she was startled to see a large tent with packs and a tarp-covered mound outside. She began to giggle in relief but didn't see Mister Tyler or his mules. She approached the tent but didn't pull back the flap as it might prove embarrassing.

When she was close, she loudly asked, "Mister Tyler?"

Cap was having his cold supper of smoked buffalo meat and a corn dodger. He quickly swallowed, set his food on the gun tarp before he half-stood then duck walked to the front of the tent and stepped through the flap.

"Yes, ma'am?"

Erna said, "I thought you were gone."

"No, ma'am. I just made my home. I said I would stay."

Erna simply replied, “Yes.”

She was going to ask him if he wanted to join them for supper but was afraid that he’d misunderstand her again. The consequences could be disastrous.

Cap wanted to put her at ease, so he just smiled and said, “Good night, Mrs. Braun. I will see you in the morning.”

He wasn’t sure that he hadn’t butchered the simple German until she returned his smile and said, “Good night, Mister Tyler.”

Erna turned and quickly walked back to the house to say grace then have supper with her children. Her children who now would be protected.

______

An hour later, Cap was lying atop the three saddle blankets wearing his heavy coat. His Remingtons were nearby, and his Winchester ’76 was on top of the tarp. He wasn’t concerned that the Lakota would return because there was no reason for them to inspect their handiwork. They’d avoid this place like the plague knowing that the army would be patrolling the area for a while. They’d attack elsewhere and then the army would go there. He wondered if they’d heard that the Northern Pacific would be laying track again soon. If they had, then the attack on the Braun family made sense. They wanted the army to send out patrols like the one he’d found on the ground earlier today. They wanted to cut down as many bluecoats as possible before the railroad started crossing their lands because it would mean more soldiers.

Before he fell asleep, he reminded himself to ask Mrs. Braun if she had any neighbors. He should have asked her before he mentioned taking her to Bismarck and leaving her at a church.

He grinned when he recalled her fiery response. For such a small woman, she certainly had grit. She was probably shorter than five feet and four inches and weighed less than a hundred and ten pounds. He was impressed that she'd been able to dig her husband's grave and couldn't imagine how distressing it must have been when she'd found his body then had to bury him. She must have kept her children inside when she first ventured out of the house after the attack knowing what she would find.

It was a measure of the strength of her character that she was still so adamant about staying. He was certain that she was still grieving inside for the loss of her husband yet hadn't abandoned his dream of building a home for her and their children. She was probably fighting more for her children than herself. A woman like that needed every bit of help he could give.

But regardless of her courage, he suspected to be hearing nightmare screams from the house as she and her children let those horrible memories invade their dreams. He hoped that his mere presence would at least diminish the power of those nightmares.

Inside the house, Erna snuggled under the blankets with Gustave on her left and Elsa on her right. Having the bedrolls between them and the wooden floor made an enormous difference. In addition to the softness, the bedrolls added a layer of insulation. It was another reason to be grateful for Mister Tyler.

But much more important was that he was staying and would protect and provide for her and her children. How long he would stay was her biggest concern.

CHAPTER 2

Just before sunrise, Cap had ridden bareback on Joe to reach Buck Creek where he quickly bathed in the reasonably warm water. After dressing, he spent a few minutes inspecting the nearby trees and found enough dead branches to make him wonder. *Why were they still here?* The small forest should have been stripped of them years ago. He'd found two stumps of trees that Mister Braun must have cut down for fuel, *but why leave the dead branches?* They were ideal for kindling. Maybe he had dragged the entire cottonwood back to his house and just cut it up there. Each of the big trees would have provided enough fuel for a couple of years, so the two trees would been enough to keep their hearth burning since they arrived. But having the dry branches would have saved time. He could have filled his wagon with as many fallen branches that Cap had found.

He realized that Mister Braun's reason for leaving them didn't matter, but it meant that he'd be able to use them to rebuild Mrs. Braun's firewood supply quickly. He'd have to take down another tree to build some replacement furniture, but his mules could help bring it back to their house.

The sun was well above the horizon when he rode Joe back to the house with Jasper and Jed trotting behind. It was rare for them to be very far apart. As he approached the house, he wasn't surprised to see Mrs. Braun and her children standing on the side of her home watching him.

He soon slid down from Joe and let his mules wander off as he stepped closer to the Brauns.

"Good morning, everyone," he said as he smiled.

Gustave and Elsa both smiled back as their mother replied, "Good morning, Mister Tyler. Have you had breakfast?"

"No, ma'am."

"Please join us inside," she said before taking Elsa's hand and walking back to the house.

Cap looked down at Gustave who was staring up at him, then offered him his hand.

Gustave placed his small hand in Cap's larger, calloused hand and after a firm handshake, they followed his mother and sister into the house.

Erna had already visited his empty tent and hadn't worried that he was gone even before she spotted him in the distance. After returning to the house, she served breakfast to her children but waited for Mister Tyler to return. She was enormously pleased to find coffee and a coffeepot in the packs he'd left with her. She hadn't had coffee in more than two years as it was an unnecessary expense.

When Cap entered, she quickly poured two cups of coffee then handed him one before giving him a plate with bacon and beans.

He smiled and said, “Thank you, Mrs. Braun.”

She nodded as she replied, “You are welcome, Mister Tyler.”

As he sat on the floor he said, “Please call me Cap.”

“You were in the army?” she asked as she sat nearby.

Cap shook his head as he answered, “No, ma’am. My name is Casper, but I am called Cap.”

“Oh. I saw the large number of guns and thought you had been in the army.”

“I was a, um…I can’t think of the word. I prepared the way for the railroad before they stopped laying tracks.”

“Why do you have so many guns?”

Cap snapped off a big bite of bacon and as he chewed, he tried to think of how to describe how he’d accumulated the weapons in German. It was hard enough in English.

After he swallowed, he said, “I traded for them and fought many Indians and some white men.”

She surprised him when she asked, “Can you show me how to shoot?”

He slid one of his Remingtons from its holster, then spread his fingers apart and displayed his large hand. He then pointed at her smaller hands and shook his head.

“You have small hands. Maybe a rifle.”

“But a rifle is heavy.”

Cap assumed that her husband had used an old muzzle loader or a single-shot breech loader like his Sharps. She probably had never seen a Winchester or a Henry.

“Not all are heavy. I have three smaller rifles. They are…um. They shoot many times.”

“Can I shoot one?”

“I think so. We will try later.”

She nodded then began eating her breakfast as Cap took a sip of the very strong coffee. He didn’t complain about it because he liked it that way. He wasn’t convinced that she could fire a pistol, but he was confident she could handle a Winchester. If she did well with the repeater, then he’d let her try a Colt.

Cap noticed that Gustave was sitting beside him watching him eat while Elsa sat beside her mother. He picked up a second strip of bacon and handed it to the boy.

Gustave looked at his mother who didn't give him permission to accept the offer, but she didn't shake her head, either. So, after a few seconds without her guidance, he took the bacon and said, "Thank you," before he snapped off a bite. Before Elsa could ask her mother for a piece of her bacon, Gustave handed the rest of the bacon to his sister.

Cap smiled at the boy and rubbed his blonde head, receiving a big grin in response.

Cap then asked, "Mrs. Braun, do you have any neighbors?"

She swallowed her mouthful of beans then replied, "Yes. At least we did before the Indians attacked. The Hartmann family had a full section of land about an hour's ride to the east."

Cap understood most of what she'd said, so he asked, "Do you know if they survived?"

She answered, "I saw smoke from their farm when I left the house, but they didn't come. So, I don't think anyone is alive."

"I'll go there this morning just to make sure."

Erna quickly asked, "How long will you be gone?"

"Maybe three hours. You will be safe. No Indians will come here again."

She wasn't sure if he was right, but if he was only going to the Hartmann farm, he wouldn't be out of sight for very long. She believed that all he would probably find was a mass of mutilated bodies, but she did want to know what had become of them.

She nodded then said, "Alright. Will you take your shovel to bury them?"

"I will take it, but I can't promise to bury them. It has been too long."

"I understand."

Twenty minutes later, Cap rode Joe away from the Braun farm heading east. He had his Winchester '76 in his right scabbard and his Sharps in his left. What was noticeable was that he didn't see the expected large flocks of buzzards overhead. Even after five days, the scavengers should be circling. He suspected that the family had been trapped inside their home as the menfolk fired through rifle slots.

When he'd first spotted the Braun house, he'd been surprised that it didn't have any rifle slots in its shutters or door. Maybe it was because Mister Braun would be alone to defend his family and had already decided to face the danger in the open. It also made him understand the wood floor and the hidden shelter. He shuddered as he tried to imagine the terror that Mrs. Braun and her children had felt as they heard the Lakota rampaging inside the house. They probably stepped right above their heads. The warriors must not have stayed long. If the raid's purpose was primarily to alert the army to send another patrol, then they would have met their objective.

He soon spotted the Hartmann farm and was surprised to see three sod houses. One was larger than the other two and he believed that he must have misunderstood Mrs. Braun when she had described the makeup of the family.

As he neared the big house, he picked up the rancid scent of death but didn't see any bodies. He did notice that the front door was open and wished the house had been made of wood so he could burn it down. He had brought his shovel but wasn't about to dig a grave for the number of bodies he expected to find.

He pulled to a stop well before the house, pulled his Winchester and dismounted. Joe wasn't pleased by the odor and trotted away but Cap wasn't worried about being stranded.

As he walked quickly toward the house, the stench became more overpowering with each step. He was close to losing his breakfast by the time he arrived and couldn't keep it down when he peered into the shadows of the single large room.

He wretched then wiped his mouth before he quickly counted the mutilated bodies. He hurriedly turned and jogged away from the big house and whistled for Joe. His mule was about a hundred yards away but simply stared at him. So, Cap resumed trotting away from the house, grateful for the cleaner air.

When he reached Joe, he slid his Winchester home and mounted. He didn't believe he'd find any bodies in the smaller houses but had to check. He walked Joe to the west of the big house and began picking up tracks. He was unable to determine the exact number of Lakota warriors, but he knew it had to be around a dozen. He noticed three sets of shod prints mixed with the others. It was more than just an odd number; it didn't make much sense. The family should have had an even number of horses or mules. Maybe one was unshod.

He set the oddity aside and approached the first small house. Its door was open as well, but he didn't need to dismount as he pulled up before the doorway. There were no bodies inside, but he was surprised that the furniture was mostly intact. There was even a mattress on the one bed. He'd have to figure out a way to bring it back to Mrs. Braun. It was better than building furniture from green wood.

Cap then walked his mule to the second small house and found it in the same condition as the first. He noted that neither of the small houses had gun slots, which made sense if they weren't going to be defended. The absence of wood floors also indicated that none of them had shelters. Mister

Hartmann must have believed that he had enough firepower to stop any attacks.

On the eastern side of the second small house, he found the family's damaged wagon. It seemed that the Sioux had been in a great rush to get to the Braun farm and hadn't done a very good job destroying the Hartmann's furniture or wagon. They had broken the spokes on one of the back wheels and tossed a flaming torch onto the bed, but it hadn't caught fire. He thought he'd be able to repair it if there was a spare wheel underneath. If not, he could turn it into a cart.

He was about to turn Joe around when he decided to finish his inspection of the property to see if the army had stopped by to check on the family after the raid. He didn't believe they had because no one had helped Mrs. Braun.

When he reached the easternmost edge of his perimeter, he stopped and stared at a set of tracks that may explain why there had only been three sets of shod hoofprints traveling with the Sioux. He found a trail left by a shod horse or mule heading east. One of them must have ridden to Fort Lincoln for help. He didn't see any marks indicating that the survivor had return, so he suspected that he hadn't made it very far before the Lakota ran him down. They may have set up a rear guard to prevent anyone from notifying the army and the sole survivor had run into them. Cap wasn't about to ride east just to find his body.

Cap set Joe to a trot and headed back to let Mrs. Braun know the grim news. It was just confirmation of what she had expected to hear, but he wasn't going to tell her with her children nearby. At least none of the bodies in the house were youngsters. But there was also the unexpectedly good news about the wagon and furniture.

———

Erna had remained outside waiting for Mister Tyler. She had no doubt that none of the Hartmanns had survived, but she was anxious that he return as soon as possible. Gustave and Elsa were inside playing with one of the empty panniers. If they left the house when Mister Tyler returned, she'd send them back inside until he'd told her what he'd found.

She soon saw him approaching and breathed a sigh of relief. He hadn't been gone that long, so she knew he hadn't dug a grave. She could understand why he didn't. It was hard enough for her to dig Wilhelm's and there were many more Hartmanns and it had been almost a week.

Cap saw her waiting by the doorway without her children, but suspected they'd pop out of the doorway when they heard Joe's hoofbeats. So, he slowed Joe to a walk and turned him toward his tent. He pulled him to stop well away from the house and stepped down. He took his mule's reins and began walking to his tent as Mrs. Braun headed that way as well.

They met a minute later and as he began stripping Joe, she asked, “Were they all dead?”

Cap nodded and replied, “Yes, ma’am. All in the big house.”

“How many did you find?”

“Two men and five women.”

Erna quickly asked, “Only two men?”

“Yes, ma’am. One went to get help but failed.”

“Why do you think that?”

Cap pulled off Joe’s saddle and set it down near his Winchester as he replied, “Marks on the ground.”

“But you did not find the last body?”

Cap slid the saddle blanket from Joe and answered, “No. Do you want me to look?”

The last thing that Erna wanted was for him to ride even further away, so she quickly shook her head. It really didn’t matter.

He removed Joe’s bridle and swatted him on his flank to let him know he could join his brothers. They weren’t really related but they got along better than most real brothers.

“Was it bad?” she asked quietly.

“Yes, ma’am.”

She glanced to the east before she asked, “Can you show me how to shoot?”

“After I put these away.”

“Then English lessons?”

Cap smiled as he replied, “More important.”

Erna smiled then left to talk to her children. She wouldn’t go into details about the Hartmann family, but she was sure that they already knew that none of them had survived.

———

In Bismarck, Franz Hartmann was now staying with the Mayers. He’d arrived in town the day after his family had been savagely murdered.

When his younger brother had spotted the Indians coming from the south, his father had shouted for everyone to get into the house to fight them off. The rest of his family had raced into the house and held the door open waiting for him to enter. But Franz had realized when his father had first described how they’d defend their farm that it would be useless. So, rather than run into the house, he’d mounted one of their four mules and ridden bareback to the east. He didn’t even look behind him to see if they’d closed and barred the door. He was already a mile away when he heard the first sounds of gunfire. He was wearing his pistol, so he had some protection if they sent any warriors after him, but he had such a lead by then that he knew he was safe.

He had spent one night sleeping alone on the prairie before he reached Bismarck the next day. When he arrived, he found help at the Lutheran church. He provided Reverend Walther with a horrific but false tale of the sudden, overwhelming attack. He related how he'd been able to escape after the rest of his family had already been killed and only when he'd run out of ammunition.

The church group had not only provided him a place to stay with one of their congregation but had collected clothing and money donations to help him replace what he had lost. They had been very generous because of his loss and his heroic defense of his family. He knew that he couldn't stay very long yet never gave a thought of returning to his farm. He was sure that sooner or later, questions would arise that he couldn't answer. He had been surprised that the reverend hadn't asked about the spare cartridges on his gunbelt nor the lack of blood on his clothing.

He had told the story to anyone who would listen and by the end of his first day in Bismarck, he almost began to believe it himself. It was better than admitting to his cowardice. He justified his despicable behavior by convincing himself that the rest of his family were fools and should have mounted the other mules and ridden away with him. He intentionally failed to recall that he hadn't shouted for them to leave the house or even asked his wife to come with him.

He had been given refuge with the Mayers on the second day and appreciated the comfort of their large home and well-cooked meals.

Josef and Magda had come to America with others from their village. Unlike those who were planning to start tilling the ground on their new farms, they chose to migrate so Josef could start his new business. Before they left Germany, he had a well-established blacksmith shop in their village a few miles outside of Stuttgart. But when a large number of the town's residents signed up for new lands offered by the Northern Pacific agent, he saw opportunity there as well. They didn't buy any of the land but took passage to the New World with the others.

He and Magda arrived in Missouri Crossing in the summer of 1872. Josef bought a house and had a new smithy built nearby. As the only other operating blacksmith in town was an Irishman, the new German settlers flocked to his smithy. When the Panic of 1873 forced the railroad into bankruptcy, it proved to be a boon to Josef as his services were in even greater demand. He hired the Irish blacksmith and added two apprentices to keep pace with his customers' demands. So, when Franz arrived, he was already one of the more prominent members of the German community in the town that was now named Bismarck.

Josef had offered him a position as an apprentice but would only pay him five dollars a month as he was staying in their home. So, after gratefully declining his offer, Franz began looking for a real job but only found frustration.

The resuscitated Northern Pacific's plan to start laying track again had lured many men to the town in hope of finding employment now that the depression was finally drawing to a close. He had no experience, so he was only qualified for manual labor. That type of work also attracted the largest number of job seekers, and he was smaller than most of the other applicants. His poor English and inability to read the language ensured that he'd remain at the bottom of that list as well. How he had reached town was another negative that he wanted to keep hidden from other men.

All he had were his mule, his Colt pistol and the $17.55 and clothing given to him by the Lutheran congregation. On the third day, he visited Schmidt's Beer Hall to have a good German beer. He hoped to meet someone who could help him find a way to improve his condition. He wasn't about to join the other prospective laborers who had accumulated in tents and shacks on the eastern end of town. It was a nasty place, and he had a much better situation with the Mayers.

———

Cap watched as Erna aimed the Winchester. Gustave and Elsa were standing close to him for protection. He'd spent over an hour using his sorry German mixed with simple

English and sign language to explain how to load and fire the repeater. After he'd emptied the carbine, he'd had her dry fire practice for another twenty minutes. Now she had a live round in the chamber and was aiming at a clump of dirt fifty yards away. He hadn't fired the Winchester beforehand to give her an idea of what to expect when she squeezed the trigger. He knew that she'd seen her husband fire his much louder and more powerful rifle, so the Winchester's lighter bark and kick should be welcomed.

Erna settled her sights on the clump and slowly pulled back the trigger. She was confident that she'd interpreted that part of Cap's instructions. When the Winchester suddenly fired, she didn't see the impact of the bullet through the cloud of gunsmoke. She had expected that the clump of dirt would explode, but that hadn't happened.

Cap did see where her .44 struck the ground and said, "You were close, Erna."

She turned to him and asked, "I was close?"

He spread his index finger and thumb apart by three inches as he replied, "This much too high. It was good."

She grinned and then levered in another cartridge without difficulty. She missed with her second shot when she overcorrected but hit the clump with her third. The ball of soil may not have exploded as she had expected, but the .44 did create a small dirt volcano.

They soon returned to the house where Cap could show her how to clean the Winchester.

As Erna, Gustave and Elsa watched him clean the carbine, Cap said, "When I went to the other farm, I found unbroken furniture in the small houses. I want to go there and bring some back."

Erna asked, "When will you go and how long will you be gone?"

"Tomorrow. Maybe four hours. You can keep the Winchester."

"Okay. How will you move them?"

"The Sioux damaged their wagon, but not as much. If I cannot fix it, I will make a cart."

"That would be useful."

He nodded as he continued to clean the Winchester. He hadn't mentioned his plans for a second trip. The one he needed to make to Fort Abraham Lincoln. He still wanted to notify the army of the destroyed cavalry company but could buy food and supplies at the sutler's store as well. It was just a few miles from Bismarck, but it was on this side of the Heart and Missouri River. It should only take him six or seven hours to reach the fort, and if he left before the predawn, he should be able to return before sunset.

After setting the cleaned carbine aside, Cap began his first English lesson. It helped that his long unused German was returning now that he needed it.

When he was sitting on the floor in a circle facing Erna with Gustave on his right and Elsa at his left, he used the open space in the middle as his chalkboard. He employed a charred stick in lieu of a piece of chalk.

Before he started, Erna asked, "Where did you learn German?"

"My mother's parents were German, but she spoke English most of the time."

"Oh. Do you still have family?"

"Only an older brother. He lives in California with his wife and children."

"You have no wife?"

He shook his head before he replied, "Let's get started."

He began their first lesson using the same methods his first-year teacher had used when he had learned to read. He didn't follow it exactly as he had found it tedious even back then. He added humor and imaginary stories for each of the words he spoke and scrawled on the floor.

The long lesson continued even while Erna prepared lunch.

They mixed English conversation in with the lessons all afternoon. They were making progress and Cap began to hope that they would be almost fluent by the time he left the farm. When that would be was still open to question.

CHAPTER 3

Early the next morning, Erna and the children returned Cap's wave as he rode east again. She had her Winchester in her left hand and wasn't about to let it out of her sight until he returned. She was curious how he would be returning. *Would it be riding his mule or driving a cart or wagon loaded with furniture?* He had told them that he'd seen two beds and mattresses in the small houses as well as two tables and four chairs.

She was surprised because all of her furniture had been turned into firewood. She had buried their mattresses with her husband because the Sioux had urinated on them. She wondered if they'd done the same to the Hartmanns'. Mister Tyler had offered his best guess about why the Indians hadn't destroyed the Hartmann furniture and she had agreed. They had been facing at least three protected shooters and after they finally killed the family, they had to quickly leave to attack her farm. After they murdered Wilhelm, they could take but a few minutes to wreck her furniture and set fire to her wagon.

As Cap headed for the Hartmann farm, he planned to do a more in-depth examination of the ground after he'd salvaged what he could from the two small houses. He didn't recall seeing any patches of dry blood on the ground, which didn't make any sense. He couldn't imagine that three men firing through those gun slots hadn't been able to hit a single Lakota warrior. Even a miss could have hit one of their horses. *So, where was the blood?*

He soon dismounted near the second small house and let Joe's reins drop. He brought both Jasper and Jed along and both were wearing their pack saddles and empty panniers in case he couldn't get the wagon repaired or converted into a cart.

Cap left his rifles on Joe as he stepped to the wagon and unbuckled his gunbelts. After laying them on the driver's seat, he slid to the ground and peered underneath the bed. He grinned when he saw a spare wheel, axle and a jack. There was even a bucket of grease. The Lakota's haste had turned into a boon for Mrs. Braun.

It took him forty minutes to replace the damaged wheel. After he unsaddled Jed and Jasper, he put them in harness and set their pack saddles and panniers onto the wagon bed.

He didn't tie Joe to the back of the wagon but drove it a few feet to the front of the second small house and stepped down. He entered the house and found a few shards of broken china but was surprised to find a Dutch oven that was still intact. There were no iron or steel cookware to be found, but he was sure that Mrs. Braun would appreciate the portable bakery.

He began with the two chairs and small table and then stripped the mattress from the bed and rolled it up before loading it onto the wagon. The bed was awkward to move, but he managed to drag it out of the house then tip it onto the wagon and slide it on its side along the bed.

He then drove it to the next house and while he didn't find another Dutch oven, he did find a bucket and a pillow still laying on the mattress. After another drag and lift operation, Cap had the other small house emptied and the wagon fully loaded. He couldn't wait to see the smile on Mrs. Braun's face when she saw the treasures he had reclaimed. Before he climbed onto the driver's seat, he took his canteen from Joe and drained it.

He hung it back on his saddle and said, "Let's go make Mrs. Braun happy, Joe."

While he was anxious to put that smile on Mrs. Braun's face, he still had to make a slow circuit of the property to see if he could find any dried blood. It had almost been a week since the attack, but it should still be there.

He donned his gunbelts then started toward the big house. He knew the smell might even be worse, but as he walked, he realized that he'd overlooked another oddity of the raid. He was startled by the revelation and thought his memory was faulty. Before he reached the front of the big house, he still hadn't seen any large black patches on the ground. But now, that was a secondary mystery. He had to look at the door again.

Despite leaving a fifty-foot-wide gap, the stench was still growing intense as he rounded the front of the house. When he spotted the open doorway, he realized that his memory hadn't failed him at all. But he'd been so focused on counting the bodies inside that he hadn't paid any attention to the door. Now he did.

He didn't care about the condition of the furniture or the even the mutilated bodies. He simply stared at the door for a good minute, not even acknowledging the rancid odor.

Cap finally turned to his left and continued his examination of the ground. He still hadn't found any large patches of dry blood but did spot a few smaller circles. Some of the Lakota had been shot, but not badly wounded. But it was the door that really disturbed him.

Ninety minutes after arriving, Cap drove the loaded wagon away from the Hartmann farm. Joe trotted alongside Jasper as the two mules pulled them along the prairie.

———

When Erna first spotted Cap driving the wagon in the distance, she giggled then said, "Mister Tyler fixed the wagon."

Gustave asked, "Did he find anything at the Hartmann farm, Mama?"

"We'll find out soon. Maybe we'll be sleeping on a real mattress in a real bed tonight."

Elsa asked, "Is Mister Tyler going to stay in his tent?"

"I think so. Mister Tyler is a gentleman."

Gustave asked, "Why does a gentleman sleep in a tent instead of a house?"

Erna smiled at her son as she replied, "Because he isn't your papa yet."

Gustave furrowed his brow as he tried to understand his mother's reply but suspected it would be a few years before he did.

———

Since he'd seen that open door, Cap had been wrestling with the question of whether or not he should tell Mrs. Braun of his discovery. The reason for the lack of blood and then finding the door open with the intact locking bar on the ground near the bodies and not broken off its hinges were the same. The Hartmann family hadn't had time to enter the house and put the locking bar in place before the Lakota reached them. That would have been impossible unless they had attacked before dawn. But Mrs. Braun had said that they attacked her farm around midday. That one set of shod hoofprints heading east was another indication that the Lakota had been spotted. They should have had plenty of time to get into the house and drop the locking bar into place. But it appeared that they only had been able to take a few hurried shots at the Sioux before they fell. *Why hadn't they been able to set up for their defense?* The Lakota warriors should have paid a much steeper price for the raid than they had.

He was still pondering that mystery as he entered the Braun property. He could already see the smiles on their faces when they saw the packed wagon. He decided to at least wait for a better moment to express his concerns. He wanted them to revel in the excitement of having their home partially restored.

He soon pulled the wagon to a stop before the house, then set the handbrake and clambered down.

"You found so much!" Erna exclaimed as she walked to the back of the wagon.

Cap was following her as he replied, "Yes, ma'am. There were even mattresses, a pillow and a Dutch oven."

She whipped around and sharply asked, "Did I understand you? You found a Dutch oven?"

"Yes, ma'am," he replied as he pulled one of the chairs from the wagon and set it on the ground.

He then climbed onto the bed and pushed aside one of the small tables to get to the Dutch oven. He carefully lifted it and turned to hand it to Mrs. Braun. He didn't want to drop it and watch it shatter after getting her so excited.

After the pottery was safely in her hands, Cap dropped to the ground and began unloading the rest of the furniture.

Erna said, "I will be back to help," then quickly stepped away to bring the precious cookware into the house.

As Cap set another chair on the ground, Gustave asked, "Can I help?"

"That's up to your mother, Gustave."

"She will say it's alright."

Cap grinned as he replied, "You can ask her right now," then pulled the first of the small tables from the wagon.

Gustave looked at his mother and decided that it would just be a waste of breath to ask.

But when Cap pulled out one of the rolled-up mattresses, he held it out to the small boy. Gustave glanced at his mother before he quickly wrapped his thin arms around the mattress and carried it to the house as he peered around the outside to avoid bumping into the side of the doorway.

Cap then handed the pillow to Elsa and she trotted after her brother.

Erna smiled at her children as they disappeared into the house and said, “They want to grow up so quickly. It seems like just yesterday that they were babies.”

While they were gone, Cap decided to ask her something very personal but needed to be answered. If he was going to stay until spring, he needed to know if he’d have to become a midwife. He was sure that even if she was pregnant, she couldn’t be that far along, but wanted to be sure.

“Mrs. Braun,” he began awkwardly, “If I am staying, I need to know if you are…um, if you are…”

He placed his right hand against his stomach and slowly began to pull it away.

No translation was necessary as Erna quickly shook her head and replied, “No. I am not with child.”

Cap nodded then let out a breath, grateful that she hadn’t seemed offended by the question or his uneasiness.

When the children returned a few seconds later, Cap had already climbed back into the wagon and began sliding the beds to the tailgate.

“I can help,” Erna said as she took hold of one of them.

“Alright. I’ll pull it out first.”

After pulling it more than halfway, he let her take the front and then once it was off the wagon, they carried it to the doorway. It wasn't that heavy, but he was still impressed that she didn't struggle with the load. Once inside, they placed it on the left side of the room and let Gustave and Elsa put the mattress in place.

Twenty minutes later, only the two pack saddles and panniers were left on the wagon's bed, and the Braun house had become a home again.

Cap drove the wagon to the back of the house and unharnessed Jed and Jasper then unsaddled Joe. He thanked them for their work then let them all wander to the creek.

After returning all of the tack to the tarp, Cap entered his tent to find some lunch. He spent almost a minute digging through his supplies before he settled on the last of his corn dodgers and four sticks of buffalo jerky. He simply wasn't that hungry, which surprised him after all that work.

As he chewed on the salty jerky, he tried to picture the Lakota attack on the Hartmann farm. He didn't want to ask Mrs. Braun for any more details. She didn't need to be reminded of that day. Having her husband's grave just outside her house was bad enough. He finished the jerky and his corn dodgers and still hadn't been able to imagine how it was possible for the Sioux to stop the family from closing that door. He finished his lunch with a cup of water from his canteen, then took his two canteens and left his tent to refill them in the creek.

Erna had finished arranging the furniture and made both beds shortly after he'd driven the wagon away. Then she waited for Cap to enter the house, but after he hadn't walked through the open doorway, she began to prepare lunch. Now she had two small tables and four chairs, so they wouldn't have to eat on the floor.

As she prepared their lunch, she kept glancing at the front door wondering where Mister Tyler was.

Cap had almost reached the river when he spotted riders coming from the east on the other side of the wide creek. It only took a few seconds to recognize them as an army patrol. There were riding in two columns and it wasn't a full company. It was only a squad of a dozen cavalrymen, but he was pleased to see them.

He waved his hat over his head to attract their attention, although he was reasonably sure that they'd already spotted him. While the lead riders didn't acknowledge him in any fashion, he noticed that they shifted their direction closer to the opposite bank. They would share a loud conversation across the twenty-foot-wide creek.

Just before they reached the opposite bank, Cap noticed that they were being led by a corporal, which spoke of their diminished manpower. He wondered if they were going to search for the missing company.

Corporal McDermott pulled the squad to a halt and walked his horse close to the creek's northern bank then shouted, "What can I do for you, mister?"

"I was going to ride to the fort to tell you what I discovered about ten miles west of here. It looked like you lost an entire company to the Lakota."

The corporal exclaimed, "Damn! The colonel expected 'em back three days ago! The captain said he didn't trust them damned Sioux scouts before he left!"

Then he asked, "Why didn't you make it to the fort?"

"I found that the Sioux attacked the farm behind me and another farm about five miles east of here. They massacred that family and killed the man of the house in this one. I've been helping out the lady and her two children. I was planning on making the ride to the fort in another day or so for supplies anyway."

"Are you plannin' on bein' the new man of the house?"

"Nope. I'm not a farmer, and my German isn't very good. I hope to find a German-speaking farmer husband for her one of these days. I'm going to see if I can hire on with the

Northern Pacific again. I was a surveyor for them before they went bust."

"Did the Sioux take Company C's guns and horses?"

"They took everything, even your boys' uniforms. You might want to be careful if you see a column of bluecoats heading your way."

"I'll let the colonel know. We still have to get out there and bury 'em. Did you bury those folks at the other farm?"

"By the time I got there, it had been a week and they were all in the house. I couldn't get close to that front door."

"I reckon not. We only arrived from Fort Omaha a few months ago, so we didn't know that anyone was out this way."

"The Northern Pacific is going to be laying track again pretty soon though. They'll probably have to build a station just on the other side of Heart River about this far from Bismarck."

"That's what I heard, but they won't be comin' so close to the river now. They're goin' due west out of Bismarck. I reckon it'll be a good ten miles north of here."

Cap was surprised and shouted, "I surveyed that route four years ago. We were told to follow the river."

"I guess their new boss figgered different. Are you still gonna head to the fort?"

"When I need some supplies from the sutler's store. How shorthanded are you?"

"We were hurtin' pretty bad before we lost C company. Now we'll only have a third of our complement."

"You haven't heard of any reinforcements heading your way?"

"Nothin' that the colonel has passed down to us lowly NCOs."

"Good luck, Corporal!"

Corporal McDermott waved, then turned his mount away and soon took his position at the head of the column. He signaled them to move forward, and the squad of cavalrymen headed west. They had four pack horses with them, and Cap noticed that each of them had two shovels. They must have expected to find what the corporal had just learned.

After they'd gone, he filled his canteens then waited for his mules. They'd been watching the horses on the other side of the river but once the squad rode off, their curiosity must have been satisfied because they turned and trotted towards him.

"Let's go back, boys," he said as he slung the two full canteens over his shoulder.

As he headed back, he hoped that the corporal's squad wasn't riding into a trap. At least he'd been warned about the possibility of finding men in army uniforms who weren't soldiers. He hoped to see them riding back to the fort sometime tomorrow.

After leaving his canteens in his tent, he headed for the house to tell Mrs. Braun about meeting the cavalrymen. He needed to start another English lesson, too.

Erna was leaving the house just as Cap turned and walked through the open doorway. They collided just two feet past the threshold and Cap quickly took hold of her shoulders to keep her from falling onto her back. Gustave and Elsa were giggling as their small mother struggled to keep her balance.

Once he was sure she wasn't about to fall, Cap immediately released her and said, "Excuse me, ma'am."

"No, it's alright. I was just coming outside to look for you. We expected you for lunch."

"I wasn't hungry, so I just had a little to eat in my tent. But I need to talk to you about meeting soldiers."

Erna stepped to one of the small tables and sat down. Gustave and Elsa were already sitting at the other table, so Cap soon joined her at her table.

"Where did you see soldiers?"

“On the other side of the creek. I told them of the bodies of the other soldiers and the attacks on the Hartmann farm and yours.”

“How many were there?”

“Only twelve. The man who led them told me they were very short of men. I hope they do not ride into a trap.”

“Will the Indians come again if they defeat the soldiers?”

“No. They have no reason to come, and they won’t attack the fort because it is too dangerous. They will wait for the railroad to come bringing soldiers.”

Erna quietly asked, “And you will be making the railroad?”

“I don’t know.”

The room fell silent for half a minute before Cap grinned and said, “Time for the next English lesson.”

The thought-inspiring silence ended when Cap stood and moved his chair to the children’s table. After Erna slid hers nearby, the next long period of instruction began.

———

In Bismarck, Franz was becoming frustrated as he sat at the kitchen table sharing coffee with Mrs. Mayer. His search for a comrade had failed. It seemed that no one wanted to even talk to him. Mrs. Mayer was trying to convince him to accept her husband's offer as an apprentice, but he wasn't listening.

If it hadn't been for his family's bodies rotting in his parents' house, he might have gone back to the farm to search for anything of value. But he knew that the Indians had probably stripped it bare and destroyed what they didn't take. He had thought about going to the Braun farm, but suspected it was just as bad as his. He just wished that Erna Braun had survived the attack.

When he had first seen her almost four years ago, he was jealous of her husband and was even more dissatisfied with his wife. Every time that the Brauns had visited, his jealousy grew more intense, and the comparison became more pronounced. But she was gone and so was his old life. He needed to find another path but knew he had far fewer choices than most of the men in town.

The only good news was that one of the parishioners had given him a set of tack for his mule. All he needed now was a Winchester but wasn't able to afford even a used one. He was glad he had his Colt though. Many of the men arriving in town were unsavory and weren't looking for work laying rails. While almost all of them lived in that tent village across from the settlers, some ventured into town and radiated trouble. While he had never fired his pistol at anyone and wasn't about to face any of the hard men, Franz felt safer when he walked the streets of Bismarck with his pistol at his side.

As Mrs. Mayer droned on, he finally reasoned that he may as well work as an apprentice for her husband until something better came along. He could use the extra five dollars a month and by the time winter arrived, he'd have his new Winchester.

Erna laughed and Cap grinned after Gustave had said, "I will milk the horse."

Gustave was horrified and Elsa had no idea what was so funny.

But Cap patted the boy on the shoulder as he said, "You ride horses and milk cows, Gustave. But you can ride cows if you want."

"I said it bad."

"It's alright. You are doing very well. So is Elsa and your mother."

"Will I talk English as good as you?"

"Probably better. You are all smarter than me."

Gustave grinned at his mother then Elsa before he said, "I will milk the cow."

Erna then asked, “Will you show me how to shoot a pistol soon?”

Without replying, Cap pulled the Remington out of his left-hand holster and emptied the cartridges onto the table. He then handed it to her and watched her small hand wrap around the grip.

“How does it feel?”

“Not too heavy,” she said as she slid her index finger behind the trigger.

He was impressed that even though she knew it was empty, Erna had kept the muzzle pointed toward the open room. He had explained that rule when he’d shown her how to use the Winchester but wasn’t sure if she remembered it or even understood his German.

“Put your left palm under the bottom of the pistol,” he said as he used his own hands to demonstrate what he wanted her to do.

Erna nodded, then slipped her hand beneath the pistol’s butt and felt more in control.

“May I try to shoot it now?”

“You must pull back the hammer all the way back before you squeeze the trigger.”

Erna nodded then tried to use her thumb but quickly realized she needed more force and used her left hand to cock the pistol. Once the hammer was back, she aimed it at the far wall and pulled the trigger. When the hammer snapped back down, she looked at Cap and smiled.

"It is okay. Can we shoot outside with bullets now?"

"We can," he replied before he said, "Your English is already much better."

She continued to smile as she handed the Remington back to Cap. He returned the cartridges to their rightful homes, then slid his pistol back into its holster.

"I will give you one of my Colt pistols. If you can fire it well, you may keep it. It uses the same cartridges as the Winchester."

Erna nodded then asked, "A cartridge is a bullet?"

Cap pulled out one of the .44s from his gunbelt and as he pointed at the head of the cartridge, he said, "This is the bullet," then as he slid his finger up and down the entire cartridge, he said, "All of this is the cartridge."

"I understand."

Cap pushed the cartridge back into its loop as he said, "Many people born in America don't know the difference."

"Now I do. Thank you, Cap."

"You're welcome, ma'am. Now let's get your Colt and see how you do."

They all rose and walked out of the house and headed for his tent. He went inside, pulled one of his spare gunbelts from the tarp and exited seconds later.

He looked at her slim waist for a few seconds, then pulled out his knife and punched a new hole in the belt.

"I am too thin?" she asked as she watched.

"You are a small woman but not thin," he replied as he handed her the modified gunbelt.

She smiled as she wrapped it around her waist and soon snugged it down onto her hips.

"It is a good fit."

He pointed to his holster and said, "This is called a hammer loop. It holds the pistol in the holster, so it doesn't fall. Okay?"

She nodded before they started walking toward the river. After they'd gone about fifty yards, Cap stopped and took Gustave and Elsa's hands.

Erna stepped another ten feet away, then released the hammer loop with her thumb and forefinger which made Cap smile. It was as if she was removing a dirty diaper from a baby.

Once the hammer loop no longer kept the Colt prisoner, she slid it from its holster and aimed it toward the creek at a hole in the ground about sixty feet away. It could have been the home of a prairie dog or a rattlesnake, but now it was her target. She cocked the hammer and as she used her left hand to support the weight, she pulled the trigger.

Erna was surprised when the Colt bounced in her hands and saw the ground six feet past the hole erupt in a dirt explosion. She expected to hear Cap comment, but when he hadn't said anything for twenty seconds, she cocked the hammer again and fired a second time. Her second shot was closer, but still high.

She glanced back at Cap whose expression didn't give her any feedback about his opinion of her first two shots, so she turned back to the undamaged hole in the ground and prepared to take her third. As soon as the pistol kicked in her hands, she saw the ground just in front of the hole erupt.

She whipped her eyes around and was gratified to see Cap smiling.

"I hit it!" she exclaimed as she slid her Colt back into its holster.

"Yes, ma'am. That's a good distance for a pistol, too. Let's go inside and I'll show you how to clean and load the pistol. Okay?"

She was still smiling as she nodded and after Cap released his grip on her children, she took their hands. As they began walking back to the house, Gustave and Elsa giggled and praised their mother for her newfound skill.

Cap wasn't surprised that she'd handled the Colt, despite her small stature. Erna Braun was a determined woman, and he was pleased to be the one who was giving her the means to protect herself and her children. But knowing that she was so determined and wasn't about to leave her farm only enhanced his dilemma. He was already growing too fond of her and the children but knew he couldn't stay. He wasn't a farmer and didn't have the desire to be one. And he didn't have the knowledge of how to make the most of the soil either. Farming wasn't a simple job, despite what many non-farmers believed. His skills and knowledge were much different.

He'd been a surveyor since he was in his teens. His father had been a surveyor for the Chicago, Rock Island & Pacific when the War Between the States began. His services were in great demand by the Union Army, so he left the family for three years to continue to employ his railroad skills while wearing a blue uniform.

His mother had died in '64 of pneumonia, so when his father returned in '65, he took his two sons to Omaha City where they were preparing to build the eastern half of the transcontinental railroad. Cap was more than happy to be with his father and had already begun learning the skills of a surveyor before his father left to join the army. His older brother, Saul, wasn't as interested and had his own plans.

As the surveyors marked the path for the tracks, Cap continued to learn about surveying and how to handle the ever-present danger of crossing the wild lands. After the Union Pacific and the Central Pacific met in Utah, Saul said goodbye to Cap and their father and continued to California. He eventually settled in San Francisco, married and now had three children. Cap and his father continued surveying more routes for the Union Pacific until his father died in Wyoming blizzard. The expected supply train failed to reach them, so half of the surveying crew had frozen to death in that early blizzard in mid-October of '70.

While Cap didn't blame the Union Pacific, he had quit the company and headed to Minnesota where he joined the Northern Pacific which was just starting its westward push through even more challenging territory than the Union Pacific had followed. By then, twenty-one-year-old Cap Tyler was an experienced surveyor and could outshoot most of the men who were there to protect the surveying crews.

They worked hundreds of miles ahead of the ground preparation and tracklaying crews. He had passed through Missouri Crossing long before it became Bismarck and faced his almost fatal attack in Montana Territory when the railroad ceased construction.

Now he hoped to return to his life a surveyor, but after the corporal had told him that the Northern Pacific's new boss had altered his earlier surveyed path, he suspected he might have to look for another employer. But what the corporal had said about the Sioux scouts made him wonder if the army would hire him as a scout. He had probably spent more time engaging the Cheyenne and Lakota than any three or four soldiers. He had traded with them when he wasn't shooting them, so he knew their ways and could communicate with them reasonably well.

As they entered the house, Cap was already adding more options to his future. If Mrs. Braun wasn't so determined to stay on her farm, she and her children could have been part of his future.

After cleaning the Colt, Cap said, "Mrs. Braun, if I'm not here, you should store the pistol in your shelter rather than wear it. You can carry the Winchester, but if you have to go down into your hiding place for some reason, it will be waiting for you."

"Why would you be gone?"

"I need to buy more supplies at the sutler's store at Fort Lincoln within a couple of weeks. I'll be gone for at least one day."

"Oh. I thought you meant gone and not come back."

He didn't commit to staying permanently, but said, "It is going to be a long winter. They are always long, hard winters on the plains."

"Yes. Worse than back in Germany and not many trees to block the wind."

He nodded then said, "I'll take the wagon to the river tomorrow and gather a lot of firewood."

She smiled as she said, "I won't burn this furniture."

Cap grinned and said, "No, ma'am."

After he cleaned her Colt, he gave it back to her before they resumed the interrupted English lesson.

———

When he left the house after supper, he was carrying his two bedrolls. Now that the house had two beds and mattresses, he could avoid spending another night on his mules' saddle blankets.

After he folded their saddle blankets and put them under the tack tarp outside of his tent, he created his new double-bedroll mattress. He would still sleep in his clothes and heavy jacket until the seriously cold weather arrived.

The winters were harsh with almost constant strong winds but not nearly as much snow as there had been in Minnesota. The summers were much hotter and more humid than folks back east would believe. The season's violent storms often spawned tornadoes that could devastate entire towns in a few minutes. Spring was iffy and usually wet and chilly. Autumn was the most pleasant season on the Great Plains, and this one seemed to be better than most. But it was the extended, almost summer-like weather that had caused some concern. He suspected that Mother Nature would soon balance the scale with a bitter prelude to winter.

He removed his gunbelts and set them on his weapons tarp before laying on his bedrolls. He imagined that the corporal's squad was still dragging bodies into a big hole that they'd dug. It was easily the worst experience those soldiers would ever have. He couldn't even enter the house with seven bodies, yet they were having to bury almost a hundred of their comrades. He just hoped that he'd see them pass by tomorrow. Maybe he'd be gathering firewood when they rode back to Fort Lincoln.

When he thought of the fort, he recalled the last time he'd visited it in '71 before he set out westward to survey the future route of the Northern Pacific. Back then, it was almost fully manned with veterans of the Civil War. After Lieutenant Colonel Custer and others had ridden onto the plains to take on the Sioux and Cheyenne, those numbers had been steadily declining. But that was the army's problem. He just hoped that the sutler's store was still fully stocked. If not, he'd have to ride another eight miles, cross the Heart River and then take the ferry across the Missouri. It would add a full day to his supply run.

The journey would become necessary within two weeks, but he had more than enough work to keep him busy. In addition to the firewood, he had to dig a new privy hole. Rather than build an outhouse, he'd erect his smaller tent over the hole to give Mrs. Braun some privacy. He was surprised that she hadn't brought up the issue.

At least finding the furniture and wagon eliminated some of the work. He wasn't going to take the newly repaired wagon to the fort because it would slow him down and if he broke another wheel, he'd have to abandon it.

Even as he began planning for the winter, he wondered what Mrs. Braun would do when he left in the spring. If he didn't find a German farmer she would accept as her husband, maybe by then, he wondered if she'd still be committed to staying. Maybe she'd want to come with him by springtime. But he still had no idea of what he'd be doing after he left.

If she stayed, he'd ensure that she had as many supplies as possible before he left and give her fifty dollars in greenbacks. That should be enough to last her a full year, but he still felt queasy even thinking about leaving her alone with her children.

Erna kissed Gustave and Elsa on their foreheads before walking to her bed and pulling back the blankets but didn't lay down. She stared at the bed and wished that she had some way to thank Mister Tyler for all he'd done. She wished he'd stay and maybe one night in the near future, they'd share the bed. But he'd made it clear to her that he wasn't a farmer and would be leaving no later than springtime.

She soon slid her feet beneath the blankets and pulled them up to her chin. The glowing embers from the fireplace created an eerie red glow in the room as she thought about the coming fall and winter months. Maybe he'd change his mind before spring and stay. But she was determined not to make him feel guilty for leaving. She suspected that he would stay if she asked him to sleep with her but wasn't going to use that immoral ploy. He had his own life to live. Besides, his decision to erect his tent outside the house demonstrated his high moral standards. As she'd told her children, Mister Tyler was a gentleman in the truest sense of the word.

CHAPTER 4

Cap hurled the two-inch-thick, eight-foot-long branch onto the wagon bed where it landed atop the growing pile. He had almost cleared the small forest and was about to create more dead wood when he spotted Corporal McDermott's squad on the western horizon. He walked to the wagon and left the axe on the driver's seat before stepping out of the trees to wait for the cavalrymen to get closer. He counted all twelve riders, so he knew that they hadn't encountered any Lakota. He assumed that if the Sioux had set a trap for the expected relief column, they had finally abandoned the plan after the long delay. He hadn't seen any signs of the Lakota when he spotted the bodies, but they may not have paid attention to a lone rider, despite his desirable arsenal.

When the column was opposite him on the creek, the corporal brought them to a halt and walked his horse closer to the bank.

Cap shouted, "That must have been pretty nasty work."

"Aye. It was as bad as it gets. We just dug a big hole and dragged he bodies to the edge. It wasn't a proper burial, but we were kinda nervous about the Indians. They never showed up, but as soon as we finished, we hightailed it outta there. We camped about three miles west of here, but we won't feel safe 'til we're back in the fort."

"I can understand why you'd feel that way with only a dozen troopers."

"Do you reckon it's a good idea for you to stay here on your lonesome with the lady and her young'uns? Maybe you oughta convince her to go to Bismarck."

"I asked when I got here, but she's determined to stay. She buried her husband herself, so I can understand why she wants to remain on her land. I don't think the Sioux are going to return, though. They did their damage and there would be no point in coming back."

"Well, good luck. What's your name, anyway?"

"Cap Tyler. And no, I wasn't an army or navy captain. It's short for Casper."

Corporal McDermott snickered then said, "Well, Cap, look me up when you come to the fort to buy those supplies."

"What's your Christian name, Corporal?"

"George, but everybody calls me Mac. I forgot the name of the family you're watchin' over."

"Braun. The lady's name is Erna, and her children are Gustave and Elsa. The boy is six and the little girl is four."

“They speak any English?”

“Some, but I’m helping them to learn the language.”

“That’ll pass some time. Don’t go teachin’ ‘em any bad words, Cap.”

Cap chuckled then replied, “I won’t. I’m having a hard enough time with cow and horse.”

Mac didn’t ask about what else he was teaching Mrs. Braun before he waved and rejoined his squad. Seconds later, the column rode east. They’d reach the safety of Fort Lincoln by late afternoon and deliver the horrific, but probably expected news to their commander.

Cap wondered if the Sioux scouts who had provided the information that led to the loss of C Company still lived near the fort. He suspected that they had been with the company and led them to the site of the ambush. He’d ask when he visited the fort to pick up the supplies in a couple of weeks.

He then moved the wagon closer to an already damaged tree to finish what nature had started. He didn’t know what had snapped the trunk almost in half but appreciated the head start it gave him. Before he stepped down from the wagon, he removed his shirt. The temperature was fairly warm, and he didn’t want to return to the house looking like one of the men who laid the rails after a hot summer day.

The cottonwood was only a foot or so in diameter, so it took just ten minutes to send it crashing onto the ground. He then chopped through the last tether of wood attaching the tree to the trunk. He'd return in a month or so and reduce the entire tree to firewood for the winter. But now he had another use for the stump.

He returned to the wagon and began pulling the long branches from the wagon. He used the stump as a chopping block and began reducing the long branches to the proper length for Mrs. Braun's fireplace.

Sweat was dripping from every pore on his body as he swung the axe into the branch and usually cut through the wood with one blow. Some of the thicker branches took as many as three cuts but after almost an hour of constant work, the wagon's bed was clear. After he had tossed all of the shorter firewood back onto the wagon bed, he walked to the driver's seat, removed his work gloves and took his canteen from the footwell. He quickly emptied its contents and set it on the seat to be refilled. He was still drenched in sweat, so he just climbed into the driver's seat and waited for the air to him dry enough so he could pull his shirt back on.

He watched Buck Creek flowing eastward and knew that it emptied into the Missouri south of Bismarck and about a mile north of Fort Lincoln. He wondered if it wouldn't be better if he built a flatboat to visit the fort. After a few minutes of toying with the notion, he laughed and pulled on his shirt. He was as close to being a boatbuilder as he was to being a farmer. He'd ride Joe and trail Jasper to get their supplies.

He drove the wagon from the trees, made a short stop at the creek to fill his canteen and let his mules drink then turned them south.

When he reached the house, he stepped down, donned his work gloves again then began stacking the firewood against the side of the house. He wondered if the Sioux had burned her supply of firewood when they'd set fire to her wagon or Mr. Braun hadn't gotten around to replenishing their supply. The wood he was unloading now should last her at least another two or three weeks.

Cap had almost emptied the wagon when Erna stepped around the side of the house.

He continued stacking the wood as she stopped near the back of the wagon and asked, "Will you be coming inside for lunch today?"

"Yes, ma'am. But first, I need to unharness my mules and wash off the woodchips and dirt. I'm pretty dirty."

She smiled and said, "You are probably cleaner than I am."

He tossed the last piece of firewood onto the tall pile then replied, "I doubt if that's true, ma'am. But I am going to get filthy again this afternoon."

“What are you going to do?”

“I’m going to dig a new privy hole and erect my other tent over it so you and your children can have some privacy.”

“That would be nice. Are you sure you can afford to lose your tent?”

“Yes, ma’am. I won it in a poker game and haven’t really had much use for it.”

She looked at him quizzically and asked, “Poker?”

Cap grinned as he pulled off his work gloves and said, “Yes, ma’am. It’s a card game that a lot of men play.”

“And you won a tent playing this game?”

“I won a lot more than the tent. I’ll tell you about it later. Okay?”

“Alright. We’ll wait for you. Thank you for the firewood.”

“You’re welcome, ma’am.”

Erna smiled then turned and walked back to the house.

Cap watched her leave then began unharnessing Jed and Jasper. After the mules walked off to join Joe who was grazing nearby and probably snickering at his brothers’ demotion to wagon pullers, Cap washed using the basin in his tent.

As he dried himself, he glanced at the empty part of the dirt floor. He would have to build a small fire pit there when he returned from his supply run to Fort Lincoln. He'd need the heat when the winter arrived in force. He was no stranger to living outside in harsh weather. Ever since his father had joined the Union Pacific push into the west, he'd endured the bitter cold and roaring blizzards. This large tent offered much better protection than most of his earlier temporary housing. Over the past decade, he'd probably spent no more than thirty days inside a real structure.

A short time later, a reasonably clean Cap Tyler reached into one of his personal packs and pulled out his well-used deck of cards, then popped out of his tent.

When he entered the house, he was impressed with the work Mrs. Braun had done to improve its appearance. The pleasant aroma wafting in the air told him that she'd made good use of the Dutch oven.

He stepped to what he now referred to as the adult table and sat down. With only two plates, a situation he would remedy when he went to Fort Lincoln, he and Mrs. Braun would share one and her children would share the other.

Erna sat down and looked at Cap expectantly. He wasn't sure what she was expecting of him until he noticed that Gustave and Elsa had bowed their heads. As he recited grace, he felt a bit awkward. Giving thanks to God for the gift of food was the duty of the head of the household.

But after he said 'amen', she smiled, said, "Thank you, Cap," and began filling their plates.

As he ate, he said, "Those soldiers passed by while I was cutting the wood. They didn't see any Indians."

"That is good news. Did they tell you anything else?"

"Only that they were happy to be going back to the fort."

As she nodded, Cap set the deck of cards on the small table.

"You will teach us poker?" she asked with a smile.

"Yes, ma'am. After I return from digging the privy hole. It will be part of our English lesson."

Gustave had watched him place the cards on the table and asked, "Do you know other games?"

He turned and replied, "Yes, sir. Many others."

"Can I learn, too?" asked Elsa.

"Of course."

Erna was still smiling as she watched her children's happy faces. For those first few days after they lost their father, she thought that they'd never smile again. Those horrible, lonely days and nights when they lived a nightmare existence in fear that the Sioux would return. Then there was the secondary, but more certain fear of starvation. She still had nightmares, but her precious children were recovering much faster than she had ever hoped. Now they were learning how to speak and write English which would give them more opportunities.

She turned her eyes back to the man who had made it possible and wished he would stay. As much as she missed Wilhelm, she had to admit that Mister Tyler was kinder to her children than their father had been. Wilhelm was a good, industrious man but was a stern disciplinarian. Gustave was his son and Wilhelm was determined to make him a strong man. She could understand his ways, but as she watched how gently Mister Tyler was with him, she believed that if Cap had been his father, Gustave would still become a strong man. He would also be a kind and generous man. A man like Cap Tyler.

After they cleaned the two tin plates, Cap left the house and headed to his tent to pick up his pickaxe, shovel and the small tent.

Selecting a location for the privy was a matter of tradeoffs. If it was close to the house, the odor would be annoying. Too far away could be dangerous come wintertime. He'd probably have to move it twice more before then, too.

He picked a spot about eighty feet north of the house and began digging. When he set aside his shovel, he began pitching the tent. Once the privy tent was up, he returned to his big tent with the tools and rummaged through another pannier and pulled out his modified canvas chair. He'd spotted it in Deadwood and paid cash money for it. It was an odd thing and he'd never seen one before. He hadn't told Mrs. Braun about it because he wanted it to be a surprise. Now she wouldn't have to worry about Elsa falling into the hole. He carried it out to the privy tent where he extended its wooden legs and pushed its feet into the ground leaving the opening in the seat over the new hole. Once he was satisfied that it wouldn't move, he left the tent.

Erna had already pushed the two tables together and had placed one chair on each side in preparation for their card-playing English lesson.

So, when Cap entered the room, he said, "You have a card table."

She slid the deck of cards to the middle of the table in front of his empty chair and said, "We can learn to play poker now."

He sat down, picked up the deck then flipped over the first card and set it on the table.

"This is the nine of spades. See the number? Then count the spots. Each looks like a tiny shovel."

Each Braun eye was focused on the cards and followed Cap's index finger as he touched the symbols. The poker English lesson had begun.

The instructive and enjoyable lesson progressed for the rest of the afternoon. The first interruption was when Elsa whispered to her mother and Erna had to take her daughter to the new privy.

When they returned, Erna exclaimed, "There was a cloth seat!"

Cap grinned as he replied, "Yes, ma'am. It'll make things better."

She and Elsa sat down while Gustave was torn between wanting to see the chair in the privy and continuing to learn about cards. He decided he'd see the privy soon anyway, so the poker English lesson continued.

When Cap returned to his tent that evening, he was very pleased with the progress they were all making. He and Mrs. Braun still conversed using a hodge-podge mix of German and English, but at least they weren't misunderstanding each other any longer. He also realized that his German was rapidly improving. He hadn't reached the point of teaching them the game of poker itself, but now they understood the cards. It helped that many German and English words were so much alike. It was the ones that sounded alike but meant something quite different that was the problem. He knew he wasn't a real teacher and wasn't about to discuss English grammar. He just needed to give them a foundation.

As he stretched out on his bedrolls, he created a basic schedule for the important things he needed to do before winter arrived. Now that Mrs. Braun had the Dutch oven, he suspected that their food supply wasn't going to last another two weeks. He pushed his trip to the fort forward a week. He'd plan on leaving for Fort Lincoln on Monday, the first day in October.

———

Franz had given up finding a willing comrade to join him when he eventually left Bismarck. The Mayers treated him as if he was an orphaned boy. He'd been working at the smithy for his five dollars but all he seemed to be learning was how to be a servant. The Irish blacksmith seemed to hate him, and the other apprentices resented him because he lived with their boss. They were all bigger and stronger than he was, which added to their distaste.

He had to figure out a way to leave the town and even began thinking about returning to his farm. Maybe if he cleaned out those bodies, he could sell the place. Once the idea popped into his mind, the only thing that kept him from following through and leaving right away was knowing that his family's bodies were still putrefying in the large house. He figured it would take another two weeks before he'd be able to clean out their remains. Then he could return to Bismarck and sell the place to a new German immigrant family. He knew how much his father had paid for the full section of land, but now it had three houses. If he asked five hundred dollars for the farm, he'd probably have a line of prospective buyers. He disregarded the fact that almost all of the new arrivals would have already bought their property from a Northern Pacific agent.

Once his time line was set, he celebrated by having a couple of good lagers. He could put up with the Mayers and those smarmy apprentices for a couple of weeks. After he sold the farm, he'd head to the Black Hills where he had heard there was gold everywhere. With his five hundred dollars, he would have a good stake and by this time next year, he'd probably be rich.

The next morning, before he started his day's work, Cap told Mrs. Braun about his revised plan. She understood the pressing need and didn't seem distressed at all. He was relieved that she'd taken the news so well and attributed it to her improved sense of security provided by her Winchester and Colt. She hadn't fired either gun since learning how to use them because she didn't want to waste his ammunition. If she'd asked, he would have given her a box of .44s as he had eight. It would have been different if she'd asked to try his '76 with its expensive and hard to find cartridges.

He spent his morning doing smaller jobs that had been neglected but when they were done, he rode Joe out to the fields to see how much grain had survived the fire. When he finished his inspection, he didn't know if there was enough to provide seed for her spring planting. He wasn't going to ask Mrs. Braun because it would probably upset her.

He still had no idea how she'd be able to keep the farm unless he found a German farmer who would become her husband. He knew that she no longer had a plow, nor had he seen one on Hartmann place. He supposed that he could buy her a new one in Bismarck when he arrived there in the spring but found it difficult to picture her working the plow. She was just so small. While she may not have been thin, she surely didn't appear to have the physical strength to plow, sow and reap a large field of wheat. Even if she did manage to do it all on her own while still caring for her children, she'd then have to transport the wheat. Now that the Northern Pacific's tracks weren't going to be just on the other side of Heart River, it would mean a longer and more dangerous journey. Despite having the two guns, she'd still be vulnerable and so would her children.

He returned to his tent with no solution to his conundrum. He knew he could drive a plow but admitted to himself that he'd feel lost. He enjoyed being with Mrs. Braun and her children very much, but this wasn't his life. He admired farmers for their patience and determination, but he could never be one. He couldn't even explain the reason to himself. He could learn how to farm, but he knew he'd never be a farmer. But that problem wouldn't arrive until after they'd gotten past the long, hard winter.

The rest of the day was spent in the house playing cards and teaching English. It had become their routine already and Cap looked forward to the afternoon sessions.

The next few days followed that routine and by the end of September, they were playing their first hands of poker.

As he dealt the cards, Cap said, "I'll leave early in the morning and may be gone by the time you awaken. I should be back by sunset."

Erna nodded as she picked up her hand but didn't reply. He'd already outlined tomorrow's trip several times over the past few days but knew he was just telling them again to reinforce their hope that he'd return. She didn't doubt that he would because he was such a good man. She wasn't even worried about any potential danger. They hadn't seen another human since his arrival.

Gustave asked, "Will you buy a lot of food?"

"Yes, sir. Enough to fill your tummy until you're as tall as me."

Gustave giggled, then looked at Elsa and said, "I'm going to be big."

Elsa laughed then smiled at her big brother before looking at her cards.

They were using small twigs as money as they played the game. Cap could have brought his pouch of coins from his tent but didn't see any advantage to using real money. He'd leave the pouch and some paper currency with Mrs. Braun when he left in the spring, but he'd be spending some tomorrow at Fort Lincoln. He'd look up Corporal Mac, too. He hadn't seen any cavalry ride west since talking to the soldier on their return trip. He could have missed a patrol or two while he was working in the house but hoped that the army hadn't suffered any more disasters like the one that had befallen Company C.

They continued playing the game while speaking as little German as possible until suppertime, then resumed after dinner. It was after sunset when Cap wished them a good night's sleep and left the house. When he entered his tent, he felt an odd sensation of loss that didn't make any sense. He would only be gone a day and he was sure that they would be safe.

He sat on his bedrolls and wondered why he felt that way. After a few minutes, he realized that it was because tomorrow would be just a precursor to the next time he rode away from the farm in the spring. Then he'd be leaving them for good. He was already beginning to feel as if they were his family and his responsibility. *How could he leave them?*

Cap finally sighed before he laid down on his bedroll. He had months to solve his ever-growing impasse.

Cap was up before the predawn. By the time the sun peeked over the eastern horizon, he was already four miles east of the farm. He was riding Joe and trailing Jed who was carrying eight empty panniers. He had decided to give Jasper a break. He was only wearing one of his Remingtons and left his Sharps and spare Winchester back in his tent as well. He didn't expect any problems and wanted to move fast.

He followed Buck Creek and crossed over to the northern bank when he found a decent ford. The sun wasn't even at its zenith when he spotted Fort Abraham Lincoln in the distance. Like most army forts, it was spread out across a wide area. There was only a small portion of the fort that was surrounded by walls. To someone not familiar with the West, it would look more like a settlement than an army post. He wouldn't be able to see Bismarck today as it was another seven miles northwest of the fort on the other side of the Missouri River.

As he approached the fort, he noticed that the Sioux encampment was much smaller than he remembered the last time he'd visited. He assumed that all of the Lakota Sioux were gone and some of the other Sioux nations' members had gone with them. There were so many different tribes in the Sioux nation that he didn't know them all. Their lands covered thousands of square miles and he knew that they were going to lose most, if not all of it over the next ten years.

But he had no control over that or much else as he turned Joe toward the large sutler's store. He hoped that its shelves were as full as it had been four years ago, but suspected that with Bismarck's growth, there wasn't the same demand as before.

He pulled Joe to a stop, dismounted and tied him off at the hitchrail. He stepped into the store and was relieved to see that it was just as well stocked as he had recalled. He'd be able to fill his panniers and then some. He had emptied his saddlebags before he left in the hope that he'd be able to fill them as well.

The sutler waved at him as he approached the counter and said, "I haven't seen you before; have I?"

"Not in six years. I was on a survey team that passed through here in '71. I was kind of left out to dry in Montana Territory when the railroad went under."

"You came back looking for a job again?"

"Maybe. I need to buy a lot of supplies. I'll bring in my panniers and line them up. Okay?"

"I only take American cash, mister. Is that alright?"

"That's fine," Cap replied before he turned and walked out of the store to retrieve his panniers.

After they were lined up before the counter, Cap started walking the aisles and returning with his selections. After the sutler marked the price of an item on a sheet of paper, Cap took it from the counter and placed it in one of the panniers. He wanted to balance the load and have the heavier things on the bottom. It was also how he was managing his purchases. Once he finished with the tins and heavy sacks of flour, beans, rice, sugar and salt, he began to move lighter items to the counter.

He shopped for more than forty minutes and the sutler's column of numbers continued to grow. Cap had been adding them in his head as he watched and was surprised that the prices that he was being charged weren't outrageous. Now that the Northern Pacific was sending supply trains regularly to Bismarck, it meant that the demand no longer exceeded the supply. He suspected that the Panic had also driven prices down and were just beginning to return to what they were in '73.

Once he was satisfied that he'd met his goal for necessary supplies, Cap added some superfluous purchases that he felt were almost as important as the ones already in his panniers.

When he finally finished, he settled with the sutler and paid the enormous $82.44 bill. The proprietor then helped him load his panniers onto Jasper and after Cap had tied them down and hung his stuffed saddlebags over Joe, he mounted his mule and headed for the army buildings. He hoped to find Corporal McDermott because he liked the man. But even if he didn't, he still needed to talk to someone about what they knew about the Northern Pacific's plans and the trouble they expected from the tribes.

As it turned out, he didn't have to search for the corporal at all. Before he reached the administration building, Corporal McDermott had spotted him and was heading towards him. He wasn't marching, but it wasn't a casual stroll, either.

Cap stepped down and grinned at the soldier before shaking his hand.

"Howdy, Corporal Mac. Glad to see you made it back in one piece."

"You ain't the only one. The good news is that we're expecting a whole regiment. That'll get us to full strength."

"I assume that's only because the Northern Pacific told them that they were going to start laying tracks again and wanted the army to protect their work crews."

"I reckon so."

"How much trouble are you expecting from the tribes?"

“It all depends on who’s talkin’. I reckon they’ll be keepin’ us pretty busy. There ain’t another fort between here and Fort Keough near Miles City in Montana Territory. I don’t figure they’re plannin’ on buildin’ any more either.”

“That’s about three hundred miles. I’ve traveled that route and you’re going to need all of those men in the new regiment to cover that much ground.”

“You got that right. If I hadn’t already spent half my life in the army, I’d just ride off into the next sunrise.”

“Were you with the same unit during the war?”

“No, sir. I was stupid enough to want to join up, but I was too young, so I missed that bloodbath. I enlisted in Nebraska City when I was eighteen and they sent me to Fort Robinson in Nebraska then Fort Omaha. I never even heard a shot fired in anger ‘til I got here a few months ago. I hope I learn enough before we run into them Indians.”

“You’ve got a good head on your shoulders, Mac. You’ll be fine. What happened to your scouts?”

The corporal snorted, then spat before snapping, “*Scouts?* The only scoutin’ that they did was for their pals out west. They rode out with Company C and most likely used the rifles we gave ‘em to kill every one of those boys.”

“Who are you using to scout for you now?”

“We’ve got three Santee Sioux that the colonel seems to trust, but most of us regular soldiers don’t. They act all friendly but so did the other ones.”

Cap nodded before Corporal McDermott suddenly asked, “Say, do you want to be a scout for us, Cap? You said you been out there for six years and four of ‘em on your own. Did you deal with them Indians a lot?”

“Yes, sir. I can’t speak their language, but I used sign language to trade with some of the tribes. I used my Sharps and Winchester to speak with the ones who weren’t pleasant.”

Mac’s eyebrows rose as he asked, “You got into fights with ‘em?”

“Quite a few, really. Most of the time it was because they wanted what I had and thought they could take them without losing any warriors.”

After a short pause, he quietly asked, “Did you take any bullets or arrows?”

Cap shook his head as he replied, “No. I did have a few near misses, but I always had an advantage in range and accuracy. The biggest danger was being caught while I slept but depended on my mules to alert me if they smelled someone sneaking up on me.”

He glanced at Joe and Jed and said, “That one with the pack saddle is really different.”

"He is, but he's a strong mule."

Mac nodded then said, "Why don't you come with me to the non-commissioned officer's mess for chow? They'd like to hear about those fights. Maybe you'll even decide to be a scout."

"I'd be happy to join you for lunch, but I still have to get back soon because I left Mrs. Braun and her children alone."

As they started to walk toward the mess, Mac said, "Oh, that's right. I forgot you were takin' care of the lady and her young'uns. Are you plannin' on stayin' with her?"

"Just for the winter. I'm in a bit of a dilemma about what to do come springtime but maybe she'll find a German-speaking farmer husband by then. I know she wants to stay on her farm, and I'll feel like a skunk for leaving her alone. But I'm not a farmer."

"I reckon that's gonna be hard. You aren't um…you know…"

Cap quickly said, "No. I'm not. I'm living in my large tent outside the house. The last thing I want to do is make her pregnant."

"That would be kinda make things worse."

"A lot worse," Cap said as they turned into the mess that was just a large dining room.

He spent almost an hour enjoying the camaraderie of military men as he ate a very filling meal and told them of his many confrontations with the Cheyenne, Crow, Blackfeet and Sioux. He didn't include the ones with the white men because he suspected that they wouldn't be interested anyway. Mac brought up the scout proposition which was reinforced by enthusiastic responses from the other corporals and sergeants. Cap explained his situation with Mrs. Braun and his plan to join the Northern Pacific as a surveyor in the spring. But the NCOs persisted in making their case for him to join them as a scout. Cap simply told them that he'd consider it but had to leave soon.

Two hours after arriving at the fort, Cap waved to Mac and set Joe westward at a medium trot. Jed was more heavily loaded than he'd ever been but seemed to be handling the weight without any difficulty. His saddlebags weren't very heavy, but they were bulging so much they almost looked like giant leather balls.

As he rode, he wasn't surprised when he realized how much he anticipated seeing Mrs. Braun again. He had bought her and her children a few presents that they hadn't expected and couldn't wait to see the look on their faces when they found them. But as that pleasant thought arrived, he soon realized that it might be better if he was in his tent when they unpacked the panniers and his saddlebags. She might be so happy that she'd embrace him and that could be dangerous.

He still called her Mrs. Braun, even in his thoughts. She had been addressing him by his shortened first name for a while now. He'd only spoken her Christian name once, and that was on the first day when they'd had so many communication errors. Even though he was sure that he could address her as Erna, he was trying to keep some measure of formality just to slow his slide toward deeper affection.

But he was still anxious to return and find them safe. He wasn't worried about any danger to himself. He had a clear field of view for most of the ride, so he couldn't be ambushed. He only had to avoid letting Joe or Jed step into a prairie dog hole.

After crossing Buck Creek in late afternoon, he knew he'd spot the farmhouse in another hour or so. He still scanned the surrounding landscape and checked his backtrail but focused his attention to the southwest.

When he did see the roof of her house in the distance, he breathed a sigh of relief. There was no flock of vultures in the sky and the only smoke was coming from the crude chimney.

He still didn't ask Joe and Jed for more speed, but kept his eyes trained on the house. He didn't see anyone outside but expected that Mrs. Braun might be cooking dinner for the children. She wouldn't have been expecting him to return so soon.

Erna had a fire burning but wasn't cooking. She'd taken advantage of Cap's absence to lead her children to the river for a bath and then washed their clothes. After she returned, she used some of the cord from the reel he'd left in the house to string a clothesline across the floor. She would have preferred to hang the wash outside but didn't have any poles. After the wet clothing was hanging over the line, she built a fire to warm the room.

When Cap was crossing Buck Creek, she took down the laundry and clothesline, changed into the clean dress and wondered if what she was doing amounted to flirting. She didn't have any way to brush her washed hair and knew it must be a tangled mess. But at least it was finally clean, and she no longer smelled like one of his mules.

When she'd walked with Gustave and Elsa to the river, Jasper had followed them as if he expected her to bathe him as well. When they finished, the mule dutifully trailed them back to the house. Maybe he thought he was their guardian during Mister Tyler's absence.

She had just decided to start cooking supper when she heard hoofbeats outside. Before she could reach the doorway, Gustave had popped up from his chair and rushed outside leaving the door open. As Erna reached their table, Elsa hopped down and took her hand. Mister Tyler had returned.

———

Cap was stepping down when he saw Gustave sprint around the corner leaving a small dust cloud as he made a sliding turn.

"Mister Tyler! You're back already!' he exclaimed in tortured English that took Cap a couple of seconds to understand.

He still grinned and waited for the boy to reach him and then surprised the lad when he plucked him from the ground and held him in the crook of his left arm as he waited for Mrs. Braun and Elsa to appear.

When she rounded the corner of the house, she was surprised to see her son grinning at her from Cap's arm.

"You returned early," she said when they were close.

"I didn't want to leave you alone for very long," he replied.

He couldn't help but notice the change in her appearance. She may have been wearing the same dress she'd worn yesterday, but it was clean. She and her children must have taken a bath as well, but he wasn't about to comment.

He set Gustave on the ground then said, “I’ll move the packs into the house, and you can unpack them while I take care of my mules. They had a long day.”

“So, did you. Did you have lunch?”

“Yes, ma’am. I ate with the soldiers at Fort Lincoln. I’ll tell you about it later.”

She smiled then said, “Alright,” before she turned and led her children back into the house.

Cap pulled his Winchester from his scabbard and left it in his tent before leading Joe to the front of the house. Before he started moving the packs, he brought the new broom inside and gave it to Mrs. Braun.

It took him ten minutes to lug the heavy panniers into the house. Erna was stunned by the amount of supplies that he’d bought. She hadn’t seen him leave with so many panniers and hadn’t even looked at the heavily loaded mule when he was holding Gustave. She didn’t offer to help him as she doubted if she could handle that much weight.

When he carried the eighth one inside, Cap had his bloated saddlebags over his left shoulder.

As he set the weighty pack on the floor near the others, she asked, “Why did you bring your bags?”

“I filled the packs and needed more room,” he replied before lowering them to the floor.

“I’ll be back in a little while,” he said before he waved and left the house.

Once outside, he quickly led Joe and Jed away from the front door. He was fighting back the overpowering urge to watch their expressions and hear their joyful voices when they discovered his supplementary purchases.

Erna looked at the saddlebags curiously but began emptying the first pannier. She opened the flap and started removing the lighter items. She was pleased to find two more heavy woolen blankets, then she moved onto the edibles. She stacked the very welcomed foodstuff along the far wall but showed the interesting ones to her children who were watching her with wide eyes. When she reached the bottom of the first pack, she found a large sack of dry navy beans and a large jug of molasses. The beans alone could feed them for a week.

She moved to the second pannier and began finding more treasures. By the time she reached the fourth one, she couldn’t imagine what else Cap had bought. *She wasn’t even halfway through the enormous order!* After removing the lighter supplies on the top, she found two big sacks of salt, slabs of bacon, two large hams and a sack of potatoes in the fourth bag. There were tins of all sorts in the bottom of the fifth as well as a large sack of flour and another of corn meal. But it was the sixth pannier that contained her biggest surprise thus far.

After tossing the flap open, she stared at the cloth before slowly extracting a new dress. She hadn't had any new clothes since they left Germany and this one was so pretty. She held it in front of her and was surprised to find that it was the right size. She looked at Gustave and Elsa and found them smiling.

Elsa said, “It is pretty, Mama.”

She returned their smile as she replied, “Yes, it is.”

After setting it on the table, she was almost shocked when she found a second dress. She didn't check its size but set it aside and then found a camisole. She felt incredibly guilty as she placed it carefully on the dresses. She was almost afraid to look inside the pannier but when she did, she found another dress, but this one was obviously for Elsa. She held it out and showed her wide-eyed daughter.

“Is it for me, Mama?” she asked breathlessly.

“It's too small for me, and I don't think your brother will want to wear it.”

Elsa giggled as her mother gave her the new dress. *It wasn't even Christmas!*

Their October Christmas continued when Erna lifted a second dress for Elsa from the pack and gave it to her. She wasn't surprised when she then discovered two shirts and two pairs of britches for Gustave. There was even a new belt.

She wasn't close to becoming jaded as she continued her exploration of the magical sixth pannier. She found new boots for each of them and six pairs of socks. At least the smaller pairs could be worn by either Gustave or Elsa. She was almost embarrassed when she found three pairs of women's bloomers but was almost as grateful for them as she was for the dresses. She found the children-sized underwear before she reached the heavy items at the bottom. She was almost as pleased to find six tins of corned beef among them.

When she moved to the seventh pannier, she expected that there would only be more supplies. She soon discovered that she was wrong when the first item on the top of the pack was a boxed game of checkers.

It was Gustave's turn to express his excitement when he exclaimed, "*Is it a game, Mama?*"

She handed the box to him as she replied, "Yes, Gustave. It is a game called checkers. It is easy to learn and I'm sure Mister Tyler will teach it to you."

Gustave stared at the fancy picture printed on the front of the box and couldn't wait to learn how to play.

She almost laughed when she pulled out two decks of playing cards. She gave them to Elsa before she continued emptying the pannier.

She was almost disappointed to find six white towels, but quietly chastised herself. Before Cap had arrived, she would have wept to find a single towel. She then found a new heavy coat for Elsa and another for Gustave. She didn't find a third one for her before she discovered a dozen bars of white soap and other cleaning supplies. The heavy items on the bottom of the next to last pannier were all kitchen related. There was a heavy steel frypan, a spatula and a large fork, two pots, four more tin plates and bowls and four cutlery sets. What made her smile was a pair of salt and pepper shakers. When she'd found the peppercorn and grinder in an earlier pack, she had wished that he'd bought a pair. They were made of tin as well, so they would last.

She found more towels on the top of the last pannier before she found her coat. When she pulled it out of the pannier, she found two boxes of matches in the large pockets. At the bottom of the last pannier, she found a dozen candles, a chamber pot and more tins of food. When she looked at the labels, she was astonished to find that there were four cans of peaches among the last collection. She didn't tell her children of the contents before she set them with the rest of the food as if they contained beets or lima beans.

Before she checked his saddlebags, she moved all the empty panniers close to the doorway. She lifted his saddlebags from the floor and set it on the table before sitting down.

Gustave and Elsa had left their treasures on their table and stood close to her table's edge to get a closer view of the wonders Mister Tyler had hidden inside.

She untied the strap to the first one and flipped the flap over the top before she stuck her hand inside. She thought she'd touched a critter of some sort and quickly yanked her hand back out. After she realized how silly her reaction had been, she tilted it toward her and looked inside. She smiled and pulled out a furry hat with ear flaps. She guessed by the size that it was for Gustave and handed it to him. He pulled it on and grinned as she took out second furry hat for Elsa. After her daughter giggled as she donned her new headwear, she found one for her that was just a bigger version of the ones he'd bought for her children.

She then found three pairs of gloves that were also fur-lined. She had never had such luxury before.

She turned the saddlebags around and after untying the straps, she opened the last vault. Erna couldn't imagine that there was anything else that she could possibly need as she peered inside.

When she found a pair of painted eyes staring back at her, she glanced at her daughter and said, "I believe you will have to give Mister Tyler a kiss, Elsa."

"Why, Mama?"

Erna pulled out the doll and handed it to Elsa who squealed before she carefully took it from her mother's hand as if it was a delicate baby.

She cradled it in her arm as she said, "I am very happy, Mama."

Gustave smiled at his sister then turned his eyes expectantly back to the saddlebag wondering if Mister Tyler had bought him a gift.

She knew that there was probably something for her son in the saddlebag but the next thing she pulled out was a heavy woolen scarf. It was too big for a child, so she knew it was hers.

After she hung it over her shoulders, she then found two more, smaller scarves and set them on the table. She thought she'd find Gustave's gift on the bottom of the saddlebags, but she found something that she knew was meant for her. She reached inside and slowly withdrew a hairbrush. It wasn't fancy but it was a hairbrush and she wondered if Mister Tyler knew that she was going to need one after washing her hair.

She set the hairbrush the table and looked at Gustave's disappointed face as she lowered the saddlebags to the floor.

“Maybe the checkers were my present,” Gustave said quietly.

“Do you want to go outside and ask Mister Tyler?”

Gustave looked at his mother as he asked, “Won’t he be mad?”

“I don’t think he’ll be angry at all.”

He started to reply, “But Papa would…” but then stopped. His father was dead, and it wasn’t right to say anything bad about him.

Erna smiled at her son and softly said, “Go and ask him. Maybe he wants to surprise you.”

Gustave shook his head as he said, “I should be happy for all the things he bought for us, Mama. It wouldn’t be right to ask for more.”

She kissed him on his forehead then said, “I’m going to make a very special supper. Okay?”

“Okay, Mama. I’m going to go outside and thank Mister Tyler.”

“You do that and take your sister with you.”

“I was going to go, Mama!” Elsa exclaimed as she hugged her doll.

Erna nodded and watched her children leave the house. She still had a lot of things to put away. When Cap said he was going to buy supplies, she could never have imagined what she had discovered in those packs. She hoped that he didn't think she was ungrateful by not being with her children when they thanked him. She was still feeling guilty for accepting so much with no way to properly express her gratitude.

Cap hadn't forgotten about buying a gift for Gustave. In fact, he had two gifts for the boy and another for Elsa. He also had one small bag of edibles for each of them, including their mother. They were all small enough to fit in his coat pockets. He hadn't added them to the pannier for separate reasons.

He had ridden Joe and Jed to the creek to refill his canteens, then after returning and unsaddling his mules, he let them loose to have a family reunion of sorts with Jasper.

He had just finished creating his small firepit and was stepping out of his tent when Gustave and Elsa rounded the corner of the house. He saw Elsa holding onto her new doll as if it was trying to escape and was sure that Gustave was disappointed even though he was trying to hide it. He wouldn't be downtrodden much longer.

He smiled and said, “Hello, young people.”

Gustave offered him his hand as he said, “Thank you, Mister Tyler.”

Cap shook his hand and replied, “You’re welcome, Gustave.”

Elsa looked up at him and wanted to do as her mother suggested, but Mister Tyler’s stubbly beard looked scratchy. But she loved her doll and wanted to tell him how happy she was to have her.

Cap dropped to his heels to be at Elsa’s eye level, then put out his hand. Elsa smiled as she shook his hand and said, “Thank you.”

“You’re welcome, miss.”

While he was at child level, he turned to Gustave and said, “I have two presents for you, Gustave.”

He pretended not to be excited, but his eyes lit up as he asked, “You do?”

“I will give you one now and the second tomorrow at noon. I have another one for Elsa, too.”

Elsa was grinning at she looked at her brother then back at Mister Tyler.

Cap reached into his coat pocket and pulled out the small penknife. It was the smallest one he’d seen at the sutler’s store with just a three-inch blade.

As he handed it to Gustave, he said, “This can be dangerous, son. Before you open the blade, you must show it to your mother. If she says it is okay for you to have it now, then you can. If she wants to wait until you’re older, you have to wait. Okay.”

Gustave nodded as he stared at the small knife. He knew it was much better than a toy doll. It was almost as if Mister Tyler thought he was a friend and not a boy.

Elsa then asked, “What about mama?”

“I am sure your mother is happy. But when you return to the house, you can make her smile even more.”

He reached into his left coat pocket and pulled out a small paper sack. He’d been careful to avoid breaking its contents.

Four small blue eyes stared at the bag as Cap slid out a thick peppermint stick and gave it to Elsa. She studied the candy almost unsure of what she should do with it. But the smell gave her a hint, so she slowly began licking the end as Cap handed a second one to Gustave.

Gustave slid his new penknife into his pocket before accepting the treat. As he slipped it into his mouth, Cap handed him the bag.

“There’s one more for your mother.”

Gustave nodded as he continued to suck on the peppermint stick. Elsa had watched her brother and soon buried her minty candy stick into her mouth as well.

Gustave pulled his treat out and asked, "Are you coming?"

"In a minute."

"Okay."

He watched the two youngsters turn and walk away. He'd miss them as much as he'd miss their mother come springtime. He stood and walked back to his tent. He really didn't have to do anything. He just needed to avoid making things worse by watching Mrs. Braun's face light up when Gustave gave her the bag.

Erna slid the six-inch stick of peppermint from the bag and wondered why Cap hadn't returned. She finally assumed that he had to have finished unsaddling his mules and whatever else he needed to do.

She absent-mindedly began sucking on the candy as she thought about him. She hadn't enjoyed the taste of peppermint since she was a girl back in Germany.

Then Gustave pulled out his penknife and as he showed it to her, he said, “Mister Tyler said that I could only keep it if you said I could. Can I keep it, Mama?”

She looked down at his hopeful eyes, smiled and said, “Yes, Gustave. You may keep it. But be careful. It is sharp and you can cut yourself.”

He broke into a big grin then said, “Mister Tyler said he will give me and Elsa another present tomorrow at noon.”

“Why would he want to wait until noon?”

Gustave shrugged as he opened the small blade.

Erna suddenly snapped, “You stay here. I’m going to talk to Mister Tyler.”

Elsa quickly asked, “Are you mad at him, Mama?”

“No. I’m very pleased with him,” she replied before stepping out of the house.

She almost forgot about the candy in her hand as she turned left outside the door but wasn’t about to go back just to leave it on a table.

Cap was in his tent oiling his Sharps when he heard Mrs. Braun ask, “May I speak to you, Cap?”

He set his rifle on the tarp, then waddled out of the tent before he stood just three feet in front of her.

“Yes, ma’am?”

“Why are you staying away?”

“I had things to do. I knew that you would be busy putting things away.”

Erna was sure that he was obfuscating, but let it go.

“You bought much more than I expected. You spent too much of your money buying us things. It isn’t right.”

“You needed everything that I bought, Mrs. Braun. I was just lucky to find them.”

“But it was too much! You spent all your money.”

“Hardly. Money is a funny thing.”

Erna looked up at him uncertain if she understood him properly. *How could money be humorous?* It was very important and the only way to buy things that couldn’t be made or obtained in trade.

“What do you mean?”

He said, “Let’s go into your house and I will explain.”

“Alright.”

She turned and Cap followed her into the house where they each took a seat at their table while Gustave and Elsa sat nearby reducing their sticks of candy into small, sharp spears.

Erna set her almost untouched peppermint stick on the table and waited for Cap to explain what he'd meant.

He pulled out a fifty-cent piece and set it on the table. He'd have to speak slowly because he wanted her to understand.

"The value of money changes by time and location. In Bismarck or the sutler's store, that piece of silver could buy a large bag of flour or that sack of navy beans and still give you a dime change. Two of them could feed a family for a week. Before I came here, I stayed in Deadwood in the Black Hills for a few months. It was a wild place. They had six saloons and there were many shootings. There were many men looking for gold and most did not find any, so some tried to take it from those who did. But many of those men who had found gold, spent time in the saloons playing poker and drinking. I didn't drink, but I did play poker.

"When I first arrived, I set aside all of the money I had earned from the railroad except for twenty dollars and began playing poker. If I lost the twenty dollars, then I'd stop and move on. But those men who had found gold didn't have to worry about losing their last twenty dollars. They continued to play poker after drinking whiskey. It's not a smart thing to do. That first day I played poker, I won over thirty dollars. I kept setting most of my winnings aside and kept playing. There were a few men who weren't happy about losing, but the ones who had suddenly become rich with their gold, didn't mind losing fifty or a hundred dollars."

Erna quickly asked, "*You won a hundred dollars?*"

"Not in one day. I'd lose some hands, but I never left the poker table with less money than I'd had when I sat down. I didn't play at the same saloon twice in a row because some of the players suspected that I was cheating. I wasn't, but it may have appeared that way because I won so often. I won because most of them gave hints of the cards they held.

"After six months, I knew that I was becoming a target of the greedy men and it was time I left. I packed up my mules and left town to go to Bismarck. I'm telling you this to explain why money has different value in different places. In Deadwood, if I wanted to buy a mule, I would have had to pay over three hundred dollars. If I bought one in Bismarck, I could have him for less than fifty. That was because there was a lot more money in the Deadwood and fewer mules."

"Oh. I think I understand. But I still feel guilty for having all of these wonderful things. Will you stay while I start cooking a real supper?"

"Yes, ma'am."

As she rose, Erna still wasn't quite sure that she grasped the concept. Regardless of how much money Mister Tyler had won in Deadwood, she still felt guilty for accepting so much from a man who was living outside in his tent.

———

Cap returned to his tent after sunset then removed his gunbelt and laid on top of his bedrolls. It wasn't cold enough to build a fire, but the nights were becoming noticeably chilly. In a few days, he'd head out to the tree he'd cut down and prepare it for reduction into more firewood. He'd strip the branches and cut the trunk into smaller logs to let the wood dry faster. Before the snows arrived in earnest, he'd start splitting the logs.

He wished that he could have made Mrs. Braun believe that his money meant much less to him than she or her children did. He had explained how money's value varied but wasn't about to tell her how much he valued her, Gustave and Elsa. That would only make his situation worse. It was only October and he had at least six more months before spring arrived. He'd only been here for a couple of weeks and he couldn't imagine how difficult it would be for him to wave goodbye when winter finally abandoned its assault on the plains.

———

It wasn't quite noon the next day when Cap sat on his heels behind the house with the sun blazing overhead. If had been cloudy, he would have asked for a postponement.

Gustave and Elsa were standing at his shoulders wondering why he had led them to this spot to give them their second gifts. Erna stood facing Cap with the same question on her mind.

Cap had created a small mound of dry grass in the middle of the human circle which only deepened the mystery.

He looked at Gustave and smiled as he said, "When I saw this in the sutler's store, I was surprised, but had to buy it."

He then reached into his coat pocket and pulled out a small magnifying glass.

"You can look through this to make things appear bigger. But it can do something else that is more impressive. Watch."

He held the lens over the grass and began drawing it higher as he watched the circle of focused sunlight shrink. When it was nothing more than a pinpoint, he held the magnifying glass in place and waited.

After just a few seconds, the grass began to smoke then burst into flame.

The children gasped as they stepped back and Erna was startled. It was almost like magic.

Cap let the grass fire burn out then stood and ground it into black dust with his boot before handing the glass to Gustave.

"It bends the sunlight, so you need to be careful when you use it outside. Okay?"

The boy accepted the gift with awe. He hadn't understood all of what Mister Tyler had just said, but the power of the lens had made its mark.

He then turned to Elsa and pulled out a small box from his left pocket and handed it to her.

Erna smiled at him before looking down at her daughter's face as she opened the box of hair ribbons.

Elsa stared at the contents for a few seconds then looked at her mother and asked, "What are they, Mama?"

Erna selected a blue ribbon from the eight that were neatly folded in the box and after pulling it straight, she stepped behind Elsa and after arranging her hair into a ponytail, she bound it with the blue ribbon.

When her mother stepped away, Elsa felt the ribbon and smiled as she asked, "Is it pretty, Mama?"

"Very pretty, and it makes you even prettier."

Elsa looked at Cap and said, "Thank you, Mister Tyler."

"You're welcome, Miss Braun."

She then took a yellow ribbon from her box and handed it to her mother.

"You should wear this one, Mama."

Erna said, “Thank you, Sweetheart. I’ll put it on later.”

“It will make you even prettier, Mama.”

Her mother kissed her daughter on the forehead before she slid the ribbon into the pocket of her new dress.

Cap said, “I’m afraid that’s the last of the surprises, folks.”

Erna smiled at him as she said, “You are the biggest surprise, Cap.”

He grinned as he replied, “That’s what my mother told me when I didn’t cause her as much grief as my older brother.”

“When did you last see your brother?”

“About seven years ago. He when left to go to California. He has a wife and three children the last time I heard from him. That was three years ago, though. He probably has more youngsters by now.”

“You don’t write to him?”

Cap shrugged then replied, “We didn’t get along that much when we were boys. When he left for California, I wrote to him a few times for the first few years, but then it just seemed fruitless.”

Erna could understand how he might feel that way about his brother. When she was growing up, she had two older sisters. They didn't try to hide their jealousy in believing that, as the baby of the family, she received preferential treatment. She didn't think that she did, but it isolated her from her sisters. Her two brothers were ambivalent about anything to do with the girls in the family, so she had felt alone in the big house.

She had married Wilhelm Braun when she was sixteen and a more than a year after giving birth to Gustave, she was actually excited to be going to America. She was infected with her husband's enthusiasm and envisioned a veritable paradise that awaited them in Dakota Territory. The Northern Pacific agent was an excellent, albeit dishonest, salesman. She was already heavy with Elsa when they left Germany, and she delivered their daughter on the ship. As it was an American-flagged vessel, she had been told that it made Elsa an American citizen even before they stepped onto the shores of the New World.

She and the children had stayed in Missouri Crossing for a few months while Wilhelm built the house with the help of the Hartmann family who were already established.

After they move to their sod house, she had been almost despondent for the first year as she cared for her baby and young son while Wilhelm broke the ground for their wheat field. There was always the threat from the Indians but after three years without being attacked, she began to believe that they were safe. Wilhelm had built the small shelter despite the Hartmanns suggesting it was unnecessary. She had only used it for cold storage until that horrible day. The day when even the difficult life she'd finally become accustomed to had vanished into nothing. For those few days after she'd buried her husband, she couldn't imagine it ever improving.

Now, as she looked at her daughter wearing her new dress and boots and with a bright ribbon in her hair, she felt more optimistic about their future than she had had ever hoped.

Cap had watched her thoughtful face and believed that she was trying to choose the right words to express her appreciation for all of the supplies and gifts once more.

When she hadn't said anything for almost a minute, he said, "I'm going to go out to the trees and start cutting the one I chopped down into smaller pieces."

Erna snapped out of her reverie and replied, "Oh. What did you say?"

"I'm going to go to the trees to do some more work. I'll be back in a couple of hours."

"Alright. Thank you for everything, Cap."

"You're welcome, ma'am."

She then gave her children her motherly stare and waited.

Gustave quickly said, “Thank you for my glass, Mister Tyler.”

Elsa immediately followed saying, “Thank you for my ribbons, Mister Tyler.”

“You’re both very welcome.”

Erna then guided her children around the corner of the house and disappeared.

Cap let out a long breath then walked to his tent to retrieve his axe and his hatchet. He had already saddled Joe and wouldn’t need Jasper or Jed because he wasn’t going to bring anything back today. He’d just be cutting the branches from the trunk and then chopping them into smaller pieces. He might have time to start working on reducing the trunk to short logs, but he knew it would take a couple of days for the job.

———

By the time he left the small forest it was late afternoon, and he was exhausted after removing all of the branches. He’d used his hatchet to clean the big branches off the smaller ones then had cut them all down to two-foot lengths for her fireplace. He’d only managed to cut two sections from the top of the trunk where it was thinner before he called it a day. The thicker end would take more time, but it had to be done if he wanted the wood to be dry enough to burn during the winter. He still had to split the logs, too.

He rode Joe to the river to wash off the dirt and wood chips and saw the tail end of an army patrol heading west. He hadn't seen them as they passed by but suspected that Corporal Mac wasn't in charge. If he had been, he would have stopped when he heard the sound of chopping wood. They were also further north of the creek than the smaller patrol. He hoped it was just a routine patrol because he hadn't seen any Lakota since he'd arrived.

But as he mounted Joe, he did spot something that attracted his attention. He slowly slid his Winchester from its scabbard and cocked the hammer. He would only get one shot and then he'd have to cross the creek if he placed the .45 accurately.

He let his sights settle then squeezed his trigger. The repeater popped against his shoulder then he lowered his Winchester and returned it to its scabbard. He nudged Joe into the water and let him worry about his footing as they crossed Buck Creek. After his mule clambered up the northern bank, Cap hopped to the ground and picked up the big tom turkey.

"Sorry, ladies, your husband is going to be roasted," he said as he looked at the flock of hens who had scattered then stood in a protective circle fifty yards away.

He was sure that another, younger tom would be more than willing to take their supper's place as he stepped into the saddle and turned Joe back to the creek.

As he approached the house, he saw Mrs. Braun standing near his tent with her arms folded. He had expected to see her after she heard his Winchester's bark. He held the big bird out wide to let her understand why he'd had fired his repeater, and she waved.

The turkey had to have its feathers and its innards removed before it could be placed on the spit, so it would be tomorrow's supper, but it would be a welcome addition to their menu.

———

The next day, Cap was back in the small forest attacking the tree while Erna prepared the turkey. The feathers from the large bird would be saved for making a second pillow. She'd use the cloth from one of her two old dresses as the covering.

He only converted about half of the remaining trunk into short logs before putting away his axe. It needed sharpening, so he'd handle that tomorrow and finish the job on Friday.

———

Fifty-four miles away in Josef Mayer's smithy, Franz was straining as he lugged a crate of scrap iron to the furnace. He had just dropped it to the ground when Dennis Cullen, the Irish smith who'd lost his German customers, approached him. He was wiping the sweat from his brow with a gray work cloth when he stopped next to Franz.

Franz asked, “What do you want, Cullen?”

Dennis didn’t take offense as he said, “I was at the Taste of Cork last night sharin’ some good ale with a friend when I heard some army boys talkin’. I heard ‘em say Hartmann, so I asked the corporal what they heard.”

Franz was suddenly very interested in what the Irishman had to say and sharply asked, “What did they say about my family?”

“Not so much about your folks other than they were all dead. But he seemed mighty impressed with some feller who was helpin’ out your neighbor. I thought you said that they were all killed, too?”

“I thought so. They aren’t?”

“He said that the man of the house was killed but the lady and her wee children were spared.”

Franz was beyond startled as he hurriedly asked, “He said there was a man there who helped them?”

Dennis didn’t quite understand his question because he’d slipped into half-German in his haste.

“Say that again in English and slower.”

Franz carefully asked, “The soldier said a man was there?”

"He did. He said the man told him he was no farmer but was just helping the lady and her youngsters. So, they asked him to scout for the army."

"Did he go to the fort?"

"I reckon not. Maybe he'd be happy to see a German farmer show up at the place, so he could scout for the army."

Franz didn't care if Cullen was using the story to get him to leave. If it was true that Erna was now a widow, he'd leave Bismarck to pay her a visit. He wasn't sure about the stranger, but he couldn't have been there very long. He hoped that the man wasn't already taking Wilhelm's place in Erna's bed.

Dennis smiled, then turned away and walked to the larger anvil to finish the set of barn hinges.

Franz approached Mister Mayer and told him what he'd just learned and said it was his obligation to protect Mrs. Braun and her children.

Josef was pleased that Franz would help the orphaned family and gave him twenty dollars for his work and to help him provide for Mrs. Braun and her children.

It wasn't quite noon when Franz left the smithy and hurried to the Mayer house to pack.

———

Early that evening, as everyone enjoyed what amounted to a feast with roast turkey, mashed potatoes and gravy, none of the diners in the Braun home knew of the dramatic changes that would happen tomorrow afternoon.

CHAPTER 5

Franz was one of the first passengers on the ferry that morning. When it bumped onto the dock on the other side of the Missouri River, he was the first off and by the time the last passenger had stepped onto the dock, he was already a hundred feet away. He was anxious to discover if Cullen had told him the truth but wasn't going to stop at Fort Lincoln to ask. Nor was he going to stop by his family farm. He was going to get to the Braun place as quickly as possible. His mule would be the one to pay the penalty for his haste.

He wasn't concerned about potential danger from the Sioux because the entire town knew that they were now raiding more to the north. He still wished he had a Winchester. He almost bought a used one with the twenty dollars that Mister Mayer had given him but didn't want to part with any more of his money. He had been down to just eleven dollars and some change before the blacksmith's surprising offer.

Late last night, Mrs. Mayer had given him food for the journey and a bag with some clothes for Erna and her children. He hadn't opened the bag but almost snickered when she told him what it contained. She was a much larger woman than Erna Braun and he assumed that she had just given her one of her old dresses. If he had looked, he would have found that Berta had asked for donations from parishioners and received much more appropriate garments.

As he rode west, he thought about that stranger who was still with Erna. While he may have hoped that she wouldn't invite him into her bed, he found it difficult to imagine how any real man could resist Erna. She may have been short in stature, but she was more woman than Marta had been. He knew that no matter what he found when he arrived, he had to control his temper. He'd have to act civilized and even thank the stranger before sending him away. He didn't know what he'd do if the man refused to leave. But the soldier had told Cullen that the man wasn't a farmer and wanted to leave. Unless the soldier was wrong or the Irishman had just made it up to get Franz to leave, then it shouldn't be difficult to persuade him to go.

He'd discover the real situation in about eight hours. He should arrive on the Braun farm in midafternoon if he kept up this pace.

———

After a turkey-based breakfast, Cap had finished sharpening the axe and hatchet while Gustave watched. As he slid the whetstone across the sharp steel they talked about knives and guns.

After a cold turkey lunch, Cap saddled Joe and with his sharpened axe in his left hand he set off to make logs.

Normally, he would have just walked, but Cap didn't like being a half a mile away if danger arrived. Gustave had asked to join him, but his mother had stepped in and told him that it was too dangerous.

He soon reached the trees and let Joe wander off to spend time with Jasper and Jed who were grazing nearby.

———

Franz had crossed the Heart River early in the day and had almost been thrown into the water when his mule had stumbled. But he made it safely across and resumed his fast tempo ride to the west. He could have avoided crossing the river if he'd taken the smaller ferry south of town, but he didn't even know it existed. Now he crossed the much narrower Buck Creek and was just eighteen miles away when Cap removed his shirt and began to swing the axe.

———

Cap found his rhythm after a few minutes and took just fifteen blows to finish one log. He was still at the narrower end and knew the cuts would take progressively longer as he neared the stump. He still expected to finish in less than three hours.

Two hours later, he finally took a break and walked to his canteen that he'd hung from a branch and opened the cap. As he drank, he admired his wooden creation.

As he created each new shortened log, he rolled it aside and soon was building a pyramid. He wanted to keep as many of them off the ground as possible. He had a row of six of them on the bottom and had added three more to the second row. He didn't expect to make a true pyramid as he estimated he only had another eight cuts left on the trunk.

He popped the cap back on the canteen and hung it back on the branch. He picked up the axe and began attacking the log before his muscles tightened.

Inside the house, Erna was resorting all the food to a more logical order while Gustave and Elsa were out in front playing with his new magnifying glass.

Elsa was growing bored as her brother continued to play with his lens when she looked away and spotted the rider approaching from the east.

She popped to her feet and quickly pointed as she exclaimed, "Someone is coming!"

Gustave stood and looked where his sister was pointing and knew it wasn't Mister Tyler.

He grabbed his sister's hand and rushed into the house.

"Mama a rider is coming!" he shouted as they entered the room.

Erna quickly asked, “Is it an Indian?”

Gustave replied, “I don’t know, Mama.”

She sharply said, “Stay here!” then grabbed her Winchester and walked out the open doorway. Her Colt was in their hidden shelter as Cap had suggested, but she wouldn’t need it.

When she saw the rider about a mile away, she cocked her carbine then raised its muzzle into the air and fired.

Cap’s axe head had just dug into the tree trunk when he heard the crack of her Winchester. He left the axe buried in the wood, grabbed his shirt and rushed out of the trees. He whistled for his mules before he hurriedly pulled on his shirt. He immediately spotted the rider who was already closer to the house than he was.

He began jogging toward the house before Joe reached him. He wasn’t even armed yet as Joe was carrying his Winchester. He had become too complacent.

Franz had seen Gustave and Elsa out front and watched as they ran inside the house. It wasn’t an unreasonable reaction. When he saw Erna leave the house carrying a repeater, he was surprised. When she fired it, he momentarily believed that she was trying to shoot him, but the distance was far too great. She might have been trying to frighten him off, but she hadn’t recognized him yet. Once she did, he expected that she would set the rifle down and welcome him with open arms. The fact that she had been the one to defend the house meant that she was probably alone, and that stranger must have already gone to the fort to scout for the army. Things were looking better already. The man was gone, and Erna had a Winchester.

The man who Franz believed to be gone was mounting his mule about a half mile north of the house. Cap pulled his Winchester and set Joe to a fast trot, knowing the newcomer would probably still reach the house before he did. If he saw the man pull a weapon, he'd have to shoot him from distance.

Erna stared at the oncoming rider and couldn't believe her eyes. He looked like Franz Hartmann. *How was that possible?* She still had her Winchester in her left hand but didn't point at the rider. She stepped closer to the corner of the house and looked toward the trees. When she spotted Cap heading her way, she felt safer.

It was only then that Franz noticed the tent in the house's afternoon shadow. Then his eyes continued to his right and he spotted a rider. The stranger hadn't left after all. He was almost to the house, so he slowed his exhausted mule and hopped to the ground.

Erna realized he really was Franz and leaned her Winchester against the wall before she stepped towards him.

Cap saw that she had abandoned her repeater, so he understood that she probably recognized the rider. He slid his own Winchester home and slowed Joe.

Franz rushed close to Erna and then shocked her when he wrapped her in his arms.

"You're alive!" he exclaimed.

Erna almost had no choice but to embrace him as well when she replied, "And so are you. How did you survive?"

Cap arrived just as they embraced and slid down from his saddle. He couldn't make sense of the massive collision of emotions that were taking place in his mind as he neared the front of the house.

Franz quickly replied, "I was riding to the creek to gather wood when the Indians attacked. They cut me off and I wasn't able to reach the house before my father barred the door and began firing. I shot two of the Indians before I ran out of ammunition and had to escape with my life. Erna, it was terrible. When I went back that day, I was horrified with what I found. They were all dead. I saw your fields burning, so I knew they had attacked your farm as well."

"Why didn't you come to check on us?"

"I couldn't bear to find you mutilated like Marta and the rest of my family had been. I didn't think there was any chance that you might have survived, Erna. If I believed for even a second that you were alive, I would have come."

Cap had been listening, but their German was spoken so quickly that he couldn't understand most of it. He only picked up a word here and there, but when he saw them still locked in an embrace, he was sure that Mrs. Braun had found her German farmer and he would be asked to leave shortly.

Franz then acted as if he was unaware of Cap's presence when he quickly looked to his right and asked, "Erna, who is this man? I have never seen him before."

She turned her eyes to Cap, smiled and said, "This is Cap Tyler. He saved us and provided for us since that day."

Then she said, "Cap, this is Franz Hartmann. He was the one who survived the attack."

Cap stared at Franz and already had many questions about his escape, but it wasn't his place to ask. Instead, he just nodded and said, "Glad to see you survived, Mister Hartmann. I'm sorry about your family."

Franz replied, "There was nothing I could do. Once the Indians came and my father locked the door, I had to use all my bullets to escape."

He'd spoken very rapidly, so Cap didn't quite catch all of what he'd said, but it had been enough to add even more questions. He wondered if he'd intentionally rushed his German to make it difficult for him to understand.

After he'd answered Cap, Franz looked at Erna and said, "He doesn't need to stay any longer, Erna. I have no one now. I can be a good husband to you and a good father to Gustave and Elsa."

Cap did understand what he'd told her this time, so he said, "Mrs. Braun, I'm sure you have much to talk about with Mister Hartmann. I left the axe in the trees, so I will go to retrieve it."

Erna replied, "Thank you, Cap."

He smiled weakly, then turned and quickly walked to Joe.

After he mounted and rode away, Franz released Erna, but took her arm as they returned to the house. Before they reached the open door, he snatched her Winchester from where she'd left it.

"Is this your rifle?" he asked.

"Yes. Mister Tyler gave it to me."

"He gave you a Winchester?" he asked.

"He gave us many things."

One step past the threshold, Franz froze and stared.

"That is my bed! And my table and chairs. The others belonged to my brother."

"Mister Tyler visited your farm to check on your family. Because the Sioux destroyed my furniture, he fixed your wagon and brought everything here."

He turned her around to face him and sharply asked, "Has he forced himself on you, Erna? I will kill him if he did."

Erna quickly replied, "No! No! He never touched me. He sleeps outside in his tent."

Franz then noticed the stacks of food but didn't ask how it arrived because he was sure that it hadn't come from his farm.

They walked to the small table and sat down.

Elsa turned to Gustave and Elsa who had been wordlessly staring at Franz. Gustave knew who he was, but Elsa couldn't recall ever meeting him. But he spoke their native tongue and her mother was talking to him as if she knew him.

Erna turned to her children and said, "Gustave, Elsa, say 'hello' to Mister Hartmann. He escaped from the Indians."

Her children didn't smile but quietly said, "Hello."

Franz grinned and said, “Hello, children,” then turned to Erna and said, “You look even prettier than the last time we met, Erna. I have a bag with clothes for you and the children.”

She ignored the compliment as she asked, “Where have you been since the attack?”

“I rode to Bismarck and lived with Josef and Berta Mayer. I was working in Mister Mayer’s blacksmith shop when I heard that you survived. I rode out here as quickly as I could. I will stay with you now, Erna.”

“What about your family’s farm?”

“We can have it, too. It’s much bigger than yours. We can talk about that later. I’m really hungry after the long ride. Can you fix me something to eat?”

“Of course,” she replied, then stood and walked to the cauldron where the turkey and rice mix had been simmering for an hour.

———

Cap picked up the axe and rather than return to his tent, he launched a vicious attack on the helpless tree trunk. Wood chips flew as he pounded the axe’s blade into the wood. When the two-foot-long log fell from the end, he sidestepped and barely missed a swing as he continued to release his confused, yet tormented emotions.

He could almost read Franz Hartmann's mind before he had told Mrs. Braun that the stranger didn't need to stay. But he wasn't sure how she felt about his arrival. The mere fact that he had survived made Cap suspicious of the man's character. The clad hoofprints he'd seen going off to the east had originated close to the house. There were no others going in that direction. He hadn't seen any return prints either, so he knew that Hartmann hadn't returned to his family's farm to check on them after the Lakota left. There was a chance that he had a reasonable explanation for how he'd managed to escape and assumed that Mrs. Braun would hear it. He was sure that if he asked, Hartmann would reply using German that would be delivered like a Gatling gun.

He finally reached the last cut and slammed the axe's blade into the stump as he breathed heavily. Sweat was dripping from his brow and it was then that he realized that he was still wearing his shirt. It was soaked, but there was no point in taking it off now.

As he gained control of his emotions, Cap began moving the logs to his pyramid. When they were stacked, he pulled the axe from the stump and walked out of the trees. He wasn't surprised to find Joe with Jasper and Jed. All of his mules were standing just outside the small forest staring at him.

He smiled and stepped over to Joe and carefully mounted with the axe in his hand. It was still sharp enough to cut Joe's hide. He looked at the house and let out a long breath before nudging Joe into a walk.

Cap was about a hundred feet from his tent when he pulled his mule to a stop and dismounted. He took his Winchester from its scabbard and carried it and the axe into his tent. He left his repeater on the tarp and the axe near his small, unused fire pit, then changed into a dry shirt.

He left his tent and began unsaddling Joe. As he removed his mule's tack, he occasionally glanced at the front of the house expecting either Mrs. Braun or Mister Hartmann to come around the corner, if not both of them. But by the time Joe was clear of his tack, he hadn't seen anyone, so he moved the leather to the outside tarp and after covering it again, he returned to his tent.

It was late in the day, but he wasn't hungry after the turkey breakfast and turkey lunch, so he began to pack his things in the belief that he was no longer needed. But even if he was going to leave, he still wanted to help Mrs. Braun. He simply didn't like Hartmann. He admitted a good part of his distaste for the man was due to his familiarity with Mrs. Braun. But the other aspect of his arrival; the inexplicable escape from the Lakota raid added a genuine distrust of Franz Hartmann. But whether he stayed in his tent or left was Mrs. Braun's decision; not his.

He didn't need to do much to have almost everything ready to go. He'd been living out of his personal panniers since he arrived. He'd be leaving almost half of them with Mrs. Braun, and he decided that he'd leave her even more. She'd need two mules to pull the wagon, so he'd give her Jed. He had only been part of the equine brotherhood for two years while Jasper and Joe had been together for more than six. He'd already given her the Winchester and the Colt, but he'd give her a box or two of cartridges. But he was now torn about giving her the money. He knew she wouldn't be offended if he offered, but almost felt as if he'd be giving it to Franz Hartmann. For some reason, that bothered him. It didn't make much sense as he was giving her Jed, but it did.

If he had a chance to talk to her alone before he left, then he'd offer her the cash and tell her that it was for her and the children and to keep it hidden. She might be offended that he was effectively insulting Franz, but he'd make the offer anyway.

———

Franz was making quick work of the large bowl of stew as he studied the house and Erna. This was so much better than he could have dared hope. Now all he had to do was to convince her that Tyler should leave.

As she sat with her children eating, Erna was facing a Cap-like dilemma of her own. She was happy that Franz had survived and come to see if she was all right, but she knew that he intended to stay and become her husband.

Cap, on the other hand, had made it clear from the day he arrived that he wasn't a farmer and would be leaving in the spring. She wished that he would stay because she was already more than just fond of him. Her children almost worshipped Cap and she wasn't far behind. She didn't know Franz that well, nor had she spoken to his wife, Marta very much. Wilhelm had known the Hartmanns much better than she had because they'd worked with him to build this house four years ago. Her husband hadn't talked much about Franz, but he was German and a farmer.

She glanced at her children and wished she didn't have to make this decision. She recalled how her husband treated Gustave and was certain that Franz would be the same kind of father. Other than his greeting, he hadn't even talked to her children since he arrived.

As she continued to slowly eat her turkey and rice stew, Erna would glance at the open doorway every few seconds, hoping that Cap would enter and help her make up her mind.

But Cap hadn't arrived by the time she collected the bowls then walked to the bucket and dropped them into the water. After washing them, she dried them and stacked three before taking the fourth to the big pot and scooping out the last of the stew.

Franz had been watching her and thought she was bringing him a second helping which didn't make sense if he'd thought about it. *Why wash his bowl if she was just going to give him more?*

She smiled at him as she walked past and said, "Mister Tyler must be hungry after all that work."

Franz didn't comment but just continued to watch her as she left the house.

Cap was chewing on a piece of smoked buffalo meat when he heard Mrs. Braun's voice outside his tent.

"Cap? I brought you some stew."

He quickly set aside his smoked meat before he leaned onto his feet and exited his tent.

After he stood upright, he smiled at Mrs. Braun as he accepted the bowl and said, "Thank you, ma'am."

"May I speak to you in your tent, Cap?"

"Of course," he replied then ducked down and reentered his canvas home with Erna following.

After he sat at the head of his double bedroll, Erna sat a few feet away and waited, expecting him to start eating.

But he set the bowl on the ground and asked, "What do you need, Mrs. Braun?"

“I am facing a difficult question and want your advice.”

“Mister Hartmann wants to stay.”

She nodded then said, “He is German and a farmer.”

To Cap, her simple statement answered his own question. She was telling him that she wanted Franz Hartmann to become her new husband and he was now a fifth wheel. He assumed that her difficulty was her uneasiness for having to ask him to leave after all he’d done for her and her children.

He slowly nodded then said, “Yes. I understand. I’ll leave tomorrow morning. I will leave you Jed, so you can pull the wagon. I’ll leave his pack saddle and panniers, too. But there is one more thing I want to give you.”

Erna had been surprised that he hadn’t even posed an argument when she’d explained the only valid reasons for Franz to stay. She had hoped that he’d offer her another path that would send Franz back to Bismarck. She was very disappointed and hurt when he hadn’t.

Cap then pulled the folded currency from his coat pocket that he’d already separated in case he did get to talk to her privately.

He handed her the money and said, “This is fifty dollars, Mrs. Braun. It’s for you and your children. You can use it to buy more seed and supplies.”

Erna accepted the bills and slowly slid them into her dress pocket. She wasn't offended at all, but she was deeply saddened. It seemed as if Cap had already prepared for his departure even before she talked to him.

Cap wanted to say much more but didn't want to make her even more uncomfortable about her decision to accept Mister Hartmann.

So, he picked up the bowl of stew, smiled and said, "The stew smells good."

"It is good," she replied before she quietly asked, "Will you leave early tomorrow?"

"I think it would be best."

"Will you not say farewell to Gustave and Elsa? They will miss you."

"Of course, I will. I just don't want to offend Mister Hartmann."

"I will send them to your tent in a little while to collect the bowl. I will tell them that you will be leaving tomorrow before they see you."

"Thank you for the stew, Mrs. Braun."

Erna nodded, then rose and left the tent. She noticed that even now, he didn't use her Christian name.

Cap wolfed down the stew just to empty the bowl. He set it down then took a long drink from his canteen. After replacing the cap, he sat and wondered if he was doing the right thing. He wished he had a looking glass that would show him the future, but then realized that knowing what would happen would be worse than not knowing.

He set his depressing thoughts aside and began to plan for tomorrow's journey. When he did, he began to think about leaving tonight. But there was a new moon, which wouldn't give him enough light to ride safely. Despite his almost overpowering urge to accept Mrs. Braun decision and just leave, he decided that he would have to wait until the predawn.

———

Gustave exclaimed, "*Mister Tyler is leaving?*"

As Erna tried to explain why he decided to leave, Franz was ecstatic as he sat nearby. He had been very concerned that Tyler would begin to question him about his survival and then convince Erna to send him away. Without even having to talk to the man, Franz had won the contest. He had Erna's Winchester on his lap as he listened. He already considered it his. Erna wouldn't need it anyway.

Erna finished her best guess about why Cap chose to leave then said, "Why don't you and Elsa go to see him and tell him goodbye. He'll probably be gone before the sun comes up."

Gustave hopped down from the chair then took Elsa's hand and left the house.

After they left, Franz said, "I'll make you a good husband, Erna."

Erna was still watching the doorway and didn't reply.

———

After a few minutes of planning, Cap had left his tent with the bowl and spoon expecting to see the children soon. It was almost sunset, and they'd be getting ready for sleep soon. He was sitting on the tarp covering the mules' tack and had his behind nestled in Joe's saddle seat when they appeared at the corner of the house.

He picked up the bowl and smiled as they approached.

As he handed the bowl to Gustave, he asked, "Have you come to say goodbye?"

Gustave replied, "Mama told us why you were going away. Do you have to leave?"

"I'm afraid so. Your mother needs a farmer for a husband and knows Mister Hartmann. It would make him mad if I stayed."

Elsa wiped the tears from her cheeks as she softly said, "I will miss you, Mister Tyler. Mama and Gustave will, too."

"I'll miss you, Gustave and your mother even more, Elsa."

Gustave then asked, "Will you visit us sometimes?"

"I'll think about it, but I don't want to make Mister Hartmann angry. If I can't visit, I'll have my friend at the fort stop by to make sure that you are okay."

Elsa sniffed then said, "It's not the same."

"Maybe you can see me when you come to Bismarck."

Gustave suspected that even if they went to the town in springtime, Mister Tyler would already be gone with the railroad. He didn't say anything because he didn't want to make Elsa sadder. He was close to tears himself but had to be brave.

Cap then rose from his tarp-covered saddle seat and dropped to his heels in front of them. He wrapped Elsa in his left arm and Gustave in his right.

He kissed each of them on the cheek then softly said, "I love you both very much. I may not be able to visit, but I will watch over you like an angel. Take care of your mother because she's a wonderful lady."

Gustave and Elsa were both crying when he finished, and he wished he didn't have to leave them. But their mother needed a farmer and now had found one, or he had found her.

He stood then smiled down at them as he said, "You keep practicing English and remember that I'm just a day's ride away."

They both nodded before Gustave took Elsa's hand then silently turned away and walked back to the house.

Cap sighed and watched the children until they disappeared around the corner. That had been one of the hardest things he'd ever had to do. He didn't know how he'd honor the promise to watch over them, but he'd figure something out.

After he returned to his tent, he sat on his bedrolls and thought about leaving in the night again. If he discarded the idea of riding all the way to Fort Lincoln in the night, he could depart in a few hours. He could just stop at the Hartmann place and stay in one of the small empty houses. He understood why it had become almost urgent that he leave. He couldn't bear the thought of Franz Hartmann sharing Mrs. Braun's bed. It was possible that she'd sleep with Elsa, but he didn't want to risk hearing the sounds of lovemaking leaking out of the house.

desperately wanted to join Erna in her bed but was still concerned that Tyler might enter. He had to wait for her to decide where he would sleep. At least for tonight.

Erna was well aware of Franz' desire for her. It had been obvious even as he embraced her when he arrived. Now she had another decision to make. Elsa was already under the blankets and Gustave was standing near the bed. She was concerned that if she slept with Elsa, then Franz might think that she was rejecting him and return to Bismarck. If only Cap had stayed, then she wouldn't be facing this dilemma. But he would be gone before sunrise and she might be alone if she refused Franz.

She then lifted Gustave onto the bed and after he slid under the blankets beside his sister, she turned and walked to the empty bed she would now share with Franz. She would become Mrs. Hartmann soon, even if they hadn't seen a preacher.

Franz was already excited when he saw Erna put her son into bed. He walked to the empty bed, sat down and began undressing.

Erna sighed before she started unbuttoning her new dress with Franz greedily watching.

CHAPTER 6

Before he left the Hartmann farm the next morning, Cap walked to the big house and was surprised to find nothing that even indicated that anyone had died there. He stepped inside and detected some of the remaining foul odor, but there was nothing else. Some of the furniture was still intact, but it didn't matter now. He wasn't about to return, at least not today.

He walked back outside and soon spotted a large mound of dirt. It looked like it had been there for about a week, and he doubted if Franz Hartmann had buried his family. He had probably never even visited the place on his way to the Braun farm. He scanned the ground and saw a lot of shod hoofprints. He was sure that Corporal Mac had led a burial detail to the place. He'd ask him when he spoke to him later this afternoon on his way to Bismarck.

He whistled for Joe and Jasper as he headed back to the small house. When they returned, he saddled both mules and began loading Jasper. It was probably close to nine o'clock when he headed northeast.

———

Erna had dressed her children and had finished making breakfast. The night with Franz had been an almost non-stop series of rutting. She hadn't even felt Wilhelm's subdued affection and it made her feel more like a prostitute than a wife. Even after the sun rose and she awakened, he had still pawed at her as if he expected her to service him again even as Gustave and Elsa stirred.

She finished cooking and carried the plates to the tables before she sat down opposite Franz. She expected him to say grace, but he began eating as soon as the food was set before him. She sighed and began to eat.

Franz was more than satisfied with his life now. He had looked outside while Erna was dressing her children and found Tyler gone. He was the only man here now and he was sure that Erna appreciated his attention. *How many men could please a woman three times in one night?*

Erna had kept the fifty dollars in her dress pocket but at the first opportunity, she'd put it in the shelter with her Colt. She wasn't sure if Franz even knew about the hideout, but even if he did and opened the trap door, he'd just see a folded towel. She'd probably lose her pistol, but it was better than having Franz take the money. He had his own Colt, but even she could see that it wasn't as good as hers.

Gustave and Elsa had remained silent all that morning as they tried to accept the fact that Mister Tyler was gone, and Mister Hartmann was going to be their new father. He had yet to speak to them and was always touching their mother. They had been awakened several times during the night by loud sounds from the other side of the room but weren't sure what had made the noise.

Franz hadn't asked about the food or new clothes and other things he hadn't expected to find as he was sure that Tyler had bought them. But that meant that the man must have had money and he began to wonder if he had left any with Erna. He wouldn't ask her yet. He wasn't going anywhere.

———

It was well after noon when Cap spotted Fort Lincoln on the eastern horizon. He had only snacked all day and would look forward to sharing the soldiers' evening mess. He was still debating about the scout job, but he wanted to ask Mac if he had visited the Hartmann farm.

When he entered the outskirts of the fort, he didn't see any increase in troop strength, so he assumed that the promised regiment hadn't arrived yet. He passed the sutler's store and headed for the administrative building hoping to find Corporal McDermott.

Again, he didn't have to search for the NCO as Mac had spotted him shortly after he rode past the sutler's store and was double timing toward the administrative building knowing that's where he was headed.

Cap soon caught sight of the corporal and grinned as he dismounted.

"Howdy, Mac. How are things in the army?"

Mac chuckled before he replied, "Messed up as always. What brings you by so soon, Cap?"

"I'm on my way to Bismarck to see if they could use me as a surveyor, unless you've got a better offer."

"I wish I did. All of us NCOs asked the captain about it and he thought it was a good idea, but the colonel kinda killed the notion. He said he'd have to get permission from headquarters. You can guess how long that'd take."

Cap nodded as he replied, "I'd guess about the turn of the century."

"That's about right. What happened to the lady and her young'uns? You didn't leave 'em did ya?"

"Well, I did leave, but a man she already knew who was both a German and a farmer showed up. He made it clear that he was going to stay, and Mrs. Braun didn't seem to object. So, I packed up and headed this way."

"I reckon that was the right thing to do."

"Mac, did you lead a burial detail to the Hartmann farm? When I checked the big house this morning, it was cleared of bodies."

"Yup. After you told me about 'em, I told the captain, and he gave me permission to go there and bury the folks. It wasn't very pleasant, but it wasn't as bad as puttin' C Company in the ground."

"Thanks for doing what I should have done, Mac. What is your schedule like for the rest of the day?"

"Well, I was gonna inspect the barracks, but I reckon I can let the boys off the hook for another day. Do you feel like a beer?"

"Sure. Let me tie off Joe and we'll head over to the club."

Mac waited for Joe to be tethered to the hitchrail then he and Cap marched away in step toward the open club. The fort was too small to have separate officer and NCO clubs, so there was one that was open to all ranks. The club still had two bars, one for the officers and the other for the enlisted men.

They picked up their beers at the bar and Cap paid the dime as he knew he could afford it better than Mac. A corporal made sixteen dollars a month and he knew that pay was sporadic at best. He smiled as he recalled explaining to Mrs. Braun how money's value changed by location and time. It also changed by occupation. When he'd been surveying for the Northern Pacific, he was paid almost five times what the army paid Mac and pay was regular. At least until the railroad went bankrupt. They still owed him two months' pay, but he doubted if he'd get a dime from the resurrected Northern Pacific Railroad.

He and Mac sat down and after taking a sip of the cold brew, Cap said, "I forgot to mention that the man who showed up at Mrs. Braun's house was a survivor of the raid on the Hartmann farm. His name is Franz Hartmann. Did you ever meet him?"

"Can't say that I have, but some of the boys who've been here for a while might remember him. How did he manage to get out of there?"

"That's one of the things that's been bothering me. When I first inspected the place, I found where the Lakota had ridden toward the Braun farm with three shod animals. I thought it was an unusual to have an odd number. But then when I checked the eastern side of the place, I found another single set of shod hoofprints heading east. I wondered if someone had survived but figured that even if he'd managed to get away from the house, the Sioux would track him down or be waiting for him."

"That is queer," Mac said before taking a deep drink of beer.

As the corporal wiped the foam from his upper lip, Cap said, "When he showed up, he was telling Mrs. Braun how he'd managed to escape, but I couldn't understand most of it because he was talking so fast in German."

"I never could understand that language. Of course, I can manage to carry on a good chat in the Irish Gaelic."

"Now that, my friend, is a true linguistic challenge."

Mac snickered before he finished his beer. Cap was well behind the Irishman but wasn't surprised. The many Irishmen who'd been building the Union Pacific and then the Northern Pacific could down enough alcohol to pickle a whole company of German soldiers. When his father had first mentioned it, Cap thought he was exaggerating. He learned differently when they reached Omaha City.

After smacking his lips, Mac asked, "Are you gonna head to Bismarck now?"

"I was hoping to share your mess again and stay the night before leaving in the morning."

Mac grinned and said, "Now that's what I was hopin' to hear. The other boys with stripes want to hear more about your run-ins with the Cheyenne and the Sioux."

"Don't forget the Crow or the Blackfeet. They can be nastier than either of them."

Cap then ordered another beer for Mac who didn't protest.

Mac continued to talk about the army and the expected arrival of the new regiment while Cap just listened. He hadn't received any more information about Franz Hartmann but wasn't surprised. The army rarely spent much time with settlers while they were still alive. But the loss of the opportunity to scout for the army meant that he'd have to depend on the Northern Pacific still needing surveyors. If they did, he'd probably have to ride all the way to central Montana Territory where they'd been when the railroad had gone bankrupt.

They left the club about an hour later and Mac led Joe and Jasper to the stables where he told the farrier to replace their shoes and take good care of them. He then arranged for Cap to stay in the half-empty NCO quarters before they headed to the mess to join his fellow non-commissioned officers for evening chow.

The meal was another non-stop session where Cap described in great detail the encounters he'd had with the different tribes. He avoided talking about the same ones he'd told them about the first time. He also included background about each of the tribes' customs and beliefs. He especially wanted to dispel any misconceptions that were common among army troops. He told them that he there was no truth to the story that the Indians wouldn't attack at night. He also told them about one of their more common tactics they used to lure army units into a trap. They let the bluecoats spot a small a small band of warriors. When the soldiers gave chase, they'd soon find a much larger and better equipped war party waiting for them.

To a man, the NCOs accepted what they were being told because Cap had been there, and they hadn't. They asked many questions, so their evening mess extended close to the lights out bugle call.

Each of them shook Cap's hand for helping them and expressed their frustration that he couldn't become their scout. They added a few barbs about their colonel as well. They all then left the mess and walked back to the NCO quarters. As Cap slid under the army issued wool blankets, he didn't have to worry about oversleeping knowing the bugler's loud reveille wouldn't be blocked by the walls.

But as he laid under a wood ceiling, he wondered how Mrs. Braun and the children were doing. He hoped that he had been wrong about Franz Hartmann but still felt guilty and selfish for leaving. She, Gustave and Elsa deserved better.

Cap was riding out of Fort Abraham Lincoln after sharing breakfast with the NCOs. Joe and Jasper were wearing new shoes and had been brushed down to look like thoroughbreds. He forded the Heart River and continued east.

He soon reached the ferry where he paid his twenty cents toll and stood on the dock waiting for it to cross the Missouri River. He could see Bismarck in the distance and wondered how much it had changed since the last time he'd seen the town when it was still Missouri Crossing. He imagined that there were a lot of men seeking work with the railroad and while it may not be nearly as bad as Deadwood, he expected it to be less peaceful than he recalled. The only saving grace would be the presence of so many Germans who were less tolerant of mayhem.

The other inhibitor would be the size and character of the lawmen. He wondered if Burleigh County Sheriff Cooper Donavan was still there. If he was, then Bismarck would be in much better shape. He had met the sheriff a few times in his brief stay and thought he was a good man. The sheriff only had one deputy the last time he'd been in town and assumed he had more now. Even though he was the law for Burleigh County, most of the counties surrounding Bismarck had no lawmen at all, so the sheriff was closer to being a territorial lawman.

The U.S. Marshal's office technically had jurisdiction, but they were headquartered in Yankton, more than four hundred miles south along the Missouri. The army was responsible for the overall peace in the territory, but Sheriff Donavan's office was expected to handle many of the criminal complaints outside of his legal jurisdiction. If he wasn't so good at the job, Cap was sure he wouldn't have lasted a year. He'd find out if he was still there when he reached town.

The enormous ferry soon bumped into the wharf and he led Joe and Jasper onto its rocking deck. Joe didn't seem to mind, but Jasper began to fidget. As the ferrymen began pulling the rope to move it away from the dock, Cap stood near Jasper's head and talked to him while he rubbed his nose.

Just a few minutes later, Cap led Joe and a very relieved Jasper from the ferry then stepped into his saddle. He'd barely left the short incline from the riverbank when he noticed the first massive change in Bismarck. The buildings were already stretching a good half a mile from where they were when he'd last visited the town. He also spotted some tall brick buildings that marked it as a prosperous and growing community. Most of the buildings were of framed lumber which had been shipped in by rail from the vast forests of Minnesota. They'd built a planing mill before he'd left to create most of the boards.

As he walked Joe toward Main Avenue, he continued to marvel at the changes. The Northern Pacific hadn't started adding more rails to its existing tracks, but he knew they'd be holding off until springtime now. There was no point in starting such an enormous enterprise with the harsh winter about to arrive.

There weren't any indications of the large number of job seekers he expected to find and wondered if many hadn't already left town when they discovered that there wouldn't be any work until next March. They could be living in tents on the other side of town out of his view.

He soon turned onto Main Avenue and headed for Groom's Boarding House. He'd stayed there for more than a month before heading west and assumed it was still operating.

He passed Mandan Street and First Street before turning left on Second Street. He soon spotted the boarding house on his right and pulled Joe to a stop then dismounted. He tied his mule to the hitchrail, swung open the gate and after passing through, he closed it and headed for the large house.

Cap stepped onto the porch and opened the door. He had no sooner closed it behind him when he heard a ruckus somewhere inside the house. He walked past the sitting room and continued down the long hallway toward the kitchen.

He heard a woman snap, "Leave me alone or I'll scream!"

Then a man laughed before he said, "There ain't anybody here, lady. Go ahead."

Cap identified the woman's voice but didn't pull one of his Remingtons. Instead, he walked quietly down the hallway and as he entered the kitchen, he found the man ripping the front of Charlotte Groom's dress.

Her eyes were closed knowing that she had no defense when suddenly, she no longer felt Harry Gordon's grabbing fingers. She didn't even have time to open her eyes before Harry flew backwards across the kitchen and slammed into one of the kitchen chairs.

Her eyes flew open and was startled to see a man she vaguely remembered picking Harry off the floor like a ragdoll.

Cap's massive frustration over Franz Hartmann's arrival boiled over as he glared at a terrified Harry Gordon.

"I should hurt you, mister."

"I…I…I was just…"

"Shut up! I know what you were doing."

Then he turned to look at Charlotte and said, "What do you want me to do to him, Mrs. Groom?"

She blinked then said, "Just get him out of my boarding house."

"Are you sure that's all you want me to do? I can drag him to the jail and have the sheriff make him sorry he ever entered your place."

Charlotte quickly replied, "No, I don't want you to take him to the jail, just make sure he leaves."

"I'll be happy to do that, ma'am."

He lowered Harry to the floor and growled, "You're getting off lucky, you sorry excuse for a man. Do I have to escort you out of here, mister?"

Harry shook his head before racing out of the kitchen. Cap listened to his hurried footsteps as he charged upstairs before he turned to Mrs. Groom.

She said, “Thank you for helping me. He knew there was no one else in the place and thought he’d take advantage of the situation.”

“You’re welcome, ma’am. I’m kind of surprised that your boarding house isn’t packed with all of the newcomers showing up in town looking for work.”

She tilted her head slightly before asking, “Have we met before?”

Cap smiled as he replied, “Yes, ma’am. I stayed here for a while a few years back before I headed west to survey for the Northern Pacific. My name’s Cap Tyler.”

She snapped her fingers then smiled as she said, “Now I remember.”

Then he asked, “Why didn’t your husband protect you, Mrs. Groom?”

“I’m a widow now, Mister Tyler. My husband died a year ago. It’s also why I didn’t want you to take him to jail.”

Cap looked at her curiously as he asked, “You’ll have to explain your answer a bit more, ma’am.”

She smiled as she replied, “Sheriff Donavan has been courting me for a month now. I know if you brought Mister Gordon to the jail and told Coop what he had done, it might have been hard for my beau to simply escort him into a cell.”

“I was wondering if Coop was still sheriff. So, tell me, was the man who was bothering you that stupid?”

“He only arrived yesterday, so he wouldn’t have known.”

“Why didn’t you tell him about Coop when he made his intentions clear?”

“I did tell him just before you entered the house, but he seemed to believe I was bluffing.”

“That doesn’t make him any smarter.”

Cap then scratched his chin as he asked, “If it’s not too rude to ask, is Coop a widower now?”

“No, it’s not rude to ask and no, he’s not a widower. In May, his wife boarded a southbound riverboat with her paramour, Foley Johnson, his older deputy. He filed for divorce in August after he was certain she wouldn’t return.”

“I met the sheriff a few times before I headed west. Sheriff Donavan is a good man and I’m sure that he’s getting a better woman. You still haven’t explained why your boarding house is so empty.”

Before she answered, the front door opened and slammed shut announcing the frustrated and frightened departure of Harry Gordon.

After the booming echo died, Charlotte replied, “The men who come looking for work usually can’t afford to stay here and the settlers who are passing through normally have tents or covered wagons.”

“Well, I’ll be a resident for a while. I’m going to visit the Northern Pacific offices shortly to see if they still need surveyors.”

“Good luck, Mister Tyler.”

“Call me Cap, ma’am. How much for a week’s stay?”

“I could just tell you that I won’t charge you because of what you just did, but you wouldn’t let me make the offer; would you?”

Cap grinned as he replied, “No, ma’am.”

“Eight dollars a week is my normal rate.”

He nodded then pulled out some bills from his pocket and handed her a five-dollar bill and three singles.

“I’ve got to park my horses in a livery and then visit the railroad office before I return.”

"Use Michelson's Livery. It's just two blocks north on Second Street and they'll give you a better rate when you tell them that you're staying here."

"I'll do that. Thank you, ma'am."

"No. Thank you, Cap. When you return, I'll give you the grand tour."

He nodded, then turned and headed back down the hallway. After he stepped onto the porch, he scanned the street for any signs of Harry Gordon. Once he was satisfied that the man wasn't about to return, he hopped down the steps and walked to the gate.

He soon mounted Joe and turned him north to Michelson's Livery. He had used the livery the last time he'd stayed at Groom's Boarding House but didn't recall getting a discount. He did know that they had a secure area for his things that made it even better than most liveries, especially now that he had so many weapons. When he'd packed before leaving the Brauns, he put all of his personal items and clothing in one pannier and his saddlebags. It was fairly light, so he'd be able to carry it back to the boarding house without any problem.

He soon stepped down in front of the big barn and led his mules inside where he was greeted by a grinning liveryman he didn't recognize.

"Mornin'. Leavin' your mules with us?"

“Yes, sir,” he replied as he shook the man’s hand, “The name’s Cap Tyler and, no, I’ve never been in the army or navy. It’s short for Casper.”

The liveryman snickered as he replied, “My name’s Arnie Roberts.”

“Where’s Larry Michelson?”

“He’s out back showin’ his boy how to break a horse to the saddle. He’s been workin’ with us since he turned fourteen, but still hasn’t figgered some of it out.”

“How long have you worked with Larry? I don’t recall seeing you before.”

“Only a year and a half. I came here lookin’ to hire on with the railroad but that didn’t work out. I was kinda lucky when Larry’s other helper ran off with some other fellers to the Black Hills to look for gold."

"I was down there a little while ago, and I’d be surprised if he finds anything but misery. I’ll be staying at Groom’s for at least a week and need to board my mules and store my packs and weapons.”

“We can do that. Charlie runs a good place. She’s gonna marry Coop Donavan pretty soon.”

"She told me when I stopped by. I'll pay for the month. Joe and Jasper both have new shoes, so all I'll need is for them to be boarded."

"That'll run you ten dollars. Is that okay?"

"That's fine," Cap replied as he handed him the cash.

He pulled his personal pack from Jasper and his saddlebags from Joe. After hanging the saddlebags over his shoulder, he walked out of the livery and headed back to Groom's. He was still amazed how much the town had grown in the few years he'd been gone, and he hadn't even explored all of it. He imagined that the buildup of immigrants from Germany and Scandinavia and out-of-work men would suddenly burst out of Bismarck into the West when the Northern Pacific began laying track again. Hopefully, he'd be part of that operation.

He soon stepped onto the boarding house's porch then opened the door and entered. After closing the door, Cap didn't have time to set his pannier on the floor before Charlotte Groom popped out of the hallway.

"Let me show you to your room, Cap."

"Thank you, ma'am."

"Please stop with the ma'am and Mrs. Groom. Call me Charlie like everyone else does except for my beau. Didn't you call me that when you were here the last time?"

“No, ma’am, I mean, Charlie.”

She smiled then led him to the nearby stairway.

As they climbed the steps, she asked, “What have you been doing since the railroad failed?”

“I was in the middle of Montana Territory with my surveying crew when the army patrol that was protecting us informed us that we were out of a job and just left us on our own. They had more important things to do than keep a bunch of ex-railroad men safe.”

When they stepped onto the upper landing and began walking down the upstairs hallway, Charlotte asked, “Where did you go after that?”

“I did pretty much whatever was necessary. I trapped and hunted and did a lot of trading. Then I spent a few months in Deadwood playing poker before I heard the Northern Pacific was starting up again. So, here I am.”

She opened the door to the last room and entered.

Cap set his pannier and saddlebags on the floor as she said, “I’m sure that there’s more to it than just that, Cap.”

“I didn’t want to bore you, Charlie,” he replied with a grin.

She smiled then said, “The bathroom is down the hallway and breakfast is in the dining room at seven-thirty, lunch is at noon, and supper is at six o'clock. As you are my only guest at the moment, those hours are flexible."

"I'd just as soon share those meals with you in the kitchen, Charlie. I assume that Coop will be joining us for most of them."

"He will when he's not busy, which is much too often now that his only experienced deputy ran off with his wife."

"He had only one deputy when I was here last, but the town is a lot bigger now and he's got all those out of work men to handle. How many does he have now?"

"He has two deputies, but both are very young. He's been authorized four, but the only ones who want the job are men who should be in jail behind bars and not wearing a badge."

"He's got a big area to cover; doesn't he?"

"That's another problem. I'm sure he'll bend your ear when you meet him. Hopefully, he'll be able to join us for dinner."

"I'm hope so. I'd enjoy having him bend my ear. But right now, I'm going to head over to the Northern Pacific office and see about that surveying job."

As they walked out of the room, she said, "Good luck, Cap."

He closed the door and replied, "I'm going to need it."

Ten minutes later, Cap stepped onto the boardwalk in front of the Northern Pacific's westernmost station. The operations office hadn't changed much since he'd seen it last. He assumed that the man in charge wasn't the same one who'd run the place before the railroad had gone under.

He entered the large office and found it surprisingly empty. He had expected to find it filled with job seekers. He approached the secretary at the desk who looked up at him with disdain.

"What do you want? We're not hiring anyone until next spring. You might as well leave."

"My name is Cap Tyler. I was a surveyor for the Northern Pacific in '73. I was wondering if they needed more routes plotted."

The secretary's face shifted from disdain to simply distasteful as he said, "We already have our survey crews on the job, Mister Tyler. We have no need for you unless you wish to apply as a tracklayer in the spring."

"Who is in charge?"

"I am. Mister Weathers only sees important people, and you are not important."

When the secretary said 'Mr. Weathers', Cap understood why the secretary felt safe with his rude behavior. The Northern Pacific had replaced the last manager with a man he knew well and disliked even more.

Cap didn't bother with any cordialities before he turned and left the office. Once outside, he pulled on his hat and wondered what he'd do next. He was jobless, but unlike most of the other men in town, he had a skill and more resources than any of them. He could ride south to North Platte in Nebraska and see if the Union Pacific could use his services. He knew that the larger and more established company was still adding routes and would need surveyors. It was just a pleasant four-hundred-mile jaunt through hostile Sioux lands with winter about to arrive. *What could be more enjoyable?*

As he began walking back to the boarding house to unpack, he wondered if his failure to find work as a scout or a surveyor was God's way of saying he should have stayed with Mrs. Braun and her children and learned how to farm. He had expected to miss them even before he left the farm. But it didn't take long for him to realize that he missed them much more that he had anticipated. He hoped that Franz Hartmann was good for them.

But now he had to figure out what he would do. If he was going to ride to North Platte, he'd have to leave soon. The snows could arrive as early as the middle of October, but even before then, the cold winds would make life on the Great Plains difficult. At least in the mountains of Montana Territory there were forests and caves to serve as shelters from the nasty weather.

He soon entered the boarding house and climbed the stairs to unpack. He knew it was lunchtime, but he wasn't hungry, and he needed to think.

After entering his room, he removed his coat and hat then began to unload his pannier. There was a nice chest of drawers in the room, so he soon filled the top three with his clean clothes. He left his dirty clothes in the pannier and would drop them off at the ubiquitous Chinese laundry.

It seemed that every town he'd ever visited in the West, even Deadwood, had a laundry that was run by Orientals who'd been brought to the country by the railroads. Some had been little more than slaves who were working off their passage across the Pacific. Despite their situation, some had built a better life for themselves by going into the business of washing clothes. While they may not become wealthy and it was still hard work, it was still better than the back-breaking and often fatal labor that had been demanded of them by the railroads.

After emptying his saddlebags of his toiletries and towels, he unbuckled his two gunbelts and hung them on the hooks along the wall beside his coat and hat. Rather than laying on the clean blankets, he sat at the small desk and began to drum its surface with his fingers.

For most of his life, he'd only been responsible for himself. Even when he was with his father and brother, each of them had looked after his own welfare. But in the past three weeks, he'd been acting as the protector and provider for Mrs. Braun, Gustave and little Elsa. He had been surprised when he discovered a deep satisfaction in that role. Logically, it made sense for him to shift that responsibility to Franz Hartmann as he would be able to till their farm or bring the family to his much larger farm. Maybe he should ride out there and tell them that the Hartmann farm was habitable again.

He thought about it for a few minutes, but soon decided that it would be disruptive for him to return so quickly. Hartmann would probably visit his family's place soon anyway.

Cap wished that the army had hired him as a scout, then he could use that as an excuse to visit. Besides, he'd told Gustave and Elsa that he would be their guardian angel.

But even as he recalled that promise, he realized that if he left to join the Union Pacific, it would be impossible to fulfill. He had to stay close to make sure that they were all safe without them even knowing he was there.

He'd seen the enormous J.M. Rittenhouse Emporium when he'd ridden down Main Avenue, so maybe he'd head over there and buy a pair of good field glasses. He could stop in the trees north of the farm every so often to inspect the place.

Then he realized how creepy that would look to anyone who spotted him. He wasn't sure he'd be pleased when he saw Mrs. Braun with Franz either. It would be even worse if he saw her with a protruding belly.

He was still absent-mindedly but rhythmically tapping his fingers on the desktop when he was startled by a loud knock on his door.

Cap popped to his feet and took three long strides to the door and swung it open.

Sheriff Cooper Donavan said, "Mind if I come in, Cap?"

"Good to see you again, Coop. Come on in and have a seat."

"I'll take the chair and you can park on your bed," the sheriff replied as he headed for the desk.

Cap closed the door and sat at the edge of his bed as he asked, "I assume Mrs. Groom told you about the incident with her guest."

"She did and I really appreciate what you did. She was right when she told you that if you'd brought him to my office, I'd probably be a tad upset."

"I'm just glad that I arrived in time."

"She also told me that you're trying to hook up with the Northern Pacific again."

"That didn't work out, I'm afraid."

"It did for me, Cap. I was kinda hoping that you'd be coming into town."

"Why would you even know I was still alive? I'd been gone for years."

"Those army boys who make use of our saloons have been talking about you and said that you were heading to Bismarck in the spring. They've also been telling stories about your skirmishes with the Indians. When Charlotte told me what you'd done, I was really happy about how you'd dealt with the man, but I was almost as pleased just to know that you'd arrived."

"I can understand why you'd be grateful that I helped Mrs. Groom, but why are you so happy that I came to Bismarck?"

"I want you to be a deputy sheriff."

"Coop, I've never worn a badge and don't even know the laws that well."

"It doesn't matter. I can help you with the laws, but Charlotte said that she'd explained my deputy shortage to you."

"She did. I was a bit surprised that you still only had two deputies."

"It's worse than that. The two I have, John Wilson and Al Hooper, are both young and inexperienced. They're good men but have a lot to learn. I won't hire any of the thugs who apply for the job because I know that enforcing the law is the last thing on their minds. The few immigrants who applied didn't speak or read English. But beyond my two boys' inexperience, each of them has another problem."

"Which is?"

"Since the Sioux started becoming more hostile, they're both afraid to leave town. I'm sure that you understand that even though I'm the sheriff of Burleigh County, the governor expects me to provide law enforcement for most of the counties in central and northern Dakota Territory. It's not a problem to the east where the railroad already operates, and the army has Fort Stephenson and Fort Berthold along the Missouri up north. My biggest problems are west and south. Fort Bliss and Fort Lincoln are both seriously undermanned and are barely holding their own. I'm also leery about sending them to the tent city east of town."

"I don't know about the tent city, but I was told that a regiment was going to reinforce Fort Lincoln soon."

"I don't think they're going to get there until spring. If you'd take the job, I'd need you to handle most of the work outside of Bismarck where my deputies are loath to go and deal with those wannabe railroad workers on the northeast end of town. I can't leave the town, especially now. I'm still looking for two more deputies, and if you'd take one of the slots, I'd really appreciate it."

Cap smiled as he replied, "I was wondering what I'd be doing after the army decided they didn't want a scout and the Northern Pacific didn't want my services as a surveyor."

"Can you come with me to my office and meet Al and John? They've heard the tales of your exploits, so they'll be happy to see you. They'll be almost giddy after they hear that you'll be joining us and handling the out-of-town jobs. Maybe I'll be able to convince them to go with you so they could gain experience and confidence."

"Okay, boss. Let's go meet your baby deputies."

Coop snickered, then stood and after his new hire rose, he shook Cap's hand before they left the room.

After stepping down the stairway and entering the parlor, Charlotte looked at the sheriff and asked, "Did you get your man, Coop?"

"I did. We're going to the jail where I'll introduce him to Al and John."

"Thank you for taking the job, Cap. Coop really needs the help."

"I hope I'm more help than hindrance, Charlie."

"You've already been much more help than you realize," she replied.

Coop stepped close to his fiancée, kissed her and whispered something in her ear that made her blush before the sheriff and his new deputy left the house.

As they walked to the jail, Sheriff Donavan said, "The job pays sixty dollars a month plus room and board. As you're already staying at Charlotte's place, that will be covered by the county. We have a contract with Mayer's livery to board our horses, too."

"Is that the blacksmith Mayer or a brother or cousin?"

"It's owned by Josef, the blacksmith. He bought the place from Pete Smith last year."

"That's handy. So, after you and Charlotte marry, is she going to sell the boarding house?"

"Nope. I'm moving into the boarding house and she'll still run it. She wanted to keep it, and I really didn't want to stay in my house after Maureen left me. It wasn't a difficult decision. Want to buy the place? I'll make you a good offer."

Cap snickered then replied, "I'll think about it, Coop. I'm still trying to adjust to living in a room with a real ceiling."

As they turned down Fourth Street, Cap began to think about Coop's second offer. He was sure that he could afford the place unless the sheriff wanted more than twenty-five hundred dollars. If he wanted that much, it must be a palace. While he really didn't need the space, he would appreciate the privacy, especially after his new boss moved into the boarding house. He expected that he wouldn't be staying in Bismarck that often anyway.

There was another reason why he might decide to buy the house. Now that he would be staying in town, he wanted to have a family of his own. He'd been surprised when he felt such deep satisfaction in caring for the Brauns. If he bought the house, he'd be able to have a place for his own family. He wished that his new family could be Erna, Gustave and Elsa, but there was little chance that she would leave her farm even before Franz Hartmann arrived. Now there was no chance at all.

He still wasn't about to search for a wife just to satisfy his new plans, but he had time now.

They soon entered the jail and Cap met Burleigh County Deputy Sheriffs John Wilson and Al Hooper. They popped to their feet when their boss entered, then looked at Cap. He had to keep from smiling because they seemed even younger than he had expected. But they did appear to be quite enthusiastic.

"Boys, this is Cap Tyler. The feller you've been hearing about. He's going to be the county's newest deputy and help me protect you from the bad men."

John and Al both grinned as they stepped close to Cap and shook his hand.

Al said, “It’s a pleasure to meet you, Cap. Those soldiers have been telling us all sorts of stories about you.”

“I’m sure they exaggerated most of them.”

John said, “We heard about how you helped that lady and her kids, too.”

Cap glanced at the sheriff before he said, “Mrs. Braun and her children were lucky to have survived. I only left when Franz Hartmann, who had survived the attack on his family’s neighboring farm showed up.”

Coop looked at Cap but didn’t ask about Franz. He’d have time to talk about him later tonight during supper. He’d heard Hartmann’s story about how he’d escaped the Sioux’s wrath, but it hadn’t made sense to him. Josef Mayer had taken him on as an apprentice, so Coop hadn’t worried about him. After he’d gone, the sheriff had almost forgotten about the man. He wondered what Cap thought about his story and why Cap left Hartmann with the woman and her children.

Coop performed a casual swearing-in ceremony and handed Cap his badge of office.

As he pinned it on his shirt, Cap scanned the weapons on the wall and asked, “Do you want a Colt and a Winchester?

I have extras that I've picked up over the past few years. They use the same .44 cartridge."

The sheriff quickly replied, "We can always use the extra firepower. Al uses a Colt New Army and I'm sure he would appreciate the cartridge-firing version."

"I'll bring them with me tomorrow."

They all sat in around the desk then Sheriff Donavan began explaining how he planned to use Cap's experience. He included a strongly worded suggestion that John and Al accompany Cap on some of his missions out in the open parts of the territory, which was almost all of it.

As Cap was being sworn in, Erna was playing poker with Gustave and Elsa. Franz had ridden Jed to his farm to see what else he could scavenge giving her some peace. He was actually planning to see if he had to move any remains from the house so he could sell the place.

"Are you happy, Mama?" Gustave asked as he folded his hand.

"Of course, I'm happy. Why do you ask?"

"You seem sad. You were happy when Mister Tyler was here."

Elsa nodded as Erna said, "It's just that I haven't gotten used to having Mister Hartmann live with us yet."

"Does he hurt you, Mama?" Elsa asked.

Erna was startled and quickly asked, "No, of course not. What gave you that idea?"

Elsa glanced at Gustave then answered, "I don't know."

Erna understood why she had asked the question but didn't want to have to explain the facts of life so soon. Wilhelm had been very subdued in his lovemaking and would only exercise his husbandly rights once a week at the most. In the two days that Franz had been in the house, he'd had her six times. And his mating habits were closer to those of a wild bear than those of a man. He was at the opposite end of the marital scale and he wasn't even officially her husband. He hadn't even used the word husband or marriage after the first hour.

After that first time with Franz, she found herself wondering how Cap would make love to her. She was sure that it would be much different from either Wilhelm's almost dutiful performance or Franz' hurried rutting. Now she wished she had told Cap that she wanted him to stay. But she knew he wanted to return to Bismarck and his almost solitary life as a surveyor.

She suddenly smiled when she recalled the first time when he'd tried to explain that he needed to go to Bismarck to join the railroad as surveyor. She'd interpreted his horrible German to mean that he wanted to join with her, and she'd come close to slapping him. Now she wished she'd dragged him into the house and experienced what she now knew was never going to happen.

But Franz was now the man of the house and before he left, he'd told her that he might move them all to his bigger farm if the main house was livable. She hoped that he found it too hideous to ever be habitable.

She then showed her winning hand and scooped up the dry beans they were using for chips. Before she'd suggested that they play poker, she'd let Gustave and Elsa go outside to burn things with his magnifying glass. While they were gone, she took out the money that Cap had given to her and folded it into a towel. She lifted the trap door and placed it under the pile of rags near the gunbelt. She didn't want her children to know it was there if Franz asked them. Even if she warned them not to say anything, she knew that young children tended to blurt out the truth. By not even letting them see her hide the money, they wouldn't need to protect the secret.

Franz was startled when he found the big house cleared of his family's bodies. The furniture in the room was heavily damaged, but he could salvage the wood if he needed it. He then checked the smaller houses and found them empty but knew where the furniture had gone. While he'd told Erna that they might move back to his farm, he wasn't keen on moving all of that furniture and supplies. He decided to stay at Erna's house for a while. The only incentive he had to move was that the children could stay in one of the small houses which would give him more time alone with Erna. She was every bit as exciting as he'd hoped. Marta was nothing but a fading memory.

He did wonder where her body and those of the rest of his family had gone. He hadn't noticed the gravesite because the mound that Cap had noticed was much flatter already.

He mounted Jed and turned the mule to the west. Franz still hadn't asked Erna if Tyler had given her any money, but he'd bring it up when he returned.

———

After leaving the sheriff's office, Cap headed for J.M. Rittenhouse Emporium. In addition to buying a good pair of field glasses, he needed to improve his wardrobe. He'd never needed to be concerned with his appearance before as he rarely stayed in a town. But now he'd be living in Bismarck and should look more presentable.

An hour later, Cap left the store carrying two large canvas bags and sporting a dark brown Stetson. He'd been surprised to find a full shelf of the popular hats and chose one that wouldn't attract the attention of anyone trying to shoot him. He hadn't liked their offerings of field glasses but had found a used nautical telescope with excellent optics. It had a greater magnification than field glasses as well, but that meant he'd have to hold it more steadily. He wondered how sailors managed it on the deck of a rolling ship.

He returned to his room and added his new clothes to the dresser drawers before sliding his new telescope into his saddlebags. It had come with a nice case and lens caps as well, so he wasn't worried that it might be damaged when he added some boxes of cartridges later.

Sheriff Donavan's offer had been almost a godsend. Not only did it give him a new livelihood that appealed to him; his described duties would give him the chance to honor his promise to Gustave and Elsa. They would become his responsibility again even if it was only in an official capacity.

That evening as he shared supper with the sheriff and Charlotte, the subject of the house resurfaced, only this time, it was Charlotte who brought it up.

As they began to eat, she asked, "Have you asked my future husband to show you his house yet, Cap?"

He grinned as he answered, "Lordy, Charlie! I just got here and you're trying to kick me out already."

"We're getting married on the seventeenth of October and I know that he wants to turn the first floor of my boarding house into our honeymoon suite."

He looked at Coop who shrugged before he asked, "Are you really that anxious to sell that place?"

"I don't even sleep in the same bedroom I shared with my unfaithful wife. I'm not sure that she and my deputy didn't use the other bedrooms, either. Every time I walk through the front door, it reminds me of what had been happening in the place. As I said, I'll give you a good price, Cap."

"Why haven't you sold it yet? I'm sure that some of these folks would be happy to buy it. What about John or Al?"

"I offered it to both of them, but they're unmarried and don't have the money anyway. The same goes for most of the men who show up in town. I wouldn't let some of them have it for ten thousand dollars. It's too pricey for most of them, but as I've already said a few times, I'll give you a discount. I got it at a very low price when the Panic hit in '73. I only bought it because my wife wanted a bigger house. She probably just needed more bedrooms to entertain my deputy."

Cap said, "We can visit the place tomorrow and you tell me how much you want. Don't go crazy. I can afford it."

"How can you say that if you don't even know how much I'm going to ask?"

“I didn’t spend much of the money that the Northern Pacific paid me to survey before they went bust. They still owed me two months’ pay when they abandoned us in the middle of Montana Territory, by the way. I spent some of it on supplies over the years, but mostly I just traded up. When I went down to Deadwood, I set aside almost all of my money and played poker for a few months. Those boys may have been good prospectors, but they were terrible poker players.”

Charlotte then asked, “What do you mean when you said you just traded up?”

“I hunted and trapped for food and fur. I’d exchange the fur for supplies at the trading posts. But between defending myself against hostile Indians or greedy white men, I’d accumulate things like horses and guns. I’d get rid of the weapons I didn’t like and keep the nice ones I liberated or trade up to newer models. I’d sell the horses and saddles because I’m happy with my mules.

“You ride mules?” Coop asked before taking a big bite of roasted potato.

“I like mules. I’ve never found a horse I wanted anyway.”

Coop snickered but didn’t insult his choice in mounts as he finally made the connection. He’d heard the legend of the ‘Mule Killer’ more than two years ago. The first time he’d heard it muttered, he thought that some crazy man with a vendetta against the critters was roaming the territory assassinating mules. He soon discovered that it was a reference to a man who rode mules and was feared, hated and respected among the tribes. He now had no doubt that Cap Tyler was the man who had earned that nickname and was even more pleased to have him as a deputy.

They talked for another hour, but the subject of Franz Hartmann never entered the conversation.

Franz hadn't challenged Erna when she said that she didn't have any money. He wasn't sure if she was being honest with him but wasn't about to anger her. She'd flared at him for simply asking the question. He was sure she wouldn't have reacted that way if Tyler didn't give her some cash before he left. He still had more than thirty dollars but wasn't about to spend it on supplies if it was unnecessary. He estimated that there was enough on hand to last them through November but had miscalculated. He was consuming more than Erna and the children combined. The large stack of supplies along the far wall also included clothing and non-edibles which disguised the total amount.

The lure of the gold in the Black Hills was still present in his mind. Each time he'd gone to have a beer at Schmidt's, that seemed to be the most common topic. Now that the main house was clean, he could sell the farm. But that would mean a trip to Bismarck and he'd most likely run into Tyler which could be a disaster. But Erna had said that he was going to work for the railroad, so by springtime, he would probably be gone.

He'd stay for the winter unless something dramatic happened or her kids became annoying. He wasn't fond of children and when Marta had said she was going to have a baby last month, he was close to heading to the Black Hills even then. The Indian raid had been providential.

When Cap entered the jail early the next morning, he found Sheriff Donavan already there with the heat stove warming the office. It was thirty minutes earlier than what he'd been told were normal operating hours, so he was surprised to find his new boss making coffee.

As he hung his new Stetson on the hat rack then took off his coat he asked, "Do you always get here this early, Coop?"

The sheriff set the coffeepot on the heat stove then replied, "Nope. I figured you'd be here before everyone else, and I wanted to show you the map to give you an idea of what will be your primary areas."

"I thought you already mentioned all of that."

"Not in detail. Come on over here and I'll show you."

Cap stepped to the far wall where there were three maps. The largest was a complete map of Dakota Territory, the middle-sized one was Burleigh County and the third was a street map of Bismarck.

He pointed to the east end of the city map and said, “Most of the settlers who are waiting to reach their land are in a tent city around here.”

Then he shifted his index finger slightly to the north and said, “This is the rougher area where the men who expected to find a job laying track call home. It’s almost a separate town and not a nice place. It’s like a miniature Deadwood by the way you described that town. They usually keep to themselves but sometimes they cause trouble in town or with the settlers. The settlers are mostly German and some Scandinavians. They’re all good, hard-working folks that were just caught up in circumstances. Some have already joined our community rather than wait.

“When we do our daily rounds, I’ve been riding through both of those areas because I don’t want John or Al to become a target. You saw how young they look. Some of those bad boys will eat them alive. My old deputy could handle them, but he handled my wife better. Anyway, now that you’re here, I’ll share that part of rounds with you. Okay?”

Cap grinned and said, “Jawohl, Boss.”

"You speak German?" the sheriff asked with his eyebrows slightly peaked.

"I was really rusty when I found Mrs. Braun and her children. I had to improve my use of the language quickly because she spoke very little English, and it led to some awkward situations when I first arrived."

"You didn't talk about them very much last night, Cap. Any reason why you didn't?"

"I was growing very fond of her and her children before Franz Hartmann arrived."

"If you were that fond of them, why didn't you bring them with you?"

"I didn't think I'd be leaving until springtime and even then, I thought I'd be working as either a surveyor or an army scout. In either case, I'd be out in the wild country. Maybe if I'd come to Bismarck for those supplies a week ago, things would have been different. But she has her land and a German farmer now."

Coop shook his head then turned his attention back to the map wall. He failed to ask about Franz Hartmann again in his anxiousness to explain Cap's new duties.

He pointed at the territorial map and traced a line from Bismarck following the north side of the Heart River for an inch or so before he stopped.

"This is the settlement of Mandan. I had to add it to the map because it wasn't there when the mapmaker drew it."

Cap quickly said, "I didn't even hear about it. When did they build it?"

"You were probably out in Montana Territory when they first started the town. Then they had to move it when the Northern Pacific changed their surveyed route."

"How big is it now?"

"About a hundred and fifty residents. It's in Morton County, but they don't have any lawmen yet. I'll want you to take a ride out there at least once a week."

"Okay, boss. I'll ride over to the east end of town to take a look at the setup in a little while. Do you want me to ride to Mandan later?"

"Give it a week or so. I want you to be seen around town and get familiar with all of the changes. When you get back from visiting the east end, I want to show you the house. It might be a bit, um, more than you expect."

"When you described it last night, I got that impression when you said that your ex-wife needed more bedrooms."

Coop snickered then said, "She probably used the kitchen, too."

"Didn't you even suspect anything was going on before she left?"

Coop parked his butt on the edge of the desk before replying, "Yeah, I knew what she was doing for a few months. I was close to shooting Foley once, but figured that if I did, Maureen would just find another man to keep herself entertained. It wasn't as if I ignored her, but she seemed to want more than I could give. Anyway, I finally told her that I knew about her affair and that I wanted a divorce. She wasn't upset at all and even laughed then said I wouldn't dare. If I did, she'd tell everyone that I wasn't even a real man and that was why she had to find one who could satisfy her. I was close to hitting her smirking face, Cap. Instead, I just promised her that I'd have John or Al follow her whenever I wasn't with her. She ran off two days later."

Then he smiled at Cap and said, "At least you haven't made that mistake."

"No, but I may have made a bigger one."

"You mean about Mrs. Braun?"

He nodded then replied, "And her children," before he quickly added, "I'll head out to the eastern side of town and see what it looks like."

Coop stood then waved as Cap grabbed his coat, and as his new deputy pulled on his hat, the sheriff took a seat behind the desk.

Ten minutes later, Cap rode Joe to the two tent cities at the eastern end of Bismarck. The line of demarcation between the immigrant's side and that belonging to the men seeking employment was clear. On his left, it was nothing but a collection of tents, shacks and lean-tos. Wandering through the open spaces were dirty, disheveled men and a few women who were probably earning the last of the grubby men's remaining cash.

On his right, the families of settlers had arranged their temporary housing neater than some of the army camps he'd seen. The tents were aligned leaving straight pathways while the covered wagons were mostly on the ends. He could see large firepits and he assumed that some of the tents were used as bathing areas and privies. He turned Joe to his right and walked him down one of the lanes between the tents. As he passed the residents, he smiled and said good morning in German. While he was sure that the blond-headed Scandinavians understood him, he wished he could speak in their native tongues. But as they could be Norwegian, Swedish, or Danish, he wasn't sure if he'd be able to tell the difference anyway.

But regardless of their birthplace, they were all Americans now and each of them smiled back and greeted him. He'd moved his badge to his coat, so they'd understand why he was there.

He couldn't help but notice the surprisingly large number of handsome young women among the families which seemed out of proportion to the young men. He suspected that their husbands, fathers and brothers acted as their shields from invasions from the savage nation across the way. That was probably one of the many problems that made the east side of town so dangerous.

After circling around the herds of horses, cattle, pigs, goats and sheep at the back of the settlement, he headed back down another pathway. He noticed that almost everyone, even the mothers with young children were busy making improvements to their temporary homes. They were preparing for the cold weather that would doon arrive. He wondered how long some had been there waiting to get to their permanent farms. He'd ask Coop when he returned.

He then crossed the end of Main Avenue which served as the boundary and walked Joe into the less reputable tent settlement. He tried smiling and greeting the men as he passed, but soon realized it served no purpose. Each man he acknowledged either ignored him or spat on the ground to let him know that he wasn't welcome. No wonder Coop was hesitant to send John or Al into this pit. He was also very aware that most of the men wore sidearms but didn't let it bother him. He was only wearing one of his Remingtons and it was hidden by his coat. If he had to act quickly, he'd grab his Winchester. He was very practiced at ripping it from its scabbard, cocking the hammer and firing it quickly and accurately. He estimated he could do it in less than five seconds. He just hoped he didn't need to find out how effective it was in this environment. Unlike his other unexpected encounters, if he needed to defend himself here, he'd be surrounded by hostiles.

He soon found a large corral with more than two dozen horses and mules inside its fences. He assumed the large shack behind the corral was for their tack but soon spotted a large, low structure at the far north end of the tent city. As he drew closer, he could hear sounds that identified it as a saloon of sorts, even at this time of the day. He imagined that the men made their own liquor rather than spend money at a real saloon. Maybe they stole it and anything else they could take without being caught. It was another topic to discuss with the sheriff when he returned.

He wheeled Joe back before he reached the saloon and soon turned west onto the end of Main Avenue. It was an educational ride, but he'd need to learn a lot more when he returned to the jail.

———

Cap's questions began as he and Coop walked out of the office and headed for his house on Mandan Street.

"Most of the settlers have been there for more than a year, but the unemployed men only started arriving in April. We've had a few incidents, but so far, we haven't had anyone shot yet. If it wasn't for a few whores moving to that place, I'm sure we would have had a killing already."

"I noticed that there were quite a few pretty blonde ladies there to attract the crude men from across the way. I reckon that their menfolk watch over them."

"They do, but they've asked me to do as much as possible to keep them protected because they don't want the place to erupt into a war. They'll all be gone one way or another by next summer."

Then the sheriff grinned and asked, "Any of those pretty blonde ladies catch your attention, Cap?"

"No, sir. I was just commenting on the number. It's unusual to see so many women and especially that many young and attractive ones. They all seemed pleasant when I greeted them. On the other hand, none of those scruffy boys seemed pleased to see me. Do you get that too, or is it because I'm new?"

"No, they're just as unhappy with me. That's why I haven't sent John or Al down that way since I hired them."

The sheriff then pointed and said, "That's my place."

Even after the sheriff had told him that it was bigger than his first house, Cap was still surprised at its size, so he sharply asked, "*You live in that place by yourself?*"

“It was bad enough when I shared it with the ex-wife, but now it’s kinda spooky. But she wanted the place, and I gave in. It took me a while to sell our first house, but like I said, I almost stole the place. Do you know how much I paid for it?”

“I’m not sure I want to know.”

“Three hundred and seventy-five dollars. When I finally sold our old house, I got three hundred and fifty but that was almost a year later.”

Cap looked at the sheriff and said, “That place is worth at least four or five times what you paid for it, Coop.”

“I know, but you were out in Montana Territory when the Panic struck. Half the men in town were out of work. This house was owned by the president of the First Dakota Bank before it failed. He wanted to get out of town as fast as he could before his depositors caught up with him. Now we have two bigger banks, the First National and Merchant’s Bank. I use the First National myself.”

They soon turned down the walkway and after he closed the gate, the sheriff said, “There’s a small barn in back but I never used it. Seeing as how you’ve got two mules; you might find it handy.”

Cap just nodded as he stared up at the house wondering if he should even think about buying the place. It was even larger than Mrs. Groom’s boarding house. Maybe he should buy it and start accepting paying guests.

They stepped onto the wraparound porch and Cap noticed that the floorboards were varnished. *Who varnishes a porch in Dakota Territory?*

Ten minutes later, they returned to the varnished porch where the sheriff turned to Cap and asked, "Well, Cap? Will you take it off my hands? I'll let you have it for what I paid for it."

"No, that's not right, Coop. I might pay you that if you emptied all the furniture and everything else. But it's so damned big! How did you manage to get enough wood for all those fireplaces and heat stoves?"

"The railroad ships in firewood from Minnesota. It doesn't cost as much as you think. But if the price bothers you, you can pay me four hundred dollars. Will that satisfy your righteous indignity?"

Cap snickered then replied, "No. I'll give you five hundred and still retain my righteous indignity."

"You must have won more poker games than I figured."

"Seeing as how you confided the situation with your wife and deputy, the least I can do is confess how much I made while I was in Deadwood."

Coop just raised his eyebrows in expectation of a silly number.

"I won just over twenty-two hundred dollars."

Coop's mouth dropped open. There was silly and then there was unbelievable.

He closed his mouth then said, "Remind me never to play poker against you."

"It wasn't that hard, Coop. Most of those prospectors couldn't keep a smile off their faces when they got good cards. When I first arrived, I was stunned how casually they tossed big bets onto the pot. It took me a month before I could afford to sit at the high stakes tables."

"Maybe I should head to Deadwood."

Cap laughed as they stepped down from the porch and said, "I'm sure that Charlotte will be happy to hear that she's leaving Bismarck."

"I would have thought that you, more than most men, would understand that when a woman says she's not moving, she means it."

"I wish I hadn't learned that lesson, Coop."

The sheriff nodded as they headed back to the jail. He had almost winced when he'd seen the reaction on Cap's face. He hadn't realized just how much Mrs. Braun and her children meant to him. He'd tell Charlotte about it tonight and ask her opinion.

As they strode along Mandan Street, Cap was still uncomfortable about buying the big house. He may be hoping to have his own family, but as Mrs. Braun and her children wouldn't be moving in, then he'd be living alone for quite some time. He may have been on his own for a long time, but not in a big house which would constantly remind him of his solitude.

———

The sheriff and Cap shared a late lunch with Charlotte at the boarding house before Cap went to his room and retrieved his money pouch. Charlotte was immensely pleased knowing that Coop was now free of the house that held so many bad memories and on the seventeenth of the month, he and Cap would be switching residences.

After lunch, they walked to the big First National Bank building where Cap opened his first bank account and deposited fifteen hundred dollars and gave Coop the payment for the house. He still kept more than five hundred dollars in cash in case there was another economic disaster like the Panic.

After they had transferred the deed at the county courthouse, Coop introduced Cap to the county prosecutor and any other officials he respected. He avoided the ones who tended to be more officious than efficient. Cap didn't have to be told why his new boss skipped some introductions.

———

That night, as Cap sat on his bed and pulled off his boots, he envisioned himself sleeping in that enormous four-poster in the main bedroom on the night of the seventeenth. He hadn't even become accustomed to sleeping in this comfortable, but normal-sized bed. He imagined that the vast mattress in his new house would be much worse.

His mind then wandered to imagining what Mrs. Braun would think of the giant bed. Then, as he stripped off his socks, he thought that there was no reason for him to keep referring to her as Mrs. Braun. He wasn't about to change it to Mrs. Hartmann, either. He'd just think of her as Erna.

CHAPTER 7

Over the next few days, nothing of consequence happened in either Bismarck or at the Braun farm. That changed, at least for Cap, on Thursday, the eleventh of October.

Cap left the sheriff's office that next morning to make his rounds of the eastern side of town. In the previous times that he'd passed through both tent towns, there had been no change in the residents' behavior. The settlers would smile and greet him in their various German dialects and Scandinavian languages. The transients on the other side of the street either ignored him or let him know that his visits weren't appreciated. He was riding Joe and wearing his new Stetson as he passed the last real building in Bismarck.

He hadn't quite reached the first of the tents when he heard loud voices coming from the settlement side. He couldn't see who was angry, but nudged Joe into a faster pace. He didn't pull his Winchester but unbuttoned his coat to have access to his Remington.

Cap soon spotted the trouble and wasn't surprised to find two of the unkempt men from the northern half arguing with three settlers. The German men were protectively surrounding a blonde-headed young woman whose blue eyes were wide with fear.

None of the three settlers were armed, which was normal. He assumed that the confrontation had just started, and soon other settlers would come from their tents carrying rifles. He knew he had to stop this before they returned, and everything turned ugly.

The pair of armed men had their backs to him, but the three settlers and the young woman suddenly looked up at him as he approached. That triggered the two troublemakers to quickly turn around. He'd seen them before and knew that the other men on their side of the road treated them with some measure of respect.

Cap didn't draw his pistol as he walked Joe closer but did release his hammer loop before he pulled his mule to a stop ten feet away from the two hostile, unkempt men.

"What's going on here?" he asked loudly but already had a good idea.

The oldest settler quickly pointed at the two men and shouted in German, "They came here and wanted to take my Anna with them! My sons and I told them to leave, but they said she was going with them or they would use their guns."

The taller of the two itinerants snickered and said, "Even if you understand that gibberish, it ain't true. We just said howdy to the girl and she acted all high and mighty. Then her old man and brothers showed up and said they were gonna hang us if we didn't leave."

Cap didn't bother insulting the man by calling him a liar but simply said, "I suggest you both just head back to your side of the street and don't return. If I see either of you over here again, I'll escort you to the county jail and you can call it home for a week."

The shorter man sneered as he snapped, "You must be feelin' all high and mighty yourself, Deputy. You sit up there on that mule thinkin' that you can scare us, but we're the bosses over there and we got friends. You're the one who oughta be afraid."

Cap expected one of them or both to go for his pistol soon to prove how tough they were, but he calmly said, "I'll ask you once more to leave quietly. Are you going to go, or do you want to issue more threats?"

Before the short man could reply, his partner did as Cap expected and reached for his Colt. But before the man's pistol barrel cleared its holster, Cap slid his Remington clear, cocked the hammer and pointed it at the taller man.

The man thought he was dead when he saw Cap's muzzle but couldn't stop in mid-draw. He finally ended his pistol's motion with the sights pointed at the roadway. But even as he began to bring his Colt back down, his partner began yanking his pistol. Cap was just as ready for the second attempt, so he shifted his sights slightly to the right but withheld his fire.

The short man had the same epiphany that his partner had just experienced and stopped short of cocking his Colt's hammer.

"Put those pistols back where they belong, then start walking back to your side of the road."

He could tell that they were embarrassed and more than just unhappy after having been humiliated. He doubted that either of them had a forgiving nature which would make future tours more dangerous. But Cap was sure that they realized how lucky they were to be alive. They slowly holstered their pistols before they began to walk past Joe.

Cap released his Remington's hammer and slipped it into his holster as he watched the two men stride past and onto the roadway. He knew he could have shot both of them, but by keeping his bullets in their cylinders, he believed that they had served a much better purpose. Those two would pass stories of Cap's ability and it should reduce the number of men who would even think about drawing a pistol. Granted, it might mean that someone would be inspired to backshoot him, but he thought it was a good tradeoff, at least for now.

Once they were across the street, he turned to the girl's father and in his rapidly improving German, said, "I know that I've seen you before, but I have not introduced myself. My name is Cap Tyler. I am a new deputy sheriff, and the sheriff has asked me to keep the peace on this side of town. If any of those men bother you or anyone else here, send someone to tell me."

'I am Oskar Wendt. These are my sons, Paul and Peter. My daughter is named Anna."

Cap smiled as he said, "Pleased to meet each of you."

Oskar then asked, "Why didn't you shoot when they pulled their guns?"

"There was no need."

"But if you gave them even one second more, they could have fired."

"I know."

Anna then stepped close to her father and smiled up at him as she said, "Thank you, Deputy Tyler. They frightened me very much."

"I can understand why, miss. Please tell everyone to call me Cap. It is much easier to remember. It is short for my Christian name, Casper."

Her father was about to say something else when two other settlers trotted up carrying rifles.

Oskar turned and said, “Thank you for coming, but Deputy Tyler sent them away.”

Before the gun-toting settlers left, Cap said, “It isn’t a good idea to face those men with guns. Many of them are hard men who may have killed before. If you bring guns, it is more likely that you will be shot. After that, many more will die. I don’t want to see a war in Bismarck.”

Oskar nodded then said, “You are right in what you say. I will let everyone know. I will have someone keep a saddled horse ready if there is more trouble.”

“Good. If I am not there, Sheriff Donavan will help.”

Anna smiled again as she said, “Thank you again, Cap.”

Cap smiled, tipped his hat and said, “You’re welcome, miss,” then wheeled Joe around and headed back to the road. He didn’t turn west but continued into the seedy enclave. He was giving them their opportunity to shoot him in the back. If they didn’t make the attempt now, then they probably wouldn’t try the next few times he rode through their shanty town. He wondered how long it would be before the two men who called themselves the tent city’s leaders would have someone attempt to backshoot him.

Five minutes later, he turned Joe west on Main Avenue and let out a long breath. It had been a tense five minutes. He’d tell the sheriff what had happened and would ask about the two men. He didn't know their names, but they thought they were in charge and each of them had distinguishing features. The tall man had a wide scar that almost looked like a brand on his right cheek. The short one wore a much longer than usual beard that had to be six inches below his chin.

While the settlers may have been surprised that he hadn't fired when the two men drew their pistols, he had already visualized the sequence before the taller man even twitched his fingers. It had always been that way for him long before he found his survey party besieged by the Blackfeet. It was as if time simply slowed down. He could see everything almost as if he was viewing the rest of the world through a giant magnifying glass. It was the main reason he'd never been shot.

But that didn't mean he was invulnerable, not by a long shot. He had to anticipate what the antagonist would do, but to do that, he had to know he even existed. If one of those men on the bad side of the road was hiding behind a tent with a Winchester, he'd learn the hard way just how much damage a slug of lead could do.

After entering the jail, he found Coop at the desk as John and Al were still doing their more sedate rounds.

He took off his hat then his coat as he said, “I had an incident between two of the hard men and some settlers that could have escalated.”

“What happened?”

Cap explained the situation then asked, “Do you know those two?”

“Yeah. The one with the scar is Ralph McCardle. He and his bearded pal, Jimmy Baker were troublemakers in town long before most of those other fellers arrived. Ralph owns that run-down place they call a saloon and Jimmy does most of the dirty work. They’re the unelected leaders of a band of hoodlums that hangs out in his saloon. They have others that come into town and steal just about anything that isn’t nailed down. It’s hard to prove and most shop owners don’t even tell me. They just figure it’s part of doing business. I’m surprised that you got the drop on them.”

“They telegraphed their moves, boss. Have they bothered the settlers a lot?”

“Not too much. Anna Wentz must have been very impressive for them to enter the settlers’ side of the road during the day.”

“She was. Do you think they’ll try again?”

“I don’t know. I guess it depends on whether or not they think they can get away with it. But I’d be more careful if I was you. Men like that don’t like being shown up.”

Cap nodded as he said, “I know. I could see it in their eyes. But I’ll make another ride through this afternoon just to let them know I’m still keeping an eye on them. Tomorrow, I’ll make that visit to Mandan. Hopefully, things are more peaceful there. When was the last time you visited the place?”

“About a month ago. I didn’t have any serious problems on that visit. Just the usual complaints about overcharging and immoral behavior.”

Cap grinned before he said, “I can live with that.”

His afternoon visit was routine with the exception that most of the settlers greeted him as Cap. He also thought that he counted more young women smiling at him as he rode past. The one with the largest smile was Anna Wentz.

While he admitted that she was a very handsome young lady, he suspected that there were more than a few young German men who would call on her. The last thing he wanted was to cause trouble on this side of the road.

But that being said, he wondered why it seemed that there was such a noticeable disparity in the number of young women as opposed to young men. It didn't take long for him to determine the reason.

The Franco-Prussian War of 1870 had resulted in over a million casualties on the French side, and while the Germans only lost around a hundred thousand men, the civilian population had then lost a quarter of a million due to a localized smallpox epidemic. Of course, the Germans blamed the French for the disease, and he didn't doubt the countries would be at each other's throats again soon. While he recalled that most of the German casualties were from one area, he couldn't remember which area it was. It didn't really matter. He assumed that the arrival of the Northern Pacific railroad agents had been seen as a godsend to many of them.

As he headed back to the jail, he wondered if that was why Erna's husband had uprooted his young family to come to America. She hadn't mentioned the war but did tell him how Elsa had been born as an American citizen before she reached the shores of the New World.

He was smiling as he stepped down and tied Joe to the hitchrail. Maybe tomorrow when he went to Mandan, he'd make a side trip to take a look at the farm through his new telescope.

———

The next morning, after making his eastern rounds without incident, Cap continued through town and headed for the giant ferry across the Missouri River on the north side of Bismarck. It was so big because it had been built to transport the rail cars and even the massive locomotives of the Northern Pacific across the wide river. It hadn't moved any trains across since it had been in operation, but it would next spring. The railroad planned to build a bridge across the river, but that wouldn't be possible for a while.

He had only learned yesterday that there was a smaller ferry operating south of the town. If he had known about it, he might have gone to Bismarck for supplies rather than Fort Lincoln. Then everything might have been much different. But he hadn't heard of its existence and he was soon going to be living by himself in that giant house and sleeping in that massive four-poster alone.

After taking the enormous ferry across the Missouri River, Cap set Joe to a medium trot and headed west. Now that he wore a Burleigh County Deputy Sheriff badge, he hadn't had to pay for the bouncing ride across the river. Today was his first trip to Mandan, but he knew that he had to start using Jasper on his rides out west to get him used to the ferry. But today, he stuck with Joe.

He had somehow missed the well-traveled road that he was sure followed the newly surveyed route for the Northern Pacific. It angled a few degrees to the north, so the Heart River would stay on his left most of the way. The distance to the river would be gradually increasing as he headed west which explained why he wouldn't have spotted the town when he'd ridden to the fort for supplies. He had first wondered why no one at the fort mentioned Mandan as he dined with the NCOs. Then he realized it was his own fault. For almost the entire time he was there, they had constantly bombarded him with questions about the Sioux and Cheyenne. He'd spent most of his two visits talking until he was hoarse.

Coop had described the young community as being a collection of folks who were anxiously waiting for the Northern Pacific tracks to reach them. Some were settlers who had bought their land as the Brauns and Hartmanns had. But unlike them, they had waited and purchased their property after the railroad had changed their route. They had probably paid much more for their land as well.

While the town was only about ten miles west of the Missouri, he knew that it would still attract a lot of business from the railroad. That was because until the Northern Pacific built that big bridge over the Missouri River, they'd have to move the trains piecemeal across its wide expanse on the ferry. That would take a day in good weather. The passengers would be sent across the river first then have to stay in Mandan until their train was reassembled and that meant customers.

The large number of ruts on the roadway made him shift Joe to the edge to avoid injury. He had his badge on his coat for the same reason he'd worn it yesterday but had both gunbelts at his waist. He also had both his Winchester and

Sharps with him because even this close to Bismarck, he could encounter hostiles.

As he rode, he glanced at the Heart River to the south. Buck Creek, which flowed past Erna's farm, was another eight miles away and carried its water on a parallel course before both waterways emptied their contents into the Mighty Missouri. He estimated that when he reached Mandan, her farm would be just another twenty-five miles south. He'd spend this visit introducing himself to the townsfolk but the next time, maybe he'd make that side trip.

On the right side were miles of rolling hills and flat ground covered in prairie grass. The only trees in sight lined the river and creek banks, but only in small clumps like the one north of Erna's farm. When he was with his father crossing the Plains of western Nebraska and eastern Wyoming, he learned that the lack of forests was due to the almost annual massive prairie fires. The hardy grass would quickly regrow, but trees never had the chance to mature.

He had only ridden a few minutes when he rounded a long bend in the road and spotted traffic ahead. For just a few seconds, he wasn't concerned. When he realized that the westbound freight wagon was stopped and two men were pointing Winchesters at the teamsters, he knew he had to do something quickly. Whoever was planning to take the wagon wasn't about to leave any witnesses.

He let Joe continue to walk closer as he slipped his Sharps from its scabbard. He hoped to get within range of his Winchester '76, but they were about five hundred yards away. If they spotted him, then he'd have to shoot one with the Sharps and hope that the other one tried to escape.

Neither Skunk Roper nor Stinky Jacobsen had spotted Cap yet. They had just stopped the heavily loaded freight wagon that they'd followed since it left the ferry. They hadn't even tried to hide from the freighters but let them become accustomed to having the two men riding behind them for a while. They'd been slowly cutting the gap until they were close enough to pull their repeaters. By the time one of them looked back, it was too late.

As Cap continued to walk Joe closer without being noticed, Skunk had his Winchester pointed at the driver and shouted, "You boys get down and leave that shotgun on the seat!"

Abner Tazwell glanced at Joe Lyons and slowly set his twelve-gauge down before the two freighters began to stand.

Stinky nodded to Skunk then began to settle his sights on Joe Lyons when he rocked violently to his right at the same moment a loud rifle report reached the wagon. Skunk stared at his partner who was still wide-eyed in shock after the powerful round had plowed into the left side of his chest. Then he slowly rolled backwards and tumbled from his saddle. His Winchester didn't go off in the fall, but it was the last of Skunk's concerns.

He forgot about the two teamsters as he turned his Winchester to the east and spotted a rider about three hundred yards away but was getting closer. The man was pulling a rifle from his scabbard, so Skunk knew he had to either run away or take the shooter down. It wasn't really a question as the bastard had killed Stinky and had to pay for it. He knew it was going to be Winchester on Winchester now, and he trusted his ability with the firearm.

But as he turned his horse toward the oncoming rider, the forgotten teamsters reminded him of their presence.

As soon as Stinky had been hit, Abner had snatched his shotgun from the seat and cocked both hammers. He thought that he might take a .44 before he could fire his scattergun, but when he looked up, he found that Skunk was already turning away.

Skunk never had a chance to get his horse moving when the roar of the shotgun reached his ears and two loads of buckshot slammed into him. The blast knocked him off the right side of his horse. The massive load of lead had only traveled twelve feet and had barely begun to spread apart, so all of the small balls of metal except for three had rammed into his left shoulder, neck and head.

Cap had just cocked his Winchester when he saw the teamster almost decapitate the second highwayman with his shotgun. His finger hadn't even reached the trigger when Skunk Roper plummeted to the ground. He released his Winchester's hammer then slid it home and started Joe at a trot toward the freight wagon.

Abner and Joe had stepped to the ground and watched as Cap approached.

As Abner pulled the two empty shells from the shotgun and tossed them aside, Joe said, "He's wearin' a badge, Ab."

Abner still pulled two new shells from his coat pocket, pushed them into the shotgun's tubes and snapped it closed as Cap pulled his mule to a stop.

"I'm Deputy Sheriff Cap Tyler. Do you know those two?"

"Yeah, I know 'em," Joe replied, then asked, "Who do you work for? Our outfit is in Bismarck, but I ain't seen you before."

"I was just sworn in by Sheriff Donavan a few days ago."

Abner said, "I don't recall seein' you in town either."

"I used to be a surveyor with the Northern Pacific, and they left us hanging out in the middle of Montana Territory when they folded. I just got back, and the railroad didn't want any more surveyors, but Coop seemed to believe I was qualified to be his deputy."

Joe said, "After seein' Stinky get blown out of the saddle from three hundred yards, I reckon he was right."

"You said you knew them, so why did you let them get so close?"

"I didn't recognize 'em until they pulled their Winchesters."

"Who are they?"

Abner replied, "The one you took down was Stinky Jacobsen, and I dropped Skunk Roper. They work Ralph McCardle. I don't reckon you've heard of him yet. But if you get close to either of those bodies, you'll find out why they earned those monikers. They seemed downright proud of bein' so foul smellin'."

Cap dismounted then said, "I met Mister McCardle a few days ago. It wasn't a pleasant introduction. Let's get them on their saddles and we'll bring them into Mandan. I'll take care of the one I shot, and you boys can handle the other one."

"Sounds fair, Deputy," Joe replied before setting his shotgun on the driver's seat.

Ten minutes later, the wagon was rolling toward Mandan again and Cap was leading two horses with the owners' bodies laid over their saddles.

It was another hour before Cap had his first view of the new settlement. It was about what he'd expected to find and could hear the sounds of new construction in the distance. The bed of Abner and Joe's freight wagon contained a lot of supplies used for building and he imagined they had a lucrative business. That would change when the railroad arrived.

When they reached town, he learned that Mandan didn't have a real mortician. But there were more than enough residents of Mandan willing to help dig a grave and drop the two bodies into the hole. Cap had to agree with Joe Lyons about their overpowering stench. It accelerated their burial as no one wanted to linger around the gravesite very long.

After they were covered with dirt, Cap met the important citizens of the new town who seemed very pleased to know that he'd be visiting them more often. The mayor told him that they would be hiring a town marshal before springtime and after hearing the story of the takedown he was offered the position. He had even offered him more money than the county was paying. Despite having just bought Coop's mansion, it was still a tempting offer. He'd stay in one town and it was a lot closer to Erna's farm. But that also meant he might be more likely to see her with her new husband, so he declined their job offer. He did accept their offer to join a few of the prominent citizens at the mayor's house for lunch so they could get to know him better.

It was early afternoon when he left Mandan to make his return ride. He was trailing the two horses and had two more Winchesters to give to Coop. He had their pistols in their saddlebags but wasn't sure that the sheriff would want them. They were old ball and cap Colts, and neither was in great condition. The Winchesters, however, were well maintained.

He wasn't sure if he should have taken the bodies back to Bismarck. But even if the sheriff chastised him for having them buried in Mandan, he still thought it was much better to leave the pair of malodorous malcontents behind. It would take a few days for their saddles to smell like leather again.

But when he'd learned that the two men worked for Ralph McCardle, he suspected that the odds of being ambushed in the shanty town had just gotten worse.

———

It was the middle of the afternoon when he entered the jail and found the sheriff and both of his fellow deputies in residence.

As he hung his hat and coat on the wall pegs, Coop asked, "What did you think of the town?"

Cap grinned as he pulled up a chair then as he sat down, he replied, “The town was fine, but I had a bit of a problem before I arrived.”

John and Al both wanted to ask but left it to their boss to pose the question.

“What happened?”

Cap explained the brief confrontation and his decision to bury the two highwaymen in Mandan rather than return them to Bismarck.

When he finished, Coop said, “I would have been mighty peeved if you’d brought those two pigs back to town. And that’s insulting hogs. I’m a bit worried because it looks like McCardle is getting bolder.”

“The teamsters said that they work for Ralph McCardle.”

“They were right about that. Those two provided a lot of the supplies for his saloon and he sells some to the other men or gives it to them to put them in his debt. Like I said before, that place is like a town all by itself.”

“I assume that he’ll be using different men for the job now.”

Coop nodded as he replied, “Maybe. But I’m not sure how many of them are really that loyal to McCardle. Did you bring their horses?”

“Yes, sir. They’re parked out front. Their Winchesters are in good shape, but the pistols in their saddlebags are a step down from what you’re wearing. Maybe two steps.”

Coop then asked, “Aside from your run-in with Stinky and Skunk, did everything else go all right?”

“Yes, sir. The mayor offered me a job as town marshal, but he didn’t include a giant house, so I turned him down. At least by next spring, they should have their own lawman.”

“That would be good. They really should have a county sheriff, though. I assume you don’t want those boys’ horses and tack; or am I wrong?”

“No, sir. You’re not wrong. For horses, they aren’t bad animals, so John and Al might want them. Just let the saddles air out for a bit and the saddlebags are a bit ripe, too.”

Coop turned to his young deputies who were both grinning and said, “You heard the man. Get out there and steal what you want.”

John and Al hopped from their chairs, and after saying, “Thanks, Cap!” in chorus, hurried to the wall and snatched their hats and coats from their pegs.

They threw on their coats and were tugging on their hats as they flew out of the jail.

“It was like they were little boys on Christmas morning,” the sheriff said as he smiled.

“We’re all little boys inside, Coop. I keep waiting to feel like a grownup, but now I’m not sure it’ll ever happen.”

“What about Mrs. Braun’s little boy, Cap? Do you still think you should have taken the whole family with you?”

Cap sighed then replied, “I wish I could have, Coop. But she was determined to stay on her farm and Franz Hartmann was a farmer and a German to boot.”

Coop snapped his fingers then said, “I’ve been meaning to ask you about him. You said that he escaped the Indian attack. I heard about that when he showed up and wondered how it was even possible. He lived with Josef and Marta Mayer, the blacksmith and his wife. He even apprenticed in the smithy for a little while. Did he or Mrs. Braun tell you how he got out of there without a scratch?”

“Nope. I hardly spoke to him, and after he arrived, I didn’t talk to Erna much at all. But I did have a lot of questions about things I found on his family farm even before I knew he had survived.”

“What did you find that made you curious?”

"The first thing was finding the bodies in the main house. The entire family had been massacred but there was almost no blood on the ground outside. If they'd been inside and were firing through the gun ports, they would have at least hit some of the Lakota horses. I found no patches of dried blood larger than a couple of inches across. Then there was the fact that the family was in the house with the door open. It hadn't been broken open; it was simply open. How did the Lakota get inside without breaking the hinges or the locking bar? Before I even reached the house, I found where the Sioux had ridden west to reach the Braun farm and they had three shod animals with them. It was the first thing that struck me as odd. It should have been an even number.

"Anyway, after I found the bodies, I did a perimeter search and found the missing shod animal's hoofprints. They trailed from the house to the east. There were no return set of prints, so I assumed that one of the family had somehow escaped but had been taken down by the Lakota or they were waiting for him."

"Why did you think that happened?"

"If he'd escaped to reach Fort Lincoln, the army would have dispatched at least a squad of troopers to the farms. But there was no sign of any shod horses coming from the east. By the way, a few days later, the army did send some men to the farm to bury the bodies."

Coop leaned back and asked, “How do you reckon Hartmann survived?”

Cap hadn’t spent any time thinking about it after Franz’ arrival because he didn’t want to think of him and Erna together, but now he was almost forced into putting the pieces together. It didn’t take long and when he arrived at the only logical answer, his stomach twisted into knots.

He quietly said, “The only thing that makes any sense was if he or someone else in his family spotted the Lakota and shouted an alarm. They would have had a plan already in place for everyone to rush into the big house which had most of the supplies and probably all of the ammunition and guns. They held the door open waiting for Franz, but he had already mounted one of their mules and run away to the east. The family must have waited too long for Franz to enter the house. By the time the father realized that Franz wasn’t going to make it in time, the Sioux were able to start firing into the house and no one had a chance to close and bar the door.”

When he finished speaking, he looked at the sheriff hoping that he had an alternative theory.

But Coop had agreed with Cap’s logical explanation, so he nodded as he said, “I think you’re right, Cap. What are you going to do about it?”

Cap was startled by his question. He may have marked Franz as a coward and might have been responsible for his family's horrible end, but he hadn't thought about interfering with Erna's life.

"I can't do anything about it, Coop. Why would you ask?"

"You seemed awfully fond of Mrs. Braun and her children, and you're okay with leaving them with the likes of that coward?"

"He's a farmer and a German. Just because the man's gutless doesn't make him a bad man. The Lakota won't be back because they've already destroyed both farms."

"So, you're just going to live in that big house while she and her young'uns live in a sod house with a man who deserted his family when they were in peril. Is that right?"

"You make it sound as if I have a choice, Coop. She told me that she wasn't going to leave, and she knew I had to go because I wasn't a farmer."

"Now I don't profess to know much about women. Hell, I was married to Maureen for four years and never came close to figuring her out. Maybe Mrs. Braun really wanted to go with you but was too proud to say so. I told Charlotte about your situation and she thinks you made a mistake."

"I don't know, Coop. She was pretty adamant about keeping her farm."

"I'll tell you what, after I leave Charlotte's place tonight to return to my mausoleum, you explain everything to her and ask her advice. I didn't know all the facts, so maybe she'll agree with you. Will you do that?"

"Sure. She's a smart lady."

"She's more than that, Cap. I'm one lucky feller."

"She's holding a winning hand herself, Coop."

The sheriff shrugged before he said, "If Charlotte straightens you out about Mrs. Braun, why don't you head down there when you make your next trip to Mandan? That can be after our wedding next Wednesday. Once you're living in that big, empty house by your lonesome, you'll probably want go down there to shoot Franz Hartmann then bring her and her children back with you."

Cap grinned but still believed that Erna could never be convinced to leave her farm. If he'd been in her farmhouse at that moment, he would have had a very different opinion.

———

Erna had just returned from Cap's tent privy and as soon as she entered, Franz closed the door behind her. She then noticed that neither Gustave nor Elsa was in the room and suspected that Franz wanted to drag her to their bed again. He had finally let her sleep two nights ago and hadn't bothered her last night either. She was convinced that he wasn't going to wait until the children were asleep. But she was wrong.

He took her hand and instead of dragging her to the bed, he pulled her to a table and snapped, "Sit down, Erna."

His tone of voice set alarm bells off in her head, but she hadn't a clue to what she had done that could have made him angry.

After she took her seat, she soon believed she understood what had set him off when he picked up her gunbelt from one of the chairs and dropped her Colt on the table. But she didn't think he'd found the money under the clothes.

He sat down opposite her and said, "I found this in that hole we dug under the floor. You didn't think I knew about it; did you?"

"Of course, you'd know about it. You helped Wilhelm build the house."

"Then why did you hide this from me?"

"I didn't hide it, Franz. Cap told me to leave it there in case the Indians came back."

"That's stupid! Why would he tell you to keep it there if you needed it to fight off Indians?"

She looked down at the gunbelt as she replied, "I had the Winchester, but if I was alone and had to take the children into the shelter, I'd have the pistol to…well, to make sure that the Indians didn't kill us."

Franz then shifted to the second, more important topic: the money.

"Did you have anything else in there that you should have told me about?"

Erna then understood that even if he hadn't found the fifty dollars, he'd probably search again. She had to assume he'd already found it.

"Before he left, Cap gave me fifty dollars. I hid it under the clothes in case I needed it."

He half-rose from his chair as he exclaimed, "You lied to me! You said you didn't have any money!"

Erna didn't bother offering an excuse but simply remained silent waiting for her punishment.

Franz slowly returned to his seat as he asked, "Why did you hide it? You weren't going to try to bribe any Indians from killing you."

She shook her head as she replied, "No. I wasn't sure if you'd stay. I'm sorry for not trusting you, Franz."

Franz was far from mollified but now had more than eighty dollars in his pockets and the whispers of the Black Hills gold fields were growing louder.

He finally said, “Alright. I’ll let it go this time. But you’d better not lie to me again. Do you understand?”

Erna nodded as she felt a wave of relief flow through her. She may have lost the money, but at least Franz hadn’t hit her.

Franz then stood, stepped around the table and practically lifted Erna from her chair and yanked her to the bed to make use of their privacy.

———

Outside, Gustave and Elsa were playing a new game they’d created by trying to toss twigs into Cap’s abandoned firepit from eight feet away. There was a chilly wind coming from the northwest that made it almost impossible.

Elsa asked, “Why did Mister Hartmann send us outside when it’s warmer in the house?”

“I think he wanted to be alone with mama,” Gustave said as he flipped his twig toward the hole and watched it curve wildly to the right as the wind took control.

“Does he hurt mama, Goose?”

"I don't know, Elsa. Mama won't talk about it and Mister Hartmann won't talk to us at all."

"Does he hate us?"

"I don't know that either. I know I don't like him at all."

"I hate him. I want Mister Tyler back. Why can't he come back and be our papa?"

"Mama said he had to leave to work for the railroad. I think she wanted him to stay, but then Mister Hartmann came, and he had to go away."

"Mister Hartmann should go away," she said before hurling her twig overhand and missing even worse than her older brother had.

Then she asked, "Is Mister Tyler watching over us like an angel, Goose?"

"I haven't seen him, Elsa. But I hope so. If he is then maybe he'll see how unhappy mama is and send Mister Hartmann away."

"He'll see how unhappy we are too, Goose. Maybe we should ask God to send him back. Should we pray now?"

"That's a good idea, but we can't let Mister Hartmann know."

Elsa tossed her remaining twigs aside, then grabbed he brother's hand before they trotted around to the back of the house so they could pray without the risk of Mister Hartmann seeing them on their knees.

———

When Cap and the sheriff arrived at the boarding house, they walked down the hallway to the kitchen as they usually did. When they entered, they were surprised to find Charlotte cooking much more food than usual.

Before they could ask, she said, "We have more guests. Two families arrived this afternoon. The Bellingers have two young boys and Mr. and Mrs. Hobart have two daughters and two little boys. Mrs. Hobart's sister is with them as well. They're all upstairs unpacking."

Coop removed his hat then stepped close and kissed her before saying, "That's quite a surge in income for you, almost Mrs. Donavan."

She smiled as she replied, "It is. But it's also an increase in my work, Mister Donavan. I can't recall having that many new guests at one time before."

Cap said, "Get used to it, Charlie. Once those rails start heading west again, your boarding house will probably be full most of the time. Maybe you should hire help."

"I thought about that. We'll see. Now both of you dirty men get rid of your coats and wash up before dinner."

Cap said, "Yes, ma'am," then turned and walked back down the hallway to go to his room.

After he'd gone, Coop explained his earlier talk with Cap. He asked her to help if she could and Charlotte was almost surprised that Coop had recognized his new deputy's dilemma. She promised she'd listen to Cap and, if possible, make some recommendations.

———

Cap hadn't seen any of the new residents as he passed by their closed doors but could hear them talking. He counted three occupied rooms but wasn't sure if the children had their own or Mrs. Hobart's sister was quietly unpacking in her own room.

He entered his room and closed the door before he took off his hat and coat. He unstrapped his gunbelts and hung them in place before stepping to the chest of drawers and pouring water into the wash basin on top. He'd have to ask Charlotte how the bathroom schedule worked now that there was a crowd of people who would use it.

———

Later that evening, he and Coop were introduced to both families. Mr. and Mrs. Bellinger were in their early thirties and their two boys were approaching their teen years. The Hobarts were younger, and their two boys and two girls ranged in age from eight to four. He couldn't help but notice how much one of their daughters looked like Elsa. He couldn't stop smiling at the cute little girl.

He soon learned that Wilma Hobart's sister, Angela Parker, was a widow and had lived with them in Minnesota before Orville Hobart was sent to straighten out and then manage the books of the Merchant's Bank. He was an accountant and once asked, spent much of the dinner explaining how critical his job was in keeping the country functional.

Angela was an attractive woman close to his age and he couldn't help but notice that she seemed interested in him. He pretended not to notice but was suddenly grateful that he'd be moving to the big house next week. Maybe he'd move earlier and live with Coop for a few days. He wouldn't have to worry about the bathroom schedule either. The big house had two full baths complete with pumps and large porcelain tubs.

———

The guests had all gone upstairs to their rooms and Coop had returned to his house leaving Cap and Charlotte alone to have their conversation. Cap hadn't asked about moving into the big house yet but would bring it up tomorrow.

Charlotte filled their coffee cups and set the coffee pot on a potholder before taking her seat.

"Coop told me about your decision to leave Mrs. Braun and her children with Franz Hartmann. He included some of the details of Hartmann's miraculous escape as well but said that you'd fill in the rest. So, Cap, tell me why you think it's a good idea to leave her and the children with a man like that? You obviously care for her and her youngsters very much. Yet you don't seem to value their safety as much as you should."

Cap took a sip of his coffee just to bide some time.

When he set it back on its saucer, he said, "I do care about Erna, Gustave and Elsa. I care about them very much. But she is determined to stay on her farm. I'm not a farmer, so when Hartmann arrived, I knew that she would prefer that I leave."

Charlotte stared at him for a few seconds before asking, "Why would she want to trade a man who had given them so much and treated them with compassion for a man who had run away from his own family? I've never met her, so before I give you any advice, tell me about her."

"She's a wonderful, caring woman who would give her life for her children. She also has a powerful, determined character that belies her small frame. I won't dismiss how pretty and well-formed she is, either. But it was her character that marked her as special."

“Yet she still preferred that coward to you?”

“She knew him much better than me, Charlie. I only stayed with them for three weeks and spent my nights outside in my tent.”

“Did she really know him that well?”

“She must have. When he showed up, they embraced as if they were old friends if not lovers.”

“And she kissed him?” Charlotte asked with wide eyes.

“No. She just hugged him. But I knew then that I had to leave.”

Charlotte closed her eyes as she tried to picture the scenario but failed.

“Forget about that scene for now. Why were you so sure that she was determined to stay on her farm?”

“When I first suggested that she accompany me to Bismarck, she practically exploded when she shouted that she wouldn’t leave her farm.”

“That was the day you found her and the children?”

“Yes.”

“But she confirmed that decision a few times over the next three weeks; didn’t she?”

Cap had to take a few minutes to review their many conversations. It was difficult as he kept seeing her smiling face and hearing her laugh. *Had he ever even asked her a second time?* He revisited as many of their talks as he could, and not once did he recall her repeating her decision to stay. He began to wonder if she hadn't just reacted that way on the first day because of their early communication problems.

He finally answered, "I'm not sure."

"Did you talk to her after Hartmann arrived?"

"Yes, but only for a few minutes. She came to my tent with some stew and said she needed my advice. I told her that I understood that Franz wanted to stay, and she simply replied that he was a German and a farmer. I understood that to mean that I had to leave."

Charlotte sighed then asked, "Did she seem happy when she entered your tent?"

"No. But she had to tell me that she had accepted Hartmann, so I knew she was uncomfortable for having to tell me."

"Really? Is that what you thought? Then why did she say that she needed your advice? Honestly, Cap, you disappoint me. I thought you were smarter than that."

"Did I misinterpret what she meant?"

"Unless I totally misunderstood what you just told me, you were as wrong as you could have been. Am I right in assuming that you never told her how you felt about her?"

"How could I? That would only make things much worse when I had to leave."

"Do you think that she cared for you as much?"

Cap cringed because he knew the answer but didn't want to admit it.

Charlotte saw his reaction then said, "She was hoping that you'd tell her that you didn't want Hartmann to become her new husband and that you'd ask her to come with you."

Cap shook his head before he asked, "Why would you think that she would want me to take her with me, Charlie? I didn't even know what I'd do after I left. Maybe if I'd known that I'd be staying in Bismarck, I would have asked her. But between her conviction to stay and my unknown future, I had no choice after Hartmann arrived."

"Well, you have a choice now, Mister Tyler. When are you going to Mandan again?"

"The day after your wedding."

"Instead of going to Mandan at all, you should ride to her farm and take her and the children to your new house. I'm sure that Coop won't protest. I'll be keeping him busy for a few days anyway."

Cap grinned as he said, "I'm sure you will, Charlie. Look, I'll go there, but only to see if she and the children are all right. If they're content and healthy, I'll just come back."

"I don't think that it's enough, but at least you'll see them again."

Cap quickly changed to a less distressing topic when he said, "I was going to move to the big house tomorrow if Coop doesn't mind the company."

Charlotte smiled as she asked, "Angela Parker makes you nervous; doesn't she?"

"Yes, ma'am."

"Even more than those blonde girls in the settlers' camp? Coop told me about your popularity among the young ladies there as well."

Cap just sipped his coffee rather than go down that road. Charlotte had driven home her point. While he wasn't convinced that she was right, he was satisfied with his plan to go to the forest north of the farm and spy on the place. As much as he hoped they were all happy, he harbored a deeper, hidden wish to find them in a very different situation.

Erna stared across the room in the low, red light provided by the dying fire. She hadn't been able to talk to her children very much since Franz had arrived but knew they were unhappy. She hoped that they weren't as unhappy as she was but knew they were confused and worried that Franz might be hurting her.

She closed her eyes and prayed that Cap might decide to pay them a visit. She didn't know why he would and wasn't even sure if he was still in the territory. If he hadn't found a job with the Northern Pacific, he might have loaded his mules onto a riverboat and headed south to Omaha to work for the Union Pacific.

She had just finished her prayer and still had her eyes closed when she felt Franz squeeze her left breast and knew she wouldn't sleep peacefully tonight.

CHAPTER 8

Cap had completed his morning rounds of the eastern end of town without incident and headed west into Bismarck. He had asked Coop about moving into the house when he returned tomorrow, and the sheriff had agreed but had also laughed because he understood his deputy's sudden need to change his residence.

As he entered the business end of Main Avenue, he pulled Joe up to a small shop and dismounted. When he'd first spotted it, he'd been amazed that it could survive with its limited offering.

But when he entered J.M Katz Confectionary, the powerful and tempting smell gave him his answer. Mister Katz offered much more than just a wide assortment of hard candies. He also had German pastries that made his mouth water by just looking at them. But what had added the most noticeable sweetness to the air was unique scent of chocolate.

He stepped to the counter and Mister Katz smiled as he asked, "What would you like, Cap?"

Cap smiled when the proprietor addressed him using his nickname. Some of the German settlers were obviously his customers.

"I need three large sticks of peppermint and two paper sacks."

"Yes, sir," he replied as he set the two small paper bags on the counter before turning and taking three eight-inch-long peppermint sticks and placing them on the bags.

"Will that be all?"

He was about to say, "Yes," when he stared at the rows of treats behind the glass and said, "Add three of the wrapped chocolate bars as well."

Johann smiled then slid the back door to the case open and took out the three bars and set them near the giant peppermint sticks.

"That will be six cents for the peppermint sticks and seventy-five for the chocolate bars."

Cap handed him a dollar bill then asked, "Do you have a pencil?"

Mister Katz pulled a stubby pencil from his pocket and handed it to him before placing the dollar note in his till and taking out Cap's change.

Using the short pencil, Cap started to draw an angel on one of the bags to let Gustave and Elsa know that he was still watching them.

Johann watched and wondered what the deputy was trying to draw but couldn't quite figure it out.

Cap finished his poor artwork and flipped it around to get the confectioner's opinion.

"What do you think?"

"Is it a crow or perhaps a vulture?" Johann asked.

Cap agreed that it was probably closer to those unappreciated birds than a heavenly apparition, so he then drew a halo around the angel's head before he showed it to Mister Katz again.

He stared at the modified image and asked, "Is that raincloud about to descend on the bird's head?"

Cap laughed as he replied, "No, sir. It's supposed to be an angel, but I'm not a very good artist."

Johann smiled as he said, "Let me try."

Cap handed him his pencil then watched as he began to create an angel on the second paper sack in smooth, gentle strokes. When he finished, he turned the bag to face Cap and looked at him.

Cap said, "That's much better than my offering. You can keep the change. Consider it an artist's commission."

"Thank you, Cap. I have many years of experience making decorations."

After the candies were all placed in the bag with his vulture drawing, Cap folded the top and slid it into the angel bag before thanking Mister Katz and leaving the shop.

He put the candy into his saddlebag, then mounted Joe and rode west until he reached the Missouri River and turned south to use the smaller ferry. He wasn't bringing Jasper because he wasn't planning on staying very long. If he was able to bring Erna and the children with him, he'd hitch Joe and Jed to the wagon and drive them back to the ferry. Everything depended on what he found when he arrived.

———

By late afternoon he reached the Hartmann farm. After making sure it was still empty, he shifted to the north to reach Buck Creek before he turned west to the small forest. He wondered if Franz had moved any of the logs from his pyramid but wouldn't be surprised to find them all still stacked exactly as he'd left them.

He soon reached Buck Creek let Joe drink now rather than when they were within sight of the farmhouse. After Joe was satisfied, he continued riding west but kept his attention to the southwest waiting to spot the Braun farmhouse. When it appeared, he searched for movement but didn't see any before he walked Joe into the trees. He noticed the smoke coming from the chimney, so he assumed that Erna was cooking their dinner.

Once among the cottonwoods, he dismounted and tied off Joe to keep him hidden. With the leaves leaving their branches he had a clearer view of the house, but it also meant that he was more visible. He wasn't that concerned about being spotted. Maybe it would be better if Franz saw him, and they had a confrontation. But that would only be a good thing if Charlotte had been right about Erna.

He removed his saddlebags and canteen, then let Joe graze on the low grass near the trees. He noticed his undisturbed pyramid of logs then shook his head before he sat on the stump.

It would be dark in another hour or so, and he hoped to see Erna and the children soon, hopefully without Franz. At least she wouldn't have a bump yet.

Cap pulled out his telescope, removed it from its case and popped off the lens caps. He then stepped closer to the open ground and raised the telescope to his eye. He studied the house and noticed there was less than a foot-high stack of firewood. Franz would have to come here to get more wood soon. He spotted Jed and another mule grazing nearby but both were hobbled, so he knew that he wouldn't have to worry about Joe's brother joining them.

He was about to lower his telescope when he picked up movement from the front corner of the house and soon recognized Gustave and Elsa. He smiled as he watched them talking and wished he could hear what they were saying. Even with the telescope, he couldn't see what they were doing, but they were wearing their heavy coats and hats and seemed happy.

He watched as they walked to where he'd pitched his big tent and then began to pick things from the ground that he couldn't make out. Then they stepped back and stood side by side and began tossing whatever they'd picked up. *What were they doing?*

Cap was close to leaving his tree shelter when Elsa suddenly threw her arms into the air and began bouncing around. When Gustave did the same and then hugged Elsa, Cap realized that they had been playing a homemade game. He continued spying on them as they resumed their game until they tossed the last of whatever they were using as projectiles.

They retrieved their weapons of choice and continued playing for another ten minutes before Erna must have called them in for supper. They dropped their imaginary spears then hurried back to the front door and soon disappeared from sight. He was annoyed that he'd wasted so much time watching when he could have trotted toward the house and attracted their attention. It would only take a minute to discover if they and their mother were happy or at least content.

But knowing that they were probably going to be eating soon meant that he wouldn't see them again today and wouldn't get a chance to see Erna at all. He closed his telescope and pushed the lens caps back in place before reentering the trees.

As the sun set, he sat on his stump having his own supper of cold mutton and beans. He didn't even think of touching the candy. He was planning to leave it as a calling card but until he'd seen the children playing their game, he hadn't figured out what to use as a post office box. Whatever they were tossing was aimed at his small fire pit. He'd leave it in the hole where only they should find it.

He'd stay in the trees until tomorrow morning, and hopefully, he'd see Erna or the children using the privy, and he'd have another chance to talk to them. But he had to return to Bismarck by tomorrow afternoon to move out of the boarding house and prepare for Coop and Charlotte's wedding on Wednesday.

If he hadn't felt as if he was an intruder or a man trying to break up a marriage, even if Franz and Erna hadn't made it official, he wouldn't have hesitated to go to the house. But he suspected that if he did show up at their door, Franz wouldn't be happy to see him. Erna might be displeased to have him disrupt their new life, but he was sure that Gustave and Elsa would be overjoyed to see him again. He'd be like a favorite uncle but wished he could be their loving papa. At least he'd be leaving them a sweet reminder of his continued affection.

He was setting up his bedroll and still debating about knocking on their front door as the sun dropped below the western horizon.

He would have been sickened if he'd known that if he had arrived just twenty minutes earlier, he would have seen Erna using his privy tent and all that followed may not have happened.

Inside the house, Erna was cooking supper while Franz inspected his new Colt. Gustave and Elsa sat at their table and were now playing checkers.

When they said that they were going outside to play, she knew why they wanted to leave the house. They had told her that they had prayed for Mister Tyler to return. While they were playing their twig-in-the-hole game, they hoped that he would come and talk to them.

But it was getting close to dinnertime and she thought that fifteen minutes was enough time for their guardian angel to descend from heaven on his winged mule. So, she'd called them back inside and resumed cooking.

Despite their prayers and her own, she was certain that Cap wouldn't return. She glanced at Franz and knew she'd made a terrible decision to allow him to stay. While she had worries about herself, she was thinking much more about her children as she always did. Almost since Franz had arrived, she had been trying to come up with a way of finding out where Cap had gone. He might still be in Bismarck and if he was, she'd ask for his help. But she was sure that Franz wasn't going to let her leave the house. When they needed supplies, he'd ride to Fort Lincoln himself. He'd spend the money that Cap had given to her and doubted if he'd bring the children peppermint sticks or anything else to make them happy. He barely talked to them at all and when he did, she cringed at his tone that dripped with disgust.

But there was that other, more troubling part of Franz' arrival that still begged questions that she wouldn't dare ask. After his first day's explanation of how he'd escaped from the Sioux, he'd quickly dismissed any conversation about the attack. Initially, she thought it was because he'd seen the mutilated bodies of his wife and family and didn't want to be reminded of the sight. But the more she understood him, the more she realized that he had little sense of compassion. That had inspired more thought about what he had done that day.

She recalled Cap saying how puzzled he'd been when he found a single set of shod hoofprints going east away from the Hartmann farm. Yet the only time Franz had talked of his escape, when he had her in his embrace, he'd said that he'd been near the creek. There shouldn't have been any hoofprints at all if he had been telling the truth.

Little by little, the clues that Cap had provided began to point to a very different explanation for his survival. But she didn't have enough information to be sure of her theory. Cap hadn't told her of his suspicions because he wasn't sure at the time. Besides there was no purpose as he believed that the last survivor had been killed by the Lakota. But he had omitted the most damning piece of evidence. He hadn't mentioned the open door. If he had, it would have cemented her growing belief that Franz had abandoned his family to their fate.

But this was her life now and as she took the skillet from the grate in the fireplace, she knew it wasn't going to be a good life. All she could do was survive and hope her children had a chance for a better life.

———

After the half-moon rose, Cap took his paper sack of candy with the well-drawn angel and walked from the trees. It was cold enough for his breath to make moonlight reflecting clouds as he crossed the open ground. He could see wisps of smoke from the chimney ahead but was reasonably sure everyone was under their blankets. He hoped he didn't hear any sounds of mating when he was close to the house but was counting on the sound-dampening sod walls to keep it from leaking outside.

When he reached Jed, he rubbed him on his nose and told him to give Franz a kick in the butt when he had the opportunity. If he missed and his hooves hit the man's privates, it would be even better. He then continued to the house hoping against hope that Erna would need to use the privy.

But no one left the house before he reached his old fire pit and dropped to his heels. He grinned when he found a small pile of twigs nearby and knew that they were Gustave and Elsa's missiles. He carefully laid the paper sack into the fire pit then stood and glanced at the front corner of the house before heading back to the trees. He wished he could see the children's faces when they found the bag. If he didn't get to watch their discovery, he hoped that they understood why there were only three peppermint sticks and three chocolate bars. The candy was for them and their precious mother. He was confident that Gustave would understand and keep the bag hidden from Franz.

He soon slipped into his bedroll and listened to the sounds of the night. He wished he could stay longer but at least he'd seen the children and they seemed happy. Maybe he'd see Erna in the morning and find that she was at least content.

———

While Cap was placing the candy just twenty feet from where she lay, Erna was still thinking. While Franz was sleeping just inches away, she was relieved that he hadn't bothered her after they'd gone to bed. While she may have been grateful for his inattentiveness, she was also concerned.

After the first few days and nights when she felt as if she was his personal prostitute, Franz had seemed to shift his attention more to what she had in the house than what she had under her dress. While he still took her violently and quickly when he was in the mood, that mood didn't arrive nearly as often as it had before. He hadn't even lived with her for two weeks and seemed to be already growing bored with his new plaything. She freely admitted to herself that she was hardly inspired by his brief, pounding lovemaking, if one dared call it that. But she refused to pretend that she cared for him at all. He was there to provide for her and her children and in the spring, he would plow and plant the fields. But his dropping level of interest made her now worry that he wouldn't stay that long. She was also very concerned about her condition. She was only a day late, but she'd been late before. Still, if she was pregnant, then she wasn't sure what the future held.

Cap was dressed and had saddled Joe as the sun rose. He didn't have much time to wait for someone to use the privy but kept his eyes on the chimney waiting for a burst of smoke to pour into the cold Dakota sky.

He knew it wasn't that frigid and was probably just a few degrees below freezing. There was a layer of frost across the prairie grass as he led Joe to Buck Creek to drink. As Joe dipped his muzzle into the cold water, Cap filled his canteen. He still didn't see any smoke, nor did he see anyone rush outside to use the tent privy.

He mounted Joe and walked him in front of the trees heading into the rising sun. He kept his head turned to the south as his mule carried him away from the Braun farm. When it dropped below the horizon, he sighed and nudged Joe into a trot.

If he'd looked back, he would have seen smoke beginning to drift from the farmhouse chimney, but it probably wouldn't have mattered. He needed to get back to Bismarck as soon as possible.

He was still uneasy about not having seen Erna, but already decided to make another trip to the farm when he could remain longer. At least he'd seen two healthy, happy children playing for a few minutes.

———

It was midmorning and Cap was fifteen miles away when Gustave and Elsa stepped outside and Franz closed the door behind them. Gustave was carefully carrying the half full chamber pot and Elsa was walking three feet away in case he tripped. Their mother usually emptied it if it had been used, but Gustave had offered to do it this morning. Erna had declined his request, but Franz overruled her saying that the boy had to grow up.

They walked past the fire pit and its semi-hidden surprise and continued to the tent privy. After Gustave dumped its malodorous contents into the equally foul-smelling hole, Elsa giggled when a stinky cloud emerged from the pit.

"It's going to get you, Goose!" she exclaimed before hurrying out of the small tent.

Gustave followed her outside into the clean air and asked, "Does mama want us to wash it, too?"

Elsa replied, "We would have to walk to the creek."

Her big brother looked at Buck Creek and was torn between returning with the dirty chamber pot or risk falling into the creek. If it had been warmer, it wouldn't have been a difficult decision.

But he didn't want to face his mother with a soaking coat and chattering teeth, so he said, "We can let it dry for a little while, so it won't smell so bad. Okay?"

"Alright. How long will it take?"

"Not too long. We can toss sticks for a few minutes."

Elsa grinned and quickly raced to the fire pit to gather her twigs while Gustave walked more slowly behind her.

He was watching as she dropped to her heels and began gathering her share of the small sticks when she suddenly stopped and stared into the fire pit.

Gustave stepped close as she pointed and said, "What's that, Goose?"

He set the chamber pot down then cautiously reached into the small hole and picked up the paper bag. Despite his curiosity about its contents, he stared at the picture for a few seconds before a smile crossed his lips.

He showed it to his sister and asked, “What does it look like to you?”

She smiled up at her big brother as she exclaimed, “It’s an angel!”

“Mister Tyler must have left it here.”

“But why didn’t he come to talk to us and mama?”

“I think he doesn’t want to make Mister Hartmann mad.”

“He’s not afraid of him; is he?”

“You know he’s not. Mister Tyler would squash Mister Hartmann like a bug if he wanted.”

Elsa still didn’t understand why Mister Tyler hadn’t come to the house and she was pretty sure that Gustave didn’t either.

She then asked, “What’s inside?”

Gustave already had a good idea of what the paper was hiding when he picked it up and felt the hard cylinders. But there was something else hidden inside that he couldn’t identify.

"Let's see," he said as he unfolded the bag and then extracted the second one.

When they saw Cap's hideous artwork, Elsa giggled as she said, "What's that supposed to be?"

"It looks like an ugly bird, but I think it was supposed to be another angel."

He then unfolded the second bag and smiled as he pulled out one of the peppermint sticks.

Elsa reached for the enormous candy, but Gustave pulled it away.

"We can't let Mister Hartmann know we have the candy, Elsa. He would take it away."

"How many are inside?"

"Three. Mister Tyler gave one to you, me and mama. They're even bigger than the first ones. But there's something else in there"

"Is it more candy?" Elsa asked eagerly.

Gustave slid his small hand past the peppermint poles and extracted one of the chocolate bars.

"What is it?" his sister asked.

"I don't know. It has writing on it, but I don't know what it means."

He then put it close to his nose and took a long sniff before he smiled at Elsa and said, "It's really sweet! Here. Smell it."

He held onto the candy bar and let her get close enough to inhale the tempting aroma. He watched her blue eyes grow as she realized the amazing taste treasure that was hidden behind the paper wrapping.

"Can't we open one and have a bite?" she pleaded.

Gustave was sorely tempted but slid the chocolate bar back into the bag before he wedged the large bag into his coat pocket. It still left a good two inches of brown paper visible, and he wished there was some way to hide it.

As Elsa watched, he unbuttoned his coat and then his shirt. He slid the bag under his shirt and after buttoning it and his coat, he looked at Elsa.

"Do I look like I'm hiding anything?"

"No. I won't tell Mister Hartmann when we go back. But how can you tell mama when he's there?"

Gustave faced another decision that was would be more difficult than his chamber pot cleaning dilemma. Once he took off his coat, the bulge under his shirt would be easily spotted and was sure to bring questions. Even if they were from his mother, Mister Hartmann would hear and then demand to know what he was hiding.

He had only spent a few seconds in deliberation when they heard the front door open and then close quickly. They were watching the corner of the house expecting either their mother or Mister Hartmann to appear when they heard their mother retching at the front of the house.

Gustave and Elsa forgot about the bag of treats as they rushed to help their mother.

Erna had tried to keep her stomach's contents where they were but as soon as she set Franz' breakfast on the table, she knew she was about to lose the battle. She hurriedly grabbed her heavy coat and rushed out the door. She barely had time to pull her arms though the sleeves when she bent at her waist and vomited.

When she stood, she was more upset by the cause of her nausea than the results. Then Gustave and Elsa popped around the corner and she tried to smile at them even as steam rose at her feet from what she'd left on the ground.

She quickly stepped toward them and said, "I'm all right. I have to clean up the mess now. Can you wait a minute before we go inside?"

"Yes, Mama," Gustave replied.

She nodded, then turned and began kicking dirt onto the mess. It wasn't really cleaning, but it would all be nothing but dirt soon enough. After she was satisfied that it was covered, she turned to her children.

"We can go inside now. Your breakfast is waiting."

Gustave suddenly said, "Mama, can you come with us first?"

"What do you need?"

"I'll show you when we're not near the door."

Erna suspected that they might have gotten into mischief and didn't want Franz to know about it. So, she simply took Elsa's hand and followed Gustave around the corner. She spotted the chamber pot on the ground and wondered if it had something to do with the portable privy pot.

Gustave stopped near the chamber pot, but then began unbuttoning his coat.

Erna discarded her theory about mischief and wondered if her son had somehow hurt himself. She glanced down at Elsa and found her staring at her brother.

Gustave soon extracted the bag from under his shirt and didn't bother closing it or his coat as he held the bag out to his mother.

“We found this in Mister Tyler’s fire pit this morning. He must have left it last night.”

Erna’s hands were trembling as she took the bag from Gustave and saw the angel drawing on its face. There was no doubt who had left the bag even before she examined its contents.

When she opened the inner bag and saw the peppermint sticks, she quickly looked north toward the trees hoping to see Cap hidden among the trunks. But it was a half a mile away and she didn’t even see his mules.

She sighed, then slid her hand deeper into the bag and pulled out a chocolate bar.

“Oh, my!” she exclaimed, “This is chocolate!”

Elsa asked, “What is chocolate?”

“It’s a very sweet and tasty candy. It melts in your mouth and the taste stays for a long time. It’s very expensive, too.”

Her daughter then asked, “Why didn’t Mister Tyler come and talk to us, Mama?”

“He probably thinks that I’m Mrs. Hartmann now and he doesn’t want to interfere. He left the candy to let you and me know that he is still here and will protect us.”

"But..." Gustave began before he stopped his argument when he knew he probably wouldn't understand his mother's answer anyway.

Erna said, "Mister Tyler didn't want Mister Hartmann to have any candy, so I'll hide it in my pocket for later. When he's gone, we can share a piece of chocolate. I'll hide the rest. Okay?"

"Okay, Mama," Gustave replied as he picked up the chamber pot.

"I'll clean that, too," Erna said as she slid the bag into her larger coat pocket before taking the chamber pot.

As they began walking back to the house, Elsa asked, "Are you sick, Mama?"

"No, dear. My tummy just didn't like its breakfast."

"Oh."

But as they approached the door, Erna was already wondering how long it would be before Franz discovered the cause of her morning sickness. She hadn't experienced it with Gustave or Elsa, so she hoped that this was just a case of stomach distress from her worries. But with the other changes that accompanied the nausea, she knew that it wouldn't be long before Franz realized that she was carrying his child. How he would react to the news was now her newest and most worrisome concern.

Cap rode into Bismarck in mid-afternoon and headed to the sheriff's office. He had thought about going to the boarding house first to make his report to Sheriff Donavan's new boss first but didn't want to face Charlotte's disapproval before it was necessary. Even though he told her he was just going to scout the farm, he was convinced that she expected him to return with Erna and the children. He was sure that she wouldn't be pleased with his decision to leave alone. He really wasn't happy about it either.

Which each yard that Joe had taken him away from the farm, his regret had grown. He was only able to deflect his displeasure by reminding himself that he'd be returning soon. This time he'd bring Jasper and more supplies because he didn't trust Hartmann to restock their pantry. While he'd brought enough food to last them the winter, it was only if they consumed it in moderation and supplemented it with hunting. He didn't believe that Franz would be out in the cold shooting turkeys and suspected that Hartmann would be consuming it at a much higher rate as well.

He pulled up before the jail and stepped down. He was sore, tired and filthy as he entered the office and only found John and Al inside. He wasn't surprised as Coop was probably at the boarding house with Charlotte going over last-minute details for tomorrow's ceremony.

John asked, "How'd it go, Cap?"

He was about to hang his hat, and as he thought about the simple question, he realized it wasn't easy to answer at all.

He looked at John and replied, "You know, I'm not really sure. I saw the children, and everything looked okay, but I feel like I made a mistake by leaving so soon."

Al said, "I don't think the boss would mind you missing his wedding if you needed to stay, Cap."

"Maybe."

He then forgot about staying and pulled his hat back on before he asked, "Is Coop over at the boarding house?"

John replied, "Yup. I'm sure he'll be grateful if you can help him get out of all the wedding chatter. Charlie has her friends visiting her to help and I think the boss is the only feller there."

Cap grinned as he said, "Maybe I'm safer here myself. But I have to move anyway, so I've got to go."

He waved then opened the door and stepped out onto the boardwalk. Once outside, he took a deep breath then mounted Joe and headed for Michelson's livery to let him have a reunion with Jasper. Maybe he'd tell his friend that he saw Jed but didn't get to chat with him.

———

Twenty minutes after leaving the jail, Cap walked into the boarding house with his saddlebags hung over his shoulder. He could hear chatter in the dining room and took advantage of the noise to quietly walk to the stairway. He was almost there when he lost his cloak of secrecy.

"Deputy Tyler, I think that the sheriff was hoping you would return."

He turned and smiled at Angela as he said, "Tell them I'll be there after I drop my things off and clean up a bit."

"I'll do that. Did you return with guests?" she asked.

"No, ma'am," he replied before he stepped quickly away then trotted up the stairs.

He wondered if everyone in the boarding house knew why he'd been gone and assumed that it was hardly a secret. He also noticed that she seemed pleased when he had told her he'd come back alone which confirmed his belief that Charlotte had expected him to do more than reconnoiter.

Cap soon entered his room, set his saddlebags on the floor near his bed, then after hanging his hat and coat, he removed his gunbelts and left them on the bed. After using the wash basin to clean up, he thought about packing his things for the move just to delay having to face Charlotte. But he knew she'd probably send Coop to find him pretty soon, or worse, she might send Angela now that he'd returned by himself.

He ran his fingers through his sandy brown hair then left his room and headed for the dining room and his showdown with Charlotte. He could hear the cacophony of voices before he reached the parlor and thought he heard a male voice other than Coop's. He thought it was one of the other boarders who had been roped into attending the meeting by his wife.

When he turned into the large dining room, the chatting stopped, and he became the focus of the four women and the two men at the table. He didn't recognize two of the women nor the man sitting across from Coop.

The sheriff pointed to an empty chair and said, "Have a seat, Cap. We were just talking about you."

As he stepped to the open place at the table, Charlotte said, "And wondering why you returned alone."

"I'm sure you do, Charlie, but I did tell you I was just going there to see how they were," he said as he sat down between Angela and one of the women he hadn't met before. He assumed she was one of Charlotte's friends.

But before he had to undergo Charlotte's interrogation, Coop said, "Cap, this is Hardy Newton. He just got into town the day you left. Hardy was a deputy town marshal over in Jamestown and heard that we were short on lawmen. I just hired him this morning and I'll swear him in after the wedding."

Cap smiled as he said, “It’s good to have another experienced lawman, Hardy. That makes two. You and the man who hired you.”

Hardy stood and shook Cap’s hand as he replied, “I hear you spent a few years fightin’ with the Injuns.”

As he returned to his seat, Cap said, “That’s true, but I still have a lot to learn about the law.”

Coop huffed before he said, “You already know more than John or Al because you’re so good at poker.”

Cap and Hardy laughed but the women didn’t seem to understand the connection.

Cap studied the new deputy and was pleased to have another experienced lawman who wasn’t afraid to go out into Sioux lands or the east side of town. He seemed friendly enough, but there was something that he was hiding that Cap couldn’t identify. It was like he was holding a pair of deuces while acting as if he had a full house. But he figured he’d find out how good he was after a while.

Hardy was grateful to be so well received. He was older than the sheriff, but he wasn’t nearly as experienced as he’d led Coop to believe. He’d worn the badge for a little over a year before he heard about the shortage of deputy sheriffs in Burleigh County and took the train to Bismarck in the hope of landing the better paying job. He’d sent a telegram to his old boss in Jamestown that morning after Coop had hired him.

He'd never faced an armed man or even had to fire his Colt or Winchester in anger or the line of duty. But he still considered himself a tough man and was capable of handling any situation.

He was also very pleased to learn that he'd be able to stay in Charlotte's boarding house for free. He'd been impressed with Angela Parker since he'd arrived, which was why he had been happy to join Coop as he sat in the wedding planning conference.

Charlotte finally looked across the table and asked, "Now, Deputy Tyler, you can explain why you left Erna and her children at the farm."

"I did tell you I was just going to check on them, Charlie. When I got there late in the afternoon, I watched the farmhouse waiting for someone to emerge. Gustave and Elsa came out just before sunset and played a game for a few minutes. They seemed happy, but Erna must have called them back inside for supper. I'll admit I was tempted to go to the house and knock on the door, but I was unsure of the reception I might get if I did."

"Why would you think that? Even if Erna was content, which I doubt, she'd at least be cordial. Surely, you weren't worried about Franz Hartmann."

"No, ma'am. I wasn't worried about Hartmann. I just…well, I didn't want to see…I mean that, maybe, if I knocked…then…"

Charlotte understood what Cap didn't want to see and why he had difficulty expressing it. She felt sorry for his discomfort but was convinced that he'd made the wrong decision. She had hoped that his trip to monitor the Braun family would have escalated into a rescue mission, but there was obviously even more to the situation than she'd realized.

She interrupted his struggling attempt to answer her question when she said, "You may have been concerned about what you might have found, but you should have at least let her know that you were living in Bismarck and had a big house for her and the children if she wanted to come with you."

"Maybe so. But everything seemed so normal. When I was riding back, I figured I'd wait a couple of weeks before I headed back there with a load of supplies as an excuse to talk to her. I had bought enough food at Fort Lincoln to last us most of the winter if we were judicious in our rate of consumption, but I'd be doing some hunting, too. When Franz Hartmann arrived that changed everything. Now, I don't think they have enough to last them through the middle of December."

"I'll forgive you this time, Cap. But you had better not come back alone a second time, unless you tell me that Erna and her children are happy and pleased to have Franz Hartmann acting as the man of the house."

Cap was relieved as he replied, "Yes, ma'am."

With the inquisition over, Cap let them continue putting the final touches on tomorrow's wedding ceremony. It wasn't going to be a fancy affair. They'd be married at the Methodist church on the corner of Thayer and Fifth Street at ten o'clock. Coop's best friend, Mike Abernathy, would be his witness and Charlotte's witness would be her friend, Lucille Flint. After the ceremony, they planned to have a casual party at the boarding house.

Just before the meeting ended, Charlotte looked at Cap and said, "I forgot to mention that I hired someone to help me run the boarding house before the railroad starts up again."

Before he could ask about her new employee, Angela said, "I just told her that I'd take care of the place while she and Coop enjoyed their honeymoon and Charlie offered me a position."

Cap turned and smiled at her as he replied, "I'm happy to hear that you'll be helping Charlotte, Angela."

"When I told Orville and Wilma about her offer, they were delighted and will be hiring a nanny to help with their children."

Cap nodded then looked back at the sheriff and said, “I’m going to move my things over to the house, but I’ll come back for supper.”

“It’s your house now, Cap. Are you going to sleep in that acre-sized four poster bed?”

“Nope. I’d probably get lost.”

Coop snickered as Cap rose then walked to the doorway. Before he reached the stairs, Charlotte and Angela had walked to the kitchen to start dinner preparation.

———

Thirty minutes later, Cap had completed his move into his new house. He’d move the rest of his things from the livery tomorrow afternoon. He’d selected the bedroom across from the main bedroom and its giant bed. It was still a much bigger room than the one he’d stayed in at Charlotte’s boarding house. He thought that the main bedroom had even more floor space than the Braun farmhouse.

After he finished putting his clothes away, he sat on the edge of the bed and thought about Erna, Gustave and Elsa. He had assumed that the children were happy because he’d seen them laughing. But he was eight hundred yards away using a telescope. *Were they really happy, or just momentarily joyful because of the game they were playing?*

But he was going to return in a couple of weeks and then he'd talk to Erna and see if they were truly happy. He did want them to be at least content. But he still hated to admit that he wished that they were miserable and would be happy for him to bring them to Bismarck.

He stood and donned his coat and pulled on his hat to return to the boarding house for supper. Then he'd return to his new house and sleep in his new bed.

———

Erna had decided that the best place to hide the bag of candy was to leave it in her coat pocket. She knew that Franz searched the house when she was outside hoping to find more money, so if she left the candy in her coat, he'd never find it. If he had discovered the sweets, he'd be angrier about how they'd arrived than the candy itself.

She wished that she could share some of the chocolate with her children because she knew how much they would love it. But she wanted some herself because she was so hungry. As much as wanted to eat even more because of her condition, she couldn't afford to add more food to her plate for two reasons. She didn't want Franz to notice her increased appetite, and their food supply was dropping much too quickly.

Franz was eating so much and if he kept it up, they'd be short of the most critical foodstuffs by the middle of December. She hadn't mentioned it to Franz knowing how he would react.

She was hoping that he'd recognize the problem himself and make a trip to Fort Lincoln. When he was gone, she'd be able to share the chocolate with her children.

But it wasn't even November yet and he might not notice the rapidly depleting food supply for another month. By then, he would surely know that she was pregnant. She suspected that when he learned of her condition, he might decide to leave her to return to Bismarck. If he said he was going to go, she'd ask him to take her and the children with her. Knowing that Cap was now living in Bismarck made it a very pleasant decision.

But all she could do was to wait. She had no control over the future.

CHAPTER 9

Even though the sheriff was going to be married later that morning, Cap still made his ride through the two tent cities on the eastern end of the town. He'd been gone two days and didn't want the boys on the northern side of the road to get their hopes up that something bad had happened to him.

When he'd talked to John and Al before he left, he was surprised that neither had known that Coop had hired Hardy Newton. They knew he had talked to the new arrival, but not that he'd be swearing him in later that day. Despite their ignorance of the sheriff's decision, they were very pleased to have another older and more experienced lawman joining them.

After making a pleasant tour of the settler side of the road, he walked Jasper across the street to the seedy side. He'd decided to give Joe a few days' rest.

He had almost reached the dilapidated saloon when he picked up sudden movement on his right in his peripheral vision. He barely had time to turn his eyes when Jimmy Baker fired. If he'd been using a Winchester, Cap knew he would have never made it to the wedding. He felt the .44 slice through the back of his heavy coat and didn't have time to get to his pistol or even grab his Winchester. But Jimmy had been so confident that his first shot would be enough that he'd lowered his pistol. By the time he realized that Cap was still very much alive, it was too late as Cap employed the only weapon that was readily available to him.

The echo of Jimmy Baker's Colt still echoed across the camp when Cap whipped Jasper to his right and slammed his heels into his mule's flanks. As Jimmy was cocking his pistol, Jasper's chest crashed into him, knocking him to the ground. His Colt went flying as he tried to avoid Jasper's hooves. For just a moment, he thought he'd survive when the mule's front hooves slammed into the ground above his head, but then he felt the enormous weight of his right back hoof punch into his chest. He wasn't in pain for very long as his ribs snapped and much of Jasper's twelve hundred pounds shoved the broken bones through his lungs.

Jasper quickly hopped off of the obstruction before Cap pulled him to a stop and hurriedly dismounted. Before he checked on Jimmy Baker, he pulled the Remington from his right holster and scanned the area for another shooter. He saw men staring, but none had his pistol in his hand, so Cap stepped closer to Jimmy. It didn't take long for him to diagnose his condition.

He kept his Remington ready as he waved to the closest onlooker.

When the man stepped closer, Cap said, "Tell Ralph McCardle that he can bury his partner and if someone else tries to backshoot me, I'll burn this whole place down starting with his saloon."

The man just nodded before Cap mounted Jasper and wheeled him back toward the roadway. It had been too close this time and he knew it was just luck that had kept his costs to just a coat. If that man wanted Jimmy Baker's pistol, he was welcome to it.

When he reached the road, he saw many of the settlers walking to their side of the street carrying an assortment of weapons. He walked his mule over the roadway and stopped when he was close to the front of the gathering crowd.

Oskar Wentz said, "We thought they had shot you and we were going to see if you needed help."

Cap looked down and smiled as he replied, "I appreciate your concern, Mister Wentz, but the last thing I'd want you to do is to cross the road. This is my job and I've accepted the risks. But if you and the others had come over there, you wouldn't be able to help me at all. You would only be risking your lives. You have your families to protect and when the railroad comes in a few months, you'll be building your farms. Let me handle those men. Okay?"

Oskar nodded as he said, "Alright. But what happened?"

"Jimmy Baker tried to shoot me in the back but missed. I charged at him with my mule before he could fire again, and he was crushed. I left a warning with them that if they tried again, I would burn them down."

"Will you do that?"

Cap grinned as he answered, "Probably not. But I'd think of some way to make them unhappy."

He tipped his hat then turned Jasper back to the road and headed into town. The settlers stared at his back and noticed the long rip across his back that hadn't been there when he'd ridden through past them earlier that morning.

While he hoped that his warning would be heeded, he suspected that Ralph McCardle would most likely try something different the next time. He'd just lost his partner and if he didn't avenge Jimmy's death, then he'd lose some of his authority as their de facto leader. He just hoped that he'd wait to make that attempt after he talked to Erna in two weeks.

———

Erna had avoided another emergency exit that morning and hoped that her morning sickness wouldn't return but believed that it was just a brief respite. Franz hadn't even asked about her earlier rushes out of the house, and he seemed to be in a better mood for some reason. Whatever had caused his improved demeanor, she was determined not to spoil it.

It wasn't that Franz was in a good mood, but his lack of crabbiness was due to a distraction. He'd noticed that the supply of food was dwindling faster than he'd expected and that meant he'd have to buy more supplies soon. He'd need to add a lot of firewood, too. But buying supplies would take money and he'd searched every nook in the house and hadn't found any more cash or even loose silver. If he bought more supplies, he'd have to spend some of his eighty-three dollars, despite knowing that fifty dollars had come from Erna.

He was weighing the advantages of sharing Erna's bed and spending money versus taking the mules and food and heading to the Black Hills. It was a long ride and if he decided to leave, he'd have to start soon before the really nasty weather arrived.

If he'd known about Erna's condition, he probably would have saddled the mules, loaded the supplies and ridden away before sunset.

"Jesus, Cap! How did he even miss?" John exclaimed as he examined the back of Cap's coat.

"He was using a pistol. He must have figured I'd spot a rifle barrel. Anyway, I've got to get over to Rittenhouse and buy a new coat before the wedding. Are you going to shut the office down?"

"Yup. Al's already gone. He had to pick up his girlfriend."

"Aren't you bringing Mary?"

"Yeah, but she always takes a long time to get ready. If I got over there before nine-thirty, I'd just have to wait anyway."

Cap just smiled before he turned and left the jail. He had to find a new coat quickly because he didn't want to be late for the ceremony. He could probably just sneak into the back of the church anyway, but it would still look bad.

Twenty minutes after leaving the jail, Cap walked out of Rittenhouse wearing his new coat with his damaged coat hung over his arm. The new one was heavier and fur-lined but didn't look anything like his last one. It was black with a thick collar where his old coat was light brown. He had tried to find one that was a closer match so the sheriff wouldn't notice then ask him why he had to buy a new coat. His answer might inspire a long conversation that wouldn't please Charlotte. This was her day. To avoid that possibility, he planned on cutting his entrance close to ten o'clock and tell Coop what happened after the wedding. By then, Charlotte should be chatting with their other guests.

After stopping at his new house and hanging the ripped coat on his varnished porch's railing, he headed for the church. While he had planned on being the last one to enter the church, that didn't happen when he was spotted by John as he escorted Mary Wilkens along the boardwalk. But it was actually beneficial because he could enter with them and then slide into the back pew.

He dismounted and as John and Mary waited, he tied off Jasper then trotted to meet them.

"Nice coat, Cap," John said when he was close.

"I like it. It cost me seven dollars, but I think it was worth the extra money just for the added warmth."

Then he smiled at his girlfriend and said, "You're looking very pretty this morning, Mary. Have you convinced John to meet you at the altar yet?"

Mary returned his smile as she replied, "He's the one who has to convince me, Cap."

John snickered then took Mary's arm and escorted her down the short walkway to the church with Cap trailing.

When John opened the door, Cap was surprised how many guests were in attendance, but realized he shouldn't have been. Coop was a well-liked and well-respected member of the community and had been their protector for years.

He waited for Mary and John to enter the back pew then took his place at the end. It was just a couple of minutes later that the organ began to play and the wedding ceremony officially started.

———

An hour later, he watched a smiling Mr. and Mrs. Donavan walk past as they exited the church. When Coop spotted him, his smile remained but his eyebrows rose just enough to let him know he'd noticed the change in wardrobe.

As he was on the end of the last pew, he was the first to follow the couple out of the church and expected them to walk around to the back where they had parked Charlotte's buggy. But as soon as he stepped into the Dakota chill, he found them waiting at the bottom of the steps to greet their guests. It was the first wedding he had ever attended and didn't understand the protocol. Maybe he should have stayed at that preparation meeting longer.

When he reached them, he smiled, shook Coop's hand and kissed Charlotte on the cheek before saying, "Congratulations, Mr. and Mrs. Donavan."

He started to leave so the other attendees could congratulate the couple when Charlotte asked, "Did you buy a new coat just for the wedding, Cap?"

"No, ma'am. I'll tell you and your new husband the reason when we're inside your warm boarding house."

Coop asked, "Is it because of official business?"

"Yes, sir."

The sheriff nodded before Cap trotted toward Jasper and mounted, He watched them greet a few more folks before he wheeled Jasper to his right and set him at a trot towards the livery.

———

He left Jasper at Michelson's with Joe but told them not to unsaddle him because he'd be back shortly. He then walked quickly to the boarding house and even after his stop at the livery, he was the first of the attendees to arrive. He quickly trotted up the stairs and entered his old room where he left his new coat, hat and gunbelts on the bed.

By the time he returned to the first floor, others began entering the parlor. It was an informal buffet and there was food and drink spread across the tables in the dining room and kitchen, but Cap didn't indulge. He wasn't planning on staying very long because the jail was empty, and he knew that John and Al wanted to spend some time with their girlfriends.

The rooms continued to fill with guests until the newlyweds entered to a smattering of applause punctuated with a few muted whistles. Not surprisingly, Coop and Mrs. Coop sought him out and soon approached.

The sheriff said, "John gave me the gist of what happened before we got here, Cap. How bad was it?"

"It was over quickly. But he almost got me, boss. I may have created more trouble than I realized. After a few quiet days, I thought they'd behave, but now it's probably worse."

"It was going to blow up sooner or later. At least you didn't get hit. The next time you go through that place, I want you to bring someone with you."

"Alright. Are you going to swear in Hardy now or later? Someone needs to get back to the office and I figure John and Al want to spend some time with their ladies."

Hardy was standing just two feet behind Cap when he'd asked, so before the sheriff could answer, Hardy replied, "He already gave be the badge, Cap. Charlotte didn't want him to do anything with his sheriff business after the wedding, so we took care of it this morning."

Cap turned and shook his hand as he said, "Welcome aboard, Hardy. Now I'm not the new man anymore."

"Maybe I'll come with you tomorrow."

Cap looked at the sheriff who was paying attention to Charlotte before he replied, "That's the boss' call."

Then he turned to the sheriff and said, "Coop, I'm going to head over to the office. After that mess I left in tent city, I don't want one of the settlers showing up and finding the jail locked."

"Okay. But if you have to go back to the east side of town because of a problem, I want you to stop by and let me know. I don't care of John or Al want to spend time with their girlfriends. Do you understand?"

"Trust me, if there's a problem, I'm not about to rush into a hornet's nest."

"Remember that," Coop replied before Charlotte tugged him away to spend time with their other guests.

Cap quickly left the room and trotted up the stairs to retrieve his new coat, hat and gunbelts.

Less than ten minutes later, he was dismounting in front of the sheriff's office. He tied off Jasper, stepped onto the boardwalk and unlocked the door. It was pretty chilly inside, so he didn't remove his coat as he built a fire in the heat stove.

It wasn't quite noon yet when he took his seat behind the desk and wished he'd grabbed some of the food from the buffet before he left. But mealtime over the past few years had always been erratic, so missing lunch wasn't unusual.

But when he set his hat on the desk, he drifted from missing lunch to Erna's food supply. He began making a mental list of the food he'd brought from Fort Lincoln. It hadn't been that long ago, so there should be more than enough to last them at least until the end of December. The great unknown factor was Franz Hartmann. If he consumed more than Cap would have and if he didn't supply them with fresh meat, then they'd need a lot more to last them until spring. He just didn't like the idea of feeding Hartmann. He's a man and should be the provider, not the consumer.

As he thought about Hartmann, Cap finally started to study him as a man and not just a German farmer. He confessed that his jealousy had kept him from just examining him as he would an opposing poker player. A man who had abandoned his wife and family to save himself. It was probably because he'd run away that his family didn't close the door in time. Franz Hartmann was a coward, but Cap had quickly identified that trait. But it was the creator of that cowardice that now surfaced. Hartmann was a selfish man who cared only about himself. That meant that he'd probably eat much more than he should and not worry about Erna and her children.

While he still didn't believe that Franz would abandon them or hurt them in any way, he was concerned about his lack of responsibility. He decided that he'd visit Erna and the children before November and bring more food and supplies. If he was wrong and found that their food and firewood supplies were adequate, he'd leave the new stock with them anyway and then return to Bismarck. But if it was as he now expected to find it, he'd react much differently. How violently he reacted would depend on Erna and the children's condition.

But now he had to shift his attention to the powder keg fuse he'd left burning on the eastern end of town. He'd make his morning rounds tomorrow accompanied by one of his fellow deputies. He wasn't sure about Hardy but if the boss said to take the new man with him, he would. Maybe he was the best choice anyway. Cap was already fond of both John and Al. He wasn't sure if he'd ever consider Hardy a friend. There was just something inside the man that Cap couldn't figure out.

As the room warmed, he removed his coat, hung it and his hat on the wall pegs then returned to the desk and pulled out a deck of cards from the top drawer. He began playing poker solitaire knowing he would always win. But he would always lose, too.

———

No one had shown up at the sheriff's office all afternoon, so after he locked it up for the night, Cap mounted Jasper and headed for Michelson's. He'd have to stock some hay and oats in the small barn behind his house when he had the chance. Then he'd move the boys to their permanent home.

After dropping him off with Joe, Cap stopped at the boarding house to see if there was any food left before he headed home. When he entered, he wasn't surprised to find the only ones still in the parlor were either residents or lawmen and their ladies. The only exception was Angela Parker, who was no longer a paying resident, but an employee. She was listening to Hardy Newton who must be relating a tale of his life as a deputy marshal in Jamestown.

As he pulled his Stetson from his head, his fellow lawmen, except for the newest one, stepped across the parlor en masse, leaving their partners to chat among themselves.

He was removing his coat when Sheriff Donavan said, “Now that you’re back and most of the others are gone, you can tell us the full story of what happened.”

Before he began, Angela and Charlotte stepped closer to listen and Hardy was almost obligated to join them.

As he provided a more detailed account, he tried to minimize how close he’d come to being unable to attend the wedding or even leave their tent domain. He simply said that he’d ruined his coat in the melee. But John and Al were well aware of how thin his margin of survival had been as they’d both seen the back of his old coat. So, as soon as he reached the point where he’d sent Jasper plowing into Jimmy Baker, John interrupted.

He exclaimed, “That bullet ripped a long stripe across the back of your coat, Cap! He almost sent you to your grave!”

Cap cringed inside as he said, “But I’m still here and Jimmy isn’t. I’m more concerned about the rest of those troublemakers.”

Coop was about to say something when Hardy quickly said, “I’ll come with you tomorrow, Cap. I wanna see what that place is like anyway.”

Cap smiled at Hardy, then looked back at his boss for comment. He suspected that Hardy had volunteered so quickly to impress Angela.

Sheriff Donavan answered Cap's unspoken question when he said, "Alright. I reckon once you get used to it, you can alternate with Cap on rounds through that mess."

Charlotte then took Coop's arm and said, "I don't care who goes into that hell hole of humanity as long as my husband stays out of there. At least until he becomes annoying."

Everyone laughed which effectively ended the discussion. They then moved back into the parlor where Cap was able to find more than enough leftover food to fill his stomach. There was even hot coffee available which was a welcome surprise.

———

It was a brisk and cloudy day threatening a cold rain as Cap and Hardy rode away from the jail the next morning. Cap was describing the layout and his routine for his circuitous ride through the two temporary settlements as they headed down Main Avenue. He explained that the southern route didn't have to vary as the immigrants were friendly and were happy to see him when he rode by. But he varied his path through the northern side to reduce the risk of being ambushed. Hardy had commented that it didn't seem to help him much yesterday, and Cap had agreed.

Shortly after they had turned south into the settler side, Hardy asked, "How come there are so many young women?"

"I think it was because of the Franco-Russian war but haven't asked. I just ride through to let them know that I haven't forgotten them."

"You don't talk to any of 'em? Not even those pretty blonde girls?"

"Sometimes, but not about the war or why they left Germany or Scandinavia."

Hardy was grinning and waved at the settlers as they passed while Cap greeted many of them by name.

They soon made a wide turn and headed back north to cross the road. Before they reached the street, Cap took the precaution of pulling his Winchester.

Hardy asked, "Is that necessary?"

"I was caught flat-footed yesterday, and it's not going to happen again."

Hardy nodded then slid his repeater from its scabbard. Neither man cocked his Winchester's hammer.

They were riding side-by-side leaving about a six-foot gap when they crossed the roadway. They entered the sorry collection of tents and shacks about fifty yards to the west of the path he'd taken yesterday.

As soon as they'd entered the settlement, Hardy pointed ahead and asked, "Is that the miserable saloon you talked about?"

"That's it. It's owned by Ralph McCardle, the partner of the man I ran down with Jasper yesterday. I'm riding Joe today because he's less twitchy than Jasper and I don't want to have to worry about what happens under my butt."

As they continued past the tents, Hardy snickered then said, "I don't know why you don't get yourself a good horse. Riding a mule is a step down."

"I turned in two good horses a while ago, Hardy. I like my mules and…"

Cap suddenly pulled Joe to a stop and yelled, "Get on the ground!"

As he leapt from the saddle, the sharp cracks of Winchester fire echoed through the cold Dakota air. Cap didn't have time to check for Hardy as he dropped into a prone position to find the shooters. It only took a couple of seconds to spot the muzzle flashes coming from the saloon.

He knew he was a dead man if he stayed where he was, so he quickly rolled away from Joe and after he'd completed three revolutions, he popped to his feet and sprinted for the nearest shack. It was about twenty feet away and as he ran, several more shots rang out and one bullet exploded into the ground just two feet in front of him.

He soon reached the shack and was breathing hard as he looked back at Joe and to see if Hardy was still on the ground. He found Joe but Hardy was gone. He didn't waste any time searching for him but scanned the tent town behind him for more shooters. When he didn't spot any, he attributed it to his use of less predictable paths. The only thing that Ralph McCardle could count on was that he'd pass by the saloon before heading back to the road. If he hadn't spotted that shooter preparing to fire from the window, they would have had much easier targets.

But now he had to go on offense. Bullets were splintering the shack and it wasn't much protection. He suspected that there were enough shooters to cover both sides of the shack, so it really didn't matter which direction he took when he made his move. The saloon was about eighty yards away which wasn't an unreasonable range for a Winchester, but that was for a stationary target. He wasn't about to make it easy for them.

He did have to worry about his ammunition supply. If he'd had a '73, he could use the .44s from his gunbelts to reload. But his '76 used the more powerful .45-75 cartridge and had fewer of them in its magazine tube to boot. He had to make every shot count.

Before he made his break away from the shack, Cap pictured the saloon in his mind and marked the location of the shooters. They had to be firing from windows or doors, so that meant he'd have no more than four targets. It was still going to be an almost impossible task. But then he realized that there might be a way to even the odds.

Their saloon had three windows along the front wall. Just behind the center window, there was a large hanging kerosene lamp. It had been the light from that lamp that had allowed him to spot the first shooter before he pulled his trigger. He now had his primary target. But before he tried to hit it, he'd take a few shots at any muzzle flashes. He knew the longer he stayed in one spot, the greater he would risk catching a .44, but he hoped to at least spoil their aim before he put one of his .45s where it would be most effective.

He cocked his Winchester's hammer, took a deep breath and sprinted away from the shack as more gunfire erupted from the saloon. He slid onto his stomach just fifteen feet from the shack and settled his sights as bullets ricocheted around him.

As soon as the next man fired, Cap slid his front sight just slightly to his right, centered on the muzzle flare and fired his first shot. When he heard a muffled scream, he knew the number of shooters had dropped by one. He then levered in a new round to take his second shot.

He was looking for another shooter when he realized that there was a brief pause as the others either ducked or attended to the injured man. Cap knew that he had to take full advantage of the break. He set his sights on the glowing lamplight outlined by the center window and squeezed his trigger.

His large caliber slug smashed through the glass and exploded into the large kerosene lamp. It shattered the cavernous brass globe that was filled with fuel splattering some kerosene into the bar before the rest poured onto the floor. The wick continued to burn behind its glass chimney, which was now Cap's next target.

But as he cycled in his next cartridge, two of the shooters resumed firing. Cap had to ignore the bullets headed his way as he steadied his sights on the upper half of the lamp. He fired just as a .44 slammed into the ground eight inches away from his right ear.

His second lamp-killing round passed through the shattered window and then blew apart the base of glass chimney and sent the remaining part of the lamp to the floor with its wick still burning.

Cap was working his lever when the kerosene covering the saloon's barroom floor ignited. By the time he'd returned his sights to the building, he could already see the flames through two of the three windows. He didn't know if they had a back entrance but was sure that none of the shooters would continue to fire. He quickly popped to his feet and set his sights on the front door. As he waited for them to race out of the door, he hoped that there weren't any women inside. He wasn't sure he'd have enough time to identify who was making an escape from the growing inferno. It was just a question of how quickly he could recycle his Winchester.

He wasn't worried about the legalities of whether or not they still were carrying Winchesters when they exited. He wouldn't have time to see if they were armed and they had already sealed their fates when they had opened fire.

Thick smoke followed the first man who ran from the saloon. He was carrying his Winchester but was coughing and probably couldn't see through his watery eyes. It didn't matter as Cap fired. The man dropped to his knees and began crawling away without his repeater before the second man raced out of the door. He probably couldn't see either, but that didn't stop him from pointing his repeater in Cap's general direction and firing. Cap fired just a heartbeat after he'd seen the muzzle flare and the shooter spun clockwise then tumbled to the ground.

He had just brought a fresh round into the chamber when a third man ran outside. He wasn't carrying a Winchester but had a pistol in his hand as he sprinted away from the saloon to the east. Cap almost let him go but then recognized Ralph McCardle. He arced his Winchester's barrel slightly to his right, leading the boss of the shanty town gang and squeezed his trigger.

Ralph thought he was going to make it to the safety of the nearest shack when Cap's .45 ripped into the right side of his neck, just above his shoulder. The slight downward arc of the bullet sliced through his right carotid artery before ripping through his esophagus, clipping the front of his fifth cervical vertebra's body and lodging in his left shoulder.

Ralph felt his warm blood shooting out of his destroyed artery as he fell face first to the ground. He couldn't even bring up his right hand to try and staunch the red geyser as his right arm didn't seem to work anymore.

Cap didn't waste time watching McCardle after he'd been hit, but quickly returned his sights to the saloon. He expected more men to escape the raging fire, but none did. He only counted three bodies outside but knew there had been four shooters. He then remembered that his first shot had hit one of them and his body was probably still inside.

He released his Winchester's hammer then turned and walked back to Joe who hadn't moved. After he slid his rifle back into its scabbard, he began brushing the dirt off of his new coat as he watched the saloon burn. He still scanned the area for more shooters but was surprised that he didn't see a single person anywhere. They must have all taken refuge in their shacks and tents.

The saloon suddenly collapsed with a roar as the fire leapt higher into the sky. It was an impressive sight. He took his canteen from Joe and took a few swallows of cold water before hanging it back on the saddle. He was reaching for his saddle horn when he spotted three riders charging along the road and all were carrying Winchesters. Cap soon identified them as Sheriff Donavan and his two young deputies. He didn't mount but turned to wait for them to reach him.

When they saw him standing beside Joe, Coop must have said something because they soon returned their Winchesters to their scabbards as they approached. They were staring at the burning saloon before they stopped a few feet away, but then shifted their eyes to him. They seemed shocked to find him standing.

"*You're alive?*" Sheriff Donavan exclaimed before he dismounted.

"I think so. I made a real mess though."

John snapped, "Hardy said you were killed!"

"He showed up at the jail?" Cap asked, then said, "I didn't know where he went after I hit the dirt."

Coop growled, "That yellow bastard! He said that they started firing and he barely made it out of there after you got hit. We would have been here sooner, but we had to saddle our horses. What the hell happened?"

Cap pointed to the burning building as he said, “We got to this point when I spotted a shooter preparing to fire and yelled at Hardy to hit the ground. I followed my own advice and ran to that shack over there. They continued to fire when I shot out from behind the shack and returned fire. I hit one, then aimed at the lamp. It took a couple of .45s to get the kerosene on the floor and then set it on fire. The rest was like shooting hogs in a pigsty. There were four shooters altogether, but one never made it out of there. Ralph McCardle tried to run away, but never got far.”

The sheriff was smoldering as hotly as the saloon as he said, “We'll let them clean up their own mess. We need to return and have a talk with Hardy.”

Cap nodded knowing that they'd be down to three deputies again, but it was better than having one who couldn't be trusted.

———

Hardy wasn't in the sheriff's office while Cap was giving his report to the sheriff. He'd ridden to the boarding house to collect his things. He wasn't sure if Cap had really died and didn't want to take the risk that he had. He'd pack and then head back to Jamestown and see if he could get his old job back.

When he entered, he quickly pounded up the stairs and hurriedly stuffed his few belongings into his saddlebags. He soon left his room and as he trotted down the stairs, he found Charlotte and Angela waiting for him near the bottom of the stairway.

Charlotte asked, “Why are you here, Hardy? Did something happen?”

As he hurried past, he quickly replied, “Ask your husband.”

The two women watched him leave the house before Charlotte asked, “I wonder what Coop did to make him so mad?”

“I guess we’ll have to wait for your husband to show up for lunch before we’ll know the answer.”

“I don’t believe we’ll have to wait that long. I have a feeling that Coop will be showing up much sooner looking for Hardy.”

———

Hardy had used the back roads to avoid running into the sheriff and was well past the smoking ruins of Ralph McCardle’s saloon by the time the three lawmen entered the established end of Bismarck.

The sheriff wasn’t surprised when he found the jail empty, but left John and Al in charge as he and Cap then remounted and headed for the boarding house. They expected to find Hardy inside telling all sorts of tall tales to Angela.

But when they arrived and didn't find Hardy's horse waiting out front, they knew he wasn't there.

Cap asked, "Do you want me to look for him, Coop?"

"No. He'll show up if he's still in town. I'm going to tell Charlotte what happened. Maybe he's already been here."

"Okay. I'll head back to the office. I've got to drop my old coat at the tailor and finish brushing down my new one."

"It's looking pretty filthy in the back, but at least there aren't any bullet holes."

Cap grinned then waved before he turned Joe away and headed back to his house to pick up his damaged coat.

Coop stepped down, tied off his gelding and marched to the boarding house. He wished that Hardy was still there, so he could let him know what a coward he was before he ripped the badge from his chest.

He had just stepped onto the porch when the door swung open and Charlotte said, "We've been expecting you, Coop."

As he removed his hat and stepped inside, Charlotte closed the door.

When they entered the parlor, he asked, “Did Hardy come here a little while ago?”

“He did. I checked his room and it’s empty. When I asked him what happened, he said to ask you in a very surly tone.”

“I imagine so. Let me tell you what happened, and you’ll understand. You’ll also realize why he’s lucky that I didn’t find him.”

He soon sat on the large couch with Charlotte and began to tell her of Cap’s second narrow escape and Hardy’s desertion. Angela sat in the closest easy chair listening and was horrified. Hardy had already made his intentions clear, and she had actually considered accepting him. She felt as if she’d missed a bullet of her own.

After dropping off his coat at Rowe & Son Tailors, Cap returned to the office. He told John and Al that they hadn’t found Hardy, and the sheriff suspected that he’d already left town, leaving them shorthanded again.

They talked about the consequences of the gunfight and if the rest of the men living on that side of the road would now act more civilized. It was a long discussion that lasted until the sheriff reentered the jail.

He almost ripped the peg off the wall when he hung his hat before he turned to his three deputies.

"The coward must have skedaddled. His room was empty, and Charlotte said he had his saddlebags full when he left. I suppose it's just as well."

"Did he leave his badge, boss?" John asked.

Coop closed his eyes as he replied, "I forgot about that. I guess it doesn't matter much."

Al asked, "What if he still pretends to be a deputy sheriff?"

Coop huffed then said, "Let him. Maybe he'll run into some hardened criminal who takes offense. That badge won't give him any courage. I'll send a telegram to his old boss to let him know what happened just in case he heads back there."

Cap asked, "Do you want me to go back out there to make sure those boys don't cross the road?"

After a short pause, Coop answered, "Let's both go. I want to let those boys understand that they've worn out their welcome."

Cap stood, grabbed his hat and followed the sheriff out the doorway. They soon were riding toward Main Avenue where they made a left turn. Before they had even reached the roadway, they'd spotted the smoke rising into the cloudy sky in the distance. But shortly after they started east on Main Avenue, they noticed the wall of settlers stretching across the southern edge of the roadway. They didn't see anyone on the northern side but instinctively set their mounts to a faster pace. As they drew closer, the two lawmen noticed that the men were mostly armed with rifles but some just had pitchforks or axes. The question was why they were even there.

When they were about fifty yards out, they were spotted and soon all of the settlers' faces turned toward them.

They pulled up near the center of the line where Sheriff Donavan turned to his German-speaking deputy and said, "Ask them what's going on, Cap."

Cap nodded then found Oskar Wentz slightly to his right and asked, "Mister Wentz, why are you all out here with weapons?"

"We heard all the shooting and then saw the fire. We did not want them coming here."

"They were shooting at me and I burned their saloon to the ground before I shot the ones who tried to kill me. You are safer now, so please ask everyone to go home."

"The bad ones are dead?"

"Yes, sir. The two that bothered Anna are both dead now. The sheriff and I are going to go there now to warn them again."

Oskar nodded then turned to the man to his left and said, “You heard Cap, Frederic. We can return now.”

Frederic Metzler nodded then shouted, “The problem is over. We can to back to our families.”

None of the men cheered or even smiled before their protective line began to dissolve as they drifted back into their camp.

Oskar stayed behind long enough to say, “Thank you again, Cap. Did you get hurt?”

“No, sir. I’m fine.”

He waved before he turned and followed the others back down the lane between the tents.

Coop looked at Cap who translated the conversation. They then turned north and entered the shoddy camp. Not surprisingly, they found many of the residents combing through the remains of the saloon. Cap assumed that the first ones had claimed the gunbelts from the dead men. The three bodies were still close to where they had fallen but had already been stripped down to their skivvies. The men who were inside the smoking ruins pulling charred beams away with shovels or picks ignored the lawmen as they searched for anything of value.

They still approached the men and Coop attracted their attention when he pulled his Colt and fired a round over their heads, and barely so.

They quickly stopped hunting and whipped their eyes toward the sheriff and his deputy.

Sheriff Donavan shouted, “You boys are on notice. My deputy told you he’d burn this place down if you tried to ambush him again, but he gave you a break and only burned down the saloon. If any of you give us or the settlers a lick of trouble, we’ll burn every one of your tents and shacks some night when you’re sleeping. The ones who are still alive come morning will be sent packing. You won’t get another warning. Is that clear?”

One of the scavengers yelled back, “Yeah. We hear ya. We didn’t care all that much about Ralph or Jimmy Baker anyway. We just miss their whiskey.”

“Just pass along the word. And tell some of your boys to take a bath sometime. The Missouri River is just a good walk away.”

When the man didn’t reply, Coop turned and said, “Let’s let them deal with those bodies. They’ll bury them when the stink gets bad enough.”

Cap replied, “I’m not so sure, boss. Remember Stinky Jacobsen and Skunk Roper called this place home, and nobody seemed to mind.”

Coop chuckled then turned his gelding around. Cap followed suit and they soon reached the road and headed back to the jail.

As they trotted west, the sheriff asked, "Did you know that Hardy was already planning to woo Angela Parker?"

"I did kind of figure that out on my own, Coop. What did she think about it?"

"Charlotte said she was about to accept him, so I guess she feels pretty lucky right now. But you do know that Hardy would have been her second choice; don't you?"

"I suspected that she might have had a notion along that line, but why are you bringing it up?"

"What if when you see Mrs. Braun and you find out that she's perfectly happy with Hartmann? Would you consider Angela?"

"Coop, I'm not going down that road unless the way to Erna is blocked by the biggest landslide you've ever seen. I've never felt this way about another woman before and I still feel like a heel for leaving her and the children. If she hadn't been so determined to stay or if Hartmann hadn't been either a German or a farmer, things would have been much different. I already planned to go there before the first of November with more supplies. Even if Hartmann is still there and she's content, I'll leave them with her."

"Then you'll start seeing Angela socially?"

Cap snickered as he shook his head then asked, "Is Charlotte driving your sudden attempt at matchmaking?"

"I reckon it's more Angela then Charlotte. Before Hardy arrived, she kept asking Charlotte about you and how committed you were to Mrs. Braun. Last night, after we consummated our marriage for the first time, Charlotte suggested that I ask you about it. I don't think she trusted Hardy as much as Angela did."

"Just let it go, Coop. The future will reveal itself when it becomes the present."

Sheriff Donavan laughed then said, "Now you're turning into a real philosopher."

Cap smiled but didn't reply as he'd just as soon drop the subject.

———

Erna had managed to convince her stomach to keep its contents inside again and was relieved that Franz hadn't noticed her other physical changes. She had maintained her limited food intake at the same level it had been which meant she was always incredibly hungry. It was almost as if she was starving.

She was cooking lunch when Franz left the house and Gustave and Elsa popped up from their chairs and hurried close.

"Can we have some chocolate now, Mama?" Elsa asked.

"Not yet, dear. Mister Hartmann might return at any moment. He probably just went to the privy."

"Oh."

Gustave then asked, "Are you feeling good, Mama?"

"I'm fine."

"You look tired. Is it because Mister Hartmann keeps you awake all night?"

"No. He doesn't bother me too much anymore. It's just the cold weather that makes me seem tired."

Gustave nodded but his mother's answer didn't make much sense. He was old enough to remember how she had been last winter when it had been much colder. She had been full of energy and seemed to do almost as much work as their father, if not more. Now she did less work but seem to be tired all the time.

Elsa then asked, "Do you want to play poker, Mama?"

Erna smiled as she answered, “Maybe after supper. Okay?”

“Alright.”

Gustave took one last, long look at his mother before he took Elsa’s hand and pulled her back to their table. They had barely taken their seats when Franz returned and plopped down onto his chair to wait for lunch.

He hadn’t visited the privy but had looked at the woodpile and knew it wouldn’t last another week. Then he’d have to head to the trees and search for more dead branches. He knew that Tyler had cut down a tree and chopped the trunk into logs, but they’d still have to be split into useable firewood.

Before he’d returned to the house, he did visit the privy tent, but only to check on the tack that was stored in the corner. With his riding saddle and the pack saddle, he’d be able to take both mules to the Black Hills. The panniers were all in the house, but that didn’t matter. All that mattered now was timing.

He had already decided to leave, so now it was just a question of when. He had briefly thought of taking Erna with him, but knew she’d never leave her children. He was becoming annoyed with the constant attention she paid to her precious brats. If she wasn’t such an impressive woman, he’d leave today. He just needed a slight nudge to make him bolt.

CHAPTER 10

After the almost disastrous day after the sheriff's wedding, things quieted down in Bismarck. For five days, nothing of consequence came to the attention of the sheriff's office. Their duties settled into delivering legal papers and stopping a few serious arguments in the town's three real saloons.

On the twenty-third of October, Cap rode out of town to make a visit to Mandan. He had picked up his repaired coat but was glad to have his new heavier coat as the weather was beyond chilly. He hadn't been reduced to wearing his furry, ear-covering hat yet, but knew it wouldn't be much longer.

After crossing the Missouri on the big ferry, he mounted Joe and headed for Mandan. He wasn't expecting any trouble and hoped to return by mid-afternoon. He soon spotted a train of three freight wagons ahead and thought they might think he was a highwayman, so he moved his badge onto his new coat in case one of them was trigger happy.

He started passing the wagons and waved at the teamsters. When he reached the lead wagon, he recognized the two he'd rescued the first time he'd gone to Mandan.

As he tipped his hat, he said, “Good morning, boys. Hope you don’t have any problems this time.”

Abner Tazwell shouted back, “Not with you around, Cap!”

Cap grinned and waved before Joe pulled ahead of the wagon.

Aside from a lunch with the mayor who spent most of the time trying to sell Cap on taking the town marshal job, it was an uneventful stay. He left town shortly after noon and headed east.

The wind had been picking up most of the day and as the cloud cover grew thicker, Cap hoped he’d be able to reach Bismarck before whatever the clouds held started coming down. It was on the border of being either freezing rain or snow and snow was much more preferable. He still left his slicker in place but was ready to throw it over his coat if whatever came down turned out not to be snow.

Franz was outside near the privy tent looking at the sky. He had the same question that Cap had about the form the precipitation would take. But regardless of whether it was freezing rain or snow, it was just a hint of what would soon be coming. It could be sixty or even seventy degrees tomorrow, but today's lousy weather was just a reminder of what was certain to arrive just a little further along on the calendar. He knew that he had to leave before the days of reasonably nice weather ended.

He walked back to the house and after turning around the corner he noticed steam coming from the ground. He stopped and realized that dirt had been kicked over vomit to cover it up. He stared at the mess and immediately realized what it meant. Marta had morning sickness before the Indians attacked. Erna was pregnant, but he was convinced that he wasn't the father. He didn't think it was possible that she could have conceived so quickly and that meant either she had lied about Tyler sleeping outside in his tent or Wilhelm had left her with a baby inside her before he died.

He stepped past the steaming pool and entered the house. After closing the door, he walked to the table and picked up the Winchester. After leaning it near the doorway, he grabbed two empty panniers and carried them to the stack of food.

Erna hesitated before she asked, "What are you doing, Franz?"

He turned to her and snapped, "You're pregnant; aren't you?"

She wasn't surprised that he'd figured it out after leaving an enormous hint in front of the door. She had only been surprised that it happened so late in the day.

"Yes."

"Who's the father? Wilhelm or Tyler?"

Erna blinked then replied, "You are, of course. I was having my monthly when the Indians attacked. I told you that Cap never even touched me."

"You're lying, Erna, and I'm not going to put up with it. I'm leaving."

She glanced at her children who were staring at her. She knew she couldn't stop him, so all she could do was to ask him to take as little food as possible.

"Are you going to leave us enough food to get through the winter?"

"You can ask Tyler for what you need," Franz replied as he continued to toss food into the panniers.

She left the fire and stepped closer not even realizing that she still carried the heavy steel spoon she'd been using.

She stopped just four feet away and said, "Cap is gone. You're taking too much, so at least leave us a mule so we can try to reach Fort Lincoln."

Franz continued transferring the food to the pannier but stopped when he thought he had enough to last him two weeks. He had only left them tins, a half-filled bag of dry beans and an almost empty bag of flour. He was about to lug them outside when he saw the heavy steel spoon in her hand and thought that Erna was about to use it as a weapon to try to stop him from taking the food.

He didn't warn her, but quickly backhanded her across the face, knocking her stumbling backwards.

Even as his mother began to regain her balance, Gustave exploded from his chair and began pummeling Franz in the stomach with his small fists.

Franz would have laughed if he wasn't already so angry. He picked up the boy and was about to throw him across the room when a furious Erna raced to her son's rescue and snatched him away.

She quickly set him on the floor near Elsa then made the mistake of turning to Franz and shouting, "You coward! You hurt small women and little boys, but you didn't even protect your family. You ran away and let them die!"

Franz' anger quickly escalated into rage. The truth can sometimes wound more deeply than lies.

He made a fist and slammed it into Erna's stomach. As she bent over in pain, he snarled, "Don't you ever call me that!"

Erna wasn't even able to whisper a response as she limped over to her children still doubled over at the waist. She managed to put her arms around Gustave and Elsa and guide them away from Franz and closer to the fire. Now she just hoped that Franz would go. As soon as he left, she'd bolt the door while she could still function.

Franz was still furious, but knew he'd done enough. He needed to leave now.

He opened the door and moved the Winchester outside before returning to the house and grabbing the two heavy panniers. He lugged them outside and set them on the ground before he walked back into the house to pick up his saddlebags and add a few more necessities.

He emptied their match box into his saddlebags, then grabbed the last box of matches, the box of .44 cartridges and a few more tins of food. Then he walked close to Gustave who was looking up at him with wide, frightened eyes expecting Mister Hartmann to try to hurt him. Erna tried to put herself between Franz and Gustave but failed when Franz grabbed her son's arm and pulled him away. She was in so much pain that all she could to was to protect Elsa.

Franz didn't intend to hurt the boy, but simply reached into Gustave's pocket and pulled out his penknife. After dropping it into his coat pocket, he then almost obscenely patted Gustave on the head before he turned and left the house. He didn't bother closing the door but picked up the Winchester and walked around to the back of the house to saddle the mules.

Once he was away from the doorway, Erna waddled to the door and pushed it closed. She then grimaced as she managed to lift the locking bar and set it in place. Once she knew Franz could no longer return, she slowly shuffled to her bed, dropped onto her right side and curled into a fetal position. The backslap had been more of a shock than anything else, but the hard blow to her stomach was still enormously painful.

As she lay on her side, she saw Gustave and Elsa walk slowly towards her. She tried to smile at them but failed.

Gustave quietly said, “I’m sorry, Mama.”

“You’re a brave boy, Gustave. I’m very proud of you. Mister Hartman was just too big.”

Elsa then asked, “Does it hurt, Mama?”

She couldn’t mask her pain, so she replied, “Yes, sweetheart. It hurts right now, but I will be better soon.”

Elsa then leaned forward and kissed her mother on the forehead because that was what her mama did when she fell and bumped a knee or elbow.

Gustave then kissed her on the cheek before he said, “I’ll stir the stew now, Mama.”

“Thank you, Gustave. It’s almost done.”

Gustave then looked at Elsa and quietly let her know that she should stay with their mother to make her feel better. He then stepped to the fallen spoon and picked it up from the floor before walking to the pot of stew. He began stirring it as he'd seen his mother do then he'd put it into the bowls.

As he stirred, he silently prayed that God would send Mister Tyler, their guardian angel, and if He had the time, to smite Mister Hartmann. Maybe God could send the Indians as his avenging angels.

After a few minutes, Erna's pain had diminished enough for her to take over from Gustave. They were soon sitting at one of the tables. Erna had said grace and as they began eating the stew, she looked at the food that Franz had left them. It was only enough for a few days, but there was another problem. Most of it was in tins and she wasn't sure how they could open them without a knife. Then there was the firewood. She was sure that Franz hadn't taken any, but there hadn't been that much left to take either. Maybe the weather would moderate. It wasn't even November, so in a few days, it could be pleasant again.

She still tried to put on a cheerful face for her children and to drive away her own deep troubles. Aside from the lingering pain in her belly, she was still concerned that Franz may decide to return, and things could get much worse. She'd keep that bar in place for as long as possible. But she had to build up her strength because she knew that they had to leave the farm before the weather turned bitterly cold. She and her children would have to walk to Fort Lincoln, fifty miles away.

———

Franz wasn't quite sure how to reach the Black Hills as he headed southwest. He wasn't even sure how far it was. If he'd known it was over two hundred miles away, maybe he wouldn't have been in such a rush to leave. But while discovering that Erna was pregnant had inspired him to go, it was her accusation of cowardice that had made him almost blind to the consequences of his hurried departure.

He rode for three hours before the freezing rain began to fall. He didn't have a slicker but thought it wouldn't matter anyway because the wind was driving it almost horizontally across the plains. He had taken the time to disassemble and pack the privy tent, so he'd be comfortable when he stopped for the night.

———

Cap had returned to the jail before the rain began and had already told the boss that the mayor was still looking for a town marshal. Coop had joked that maybe he should hire Hardy Newton.

When they closed the office for the night, Cap headed to his house riding Joe. He'd arranged to have some hay and oats delivered to his small barn before he left. Tomorrow, he'd retrieve Jasper from Michelson's.

After introducing Joe to his new home and stripping his tack, he braved the freezing rain for just a few seconds before he hopped onto his back porch and entered the kitchen.

Before he took off his coat or even his hat, he quickly started a fire in the fancy cookstove to get some heat into the house.

By sunset, the house was much warmer after he'd built fires in two of the four fireplaces. He had cooked a fairly decent supper and had enough leftovers for breakfast. But living alone in this big house made him feel more isolated than when he'd slept under the open sky on the Great Plains without another human within fifty miles.

He knew he couldn't endure this kind of life much longer. He either had to return to his earlier plan to try to hire on with the Union Pacific or find a wife. He didn't doubt that he'd enjoy the company of Angela Parker. She was a handsome, well-figured woman with a good sense of humor and a fine mind. She was pleasant company, and he knew she'd be more than willing to accept him. But to Cap, this wasn't a matter of logic. He knew he loved Erna and her children, and she was the only one who could turn this mausoleum into a home.

He poured a cup of coffee and walked down the hall, crossed through the well-furnished parlor then entered the foyer where he opened the heavy front door. He stepped onto his varnished porch and closed the door.

It was colder than it had been earlier, and the freezing rain had changed to snow. As he sipped his coffee and stared out into the darkness watching the hard snow being whipped past his house, he decided he wasn't going to wait until November.

He was about to step to the edge of the porch to toss his coffee away but knew it was a bad idea because the intense wind would probably blow it back into his face. So, he turned around and reentered his warm house. He'd talk to the sheriff tomorrow. If the east end of town was quiet, he'd head out to the Braun farm the next day. The only thing that would keep him in Bismarck would be if the weather worsened. It wasn't likely, but it was possible.

———

Franz had struggled setting up the tent. He'd never pitched one before and thought it would be easy. It took him almost an hour to do a job that Cap could handle in five minutes. But after he'd hammered the wooden stakes into the hard ground, he tied his mule and Jed to one of them and then unsaddled both mules and dragged his supplies into the tent for the night.

The wind was whipping the tent's canvas as he built a small fire inside and decided to have something to eat. He had been in such a rush to leave that he hadn't taken any pans or even tin plates. So, he used Gustave's penknife to open a tin of beans and dumped them onto the flap of his saddlebags.

As he ate, he swore at Erna and those brats of hers. He should have just sent them to his parents' farm with only the clothes on their backs. *How dare she call him a name and accuse him of making her pregnant?* Maybe he'd ride back in the morning and take the rest of the food and the pans and plates he'd need to make it to the Black Hills gold fields.

He kept scooping the beans into his mouth as he thought about it. As he pondered his decision, the blowing snow was covering the ground across the plains. It was less than an inch of the granular frozen water, but it covered a sheet of ice and between the two, even an expert tracker would have a difficult time following the trail beneath. And Franz Hartmann was a farmer, not a tracker.

———

Erna tucked her children into bed and kissed each of them on the forehead.

Elsa smiled at her mother and asked, "Can we pray now, Mama?"

"Yes, sweetheart. We will pray to thank God. You will be safe because He won't let harm come to His most perfect creations."

"Will He send Mister Tyler to help us again?"

"I don't know, dear. Only God knows what will happen. We can only pray."

Gustave asked, "Are you better now, Mama?"

She smiled and said, "Much better."

She still had an troubling ache in her abdomen, but she had been able to eat without any problem, so she thought she'd be all right.

She knelt beside their bed and as she looked at their innocent faces, she prayed for their safety but stopped short of asking for God to punish the wicked man she'd allowed to enter her home.

The horrid weather had somewhat abated the next morning when Cap rode east out of Bismarck on Joe. It was still cold and windy, but the clouds were no longer sending gifts of water in one form or another. He had shifted to his furry hat that covered his ears and as he left the buildings behind, he figured it was time to add a heavy wool scarf to his wardrobe.

He had told Coop about his decision to leave as early as possible to visit the Braun farm, but didn't explain why he had advanced the timing. He didn't think the sheriff cared anyway. Maybe he even understood the reason.

During his ride through the settler camp, he waved to the heavily bundled folks and greeted many. When he found Oskar Wentz, he asked if they'd had any problems and Oskar had told him that everything was quiet. He then proceeded to the other side of the street and found very few men outside. The bodies were even gone, but Cap suspected that they'd just been dragged into the piles of ash and burnt wood that used to be their saloon.

But the peaceful nature of the place was a relief and he hoped that they'd finally behave themselves. Maybe dragging those dead bodies away made them realize that it was safer to obey the law.

He turned Joe back toward town and headed for Michelson's. He'd have to move Jasper to his small barn and then buy some more food for his pantry as well as that heavy scarf. While he shopped to stock his house, he'd buy food and supplies for Erna and her children.

When he left Michelson's trailing Jasper, he looked at the sky and wished those clouds would head east and torment the folks in Minnesota. Tomorrow morning, he hoped to be able to at least see the sunrise. If it was a few degrees warmer, he wouldn't complain either.

———

Erna had difficulty getting out of her bed that morning but managed to use the chamber pot and then dress with just a moderate amount of discomfort. But after she pulled on her heavy coat and hat that Cap had provided, she walked to the fireplace. Her breath was making clouds in front of her face reminding her of how cold it was in the house; just in case she hadn't noticed. She tossed some dry grass onto the cold remnants of yesterday's fire then turned to the right to open the matchbox. But it wasn't there. *Why had Franz had taken their matches?* But she knew that Cap had left her another box, so she hopped to her feet and stepped to the small stack of remaining supplies. In the darkened room, she quickly began shifting the tins, towels and spare clothing but couldn't find the matches.

After five minutes of searching, she knew that he'd taken that box as well. She walked to the nearest chair and sat down. She looked at her sleeping children and smiled. Gustave and Elsa were still snug and warm under their blankets. But as she looked at her son, she remembered Cap showing him how to make a fire using his magnifying lens. She knew that the sun wasn't out because there wasn't enough light shining through the gaps in the window shutters. Cap had waited to give the glass to Gustave until noon the next day because it needed to concentrate the power of strong sunlight to start a fire.

She sighed before she stood and walked to the fireplace. They'd finish the last of the cold stew for breakfast and hopefully the sun would emerge soon, and they could build a fire. As desperate as their situation was becoming, she still kept the door barred to keep Franz from entering. He could promise her a feast of roast turkey, but she wouldn't open the door. If he hadn't returned by this afternoon, she'd go outside to scan the horizon and bring the last of their firewood inside. Maybe the sun would break through the clouds by then.

When Franz crawled out of his tent that morning, it didn't take long for him to realize he wouldn't be able to follow his trail back to the house. He snickered knowing that Erna had no matches and not much food. He looked at the sky and saw the disk of the sun behind the clouds and made a half-turn to face in the opposite direction. He picked out a distant outcrop on the horizon and marked it as his next destination. He needed to head southwest and that jutting point of earth was in that direction.

He then returned to his tent to have his breakfast. Then he'd saddle his mules, take down the tent and head southwest. He expected to be in the Black Hills in less than three days.

Unfortunately for Franz, the outcrop wasn't southwest of his tent. It was closer to west than southwest. Even if he had been correct in his guess of the direction, he wouldn't have reached Deadwood for another week.

Erna had finally opened the door in midafternoon then quickly stepped outside to make sure that Franz wasn't in sight. Once she was satisfied that he was gone, she closed the door and hurried around to the left side of the house to retrieve some firewood.

She bent over and picked up two branches. But as she reached for the next one, she felt a sharp stab of pain in her lower gut and thought she was about to retch. But it wasn't the same. She hurriedly snatched one more branch then awkwardly walked back to the house as the cramping intensified.

After passing through the doorway, then closing it behind her with her foot, she struggled to walk normally as she carried the three branches to the fireplace where she simply dumped them onto the few pieces of firewood that were there.

She was still wearing her coat and hat as she waddled to her bed and hurriedly laid down and curled up. She knew that what she was experiencing wasn't morning sickness. She was losing her baby.

Gustave and Elsa had been standing beside one of the tables when their mother entered the house and couldn't help but notice her odd gait. When she suddenly took to her bed still wearing her coat and hat, they rushed to her bedside.

Gustave asked, "Mama, are you sick again?"

Erna closed her eyes and grimaced as a wave of pain swept through her and couldn't answer for a few seconds.

When it passed, she said, "I'm having lady problems."

Elsa began to cry and tried to hug her mother, but she couldn't get her small arms around her.

Instead, she kissed her precious mama on her lips, then in a quivering voice, she whispered, “Don’t die, Mama.”

Gustave felt helpless as he looked at his mother and wished he could do something to help. But all he could do was be strong for her and Elsa.

“What can I do, Mama?” he asked.

“Do you still have your looking glass?”

“Yes, Mama. Mister Hartmann only took my knife.”

“When the sun comes out, can you make a fire? We have no matches.”

“I’ll try, Mama.”

“I know you will, Gustave. I need to rest now.”

Elsa asked, “Can I cook, Mama?”

“No, dear. We only have tins of food now. The only way to open them is with the axe and it’s too heavy for either you or your big brother to use. I’ll do it when I feel better. But when you get hungry, you can eat this.”

She then reached into her coat pocket and pulled out the paper sack and handed it to Gustave.

He looked at the angel on the front of the bag then showed it to Elsa.

"Mister Tyler will come and help us, Elsa. He will still be watching over us like this angel."

Elsa stared at the angel image as she said, "He will come; won't he?"

Gustave nodded then said, "We'll save the chocolate for later. But do you want to have a peppermint stick now?"

Elsa grinned as she held out her small hand and Gustave slipped one out of the bag and placed in onto her palm.

He then carried the bag to the table and set it down. He pulled a second stick out and snapped it in half on the corner of the table. He returned to his mother's bedside and handed the broken half to her.

"This will make you feel better, Mama."

Erna accepted the candy knowing that it would please Gustave. She began to suck on the end before Gustave and Elsa started on theirs.

Elsa felt guilty for having a full-sized peppermint stick but planned to give it to her mother before she finished.

As her children returned to the table, Erna experienced more cramping and knew it wouldn't be long before they would learn the true nature of her 'lady problem'.

She thought the best she could do now was to prepare for the miscarriage, so she asked Gustave to bring her three towels. She couldn't use any of the water in their two buckets because she didn't want to send Gustave to the creek a half a mile away.

After she had the towels, she asked them to turn around. When they were no longer looking, she layered them in place and then after pulling the blanket over her, she told them they could turn around again.

She couldn't help lurching in pain as they watched. As bad as this was now, she was much more concerned about the aftermath, especially if she couldn't stop the bleeding. Even if she passed the most dangerous point, she knew she'd be weak and unable to help her children much longer. If it hadn't been for the sharp pains, she would have wept.

The rest of Cap's day was routine, but he was able to stock his pantry and fill four panniers with supplies for Erna and the children. The loaded packs were aligned near the back door of his large kitchen. He even made a large batch of hash browns and filled two quart-sized Mason jars.

He hoped to be loading everything onto Jasper tomorrow morning and as he prepared his supper that evening, he kept glancing through the window to see if there was any sign of a break in the weather.

The sun was still hidden, but the wind seemed to be dropping. While it wasn't as heartening as the sun making an appearance, it convinced him that he'd be riding west in the morning.

———

Franz had continued riding after passing his outcrop then picked out another distant waypoint. It was more to the southwest, but not enough to correct his initial error.

But it wasn't his poor navigation that was his biggest problem. It wasn't even the bad weather. It was a combination of bad timing and having Jed trailing behind his mule. Jed's unusual markings came from his father, an Appaloosa. His distinctive coloring was passed on to his offspring. Jed's coat was a mottled gray with white splotches that was much different than almost any other mule.

As he rode across the prairie, he was spotted by a Lakota hunting party. They were almost a mile to his northeast, so he didn't even notice them. If he'd just been another white man heading to Montana Territory, which was where he would find himself soon, they might not have cared. But even at that distance, they identified Jed. They didn't stop hunting for game but sent one warrior to the village to tell the war chief of their discovery. They would finally have their revenge against the Mule Killer.

———

It was almost evening when Erna lost the baby. Her children watched in fear as she suddenly grunted, then closed her eyes. For a moment, Gustave and Elsa thought she had died, and both erupted in tears, but were too afraid to step closer to her bed. They didn't want to know that they'd lost their mother.

But less than a minute later, Erna opened her eyes and found them weeping nearby. She knew she had to clean herself but didn't want them to see the blood.

When they saw her open her eyes, both children rushed to her bedside.

Gustave quickly asked, "What happened, Mama?"

She found it difficult to speak, but managed to quickly reply, "I told you. It is a woman problem. I need you to do something for me. I want you to get more firewood. Both of you."

Gustave glanced at Elsa before he asked, "You want firewood, Mama?"

"Yes, dear. Go now."

He took Elsa's hand and had to pull her away from the bed. He opened the door and led his sister outside then closed the door.

Once outside, he turned to Elsa and said, "I think mama is pretending she is all right. We have to take care of her better."

"What is wrong with mama, Goose?"

"I don't know. But we have to watch her all the time now. Okay?"

"Is mama going to die?" Elsa asked quietly.

Gustave shook his head as he replied, "No, Elsa. Mama won't die. We prayed for God to send Mister Tyler and he will come to help her."

Elsa smiled as they turned and began to walk to the woodpile.

After they'd closed the door, Erna tossed off the blanket and started removing the bloody towels. As she pulled each one away, she tossed it onto the floor on the near wall so the children wouldn't see them. After the towels were gone, she slowly pulled down her underpants with much more difficulty and tossed them onto the bloody towels. She couldn't even look at them knowing what was probably embedded in the fabric. With nothing covering her privates, she needed see if she was still losing blood. So, she slid her legs from the bed and carefully stood. She stepped gingerly to the other side of the room and picked up one of the few clean towels and a new pair of underpants, then returned to her bed. She folded the towel and after cleaning herself as much as she could she turned it over and left it in place for a few seconds. When she removed it, she breathed a sigh of relief. She wasn't bleeding.

But her relief was short-lived. She had to remove the blood-soaked towels and underclothes but didn't know where to hide them. She didn't want to walk outside and let the children see them. So, after she struggled to pull on the clean underpants, she laid across the bed and picked them up from the floor. She carried everything to the cold fireplace and used the same spoon that had used to empty the stew to shift the ashes aside. She put the all the bloody towels and the underpants into the shallow black hole and then covered them with the ashes before she added some branches to hide the white and red that still showed. It wasn't perfect, but if they could start a fire the towels would become nothing but fuel.

She was still weak from her exertions and loss of blood, so she walked back to her bed to rest and waited for Gustave and Elsa to return.

As she lay on the bed in her coat and hat, she made a short inventory of their food and firewood. It wasn't a very long list. To make matters worse, she was the only one strong enough to use their axe to open those tins. She wished she could use her strength of character to overcome her body's weakness, but knew it wasn't possible. She needed food and to obtain their only source of nutrition required her to be physically strong. It was a terrible conundrum. But beyond that critical problem, she knew that her loss of blood and lack of food were combining with the cold to drive her ever closer to death.

When Gustave and Elsa returned with their small arms clutching the last of their firewood, she watched as they lugged their loads to the fireplace and dropped them nearby. She hoped that they didn't notice the towels and was relieved when they didn't spot them.

Gustave rushed back to close the door while Elsa walked close to her bedside.

"Are you better now, Mama?" she asked.

"Yes, dear. I just need to rest now."

Elsa smiled, and if there had been enough room, would have crawled into bed next to her mother.

After he closed the door, Gustave lifted the locking bar in place. He didn't want Mister Hartmann to be able to enter the house.

It was getting late, and Erna knew they were hungry, but knew that she didn't have the strength to wield Gustave's penknife, much less the axe. She looked at the table and saw the last peppermint stick protruding out of the bag. She knew it wouldn't help her children, but the chocolate bars further down in the bag would.

As Gustave joined Elsa, Erna said, "Gustave, why don't you get a chocolate bar from the bag. I won't be able to open a tin yet, but the chocolate will help."

Gustave nodded then left her bedside, retrieved a chocolate bar and carried it back to his mother. He gave it to her and watched her peel back the waxed paper covering.

Erna broke the bar into two large pieces and handed one to Elsa then the second to Gustave.

Neither of them took a bite before Gustave asked, “Do you want me to get another one for you, Mama?”

“No, dear. My tummy is still upset. I’ll have some later. Okay?”

Gustave nodded then he looked at Elsa before each of them sunk their teeth into the dark chocolate. Under any other circumstances, they would have squealed in unrestricted joy when the incredible flavor touched their tongues. But now it was just food. It was very tasty food, but they felt guilty that they were eating, and their mother wasn’t.

Erna watched until the chocolate was gone then said, “Now go and drink some water.”

They both quietly turned and headed toward their table where Gustave took one of their tin cups before they walked to the buckets.

Erna then closed her eyes. She’d have them sleep wearing their coats and hats tonight even though they’d still have two heavy blankets. She’d do the same and maybe by tomorrow, she’d be strong enough to open some tins of food. She knew that she was being overly optimistic, but she had to be strong for her children until she breathed her last.

———

Cap blew out the lamp then slid beneath his heavy quilts. He didn't care if there was a raging blizzard tomorrow. He'd load the supplies onto Jasper and then head south to use the small ferry. He didn't understand his sudden overpowering urge to go to the Braun farm. His logic told him that Gustave and Elsa were already warmly snuggled under their blankets with a roaring fire blazing a few feet away. He still didn't want to imagine Erna sleeping with Hartmann, but still believed that she was at least content. It made his decision to leave regardless of the weather more than just illogical. It seemed downright silly. But he knew that if he delayed his departure that nagging voice would only grow louder and more insistent.

———

As Franz ducked into his tent just after sunset, he thought that he might see the Black Hills on the horizon by late afternoon tomorrow. He had created a bowl of sorts out of an empty tin of beans and celebrated by opening some corned beef to go along with another tin of beans.

He was in a surprisingly good mood despite the frigid cold. The wind had died down enough to lead him to believe that warmer days would soon arrive.

If there had been more daylight, he might have spotted the six Sioux warriors who were two miles away and riding closer. They weren't going to attack him in his sleep. Despite their hatred of the man, they still regarded him as a fierce warrior. It would be more honorable to face him and risk death than to sneak into his tent while he slept and murder him. They were proud warriors, not women. Nor would they act as some of the bluecoats did when they attacked their villages. They considered themselves to be better men.

They set up their camp a mile away and would face the Mule Killer in the morning. Each of them had a rifle but knew he had several, including repeaters and one that could kill from a long distance. It would be a fair fight, but he would die. Then those who lived could return to the village in triumph leading his oddly colored mule as proof of their bravery.

———

Erna closed her eyes and listened to her children's quiet breathing. Her stomach had stopped growling hours ago as it seemed to have given up. She was sorely tempted to get out of bed and eat one of the chocolate bars, but they were all Gustave and Elsa would have to eat if she didn't improve. She knew she couldn't walk across the room now even if she gave into the temptation.

She felt tears dripping onto the pillow as she tried to think of some way to save her children. She no longer mattered.

CHAPTER 11

Cap yanked the legs of one of his wool Union suits over his feet then after he buttoned it closed, he pulled on his heavy canvas britches. He had two pairs of thick socks under his boots as he stood and slid his arms though the sleeves of his warmest flannel shirt. He added his gray woolen sweater then strapped on his gunbelts before he left his bedroom. There was a reason for his almost excessive bundling.

When Cap had opened the window that morning, it seemed to be even colder than it had been yesterday. The clouds were still thick overhead and the wind had picked up slightly, but he was determined to leave.

He exited the back door of his house carrying his Winchester and Sharps. Once in his small barn, he saddled Joe and Jasper then slipped both rifles into Joe's scabbards. He then led his mules close to the porch and tied them off at the hitching post near the steps before reentering his house.

It took him twenty minutes to load the packs onto Jasper then mount Joe and start his favorite mule away from the house. He soon turned south and hoped that the ferry was running. The Missouri would be choppy and ice flows would be flowing downriver, so the ferryman might not take the risk. He was also worried that Jasper wouldn't tolerate the crossing.

The small ferry had a much bouncier ride than the much bigger one north of the town. He'd have to talk to Jasper the entire time, assuming the ferry was operating.

His worries about the ferry and Jasper proved unfounded and just forty minutes later, Cap mounted Joe again and waved to the ferryman as he headed west. He'd given the man a quarter even though he didn't need to pay for the crossing. It wasn't official business, but he was very grateful to be able to cross the angry Missouri quickly.

———

Erna's hopes for improvement in the weather or her condition were dashed before her children stirred. She had been awakened by an urgent need to use the chamber pot. After tossing the blanket aside, she'd tried to sit up but was so dizzy that she had to drop back to the mattress. She waited for almost a minute before laying onto her right side, then sticking her legs off the bed. She then rolled into a sitting position hoping that the dizziness wouldn't arrive. It may not have been as strong, but it still kept her sitting on the edge of the bed. She didn't want to risk standing and then collapsing to the floor.

After she thought it was safe, she leaned forward and started to rise. She almost stood upright before her weak legs buckled and she crumpled to the floor by her bed.

The noise startled Gustave and Elsa awake, and they bolted out from under the blanket.

"Mama!" Gustave shouted as he dropped to his knees beside her.

Erna softly said, "I just tripped."

She could see the fear in their eyes and wished she could smile and reassure them but wasn't even sure that she could make it back to the bed. She then rolled onto her back and took a deep breath to prepare herself for the difficult task of sitting up.

She grabbed the bed's siderail with her left hand and used almost all of her remaining strength to sit up. She had barely pulled herself from the floor when her bladder let loose. She fought back the urge to start sobbing as she sat in her own waste in front of her children.

Gustave then said, "I'll get you a towel, Mama."

He then hurriedly walked to the other wall and picked up their last towel, wondering where the others had gone. He knew that Mister Hartmann hadn't taken them. But he let that question go as he trotted back to his mother and held out the towel.

She said, "Hold onto it for now, Gustave."

Then she took another deep breath and crawled onto the bed where she collapsed. She no longer cared about the smell or discomfort. She was just so incredibly tired and weak.

As his mother closed her eyes, Gustave began wiping up the mess. When it was as clean as he could make it, he carried the towel to the door and pulled the locking bar free and lowered it to the floor. He opened the door and tossed the towel outside as a mass of cold air rushed into the house. He slammed the door and replaced the bar before walking back to his mother's bed.

"It's all clean, Mama."

"Is the sun out?" she asked quietly.

"No, Mama. It's still cloudy and cold."

She closed her eyes and whispered, "You should share another chocolate bar now. I can't eat yet."

Elsa looked at her brother with terrified eyes hoping he had some way to help their mother but saw the same despair in his blue eyes.

Gustave then took her hand and walked with her to the table. He took out the second chocolate bar and broke it in half. After giving her the bigger half, they stood staring at the candy as if it was leather. They wanted their mother to have all of it but knew she wouldn't take it.

After almost a minute, Gustave took a small bite from the corner. Elsa then took a bite and they soon finished their candy breakfast.

When they returned to their mother's bedside, they simply stood and watched her. She appeared to be sleeping, but each of them began to believe that they would soon lose their wonderful mother. While Elsa was overcome with sorrow, Gustave's anguish was mixed with deep loathing of Mister Hartmann. He was the one who'd hurt his mother and Gustave wished he was a real man with a Winchester.

———

Twenty-eight miles to the west of the farmhouse, the man who'd punched his mother was facing his own problem. When he'd left his tent to relieve himself that morning, he found six mounted Lakota warriors in a line about four hundred yards away. He never had the chance to unbutton his britches as he stared at the Sioux wondering why they didn't attack.

He didn't waste any time pondering the question as he hurried back into the tent to retrieve his Winchester. He cocked he hammer and hurried behind his mule which was the only protection he had.

As he set the carbine's forearm across his mule's back, Burning Light turned to his lieutenant and said, "He hides behind his animal. This man has no honor. He deserves to die."

Yet even as he raised his cocked repeater over his head and screamed his war cry releasing his five warriors, he had questions about the identity of the man. From all the tales he'd heard of the Mule Killer, he had been described as a worthy adversary. Then the behavior of the man hiding behind his mule for protection added more questions about his identity.

As they charged toward Franz, he began rapidly firing before they were within two hundred yards. He barely took time to align his Winchester's sights at any of the Sioux, but they held their fire.

By the time they were within effective range of his Winchester, he'd already expended nine rounds. If he'd reloaded the carbine after his last target practice, he would still have six more shots. But he was down to three and didn't realize it yet.

The Lakota were much more concerned about wasting ammunition, so they still didn't open fire as they drew closer. But when they finally decided they were close enough, Franz Hartmann's hammer fell on an empty chamber.

When he realized he was empty, he opened his coat to get to the spare .44s on the gunbelt but kept his eyes on the Indians.

He fumbled the first cartridge that he pulled free then decided to use the loaded pistol. So, he tossed his Winchester aside and grabbed his Colt's grips. He yanked it, but the pistol wouldn't budge. In his panic, he forgot to release the hammer loop.

By the time he freed his pistol, he may as well have been holding a peppermint stick.

Cap was making good time as he trotted Joe across the frozen ground. He was reasonably comfortable in his multi-layered getup which was augmented by Joe's body heat. He still felt somewhat foolish for rushing this way, but at least he'd given his mules two breaks and let them drink when they passed over a small creek.

It was early afternoon when he spotted the Hartmann farm and would have stopped if there had been smoke coming from one of the houses. He wouldn't have been surprised if Hartmann had moved Erna and the children to the bigger farmhouse.

But the sight of the three houses meant that in a few more minutes, he'd spot Erna's house. He expected to see smoke pouring out of their chimney and Jed tethered nearby. He was sure that Joe and Jasper would be happy to meet their brother again.

When he did pick up the roof of the Braun farmhouse, he was immediately troubled by the lack of smoke. Even if they'd already run out of the branches he'd added to the pile, Hartmann should have gone to the forest and picked up the ones he'd cut. He would have been amazed if the man split the logs.

As he continued to see more of the farmhouse, he noticed other even more troubling signs. He didn't see Jed or Hartmann's mule, nor was the privy tent still in place. The sight of the snow-covered wagon was even more disturbing.

The farmhouse was growing closer, and his stomach threatened to shrivel into a walnut as he began to suspect that Hartmann had murdered Erna and her children then run off. He couldn't imagine Erna not having a fire going to keep her children warm. Hartmann may not have gone to the woods to get more wood, but Erna would have.

He nudged Joe into a faster pace as he continued to examine the house for any clues to what he might find when he opened the door. But the ones he'd already noticed were all he had as he drew nearer to the quiet house.

Cap pulled Joe to a stop and quickly dropped to the ground, letting Joe's reins drop. He trotted to the closed door and pushed on it, but it didn't budge. That meant the locking bar was in place and that added confusion to his growing concern.

Inside the house, Gustave and Elsa had been standing watch over their mother for hours. They hadn't eaten the last chocolate bar because they were saving it for her when she woke up. But she had never opened her eyes and even though they could see the clouds forming over her when she exhaled, they were sliding ever deeper into depression knowing that she may never awaken.

They were wearing their heavy coats with their ear-covering hats, so they hadn't heard the hoofbeats announcing Cap's arrival. So, when there was a loud pounding on the door, they both jumped and had the same thought. *Mister Hartmann had returned!*

Despite their deep worries about their mother, they both understood that she wouldn't want them to open the door and let him in. But they did turn to stare at the door, hoping it would hold if he tried to break in.

Cap waited for thirty seconds after his heavy knocking, but when no one even called out to him from inside, he feared the worst. He wasn't about to break the door down but was hesitant to call out. He didn't want to hear continued silence after he shouted his name.

He finally let out a long, frosty breath then sucked in the frigid air and yelled, "This is Cap Tyler! Are you okay?"

Gustave and Elsa immediately hurried to the door and their small hands pushed the locking bar away and let it crash to the floor.

Cap heard their footsteps and the locking bar sliding up and then the bang when it hit the wooden floor. He was about to push the door open when Gustave beat him to it and yanked it away.

"Mister Tyler!" he exclaimed as Cap entered and searched the dark, cold room for Erna.

"Mama's sick!" Elsa cried as Gustave closed the door.

Cap found Erna on her bed covered in blankets yet still wearing her hat and coat.

As he walked to her bedside, he asked, "What happened, Gustave?"

Gustave and Elsa trotted behind him and as Cap took a knee near Erna's bed, Gustave replied, "Mister Hartmann left and took everything. He hit mama in the tummy, and she was sick. She can't get up."

Cap had to delay his fury and his feelings of guilt for leaving them with that bastard as he leaned close to Erna's face.

"Erna, this is Cap. Can you hear me?"

Erna had been fading in and out and no longer had the energy to do anything. She felt as if she was floating in the air. When she'd heard the loud banging, she wasn't sure if it was Franz returning or Death himself coming to claim her. Then she heard Cap's shout and thought she was dreaming. It was only when his voice was so close that she began to believe that he really had returned.

"Cap?" she whispered.

"Yes, Erna. I'm so sorry that I didn't come sooner."

She managed a weak smile as she softly said, “You called me Erna.”

“Yes. I will always call you Erna now.”

She opened her eyes and found his green eyes looking at her as she said, “Take care of my children. Promise me.”

“No. I won’t take care of your children, Erna.”

For just a moment she thought he was refusing to help Gustave and Elsa and believed that she’d misunderstood him.

Cap then said, “I will take care of our children, Erna. But first I will take care of you. Then I will take you and our children to Bismarck to live in my house. You will be my family.”

He thought that he’d misused his German when she slowly rocked her head on her pillow.

“Just children. Not me.”

“You need to come to take care of our children, Erna. Why would you not want to come to Bismarck?”

“I…I…” Erna started to speak but couldn’t muster the energy to confess what had put her into such a weakened state.

Cap stood then said, “Let’s get a fire going and then I’ll cook a hot meal.”

Gustave pointed at the row of tins and said, "That is all he left us."

"I have a lot of food outside. I'll start the fire first. You and Elsa stay with your mother."

The children nodded and stepped back to their mother's bedside as Cap strode to the fireplace and dropped to his heels. After taking off his gloves and dropping them to the floor he grabbed one of the branches. As he placed it onto the ones that Erna had already dropped there, he noticed the bloody cloth half-buried under the ash. He tugged on one corner and then saw the blood-stained underpants before he added the branch. He placed four more on top then reached into his coat pocket and pulled out a match. A minute later the fire was already strong enough to demand more fuel. He tossed in the last of the wood nearby then stood and walked to the children.

He may not have known much about women, but after what Gustave had told him, he had a good idea why the towels were bloody. It also explained why Erna had tried to hide them from her children. He had been angry enough at Franz Hartmann for abandoning them, then for striking Erna, but he had also murdered her unborn child. He didn't know if the baby had been her husband's or Franz', but it didn't matter. After he was sure that she and the children were healthy and safe in Bismarck, he'd track down that murdering son of a bitch. But he soon realized that it may not even be necessary because he was trailing Jed.

"Has your mother eaten anything today?"

They both shook their heads as Gustave replied, "No. She hasn't had anything to eat for a long time. She wouldn't even eat the chocolate. We saved the last one for her."

He smiled and said, "Well, you start giving her pieces of the chocolate bar and tell her I told her to eat them. Okay?"

Gustave and Elsa smiled then hurried to the table as Cap opened the door and went outside to unload the supplies. After he closed the door, he wanted to scream but managed to rein in his anger. He understood why Erna was so weak and hoped that she hadn't lost too much blood. But it was her last weak words that bothered him. She seemed to blame herself for what had happened to her. And now that she knew her children were safe, it was almost as if she had given up and was content to simply surrender her life.

He unloaded the first two packs and lugged them into the house. After leaving them inside, he returned for the second pair. After bringing his bedroll inside, he left the house again and walked around the side of the house to see how much firewood was there. It wasn't much, but he gathered the last of it and carried it into the house.

Cap added the last of the wood to the fire and planned to ride out to the forest to collect more before sunset. But now he had to cook something warm for Erna and the children.

When he'd entered the first time, he was gratified to see that Gustave and Elsa were able to convince their mother to eat the chocolate. It had a lot of energy and should trigger her appetite. He also needed to convince her that she had a lot of reasons to live, starting with the two small ones who were still feeding her bits of chocolate.

Erna had tried to refuse Gustave's offer of the chocolate but couldn't even muster the energy to tell him. She finally relented and opened her mouth just enough to let him insert a small piece of chocolate. Then the incredible taste exploded from her tongue and seemed to flood her entire being. Even as she reveled in the extraordinary sensation, she remembered the hand-drawn angel on the bag that had protected the chocolate. Maybe the angel was real and that was why she felt so incredibly exhilarated after just a taste of the chocolate.

She opened her mouth again and after Elsa placed the second piece on her tongue, she didn't have the same powerful reaction, but it was still comforting. Yet despite the delightful effect, she was still ashamed. She believed that God had sent Cap to save her children, but not her. *How could she be with him in Bismarck?* She wasn't a good woman.

Despite her self-loathing, Erna was so hungry that she couldn't help waiting for the next bite.

Bit by chocolaty bit, Gustave and Elsa fed their mother while Cap began to cook. He didn't dare bring any eggs, but he had bought lots of the sausage that he knew they liked. He opened one of the jars of hash browns before he set his large skillet on the cooking grate and after the dollop of butter melted, he dumped the entire jar of hash browns onto the pan. He slid his big knife from its sheath and began slicing three sausages onto the hash browns.

As it began to simmer, he quickly walked to his panniers. He unloaded four tin plates and some utensils and set them on one of the tables. He trotted back to the fire, stirred and flipped the hash brown and sausages, then returned to finish setting the table. He was sure that Erna couldn't stand but would place his bedroll behind her to lift her into a sitting position.

After he donned one of his gloves, he pulled the skillet onto the rocks near the fireplace. Next, he filled four tin cups with water from one of the buckets, set them on the table then stepped to his bedroll and plucked it from the floor.

"Gustave, you and Elsa can sit at the table now. I will help your mother."

Gustave nodded, then automatically took Elsa's hand before they walked to the table.

Cap then stood over Erna who still had her eyes closed and said, "Erna, I'm going to lift you then put my bedroll behind you so you can sit up to eat."

Erna just slowly rocked her head.

Cap was surprised because he thought his German had improved significantly since he'd first found them, so he said more slowly, "I will help you sit up."

Even though she shook her head again, he knew she'd understood him. He didn't repeat it a third time but set the bedroll on the floor and took hold of her shoulders and lifted her from the pillow. He knew she was a small woman but was still surprised by how easily he was able to lift her.

Once he had her upright, he held her with his right hand and grabbed his bedroll with his left and placed it on top of her pillow before lowering her gently.

While she still didn't even open her eyes, Cap left her in her half-sitting position and walked to the skillet. He put on his left glove again, then grabbed the big spoon with his right and carried the steaming sausage and hash browns to the table.

After he filled the four plates, he said, "Gustave, you say grace while I take food to your mother. Okay?"

"Okay."

As Gustave said grace, thanking God for the food and sending Mister Tyler, Cap moved one of the chairs close to Erna's bed. He returned to the table, took one of the plates and a cup of water then sat down near Erna's head.

"Erna, open your eyes. You must eat."

Her blue eyes slowly revealed themselves and she turned to look at Cap.

Despite the loud rumbling from her demanding stomach, she said, “Not until you promise me.”

“And what is this promise you demand of me?”

Her voice was still weak when she replied, “Leave the supplies for me…take…take my children to Bismarck.”

“I cannot make that promise, Erna. I already promised God and myself when I left this morning that if I found you unhappy, that I would never leave you again. Would you have me break my vow to God?”

She answered, “But I am a…I…I cannot go with you,” then after a pause to build up her strength, she said, “God calls me to His judgement and will not hold you to your promise.”

Cap was concerned that the same determination that had convinced him that she would never leave the farm would now allow her only to leave the house when she left this life. He had to use the only argument that he knew would convince her to eat.

He said, “Then let Him decide. But you must eat, and I will not leave until you do. As much as you have already done to protect your children, do you now wish to allow them watch you starve to death?”

She looked at him and realized that he wouldn't leave without her, so she reluctantly nodded.

Once he had her consent, he put the tin of water to her chocolate covered lips because she needed the liquid. After she'd emptied half of the cup, he set it down on the floor and began to feed her.

As he watched her chew and swallow, he knew it was just the first step of returning her to good health. But healing her body would be much easier than repairing the damage to her soul.

After she emptied the plate, he gave her the last of the water. He then stood, lifted her slightly and removed the bedroll before laying her back down.

He quietly said, "You rest now."

She nodded and closed her eyes before Cap turned and walked to the table and sat down.

Gustave and Elsa had already finished their food, so he asked, "Do you want more?"

They both shook their heads before Gustave asked, "Is mama going to be all right?"

"Yes, she will. She needs more food and rest. We will stay here tomorrow and the next day, we will go to Bismarck. You and your mother will live with me in my house."

As Cap began eating, Gustave asked, “You have a house? Mama said you were going away.”

After swallowing, Cap replied, “I thought I was, too. But now I live in Bismarck. I wear a badge of the law to protect the people.”

He then opened his coat and showed his deputy sheriff’s badge to the children before taking another bite.

“Will you be our new papa?” Elsa asked as she stared at the badge.

He smiled as he answered, “I hope so, Elsa. I have to ask your mother to marry me first.”

Gustave snapped, “I didn’t want Mister Hartmann for a papa. He hated us.”

Cap didn’t want to have any more reason to despise the man, so he asked, “Do you know where he went?”

Gustave replied, “He talked about a place called the Black Hills sometimes.”

“That’s what I thought. They found gold there and many men are going there to find it. It’s not a nice place.”

“Are you going to arrest him for hurting mama?”

“I’ll worry about him after I get you and your mother to Bismarck. But I don’t think that I’ll have to search for him. Even if he even makes it to the Black Hills, I don't think he will do well with all the bad men there."

Elsa asked, "Is it far away?"

"It took me a week to get here, and I knew the way. But that long ride is hard, and he took my mule with him; didn't he?"

Gustave nodded then asked, "Can you arrest him for stealing your mule, too?"

Cap smiled then replied, "I could, but that's not why I asked if he had my mule. I named the mule Jed. Did you see how different Jed looked?"

Gustave grinned as he answered, "He had spots."

"He had very unusual coloring. I've had him for two years now and everyone who sees him comments on his spots. If Mister Hartmann is seen by Indians, they might think he was me. Many of the Indians are mad at me and would chase him. He might make it to the Black Hills but there are too many, um…problems in his way."

Cap hadn't come up with the German word for obstacles, but figured he wouldn't need it in the future, so it didn't matter. By the time Gustave started school next September, he would be speaking English as well as any of the other first years.

———

Thirty-six miles southwest, Burning Light sat across from Chief Standing Buffalo and explained what he'd learned from the white man. The white man he had discovered not to be the Mule Killer, but just a coward.

He'd told him of his cowardly behavior and how when his warriors reached him, he was on his hands and knees begging for his life.

"His English was not as good as mine. But when I asked him how he had the mule, he told me the Mule Killer left it with a woman and two children who had survived our raid. He said the Mule Killer would return to that house now."

"Was he telling the truth?"

"He described the Mule Killer very well. He also talked about his many guns. It was one of the reasons I was sure he was not the Mule Killer."

"What do you propose?"

"I want to go back to that farm to see if anyone is inside. If it is only the woman and children, then I will return. But if I see more mules, then I will kill him once and for all."

The chief asked, "How many warriors will you take with you?"

"I will go alone. I will take the coward's Winchester rifle and ride the Mule Killer's animal. If I do not return in three days, send a large war party."

Chief Standing Buffalo understood his war chief's desire to build his own legend for killing the Mule Killer on his own but thought it would be better for him to take at least four warriors with him.

He finally gave him permission suspecting that Burning Light would still leave before dawn whether he had received the authorization or not.

Cap cleaned the dishes, then after checking on Erna, he carried the two buckets out of the house and mounted Joe. He didn't bother detaching Jasper as he rode toward Buck Creek. He'd load Jasper with enough firewood to last another day before filling the buckets with fresh water.

It was almost sunset minus the sun when he rode back to the house holding a full bucket of water in each hand as he let Joe find the way. He managed to dismount without spilling any significant amount then carried them into the house before going back outside to strip his mules. He left the branches he'd gathered near the door before he unsaddled Joe and then Jasper. He let them wander off and carried their tack inside. After taking the wood inside and stacking it beside the fireplace, he turned his attention to Erna.

He didn't know if she was sleeping or just pretending so he didn't talk to her. He placed his hat and scarf on one of the tables, then removed his gunbelts and set them on one of the empty chairs.

He smiled at the children who'd been silently watching him and said, "Let's get you ready for bed."

Gustave replied, "Okay. Do we have to keep our coats and hats on?"

"No, Gustave. I'll keep the fire going."

He helped them remove their outerwear and then change into the nightshirts he'd bought at Fort Lincoln's sutler store. After he tucked them in, he added another blanket then kissed each of them on the forehead as he'd watch Erna do when she put them to bed.

"Good night and have pleasant dreams," he whispered.

"Thank you for coming back," Gustave said softly.

"I should have brought you with me the last time I was here, but all I did was leave you candy."

Elsa smiled at him as she said, "And an angel."

He nodded then turned and walked to Erna's bedside where he took a seat on the chair he hadn't moved back to the table.

Her eyes were closed, and she seemed to be sleeping, but he knew that even if she was, she'd have to leave her bed to use the chamber pot soon. He hadn't missed the acrid scent of urine when he was close to the bed and found it hard to imagine her agony and frustration for what had happened to her. He suspected that she might be awake and in addition to needing to use the chamber pot, would need to be cleaned. He'd brought more towels from Bismarck and wasn't surprised to find that Hartmann hadn't taken the bars of soap when he'd stolen most of their supplies.

He leaned closer and whispered, "Are you awake, Erna?"

Erna had been awake for some time and had heard him put her children to sleep. She felt marginally better but wasn't sure she could leave the bed yet despite her driving need to use the chamber pot. She knew that she had dried blood stains on her dress and didn't want Cap to ask how they had gotten there. But her bladder's demands took priority, so she opened her eyes and turned to look at him.

"Can you bring me the chamber pot?"

"Yes, ma'am."

He stepped to the other side of the room and retrieved the recently emptied and cleaned chamber pot. When he returned, he reached for her blanket to pull it away, but she clutched it with both hands.

She quickly said, "I can do it alone."

Cap wasn't surprised by her desire to hide under the blanket, but the strength of her voice was a noticeable and very welcomed improvement.

"I don't believe you can, Erna. But if you want to try, I'll leave it on your bed and turn my back. If you can manage, just let me know when you are done."

He set the chamber pot near her head then stood and turned to face the other wall. He hadn't moved because he was sure that she'd soon need his help.

Erna released her grip and pulled the chamber pot under her blanket. She knew it was going to be difficult, but soon discovered another problem. After hiking up her dress, she realized that she was still wearing her soiled undergarments. It had been difficult removing the first pair, but now she was even weaker. She suddenly understood that she would need Cap's assistance.

She left the chamber pot under the blankets as she prepared to ask for his help. She thought it was ironic that she'd let a man she didn't respect or even like act as her husband yet was now behaving as if she was an innocent virgin. The only good to come of what he saw when he pulled back the blankets was that he'd understand why she couldn't go to Bismarck.

She sighed then said, "I need your help, Cap."

He turned around and as he reached for the blankets, Erna grabbed them again before she asked, “Can you bring a towel and water?”

“Yes, ma’am.”

He stepped away from the bed and took two towels from one of his panniers before he grabbed one of their bars of soap. He dunked one of the towels in the bucket and after wringing it out, he returned to the bed and set both towels and the soap on the chair.

Erna had watched him prepare two towels and had already released her grip on the blankets by the time he’d returned. She didn’t close her eyes again because she wanted to see his reaction when he pulled back the blankets. She expected him to be shocked with what he saw then question her about the blood stains.

Cap did neither as he tossed the blankets aside, then without saying a word, slid her underpants down her legs, pulled them off and tossed them aside. He picked up the chamber pot and took hold of her coat.

“Ready?” he asked.

Erna was still befuddled by his lack of a reaction but assumed he hadn’t seen the blood stains in the dark room, so she replied, “Yes.”

He lifted her middle using the coat and once it was eight inches from the mattress, he slid the chamber pot where it belonged.

Once she felt the cold steel beneath her, Erna quickly relieved herself. When the sound ended, Cap lifted her again, then slid the chamber pot away and slowly lowered her to the mattress. After setting the chamber pot on the floor, he picked up the wet towel, then worked the soap into a lather. Without asking her permission, he lifted her using her coat again and washed her behind, then her private area before he lowered her to the mattress and continued down both of her legs.

Erna was too stunned to feel ashamed or anything else other than the cold water that Cap was using to wash her.

When he'd reached her socks, he tossed the damp towel aside and picked up the other towel and quickly dried her. Then he pulled her dress back down before covering her with the blankets.

After Erna had recovered from her initial shock of his actions, Cap's quiet, unemotional actions had seemed almost medicinal. She didn't understand why she felt so much better, but she did. She looked at him as he pulled her blankets back into place and decided that she had to tell him what had happened.

Cap was about to take the chamber pot outside when Erna said, "Cap, I need to talk to you."

He sat back down and waited for her to tell him what he probably already knew.

She said, “It was too dark, so you didn’t see the blood stains on my dress. It is why I am so weak. I want you to know why they were there.”

“You don’t need to tell me, Erna. I saw them and I understand. I also found the towels and your undergarment in the ashes.”

Erna thought he’d assumed she was having her monthly, so she hurriedly said, “No, you don’t understand at all. Franz gave me a baby and I lost it. I sinned and God punished me.”

She closed her eyes and as tears slid across her cheeks, she waited for Cap to express his disgust.

Instead, she felt his fingertips brush across her damp cheek as he said, “I know, Erna. But you didn’t sin. And God surely wouldn’t punish you for being a good woman.”

Her eyes popped open as she snapped, “But I’m not a good woman! I gave myself to him and he never even said he was going to marry me. Don’t you understand? I am little more than a whore!”

She’d spoken so rapidly that Cap had to take a few seconds to review her rushed German.

He then took her hand and asked, "Why did you let him into your bed, Erna?"

She sighed then softly answered, "I was alone and needed a man to provide for me and my children. You had to leave to work for the railroad."

"Then it was my fault, not yours. When you came into my tent before I left, we both misunderstood what the other really was saying; didn't we?"

"You wanted me to come with you?"

"Yes, but you had seemed so determined to stay on your farm and I wasn't sure what waited for me in Bismarck. When you said that Hartmann was a German and a farmer, I believed that you wanted me to go."

"I wanted you to stay, but knew you weren't a farmer. You told me so."

"If my German was as good then as it is now, then maybe we would have been able to understand each other better."

"Why can you speak better German now?"

"There are many German settlers in Bismarck waiting for the railroad to start again. I speak to them almost every day in my new job. I am a lawman now. I carry a badge and have a house in Bismarck. Will you come with me now?

She hadn't heard him tell her children about his new job or house, so she was surprised when he told her. While it was an incredible temptation, she still wasn't convinced that she was free of guilt for what she'd done.

"Why would you want me to come with you? Aren't there many women in Bismarck?"

"There are many young German and Scandinavian women with their families. The Franco-Prussian war took too many young men."

"Then why would you want to be seen with a woman like me when there are so many unsullied women available?"

"I love your children, Erna. And I know that I've never told you, but I love you even more."

Erna was startled into silence. *Did he really mean it?* She knew how much she cared for him, but she'd never dared to believe that he loved her.

She quietly asked, "Why would you? I'm not a good woman."

"The first day I was here when we had our problems understanding each other, you said that you were a good woman. I knew that you were and nothing I've learned since has changed my opinion. I think that you are the finest woman I've ever met or ever will meet."

"But why? Why would you still believe that after what I did?"

He softly replied, "Look behind me, Erna. See your sleeping children? Everything you've done since I've known you has been for them. You gave yourself to Hartmann to provide for them after I foolishly left. You even let them have the chocolate bars when you were incredibly hungry. You have so much love for your children that you even asked me to take them away from you knowing it would break your heart. You placed their well-being above your own life. A woman with that much love is nothing less than God's most perfect creation."

She closed her eyes and Cap wasn't sure if he'd massacred his reply. He sat watching for more than two minutes without a reply.

He hadn't botched his answer, but Erna still found it almost impossible to believe that he actually meant what he'd told her. But as she thought about it and soon realized that he wouldn't say such a thing unless he actually believed it, she made her decision. But by then, she began losing focus and the need for rest took control driving Erna into a deep sleep before she could agree to return to Bismarck with him and her children. With her full stomach and the warmth from the large fire, she simply couldn't stay awake.

Cap then stood to add more wood to the fire and prepare his bedroll. It was fairly comfortable in the house now, but he had to ensure the fire stayed strong while he slept.

When he returned to her bedside and found her breathing softly, he knew that she wasn't going to continue their conversation. It must have been hard for her to talk as much as she had.

He left the chair in place and laid on his bedroll. He hoped that in the morning, she'd be strong enough to talk more. He had so much to tell her and knew he still needed to convince her to come to Bismarck with him.

CHAPTER 12

It was just after dawn when Burning Light set out on Jed with the Winchester that Cap had given to Erna. He planned to swing well south of the farm and approach from the east. If the Mule Killer was there, he wouldn't be expecting danger from that direction. He didn't believe that it was likely that the Mule Killer was there, but if he found more mules outside the house, he'd pull back and make his plans for his attack. His long, looping approach would take him more than eight hours.

After he'd gone, Chief Standing Buffalo decided he wouldn't wait three days before dispatching a war party. If Burning Light didn't return after two days, then he'd send twenty warriors to avenge his death. The chief was giving Burning Light one day to complete his mission.

Cap had been pleased when Erna was able to use the chamber pot on her own. He carried the pot outside to empty it when he escorted Elsa and Gustave to the privy pit and let Elsa walk the last fifty feet while he waited with Gustave and they used his old fire pit.

The weather may not have returned to the pleasant temperatures it had been the week before, but it had moderated enough to start melting the snow and ice. It made for careful walking and Cap was relieved when Elsa returned from her private time.

He led the children back into the house and after leaving them with their mother, he walked to the fireplace to rebuild the flames.

“Are you feeling better now, Mama?” asked Gustave.

She smiled at her son as she replied, “Yes, Gustave. I feel much better. I’m sorry I frightened you and Elsa.”

Elsa quickly said, “It’s okay, Mama. We understand. Mister Hartmann hurt you before he ran away. He’s a bad man, but Mister Tyler is going to be our papa now; isn’t he?”

Gustave glanced as his sister before saying, “Mister Tyler said he could only be our papa if you agreed to marry him. Will you marry him, Mama?”

Erna nodded then replied, “If he asks.”

Gustave and Elsa both turned to look at Cap as he added more firewood to the growing flames. Elsa then whispered to her brother, who then shook his head. He didn’t think that he should tell Mister Tyler to ask his mother to marry him. It was a grownup question.

Cap had heard most of the conversation and had been surprised by Erna’s answer. After she’d drifted to sleep, he was still unsure if she would agree to come with him. He didn't realize that his last argument about why she should stay with her children had struck home.

When he turned to look at them, he saw Gustave and Elsa staring back at him with their blue eyes almost pleading for him to ask their mother to marry him.

Cap took three long strides away from the fireplace and took his seat at Erna's bedside, flanked by Gustave on his left and Elsa on his right.

"You seem much better this morning, Erna."

"I feel much better, Cap. And I haven't even had breakfast yet."

"I'll cook you and our children a good breakfast soon, but before I do, I need to ask you something."

Erna's heart picked up a few beats as she waited for his question.

Cap took her hand and asked, "Would you rather have bacon or sausage?"

She stared at him dumbfounded as both Elsa and Gustave simply stared in confusion.

He then laughed, took her hand and said, "I was hoping to hear you laugh, but I guess it wasn't the right time. Will you marry me, Erna? Will you come with me to my house in

Bismarck and turn it into a home where we can raise our children?"

A giant smile erupted on Erna's face as she nodded and replied, "Yes, Cap. I'm sorry I was so selfish in what I told you. Now that I'm feeling stronger, I see how incredibly stupid it was."

"You were so tired and hurt that you weren't thinking right. It's nothing to cause you shame. I don't want you to walk until you've fully recovered. But tomorrow, I'll harness the wagon and we'll head back to Bismarck."

"Why can't we wait until I'm well enough to sit beside you?"

"Because I'm a lawman now. I have to return as quickly as possible."

"Oh. I forgot about your new position. Is it so terrible in Bismarck that they can't miss you for another day?"

"Not so much now, but I still have to watch the east side of the town. There are many men who are waiting to work for the railroad. They live in a camp on one side of the road and German and Scandinavian settlers live on the other side. I am the only lawman who can speak any German at all, so I am necessary."

She smiled as she said, "Your German is much better now, but I must improve my English."

"We'll continue our English lessons soon."

Neither of them had noticed the restrained joy in Gustave and Elsa as they managed to keep from bouncing and laughing.

Before he stood to start making breakfast, Cap took her small hand then leaned forward and kissed her gently.

Erna was stunned by the amount of emotion that soft kiss had generated within her. For the two seconds that his lips touched hers, it was as if a whole new world had been opened to her. After he stood and smiled back down at her, she realized that it was exactly what had happened.

When he stepped away from her bedside to prepare breakfast, Gustave and Elsa stood as close to their mother's face as possible without climbing onto her bed and they began rapidly expressing their happiness that she was coming with them to Bismarck. They verbal assault included questions about living in a real house, which neither could even imagine. While Erna explained as well as she could, she had no idea that the house they would soon inhabit was four times larger than the house she grew up in Germany.

As he fried the bacon which would then cool while he warmed the hash browns in the bacon grease, Cap was immensely happy that Erna seemed so much better. He had expected her to be immobile for at least three more days. But he wasn't about to risk having her sit in the driver's seat for that long ride to Bismarck. He'd have her lying on a mattress in the wagon's bed with Gustave and Elsa acting as heaters. He'd have to line up the supplies he'd bought as well as Joe and Jasper's tack on the other side of the wagon's bed, but it should all fit.

But as he planned the trip back to Bismarck, he wondered why he hadn't seen any wheel ruts. They had a wagon before the Lakota burned it and so did the Hartmanns. *So, where were the ruts that they would follow to go to either Fort Lincoln or Bismarck?*

When he shared breakfast with Erna as Gustave and Elsa ate at the table, he asked her about the missing wagon tracks. Erna explained that the few times she'd gone to Bismarck, Wilhelm had taken different routes as he tried to find the best path. The Hartmanns had done the same. She said that the last trip they'd taken in May had been the best one they'd found.

Cap still thought he should have seen some tracks, but let it go. As a surveyor, he had an eye for the lay of the land and had marked his own trail from the ferry to the farm. He'd follow the same path back tomorrow. If they left early enough, they could reach the ferry well before sunset.

It was a pleasant morning, but Cap wanted to start preparing for tomorrow's journey. So, after a filling lunch, he left the house and walked to the wagon to get it ready for the trip.

The wheels were all well-greased and the leather was good enough, so all he needed to do was to figure out the loading. He knew the width of the mattress, so he moved Joe and Jasper's tack to the front on the right side of the bed. Then he started moving some of the supplies from the house but left enough behind for supper and breakfast.

As he lugged the loaded panniers from the house, Burning Light was riding past the farm just four miles south. While he couldn't see the farm, he spotted the smoke from the fire and knew he only had a short ride before the looped back to the east. The fire meant that someone was in the house and he hoped that the Mule Killer had returned. He was already envisioning their heroic confrontation. It would become legend.

Burning Light's only concern was the rifle that the Mule Killer used to kill from a long distance. He had to be careful when he approached but he had learned that as long as he was far enough away that if he saw the Mule Killer fire his long rifle, then he'd have enough time to avoid the deadly bullet. If it was Winchester on Winchester, then it would be a fair fight.

———

While he had been loading the wagon, Joe and Jasper had stood nearby just watching. Cap wondered if they realized what they would be doing tomorrow then snickered. They weren't that smart.

He couldn't move the mattress and blankets until the morning, so before he finished loading what he could, he did one final inspection of the wagon. He couldn't afford to lose another wheel or have any other serious issues like a broken axle. He took off his hat and set it on the wagon's bed before dropping to the ground and sliding under the wagon. He carefully checked both axles for cracks and then inspected the yoke. All were in good condition and shouldn't give him any trouble tomorrow.

When he slid out from under the wagon, he removed his new coat and beat the dirt that had accumulated before pulling it back on. The sky was still cloudy, but the temps were improving. He wished that the sun stayed behind those clouds for one more day because he wanted to be able to see where he was going as they traveled east.

He then climbed into the driver's seat and looked to the east to look for landmarks to the north or south that would help him navigate if the sun tried to blind him. He spotted the trees along Buck Creek that the Hartmanns used for their firewood, then slowly shifted his eyes to the south for another landmark. Then he spotted a lone rider just at the edge of the horizon. He was so far off, that Cap couldn't determine anything about him or his mount. His telescope was in his saddlebags, but by the time he retrieved it, the rider would be gone. He continued to watch to see if there were more riders, but he only saw the one until he disappeared. There could have been more with him, but it was where he was that bothered Cap.

There were no settlers south of the Braun or Hartmann farms because they were at the far end of the Northern Pacific's land grants. The only other settlements were north and east. The rider could have been part of an army patrol, but he found it hard to imagine seeing one army cavalryman without seeing many more.

That meant he was probably a Lakota. *But why was he there all by himself?*

He hopped down from the wagon and pulled on his hat as he tried to come up with a reason for the presence of a Lakota warrior so far from his village. He could be scouting, but that didn't make any sense because they had recently raided both farms and knew that there was nothing left.

Cap sat on the back of the wagon and looked to the east where the Indian was riding. All that was in that direction was the Hartmann farm. The moment the name Hartmann reached his mind, he made the connection to Franz. He wouldn't have been surprised if Franz had run afoul of the Lakota, even if he hadn't been trailing Jed. Maybe he told them some tall tale of undiscovered loot at his family farm in the hope that they'd let him live. But even if they had believed him, they wouldn't have sent a lone warrior to investigate his claim. It wasn't perfect, but it was as close as he could get to a solution to the riddle.

He'd continue with his preparations, but now the possibility of another Indian raid was planted in his mind. He'd have to be ready to protect his new family. If they were able to leave in the wagon tomorrow, he'd have to be more vigilant than usual, and the sun could be his biggest enemy if it finally came out of hiding.

As he walked back to the house, he was unsure of whether or not he should tell Erna about what he'd seen. He quickly decided that it made no difference if she knew. She was still weak and now with the prospect of a new and better life for her and the children, he wasn't about to add uncertainty to that future. He'd deal with the Lakota if they came.

———

Burning Light hadn't realized that he'd been spotted and soon made his wide loop to the north and then west. Just before he made the turn westward, he pulled Jed to a stop and looked down. He smiled when he saw two sets of shod hoofprints that were less than three days old. The Mule Killer had returned after all. *But what was he planning to do now that he was here?* Even Burning Light knew that the man wasn't a farmer, so he had to have come to bring the woman and her children away to the big town.

He followed the tracks westward and kept watching the smoke rising into the cloudy sky ahead. When the roof of the house appeared, he stopped and dismounted. He walked another two hundred yards until the distant farmhouse came into view. When he stopped walking, he studied the structure and noticed the wagon parked nearby. He wanted to avoid the risk of being seen but had to know what the Mule Killer was going to do. So, he mounted Jed again and walked him closer to the house. The added height and closing distance soon gave him his answer. He quickly turned the mule around and trotted away. He kept riding because he knew where he would stay the night. The coward's farm was just ahead, and he would stay in one of the small houses and make his plans for tomorrow's confrontation with the Mule Killer.

In Bismarck, Cap's extended absence was causing some measure of concern with Sheriff Donavan. They'd expected him to return yesterday. But Charlotte had told him to be patient as Cap was probably trying to convince Mrs. Braun to come to Bismarck.

While he understood her reasoning, there was another reason for his worries. Since the saloon had been burnt to the ground, everything had remained quiet for two days. He'd been doing the rounds on the eastern side of town since Cap had gone and this morning, he'd noticed a return to the open hostility from some of them that he had hoped never to see again. He didn't know what had changed but would feel a lot better if Cap was back. If he knew the reason, he might have been even more worried.

After Hardy returned to Jamestown in the hope of reclaiming his job, he was more than just rebuffed by Marshal

Rushton. He was close to being ridden out of town on a rail. It seems that Sheriff Donavan had sent a telegram to his old boss with an accusation of cowardice under fire.

He didn't wait for anyone to find a riding rail and quickly headed back west with no idea where he'd go. He thought about that marshal's position in Mandan but knew that the sheriff would probably stop that from happening.

As he neared Bismarck, he noticed the still smoldering wreck of the saloon and pulled up. He'd heard stories in Jamestown of that gunfight and how Cap had killed the leaders of the camp. Maybe they needed a new man to take charge.

He turned his horse into the camp and studied the men who stared at him. He doubted if any of them remembered him from his brief visit the last time, but they weren't exactly happy to see him. They probably saw him as competition.

It took him more than an hour to find the two men who were trying to establish their control over the others. They were closer to shooting him than listening when he first began explaining the advantages that they would gain by letting him join their partnership. He talked quickly, telling them that he knew all the lawmen, including Cap Tyler, and would be able to show them the best way to deal with all of them. Once the badge wearers were gone, then they'd have free reign over the town.

While Hardy himself didn't believe that he'd be able to deliver on his promises, he was a good salesman. Fred Thomas and John Wickersham eventually agreed to let him stay the night to convince them that he could do what he said he could.

It had taken him another full day before he had been accepted as a partner and then they began recruiting more men to their side. There weren't as many as Hardy had hoped because most of the men weren't troublemakers and many of those who were had witnessed Cap's shootouts.

Coop never spotted Hardy as he rode through the camp, but he'd been watched by his short-term deputy as he passed by. Soon, Hardy would have his revenge on the sheriff for that telegram. He wasn't going to be gentlemanly about it, either. He learned that the sheriff had been making the rounds as Cap Tyler had gone off somewhere. Now he planned to take advantage of Tyler's absence.

———

Cap had everything ready and after scanning the horizons, he entered the house and put the locking bar in place.

After he cooked and served their supper, he explained his plans for tomorrow. After he harnessed Joe and Jasper, he would move the children's mattress, pillow and blankets to the wagon. Then after they had a quick breakfast, he'd carry Erna to the wagon and set her on the mattress. Gustave and Elsa would snuggle close, and he'd cover them with the blankets. Then they'd start the long journey to the ferry south of Bismarck.

He didn't talk about what he'd be doing with his rifles. When he'd found the horizons empty, he was reasonably sure that they'd be able to leave the farm without a problem. It was when they approached the Hartmann farm that he expected to find trouble. He wasn't sure how many Lakota he might encounter, but he'd have his Sharps and his Winchester '76 close and he'd be wearing both of his Remingtons. The Lakota would have to have a large war party to get past him, and he didn't think that there had been that many hidden from his sight yesterday.

After tucking the children into bed and kissing them on their foreheads, Cap stepped to Erna's bedside and sat down.

"Is this really happening, Cap?" she asked quietly.

"Yes, Erna. It is real. Tomorrow night, you will be sleeping in a bed that is half the size of this room."

Erna thought he was joking, so she laughed before asking, "And this new house where you will take us is so big that it fills a city block all by itself?"

"No, but it is much bigger than you might expect. I didn't even want to buy it because it was so big, but my new boss wanted to get rid of it, so I did."

She then asked, “You weren’t making a joke about the size of the bed?”

“I might have made it sound too big, but it is much larger than any I’d ever seen before.”

Erna’s joyous mood evaporated as she slowly said, “Cap, I can’t be a wife to you until I’m healed.”

He took her hand and replied, “I know we can’t share the bed until you have recovered, Erna. I just want you to be warm and happy. You can tell me when you are sure that it won’t hurt. Okay?”

She nodded then asked, “What if I never recover enough? Have you thought of that?”

“No, I won’t lie and tell you that I’ve already accepted that possibility. But don’t worry about what is in our future, Erna. We will meet any problems that await us.”

Erna smiled before she asked, “Will you kiss me again? Only longer?”

Cap stood then bent over and slid his hand behind her head before he kissed her much more passionately than she probably expected. He needed to let her understand in a language that needed no translation.

Erna had put her left hand behind Cap's neck when his lips met hers and soon was engulfed with newfound emotions that threatened to overwhelm her.

When they separated, she whispered, "Thank you, Cap. It was wonderful."

"You deserve all the love I can give to you, Erna."

She was still in ecstasy over that one kiss as she smiled at him. She prayed that she wouldn't have to wait for very long before they shared their marital bed. The amount of passion they had exchanged made that special night incredibly promising. Yet was just as important to her was that even as she recognized his desires as a man, she felt his tenderness. It was almost startling.

Cap then prepared for sleep by stretching out on his bedroll in his coat. The fire was still strong, but it would be just glowing embers come morning. He wasn't going to rebuild it for breakfast because he wanted to be able to begin rolling as soon as possible. He'd make a quick survey of the landscape for the Lakota but wouldn't be surprised not to find them. If they were still in the area, they'd be east, near the Hartmann farm.

He had his gunbelts and his Winchester on the floor by his right side but was confident they wouldn't be necessary tonight. Hopefully, he wouldn't need them tomorrow, either.

———

Burning Light had brought Jed into the house with him for the night. The mule would keep the house warmer. He had packed enough food to last three days, but strongly believed that tomorrow evening, he'd be having his meal in his own lodge after having taken the life of the Mule Killer.

———

Cap had exited the house in the predawn and after a quick scan of the empty horizons and using his firepit one last time, he whistled for Joe and Jasper who were grazing a good three hundred yards away. They might have been annoyed for having their breakfast disturbed, but they didn't complain before they quickly trotted to the house.

Cap rubbed their necks as he said, "Sorry for the demotion, boys," then guided Jasper into the right side of the harness.

After placing the collar over his neck and attaching the straps and reins, he brought Joe in beside him and soon had them both in harness. They still didn't complain, and Cap appreciated their patience.

He then returned to the house and after serving his cold breakfast, he rolled the blankets, pillow and mattress from the children's bed and carried it out to the wagon. Once they were all in place, he returned for his most precious cargo.

He smiled down at Erna and asked, "Are you ready for the long ride?"

She smiled back as she replied, “Very much.”

Cap then rolled her two blankets and set them on the floor. Gustave struggled to pick them up, so Elsa took one end of the roll while Cap slid his arms under Erna and lifted her easily from the bed. She rested her head on his shoulder and felt as safe and comfortable as she'd ever been in her life.

He followed the children out the door leaving it open because it no longer mattered. He soon reached the wagon and gently laid Erna on the mattress before hopping inside and sliding her to the top. He then took the rolled blankets from the children before helping them into the bed and waited for them to almost burrow into their mother's coat before he covered them with blankets. Elsa was still clutching her doll which made him smile. He reminded himself to buy Gustave another penknife. Maybe one with a slightly bigger blade. He was about to lay the last two blankets on top, but it was reasonably pleasant, so he just tossed them with the rest of the supplies.

Before hopping down, he looked at the three blonde heads peering out from under the blankets and asked, “Ready to go?”

Each of them nodded and Gustave shouted, “Let's go to Bismarck!”

Cap grinned then dropped to the ground and walked to the front of the wagon and climbed into the driver's seat. The sun had made its appearance which would have been welcomed just a few days ago, but its timing was terrible. He couldn't do anything about it, so he snapped the reins, and Joe and Jasper began pulling the wagon into the blazing sun.

Four miles east of the wagon, Burning Light had mounted Jed and with his Winchester in his hand, set off to the west following the same trail he'd used yesterday. He hoped to catch the Mule Killer driving the wagon but if he was still in the house, he would call out to him with a challenge. Either way, he'd have the advantage of having the blinding sun at his back.

He'd only ridden for a few minutes when he spotted the wagon and knew that the gods were smiling on him. He didn't see the woman or her children, but they didn't matter. He only wanted the Mule Killer.

Cap hadn't spotted Burning Light because of the sun, but because the way ahead was his only blind spot, he was employing the only method he knew how to block the sun. He would lower his eyes and use his palm to block the sun then raise his head until the first rays reached his pupils. Then he'd drop his head slightly until he could see ahead. Joe and Jasper seemed to have accepted their new duties well and had the wagon moving at a good clip as they rumbled eastward over the rough ground.

It was only when he was within a thousand yards of Burning Light that Cap spotted him and immediately pulled the wagon to a stop.

He reached into the wagon well for his Sharps but didn't cock the hammer as he watched the Lakota warrior. He couldn't see any others with him, so he was puzzled by the man's behavior. He was still walking his horse closer and had his rifle in his hand. This wasn't a situation that he'd come across before and as he watched the lone Sioux warrior get within four hundred yards, he was about to cock his Sharps hammer when he realized that he wasn't riding a horse. He was riding Jed, and that clarified everything in an instant. The Lakota wanted to challenge him one on one.

Erna felt the wagon stop and after it had remained motionless for thirty seconds, she asked, "Cap, is there something wrong?"

"I have a visitor approaching. I have to meet him. I'll be back soon."

He didn't clarify his answer before he lifted his Sharps into the air, then returned it to the footwell before he grabbed his Winchester, showed it to the warrior and clambered down from the driver's seat. He wanted the Sioux to believe that he was offering him a fair fight, but he didn't mind being accused of cheating. He had his family to protect, and the advantage provided by his more powerful '76 was his ace in the hole.

Burning Light had seen the man raise his long-distance rifle then set it back down before leaving the wagon with his Winchester. He knew that he was now facing the real Mule Killer and not that coward who had his mule. This man had courage and was so arrogant that he was going to face him with no advantage while he had the sun at his back. For a man who had survived so many fights with the Sioux and the Cheyenne, he was behaving foolishly.

He slid down from Jed and cocked his Winchester's hammer before he began walking toward the Mule Killer. He kept his long shadow pointing at his opponent ensuring that the sun would protect him.

Cap watched the Lakota drop down from Jed and was surprised that he'd chosen to leave his mule. He still had his left palm over his eyes to block out the sun, so he was able to watch Burning Light as they drew within three hundred yards. He knew that the moment he had to fire, the sun would be almost directly over the Lakota's head. He'd have to aim low at his feet, the raise the sights just a bit before he squeezed his trigger. He knew that he'd only get one shot before the Sioux realized he was at a disadvantage. If he missed, then he'd have to use his second surprise that had just entered the picture.

The adversaries were about two hundred yards apart and Burning Light continued his slow walk keeping his shadow pointed at the Mule Killer. He expected to take his first shot in about a minute or so but knew that the Mule Killer wouldn't waste ammunition and believed that he'd let Burning Light take the first shot.

Cap knew he was within range but waited for the Lakota to start bringing his repeater to bear. Once he saw that Winchester move, he'd take aim at the warrior's feet and make his adjustments. He expected to hear the crack of a Winchester '73 before he fired.

Burning Light was annoyed when he discovered that he was growing anxious. He'd been in many battles before and hadn't even given a thought to the danger yet facing the Mule Killer alone was much different. He suddenly stopped walking and whipped his Winchester into a firing position.

The moment the Lakota had stopped walking, Cap lifted his Winchester and set the sights on the warrior's feet. He was bringing the barrel up two inches when Burning Light fired. Cap felt the .44 whiz past his right ear before he pulled his trigger. His .45 raced across the hundred and twenty-two yards of Dakota prairie and nicked the left side of Burning Light's pelvis. He rocked a half-turn counterclockwise but didn't fall. He felt blood soaking his buckskin but still prepared for his second shot.

The Lakota's first shot had been much more accurately placed than Cap expected, so even though he'd seen his shot strike the man's left side, he knew he was in danger and decided to rely on his secret weapon to distract the shooter. He suddenly whistled loudly as Burning Light was preparing to fire. The Lakota warrior was momentarily confused by the Mule Killer's whistle until he heard the pounding hoofbeats then turned his head as Jed raced past him.

In that brief moment of distraction, Cap again sighted on his target's feet and after bringing the muzzle up another two inches, he fired. His second .45 struck Burning Light in the right side of his torso, just below his rib cage. The slug of lead ripped through his liver, destroying arteries and veins before it exited his back.

He dropped to his knees and didn't feel any pain before he fell face forward into the dirt.

Cap immediately turned and jogged back to the wagon. He couldn't risk the possibility that more Lakota were nearby. He soon hopped onto the driver's seat and snapped the reins.

As Jed reached the wagon, he turned and began matching Joe's strides.

Erna exclaimed, "*What happened, Cap?*"

"A Lakota warrior must have wanted to kill me and challenged me to a duel. He lost. We need to keep moving in case he had friends. I'll tell you more when I feel we're safe. Okay?"

"Alright," she replied as she hugged her children.

Cap slowed when he reached the dead warrior, then stopped the wagon, hopped down and recovered the Winchester. He soon returned to the driver's seat and as Joe and Jasper continued pulling the wagon east, he examined the Winchester and wasn't surprised to find it had been the one that he'd given to Erna. It had an easily remembered serial number that ended in three sevens. With Jed trotting next to Joe, it was the final bit of proof of what had become of Franz Hartmann.

They soon passed the Hartmann farm and continued east at a brisk, but rugged pace. It wasn't quite noon when Cap felt that they were out of danger because they were too close to Fort Lincoln for the Sioux to dare to attack. He had already explained much of what had happened, so now he just needed to feed his family.

He pulled Joe and Jasper to a stop, then stepped down and walked to the back of the wagon. After he climbed onto the bed, he crawled between the supplies and the mattress and laid down on his side with Gustave's face between him and Erna.

"Are we safe now?" she asked.

"Yes, ma'am. Fort Lincoln is just about fifteen miles northeast of where we are. We have another four or five hours before we reach the ferry. I'll give you all something to eat and if you need to water the prairie, let me know."

Gustave giggled, then slid carefully out from the blankets and made his way to the back of the wagon before dropping to the ground.

When Elsa slipped out from the other side, Cap had to leave quickly to help her from the wagon, but once she was on the ground, he returned to get the chamber pot for Erna.

With everyone's bodily needs satisfied, he quickly went through the panniers and began giving them corn dodgers and slices of ham. It wasn't a feast, but it was more than they'd had before he reached their house.

The sun was low in the sky when he spotted the ferry in the distance and told his family that they'd be across the Missouri River soon. He half-expected to find the ferry already closed for the day to balance all of the good luck they'd had so far that day. But the ferryman was still at his post, so when they reached the ferry, he paid the man a dollar even though the normal fee for a wagon and spare mule would have been forty cents.

It was approaching sunset when Cap drove the wagon onto Main Avenue. He was debating about stopping by the sheriff's office to let them know he was back when he soon realized it was unnecessary. Sheriff Donavan had just reached Main Avenue to make his evening rounds of the east end when he spotted Cap and changed his direction.

Cap pulled the wagon to a stop and waited for his boss to reach him.

When he did, Coop asked, "What happened, Cap? We expected you to get back yesterday. And why didn't you bring Mrs. Braun and the children? Charlotte is going to let me have it."

Cap grinned then said, "Erna, say hello to Sheriff Donavan. Call him Coop."

Erna laughed then said, "Hello, Coop. I'd sit up but my arms are full of children."

Coop grinned as he shook his head then said, "You go ahead home. You can tell me what happened tomorrow. I was going to make your rounds on the east side, but I figure they can go a day. I'll tell Charlotte that you returned with your new family."

He then wheeled his horse around and headed for Second Street before Cap turned the wagon toward the big house, hoping that it didn't scare Erna.

Neither of them would ever know that Cap's timely arrival had saved Coop's life.

———

Cap soon turned the wagon down the drive along the northern side of the house but none of his passengers could see it in from behind the wagon's sideboards. The light was already fading, so all they could see were large shadows overhead on their right.

He pulled the wagon to a stop, set the handbrake, then hopped down.

"I have to unlock the door and I'll be right back," he said loudly before he bounded up the back porch stairs.

After unlocking the door, he left it open and hurried back to the wagon.

"Gustave and Elsa, we're home now."

They crawled out from under the blankets being sure to leave them over their mother before sliding toward Cap. He lowered Gustave to the ground first before lifting Elsa and her doll from the wagon. Both stood looking up at the massive structure with both their eyes and mouths wide open.

Cap then tossed aside the blankets, slid the mattress and Erna from the bed until her lower legs were hanging over the edge.

Erna was watching him as he slid his long arms under her knees and back and hadn't noticed the house yet. As he lifted her from the wagon, she rested her head on his shoulder and closed her eyes. She was so incredibly content being in his arms that she simply wanted to live in the sensation.

Cap carried her carefully up the steps and crossed the varnished porch with Gustave and Elsa walking behind them. He turned and sidestepped through the door to avoid banging Erna's head before entering the dark and chilly kitchen. Leading the children, he passed through the kitchen and turned into the first of the two first-floor bedrooms. He laid her gently on the normal-sized bed before Elsa and Gustave arrived to stand by her bedside.

She finally opened her eyes and smiled as she said, "This is very soft."

"I have to unharness the mules then move things inside. Before I do that, I'll light some lamps and start a fire in the heat stove. Then I'll cook us supper."

"Thank you, Cap," Erna said.

"You're welcome, ma'am."

Then he turned to Gustave and Elsa and said, "I need you both to stay with your mother until I light those lamps. Okay?"

They both nodded before they began scanning the shadowed room that was bigger and fancier than anything they'd ever seen before. Yet it was the small bedroom of the housemaid employed by the bank president who must have believed himself to be a prince of industry before the Panic.

Cap quickly lit the lamp in the bedroom, then started a fire in the room's small heat stove. He left the room and walked to the kitchen where he lit another lamp then started a fire in the elephantine cookstove.

He left the back door open and began transferring the supplies to the house, leaving his mules' tack for storage in his barn. It wasn't as small as one would expect on a private residence and had enough room for four horses and a carriage. Today, it would house three mules and a wagon.

It took him just ten minutes to move the wagon to the barn and let his three mules loose to enjoy the oats and water waiting for them.

As Cap was unloading his wagon, Charlotte was unloading on her new husband.

"You didn't even ask how she and her children were doing?"

Coop sheepishly replied, "She sounded all right to me, Charlotte. Cap didn't say she was doing poorly or anything."

"Then why wasn't she sitting in the driver's seat with him, sir?"

"Um, I reckon that she wanted to be with her youngsters."

Charlotte snapped, "We'll take some hot food over there shortly. They must be starved after that long journey."

"Yes, ma'am."

Charlotte wasn't really as angry as she made herself appear. She was enormously pleased that Cap had brought Mrs. Braun and her children to Bismarck and wanted to hear the story. Bringing them warm food was just her entrance ticket.

———

On the east end of town Fred Thomas and John Wickersham had already grown suspicious of Hardy's claims and plans. When the sheriff failed to even show up for his rounds, they were close to booting him out their large tent which served as a temporary replacement for the destroyed saloon.

"Give me one more day, boys! I'll take him out when he comes by in the morning. Then we'll just have those two kids to deal with."

Fred snarled, "It ain't the kids we're worried about, Hardy. What will you do if Tyler shows up in the mornin'? Are you gonna put a .44 into him or are you gonna pee in your britches?"

"I'm not afraid of him or anyone else. If he shows up, I'll kill him. You'll see."

John looked at Fred and asked, "Do we give him one more chance?"

Fred huffed then replied, "I don't think he's got the guts to do it, but maybe he'll get lucky and one of those baby deputies will show up."

John then glared at Hardy as he said, "We'll give you one more chance to prove yourself. If you pull it off, then we'll let you join us."

Hardy tried to smile but only managed a grimace as he nodded. He realized that he may have bit off more than he could chew. He debated making a break out of this hodge-podge village in the night but suspected that they'd put a bullet in his back if he tried. He had to build up his confidence that he could backshoot the sheriff tomorrow. He'd never even shot at a man before but was sure that he now had more than enough motivation to go through with it.

Cap was in the kitchen and had finally removed his hat, coat and Remingtons. He reminded himself to make use of one of the two bathtubs as soon as possible.

After lighting a few more lamps, he'd given permission for Gustave and Elsa to explore the first floor but told Gustave to hold his sister's hand, so she didn't trip over the rugs.

He had just set the frypan on the stove when he was startled by loud knocking at the front door. He knew it had to be the sheriff because no one else knew he'd returned.

Elsa and Gustave were in the big parlor running their small hands over the upholstered furniture when Charlotte and Coop stepped onto the porch. Before Coop even knocked, they had turned and hurried back down the hallway and almost plowed into Cap.

He caught them and said, "It's probably my boss."

Gustave exhaled in relief then said, "Okay," before they continued back down the hallway, across the parlor and entered the foyer.

When Cap opened the door, he smiled when he saw Coop and Charlotte. Charlotte was carrying a covered platter and Coop held a large basket in his hand.

"Please come in," Cap said.

As they passed, Charlotte smiled at him and Coop made one of those 'not my idea' faces.

Charlotte's eyes immediately latched onto Elsa cherubic face as she clasped her doll close. It was as if she feared that the strange lady would take it away. She then smiled at Gustave, but even Cap could tell that she'd fallen in love with Elsa.

Charlotte pried her eyes from Elsa then turned to Cap and said, "We brought food because I wanted to make sure that you fed your new family."

"I was just about to start cooking, but I'm sure whatever you brought is much better."

"Where is Mrs. Braun?" Charlotte asked as she peered down the hallway.

"Erna is in the bedroom on the left near the kitchen. I found her and the children in a bad situation and she's still weak. She's recovering quickly, so I'm sure she'll be back to normal soon. I'll explain after I introduce you."

Erna had heard them talking and picked up most of what Cap had said, so she prepared herself for their arrival. Cap had already helped her out of her coat. She had burned the bloody dress, which was a hideous reminder of that horrid time, but she still felt ill-prepared to meet Cap's boss and his wife. Cap hadn't talked about them much because they had so many other things to discuss. But she decided that if Cap liked them, they must be good people.

She heard them coming down the hallway and soon Gustave and Elsa popped into the room followed by Cap, but their visitors continued past to the kitchen.

He sat at the chair he'd set near her bedside and took her hand.

"My boss and his wife brought warm food for supper. They'll leave it in the kitchen and will come to visit soon. Call him Coop and his wife is Charlotte."

"It will be acceptable to use their Christian names?"

Cap smiled as he replied, "Yes, Erna. It is acceptable."

Just as he finished assuring her of the proprieties, Charlotte entered the room and smiled at Erna as she approached the foot of her bed. Coop trailed behind.

She stepped around Cap and said, "Welcome to your new home. May I call you Erna?"

Erna smiled as she nodded then said, "My English isn't very good."

"I understand. It's better than my German which is non-existent. We won't stay long because we know you must be tired from your journey."

Erna was still uneasy by addressing her as Charlotte, but still replied, "Thank you, Charlotte. I am better now but tired."

Charlotte glanced at Gustave and Elsa and said, "You have beautiful children."

"Yes. I am fortunate."

"Let me feed them and you and maybe I'll let Cap eat a little," she said before turning and walking out of the room.

Coop wasn't sure if he was supposed to go with her, but Charlotte took his elbow and made the decision for him.

After they'd gone, Elsa said, "They seem very nice."

"They are good people," he replied, then chose his German carefully when he asked, "May I tell Charlotte of your difficulties? She is an understanding woman and can help you much better than I."

Erna was initially horrified at the idea but after searching Cap's caring eyes for a few seconds, she slowly nodded.

"Perhaps she could help."

He sighed in relief that she hadn't been hurt before he smiled and said, "I'll share supper with you shortly."

After kissing her gently, he guided Gustave and Elsa from the room.

Erna had only agreed because Cap had asked, and she knew that she would never be able to repay the enormous debt for all that he'd done for her and her children.

Cap stepped into warm kitchen where Charlotte and Coop had already set the table. She was reheating the roast beef and spiced, boiled small potatoes and already had the coffeepot on the stove waiting for the water to boil.

Gustave had to help Elsa onto her tall chair before he took his seat. They both continued to scan the kitchen with its walls of pots and cookware, shelves of china and glassware. They saw the heavy door to the cold room and wondered what was hidden inside. It was almost like being in an enchanted castle.

Cap stepped closer to Charlotte and Coop before he said, “Charlotte, I need to ask you for your help caring for Erna.”

She turned and replied, “I thought you might.”

Coop listened as Cap said, “When I arrived, I found that Franz Hartmann had abandoned them. He’d taken all their food except for some tins that they couldn’t open. If that wasn’t bad enough, before he’d gone, he backhanded Erna and then when she accused him of being a coward, he punched her in the stomach.”

Charlotte snapped, “That bastard! He should be hanged!”

“There’s no need. The Sioux caught up with him. I’ll explain that later. But the reason he struck her was that he discovered that she was pregnant. She…”

Charlotte wished she had a gun in her hand rather than a spatula when she interrupted him again by growling, “Hell is too good for him!”

“I agree with you, Charlie. But she was so injured by that blow that she lost the baby. The combination of the injury, miscarriage, cold and lack of food for two days brought her close to death. You can see how small she is. When I arrived, I wasn't sure I could save her. I did all I could, and she seems to be recovering much more quickly than I could have hoped, but I'm over my head now. She needs to see a doctor and have a good woman to help her."

"Don't worry, Cap. I'll help all I can. Angela can watch the boarding house in my absence, and I'll have my husband fetch Doctor Bloomberg in the morning. You need to get back to work and reign in that east side of town again. Coop has been making those rounds and it's making me nervous."

Cap smiled as he replied, "He's been doing this job much longer than I have, ma'am."

"That's true, but you seem to have a knack for dealing with those troublemakers. Even Coop says that you can handle them better than he can."

Cap looked at the sheriff who just shrugged.

"Thank you, Charlotte. It'll put my mind at ease knowing that Erna will have a kind heart to watch over her."

"She already has a kind heart, Cap."

"But if I'd taken her away from that farm on my last visit, she wouldn't have been hurt so badly."

Coop said, “Don’t blame yourself for what Hartmann did. We’ll talk in the morning when you return from your rounds. Okay?”

Cap nodded as Charlotte began moving the food to the plates. After filling two, she carried them to the children and set them on the table. She smiled at Gustave and Elsa and expected them to dig in, but they didn’t. She didn’t ask why before she turned back to the stove.

After she’d stepped away from the cookstove, Cap slid the hot coffeepot from the hotplate to one of the warming plates and dumped in a half-full measuring cup of ground coffee.

Charlotte then asked, “Why aren’t the children eating?”

Cap glanced at Gustave and Elsa as they patiently sat before their loaded plates knowing that their small stomachs were probably loudly protesting.

Without answering her question, Cap stepped over to the table, took a seat and nodded to Gustave before bowing his head.

Gustave then said grace and didn’t even rush the words. When he finished, he smiled at Charlotte and then surprised her again when he began cutting Elsa’s meat.

Charlotte hurried to their table and took over the job letting Gustave start his attack on his own food.

Cap then filled two more plates and placed them and the necessary cutlery on one of the large trays. He filled two cups with hot coffee and carried it out of the kitchen.

When he entered the bedroom, he found Erna staring at him with questioning eyes. He suspected that she'd only been able to understand some of the English spoken in the kitchen and was desperate to know how much he'd told Charlotte.

He set the tray on his chair and pulled a second one beside it before taking a seat.

"Can you sit?" he asked.

"I think so."

He wanted to help her but hoped she could manage it on her own. So, he simply placed his left hand under her right shoulder but didn't lift as she began to rise from the bed.

When she reached a sitting position, she smiled and said, "It wasn't as bad as I had expected."

"I'm happy that you're doing so much better, Erna."

He then moved the tray to her lap and moved his supper to the chair.

Erna inhaled and said, "The food smells very good. Is it beef?"

"Yes, ma'am."

As much as she wanted to ask about his conversation with Charlotte, she couldn't resist the power of the nourishment sitting on her lap. She still managed to control her desire to inhale the aromatic beef and potatoes. There was even a small crock of butter and a biscuit alongside the plate. It was almost a feast. Then she remembered the last time she'd had a feast. It was the turkey that they'd shared before Franz had arrived and ruined everything. She pushed aside that memory and began to empty her plate.

Cap watched her as she ate as he was concerned that she might fall back before she finished. But she seemed to be doing well and after she was halfway done, he was confident she would be all right.

She hadn't quite finished when she sighed, then picked up the china cup of coffee and held it tightly in her hands as she took a sip.

After taking a second sip, she set it down then looked at Cap and asked, "Did you tell Charlotte?"

"Yes, Erna. I told her what Hartmann had done to you and how he'd hurt you. He was probably fortunate that the Lakota discovered him before she did. She told me that she will come here in the morning to help you and that she will have a doctor come as well."

"Why do I need a doctor? I am improving."

"Just to be sure that you will grow stronger. But when she arrives, I need to go back to work. I think something bad is happening at that camp I told you about."

Erna set her cup down and asked, "You have to stay safe now, Cap. Please be careful."

"I'm always careful. But now I'll even be more so because I have a family to protect and provide for. I'll stop by at lunch time to see how you are doing just to make you feel better and hear what the doctor said. Okay?"

Erna slowly nodded as she began to pick at her remaining food. After all they'd gone through, she had a horrible sense of dread that something terrible was about to happen.

Cap soon finished eating, then loaded the tray again. After she laid back down, he kissed her then carried the tray from the room.

As he entered the kitchen, Charlotte asked, "Which of those packs contains Erna's personal things?"

He pointed to the second one from the end before Charlotte quickly stepped to the pannier, opened the flap and rummaged through Erna's belongings until she found what she wanted and carried them from the kitchen.

Erna's bedroom door soon closed, so Cap said, "Gustave, I think it's time for you and Elsa to get some sleep. I'm going to let you share the second bedroom on this floor for the night. Okay?"

Gustave nodded then said, "Okay," before he dropped to the floor and helped Elsa from her perch.

Cap found their nightshirts, then walked with them to the second bedroom. After lighting a lamp, he helped them undress and put on their nightshirts before lifting Elsa onto the bed. While it was no bigger than the bed that Erna was using, it was still a good foot wider than the one they shared at the farmhouse.

But it was the multicolored quilt that seemed to impress Elsa. After she was snuggled under the blankets and the quilt, she hugged her doll with her right arm and ran her fingers over the quilt's decorative patches.

"This is pretty," Elsa said as she continued to stroke the quilt.

"It will keep you warm, too," Cap said as he let Gustave climb into his side of the bed.

After they were both covered up to their chins, he kissed each of them on the forehead before blowing out the lamp. When he turned, he found Coop watching from the doorway.

Cap left the door open and followed Coop down the hallway past Erna's closed bedroom door. They each filled a cup with coffee before sitting at the table.

Coop grinned as he said, “I think that cute little girl will give Charlotte some ideas about having her own.”

Cap asked, “She never had any children with Mister Groom?”

“Nope. She thinks that she’s barren, but I hope she’s wrong. She’d be a wonderful mother.”

Cap then asked, “So, what’s going on with the bad boys out east?”

“Everything was okay for a couple of days, but then the last time I visited, they seemed angrier. I do know that a couple of them have set up a temporary saloon of sorts in a large tent just about fifty yards east of the one you burned down. I haven’t had any incidents, but I can’t speak to the Germans across the way to ask.”

“Some can speak some English and they would have come to the jail looking for me if they had a real problem. I’ll talk to them in the morning.”

Coop nodded then said, “Before Charlotte comes back, can you give me a quick rundown of what happened?”

Cap had already told them what Franz Hartmann had done, so he picked it up from their departure and the facedown with the Lakota warrior who had ridden Jed for the confrontation. It didn’t take long, but Coop had to agree that it was an unusual situation.

“Do you reckon more Sioux will be showing up looking for the one you killed?”

“I’m sure they will, but when they find his body, I don’t think that they’ll head this way. It’s too risky because they’d pass so close to Fort Lincoln. They may be shorthanded, but it’s still a big risk for no gain. I’m just glad that there aren’t a lot of settlers west of here yet. I’ll ride out to Mandan later this week to make sure they’re safe.”

“We’ll see.”

Charlotte had helped Erna change into clean underclothing and put on her nightdress. Erna had been uncomfortable at first, but not because of what had happened to her or even because she was naked. She wasn’t sure how to behave with a woman who owned her own business and was now the wife of the top lawman in the area. She felt almost unworthy of Charlotte’s ministrations.

Charlotte had been talking quietly to Erna since she entered the room but had avoided any difficult topics. She mostly praised Erna’s children and told her that Cap was a good man and would take good care of her and their children.

But as Erna slid beneath the blankets, Charlotte knew that Erna was still concerned about something and knew it wasn’t anything to do with Cap Tyler.

She sat in Cap’s chair and asked, “How can I help you, Erna?”

Erna wasn't quite sure how to express herself in English, but replied, "I am not important. I am a German woman and a farmer's wife."

Charlotte smiled as she said, "You are not unimportant, Erna. Soon you will be Mrs. Tyler, and everyone will admire and respect you. You will become the anchor for Cap's life. Cap loves you and your children very much. When he arrived, you were all he talked about. Even as other women made it clear that they sought his attention, he only thought of you. You have every reason to believe that you are now much more important that you could ever have imagined."

Erna took a few seconds to work through Charlotte's English before she grasped the idea. *Was she really the woman Charlotte had claimed her to be?*

Charlotte waited until Erna slowly replied, "Thank you, Charlotte. I will help Cap as much as possible. I will never be able to pay the debt I owe to him."

Charlotte smiled as she stood and said, "I think that you have already repaid that debt just by coming back with him, Erna. Now get some rest and I'll see you in the morning."

Erna smiled and nodded before Charlotte scooped up her dirty clothes and left the room.

She dropped Erna's clothing in a hamper in the downstairs bathroom then returned to the kitchen. Coop stood when she entered then walked to the coatrack and took down her medium jacket.

Cap stood and asked, “What can I do for her tonight?”

As Charlotte slid her arms though her jacket’s sleeves she replied, “Just let her rest. She seemed to believe that she wasn’t very important, but I hope I changed her mind.”

“Thank you, Charlie. She’s a very special lady.”

“She is. But now that she’s here, you’d better think about arranging for a marriage before the wagging tongues get carried away.”

“I was planning to talk to her about that tomorrow. Thank you for stopping by and helping.”

“You’re welcome. When I get back, I’ll tell Angela that she’ll be running the place for a few days. Luckily, we only have two guests right now.”

Coop had donned his coat and hat and after Charlotte pulled her bonnet onto her head, Cap kissed Charlotte on the cheek, then shook Coop’s hand.

Ten minutes later, after some minor cleanup, he quietly entered Erna’s bedroom and found her sleeping. He added more wood to her heat stove and was pleased that he hadn’t disturbed her before he tiptoed out of the room and closed the door. He hoped that Doctor Bloomberg didn't discover any serious injuries when he did his examination.

The house was still chilly, so he built a big fire in the parlor's enormous brick fireplace that even had an iron housing. With the heat building quickly, he climbed the stairs to the second floor and entered the upstairs bathroom. After lighting a lamp, he pumped the tub half-full of cold water and let it sit while he disrobed. He took a quick bath to wash off the grime before going to his room. He'd move the children and Erna upstairs tomorrow. He had been surprised that Erna hadn't commented on the size of the house yet but doubted if she'd remain silent when she saw the enormous four-poster.

It must have been after ten o'clock when he finally slid beneath the blankets and quilts. He was very grateful for Charlotte and Coop's help and was sure that even after Erna was strong again, Charlotte would be a regular visitor.

CHAPTER 13

Cap almost overslept, but was fortunate, in a manner of speaking, when his overfull bladder reminded him that he needed to exit from the warmth of his bedding unless he wanted to make it moist as well.

He quickly made use of the chamber pot before hurrying into the bathroom to wash and shave. He hadn't heard anyone stirring on the first floor, but that didn't mean they weren't already awake.

After he dressed, he left his room and trotted down the stairs. He was relieved when he peered into each of the downstairs bedroom and found everyone still sleeping. He could understand why they were taking advantage of the soft beds. He then added more wood to the fireplace and then started one in the cookstove. He wasn't sure how early Charlotte would arrive, but suspected she wasn't going to delay her departure from the boarding house.

As Cap prepared for Charlotte's arrival, Hardy was already preparing for a much different welcoming for Sheriff Donavan. He was loading his Winchester under the watchful eyes of

Fred Thomas and John Wickersham. He was still nervous and was trying to hide it from their scrutiny.

He tried to use excessive bravado as his shield as he said, “I probably won’t need more than one shot to put him down. When he’s on the ground, I get his badge and gunbelt and you boys can take his horse and Winchester.”

John looked at Fred and arched his eyebrows before he replied, “I reckon that badge you got ain’t good enough, Hardy. I don’t know why you want another gunbelt unless you wanna look like Tyler. He wears a pair of Remingtons; don’t he?”

“Yeah, but he ain’t here. I’ll deal with him after Donavan’s dead.”

Fred avoided smirking as he said, “We’ll leave him to you, Newton.”

Hardy didn’t notice their derision as he focused on sliding .44s into his repeater’s loading gate. He’d just finished cleaning and oiling the carbine to make sure that it didn’t fail him.

There wasn’t even a real plan. Without realizing it, he would use the same method that Jimmy Baker had tried. He’d set up behind another tent that was closer to the roadway and wait for Sheriff Donavan to pass before backshooting him. He hadn’t been there when Jimmy came face-to-face with Cap’s charging mule, so he didn’t know of Jimmy’s failure because no one had told him. It probably wouldn't have mattered anyway.

By the time Charlotte walked through the back door of Cap's mansion, Hardy had left the big tent and headed for his ambush site. Many of the other men who weren't involved watched him as he passed and knew what he was going to do, but it wasn't their business.

It was just before eight o'clock when Cap kissed Erna goodbye, then waved to Gustave and Elsa as they sat at the kitchen table gouging themselves on butter and honey-laden oatmeal. Doctor Bloomberg would be stopping by soon.

He decided to ride Jed today as Joe and Jasper had done all the work over the past few days while Jed had just carried the Lakota warrior to try to kill him.

He didn't go to the jail but thought he'd have plenty of time to talk to his fellow lawmen after his rounds. He was anxious to talk to the settlers and try to get a read on the resurgence of hostility on the north side of the road.

It was a chilly morning, but the sun was bright in the sky as he rode east wearing his heavy coat and Stetson. He also wore his well-worn gloves to fight the morning chill. Jed was carrying his Winchester '76 in his scabbard and Cap was wearing both Remingtons. Despite Coop's concerns, he wasn't expecting trouble. At least not on the morning rounds. If there was going to be any, it would most likely show its face on the evening rounds.

He soon reached the east end and turned Jed to his right and entered the settlers' camp. He smiled, waved and greeted the folks as he passed and didn't see any signs of fear. When he found Oskar Wentz, he asked him if everything was quiet. Oskar replied that they hadn't been bothered since the fire and thanked him before Cap continued. After making his wide turn, he headed north to the other side of the road.

John and Fred had been standing near the front of their saloon tent watching the road waiting for Sheriff Donavan to arrive.

When they spotted Cap heading into the settler side, Fred snickered then said, "This outta be fun."

John didn't smile but waved to Hardy who was watching them for a signal. After Hardy acknowledged John's warning and turned away from them, John allowed himself a chuckle.

Hardy had been waiting for almost an hour and hadn't brought a canteen with him. His mouth was parched from nervousness, but it was too late to get some water now. He cocked his Winchester's hammer and waited for Sheriff Donavan to pass. He kept telling himself that it would be an easy shot and it was no different than taking down a buck deer.

John kept his eyes on Cap as he crossed the road and headed straight for them, but Fred couldn't resist watching Hardy.

After entering the disorganized compound, Cap didn't pull his Winchester or even unbutton his coat or remove his gloves. He didn't see any indication of danger as he walked Jed closer to the charred rubble at the north end. But then he felt a tingle at the back of his neck when he realized that most of the residents were out of sight. He still didn't pull his Winchester but focused on the only men who were still visible. The two who were standing before the large tent.

As Jed stepped closer, Cap noticed that only one of them was looking back at him and the other was looking to his right. He glanced in that direction, didn't see anyone and suspected that there was a shooter behind the next tent. The question was, *how would he handle it?*

He quickly turned Jed to his right and walked him between the two tents and circled around the back of the one that was probably hiding the assassin. He quickly yanked off his gloves then pulled his Winchester and cocked the hammer just before he spotted Hardy.

Hardy had been concentrating so closely on the expected arrival of Sheriff Donavan that he'd paid no attention to the sound of Jed's hooves. The presence of the nearby corral had also helped to mask Cap's approach.

When Cap recognized Hardy, he lowered his Winchester's muzzle to the ground before he pulled Jed to a stop just ten feet behind him.

"Morning, Hardy. Planning to shoot somebody?"

Hardy was more than just startled to hear Cap's clear voice and forgot he had a cocked Winchester in his hands. He whipped around and as he did, his index finger yanked back the trigger. The Winchester fired, sending its .44 through the canvas roof of the nearby tent as he shook, knowing that he was about to die.

Cap had been momentarily startled when Hardy had fired, but his Winchester's muzzle hadn't been close to pointing in his direction. He left his repeater pointing at the ground knowing that he had more than enough time to shoot Hardy if he was foolish enough to cycle his Winchester. Before he said another word, Cap glanced at the two characters who were still watching. Their arms were folded, so they weren't a threat. He'd deal with them later. Now he had to have a chat with Hardy Newton.

He didn't move Jed any closer as he said, "You need to drop that Winchester, Hardy."

Hardy didn't argue as he opened his hand and let the repeater drop to the ground.

"Can I guess that those two boys over near the big tent knew what you were going to do?"

Hardy thought he was helping his case when he replied, "I didn't know you were back, Cap. I thought Coop would be making the rounds."

Cap was stunned by his bizarre apology and said, "Drop your gunbelt, Hardy."

Hardy quickly unbuckled his gunbelt and let it fall before Cap dismounted then said, "Step back ten feet."

Again, Hardy quickly complied as Cap snatched the gunbelt and Winchester from the ground. He kept his eyes on the two men who were still just watching the show with their arms folded as they seemed to believe they were immune from prosecution.

After sliding Hardy's Winchester behind Jed's saddle, he dropped his gunbelt into his left saddlebag before walking back to Hardy.

"Let's go talk to your friends," Cap said then waited for Hardy to start moving.

As he got into step leaving a six-foot gap between them, Jed slowly walked behind him. He didn't release his Winchester's hammer in case either of the two tried to resist arrest. He doubted if they would.

But when he began crossing the trash-strewn ground, Cap noticed that some of the other men were emerging from their tents and shacks. They all seemed more curious than dangerous, and he thought this might turn out to be his best chance at ending the difficulties created by the hard men once and for all.

He stopped ten feet in front of the two onlookers and asked, "What are your names?"

John replied, "I'm John Wickersham and this is Fred Thomas. I see you got your man, Deputy. Are you gonna hang him for tryin' to backshoot you?"

"That's not my call. What I want each of you to do is to use your left hands to unbuckle your gunbelts and let them drop to the ground. If you notice, my Winchester's hammer is already back and if you decide that you want to risk trying a shot, I'll put a .45 through your chest before you touch your grips."

"*Why would you want us to do that?*" Fred exclaimed.

"Because I'm arresting both of you as accessories for attempted murder."

John loudly protested, "We didn't do nothin!"

"That's not much of a defense. You both watched with your arms folded while Hardy prepared to shoot me. Even if you didn't help him set it up, you failed to stop him. Just drop your gunbelts and we'll see what the county prosecutor decides."

John glanced at Fred but neither dared to challenge Cap as they unbuckled their gunbelts and let them drop.

After he had them step away and stand with Hardy, he picked up their gunbelts and stepped back to Jed where he put their gunbelts into his saddlebags before mounting.

Before he marched them back to the road, he looked at the gathering crowd of men. It was time to issue his final warning.

He shouted, “This is the last time I want any trouble from anyone in this camp. Most of you boys are waiting for the Northern Pacific to start laying track again. I know you’ve had a rough go of it and want to just earn a living. I used to work for them before they failed, and I know many of their senior officers. If you ever hope to land a job in the spring, clean this place and start behaving like men. The railroad doesn’t like troublemakers any more than I do.”

He saw many nods, but no one replied before he looked down at his three prisoners and said, “Let’s start walking, boys.”

Fred Thomas, John Wickersham and Hardy Newton began stepping south toward the roadway with Cap riding Jed a few feet behind. He released his Winchester’s hammer and slid it home but continued to scan the watching faces for any signs of danger. By the time they reached the road and turned west, Cap was reasonably sure that his message had finally been heard.

It took another twenty minutes before he dismounted and opened the door to the jail to let his three prisoners enter. As he followed them inside, he noticed the shocked expressions on his boss and fellow deputies.

Without explanation, he guided the three men into the nearest cell and closed the door.

"*What the hell happened? What is Hardy doing here?*" the sheriff asked loudly.

Cap removed his hat, hung it on a peg and replied, "Hardy must have come back thinking he could be the new boss of the nasty tent town and was planning to ambush you, Coop."

He hung his coat as the sheriff exclaimed, "*That bastard was going to backshoot me?*"

"I'm not sure he would have been able to do it, but that was the plan. Those other two, Fred Thomas and John Wickersham helped him set up and just watched. I reckon it was just a show for both of them. I'm still not that familiar with the law, so I'll let you and Mister Johnson figure out the charges."

"You're damned straight I will," Coop growled before he turned to glare at his prisoners.

Cap then sat down to write his report for the prosecutor while he continued to explain what had happened to his boss, John and Al.

When he finished, Coop snatched his report from the desk then pulled on his hat and hurried out the door to talk to Harold Johnson, the county prosecutor. In his rush, he didn't even bother donning his coat.

After their boss made his explosive exit, Cap stood and unlocked the cell before he said, "Hardy, I think you'll be better off in the other cell by yourself."

Hardy needed no encouragement and hurried out of the first cell and grasped a bar to swing into the neighboring cell before Cap closed both doors and returned to the desk.

John glanced at the prisoners and asked, "Where are their guns, Cap?"

"I've got their gunbelts in my saddlebags and Hardy's Winchester stuck behind my saddle."

Al quickly said, "I'll go get 'em," then hurried out of the office.

John then asked, "Do you reckon they'll hang, Cap? I imagine the boss is asking Mister Johnson that question right about now."

"I don't think it reaches that level, John. But I'm still learning the law. Do we even have a territorial prison?"

"Nope. Not yet. I hear that they're talking about building one, but right now we send our prisoners down to Nebraska Territory on a steamboat."

As they were talking, their three prisoners were paying rapt attention. At least Hardy expected to be sent to prison. It was John's casual reference to hanging that surprised him. Meanwhile, his erstwhile partners were almost stunned by the discussion in general. Until they had heard the deputies, they had still believed that they'd walk out of jail and head back to their tent with their gunbelts at their waists.

Cap replied, "That seems like a waste of the county's money. When is the next boat heading south?"

"Not for another week or so. The schedule is posted at the docks. It's good timing, though. A trial, a twenty-five-year sentence and off they go."

"I assume one of us has to escort them down to Nebraska Territory. Is the prison on the Missouri?"

"Nope. You have to get off the boat at Omaha and if you're lucky, the prison will send some guards from Lincoln, that's about fifty miles west of there."

"I've been there a while ago. Then the escort has to wait for another boat heading north."

"Unless there isn't one for a while. Then you can take a Union Pacific train east and north then hook up the Minnesota

Pacific trains that have been using the Northern Pacific's rails while they were sorting out their money problems. The only time I had to take anybody down there, it took me two weeks."

Cap nodded and even though he suspected that Coop would send John or Al as an escort, he thought it was still a waste of time and money. Hardy was as ineffective as a man as he was as a deputy and the other two would never rise above the level of troublemakers and instigators.

Al soon returned with their weapons, placed Hardy's Winchester on their gunrack, then pulled open the large drawer underneath and dropped in their gunbelts.

"They're alright, but I wouldn't trust those pistols without a good cleaning," Al said as he pulled up a chair.

They continued to chat about the future of their prisoners without any input from the men in the cages until Sheriff Donavan entered the room.

He hung his hat and beckoned for Cap to follow as he passed by the cells heading for his small office.

After Cap entered, Coop said, "Close the door, Cap."

"Yes, sir," he replied before he pulled it shut then took a seat.

"What did Mister Johnson recommend?"

"He said he'd like to hang them, but he'll charge them with conspiracy to commit murder which carries a maximum twenty-year sentence. But he said to ask you what you wanted him to do because you were the one who almost took a bullet in the back."

"I've been thinking about that. John explained the process and it sounds like a waste of time and money to prosecute those idiots and then take them five hundred miles downriver just to let them take more of the taxpayers' money for a couple of decades."

Coop arched his eyebrows as he asked, "You want to let 'em off?"

"Kind of. I think it'll be a lot easier if we just give them until sundown to get out of town or we'll arrest them again. We won't give them back their guns, but I'm sure that they all have horses back in their camp. I'll even follow them if you want. Personally, I think they've worn out their welcome back there anyway."

"Do you really think they'll skedaddle?"

"Pretty sure. You had to see Hardy's face when I found him with that Winchester, Coop. He was terrified. I don't think he's ever fired a gun at anyone before. The other two impress me as being nothing but hot air. What do you think?"

"It's alright by me. At least we won't have to feed those bastards. Do you want to tell 'em?"

Cap grinned as he replied, “Sure. It’ll be a pleasure.”

After opening the door, Cap left the office and Sheriff Donavan followed Cap to the cells. He’d watch the three prisoners’ reactions to the offer. He wanted to believe that Cap was right.

The reason Cap felt confident in his decision was based on his poker skills. He was almost able to read each of the men’s thoughts when he’d first confronted them. He would have been surprised if they weren’t ten miles out of town by sunset. He assumed that they’d head east toward Jamestown rather than risk bumping into the Lakota. He suspected that the Sioux wouldn’t be happy when they found their dead warrior.

John and Al watched from the front desk as Cap faced the prisoners and said, “Boys, I feel generous this morning. The sheriff and the county prosecutor both want to send you to the Nebraska Territorial Prison for a couple of decades. Personally, I don’t think any of you are worth the expense, so I’m going to give you until sundown to get out of Bismarck. If we ever see your faces again, we’ll toss you right back into those cells and you’ll soon be heading south to spend the next twenty years behind bars. It’s your choice.”

There were thirty seconds of silence before Fred Thomas asked, “What about our guns?”

“I’m not about to give you another chance to shoot me in the back. You can get out of town without firearms or face a trial tomorrow. I don't reckon that any of you have much of a chance of walking out of that courtroom a free man; do you?"

Fred and John went into a whispered conference while Hardy just sat staring at the bars. Cap knew he'd already made up his mind and it wasn't to face an angry jury.

Fred finally asked, "We get to keep our horses and the rest of our gear?"

"I don't care if you steal everything in that place as long as you're gone. But if any of you set one toe onto the settler side of the road, you'll lose the whole foot because I'll be watching."

"Alright. Let us outta here," Fred unhappily replied.

Cap yanked the key ring from the peg and unlocked Hardy's cell.

As he shuffled past, Cap said, "I'm giving you a ten-minute head start, Hardy. Make good use of it."

Hardy didn't even look at anyone, but his step became much livelier as he hurried to the door and quickly left the jail.

Cap didn't have to explain his reason for giving Hardy a lead to the sheriff or the other deputies. He was sure that they understood that Hardy was in greater danger from the two men who still sat in their cell than anyone else in Bismarck. But just to be sure that Hardy didn't try to take Jed, Cap headed to the window and looked outside. Once he saw Hardy trotting toward Main Avenue, he returned to the front desk.

He looked at the sheriff and said, "I'll follow the other two back to the camp and if it's okay with you, boss, I'll head home for lunch and see how Erna is doing."

"I'm surprised that you didn't just toss them in jail and hurry over there. I know that Charlotte was anxious to help her as much as possible."

Cap nodded then leaned on the desk and glanced at the wall clock. It was already 11:25, so he wasn't going to be that early when he returned to the house. He wouldn't be surprised to find Erna in a much better frame of mind when he returned and was anxious to hear Doctor Bloomberg's diagnosis.

Thirty minutes later, he sat on Jed in the middle of the road and watched Fred Thomas and John Wickersham hurry into their big tent. They'd walked as fast as they could to reach the sordid settlement and hadn't said a word. Once they entered their tent, though, he heard a loud litany of cursing, but it wasn't just from John and Fred. He assumed that after they'd been arrested, other men had invaded their temporary saloon and made off with much of their property. The scroungers must have waited long enough to be sure that they wouldn't return, or the owners would have found an empty tent.

Cap smiled as some men rushed out of the tent still clutching their booty but after another minute, it was Fred and John who made a hasty exit. Their arms were full of their clothes and some other personal property, but not much. They carried them to the corral where they saddled their horses.

When they left the camp, they didn't ride directly toward Cap, but headed east before turning onto the road. They never looked back as they trotted away. They had a long ride ahead and had no protection.

He hadn't seen Hardy leave, but was sure he was gone, so once the other two were a couple of miles away, Cap wheeled Jed around and headed west.

As Cap was riding back into town, fifty-two miles west, Tall Horse had two of his warriors pick up Burning Light's body from the ground and place it over the spare horse they'd brought with him. Standing Buffalo had instructed him what to do if they found the war chief's body, but Tall Horse couldn't see any signs of the Mule Killer. He saw the wagon wheel tracks heading east and was sure that the Mule Killer had repossessed his odd-looking mule before he returned to the big town. He wasn't about to risk any men to follow. He knew about the expected arrival of more bluecoats and the railroad. They would need every warrior for the battles to come. He thought that Burning Light's mission was nothing but foolish vanity.

After the war chief's body was lashed down, he ordered his band to ride back to their village. He would be the new war chief and would be much wiser in the use of his men.

Before he went home, Cap made a quick stop at Michelson's and picked up a nicer, ivory-handled pocket knife with a four-inch blade. He didn't think that Erna would object.

With the replacement gift in his pocket, Cap headed to the house and soon pulled up near the back porch and dismounted. He tied Jed at one of the three fancy hitching posts before hopping up the stairs and crossing his polished porch floor.

He was removing his hat as he entered the kitchen and almost forgot about hanging it when he found Erna sitting at the table with Charlotte and smiling at him. Not only was she out of bed; it was obvious that she'd bathed, shampooed her hair and was even wearing one of the hair ribbons he'd given to Elsa.

He slowly hung his hat on the coat rack as he stared at Erna.

She said, "Welcome home, Cap."

Cap recovered from the surprise and noted that when she spoke English, she actually said welcome with a 'w' and not a 'v'. He assumed that Charlotte had somehow managed to help her make the transition.

He said, "You look very pretty this morning, Erna."

"Thank you very much. The doctor said I was doing very well. After he left, Charlotte helped me bathe and I feel much better. I even walked without help."

Cap glanced at Charlotte who was just grinning like she was holding a royal flush before he walked to the table and took a seat across from Erna. As far as Cap was concerned, Charlotte had earned the privilege.

He had been so entranced by Erna's transformation that he had missed Gustave and Elsa who were playing checkers at the other end of the long table.

That changed when Gustave said, "Mama is almost herself again."

When Cap turned to look at the children, he remembered the pocket knife. So, he pulled it from his pocket and set it on the table near Gustave.

"This is to replace the smaller one."

The boy's eyes popped into round blue circles as he carefully picked up the knife.

As he rotated it in his hand, he said, "Thank you, Mister Tyler. It's much nicer than the other one."

Cap rubbed his head then turned his attention back to Erna.

Before he could say anything, she asked, “Did you have a quiet morning?”

Rather than use his almost decent German, he replied in English when he said, “No, ma’am.”

Then he asked, “Do you want me to explain in English?”

She nodded, so Cap smiled and slowly said, “When I went to the bad men’s camp, the man who Coop hired as a deputy was waiting with a Winchester.”

Charlotte snapped, “*That bastard was going to drygulch you?*”

Cap shook his head before replying, “No, Charlie. He thought that Coop was going to do rounds this morning. Two other troublemakers must have nudged him into the attempt, but I saw one of them looking in Hardy’s direction. I didn’t know who was there but rode around the tent he was hiding behind and found Hardy with his Winchester cocked.”

Charlotte flushed into a deep red and was almost apoplectic as she shook and asked, “He…he was going to shoot Coop?”

“He may have planned to, but I don’t think he would have pulled the trigger. I didn’t even have to point my Winchester at him to make him drop his repeater and gunbelt. Then I marched him to his two new friends and I disarmed them as well. They figured they were safe because it was Hardy who was holding the cocked Winchester. After I walked them back to the jail and locked them up, I think Coop could have fried them all with the fire from his eyes."

Charlotte more calmly asked, "Are they going to hang?"

"No, ma'am. At best, they'd get twenty years, but after talking to Coop, I decided to just kick them out of town."

Charlotte exclaimed, "*You let them go?*"

"When you talk to Coop about it, you'll understand. I doubt if we'll see any of them again. They left town without any weapons."

He then looked at Erna and asked, "Did you understand what I told Charlotte?"

"Most of it. I am getting better with English."

Charlotte would definitely be talking to her husband when she returned, but thought it was time to bring up the subject she had expected to be the primary topic when Cap stopped by for lunch.

She looked at Erna and said, "You can ask him now."

Erna nodded then took Cap's hands and asked, "When can we be married?"

"Whenever you wish, Erna. Where do you want to have the ceremony?"

"Can we have it here tomorrow afternoon? Charlotte said that Reverend Walther would be pleased to come. She and Coop can be our witnesses. Is that alright?"

He smiled as he replied, "Of course, it is. Will he be coming by earlier so we can talk?"

Erna looked at Charlotte who said, "He'll be stopping by at three o'clock."

Cap chuckled then said, "I guess what I thought didn't matter anyway, but I won't object. Does Coop need to be here?"

Charlotte said, "I'll tell him in a little while after he explains why you both thought letting those three assassins leave town without any punishment was a good idea."

"There's no point in my returning to the jail then. Has everyone already eaten lunch?"

"We have, but I saved yours in the oven. I'll take it out and then I'll head to the jail and chat with my sheriff husband."

As Charlotte left the table, Cap looked at Erna and asked, "Have you explored the house now that you can walk?"

"No. I didn't trust myself to walk up the stairs. I was already surprised by the kitchen and the bathroom. It is much bigger than you said."

"Coop warned me before I saw it and I was still shocked. When you feel stronger, I'll help you up the stairs."

Erna glanced at Charlotte before she quietly said, "I don't know if I'm ready for the big bed."

"I wasn't worried about it, Erna. But it is almost scary all by itself."

Charlotte set his plate of warmed pork roast and boiled potatoes before him with utensils and a cup of coffee before she turned and pulled on her hat and coat.

"We'll see you in a couple of hours," she said before exiting through the back door.

Cap was surprised at the menu and said, "This looks good. When did she have time to make this?"

"She heated water for my bath and roasted the pork and cooked the potatoes at the same time."

Cap began eating his lunch but kept glancing back at Erna who seemed even younger than her twenty-two years. She was small but so perfectly formed and handsome. It was only now that he suddenly found her so desirable and was almost embarrassed when he realized the impact that she had on him.

Erna noticed the distracted look on his face and asked, “Is there something wrong, Cap?”

He smiled as he answered, “No, Erna. I’m just so happy to find you sitting there.”

For a few seconds, the only sound at the table came when Gustave executed a loud triple jump followed by Elsa’s louder sigh.

Erna then asked, “Are you sure the bad men are gone?”

“Yes, I watched them leave.”

He returned to eating and managed to keep his eyes on his food rather than taking surreptitious looks at Erna. He was almost angry with himself for thinking that way about her.

He quickly finished his lunch and risked smiling at Erna before he stood and carried his empty plate and dirty cutlery to the sink.

When he returned to the table, he picked up his cup of coffee and asked, “When did you start walking?”

“Charlotte helped me out of bed but after I reached the hall, I was able to walk to the bathroom. She helped me in and out of the tub, but I have not needed help after that.”

Cap smiled and lost his ability to speak as Erna smiled at him. *What was wrong with him?* He'd seen her almost naked when he'd cleaned her and hadn't been affected at all. He didn't know if it was because of their impending marriage coupled with their likely inability to consummate the marriage for a while. But whatever the reason, he found it extremely difficult to avoid letting his eyes follow her womanly curves.

Erna hadn't fully accepted his first excuse for his distraction and as she smiled at him, she noticed his eyes drifting down then popping back up to look at her face. It soon became obvious what the real reason for his distraction was. She just didn't understand why he was suddenly paying attention to her as a woman and not an injured puppy.

She took his large, calloused hand and said, "It's alright, Cap."

He blinked then asked, "What's alright?"

"It's alright that you want me as your woman. I've wanted you as my man long ago. I actually like it when you admire me as you do now. There were times when I wondered if you would ever see me as a woman."

"I don't know why it suddenly became so obvious. I've always thought of you as a handsome woman with a wonderful figure. But now…well, now I am almost overwhelmed."

She smiled as she whispered, "Soon, Cap. Soon."

He took in a deep breath then pulled her hand to his lips and softly kissed her fingers.

Erna was taken by surprise when she felt a chill slide down her back. It was such a simple gesture, yet it stirred her much more than she had anticipated. As Cap lowered their hands to the table, Erna wondered how she would be able to know when she was fully healed.

It was Elsa who broke the spell when she shouted, “You can’t do that, Goose!”

Erna and Cap both turned to look at the checkerboard end of the table and saw what had driven Elsa’s complaint. Gustave had crowned one of his black pieces with one of her red ones. While Elsa may have been offended, Gustave seemed immensely pleased with his construct which now sat on Elsa’s end of the board.

Elsa pointed at the offending pair of checkers as she looked at Cap and asked, “Can he do that, Papa?”

Cap was about to answer when he realized that Elsa had addressed him as ‘papa’. Gustave had called him Mister Tyler just minutes ago when he’d given him the pocket knife, so he assumed that Elsa had decided on her own that he was her father now.

He didn’t comment as he said, “No, he should use his own black pieces. When he did that, he accidentally made his black king your red king. So, now the odd one is yours to move.”

Cap had just made up the rule, but his answer made Elsa break into a big grin before she turned and stuck her tongue out at Gustave.

Gustave didn't seem to care as he was still in control of the board even after Elsa used her new king to jump one of his pieces.

While Erna watched Elsa use her traitorous king to jump Gustave's unsuspecting piece, Cap looked at her left hand and was almost relieved that she wasn't wearing a wedding band. He didn't see any indication that she'd worn one at all, so he'd pay a visit to Kitsch's Jewelry tomorrow morning.

———

Four hours later, Cap and Erna waved to Reverent Paul Walther, Coop and Charlotte as they stepped down the front porch steps. After he closed the door, Cap walked with Erna back to the large, brocaded couch and sat down beside her. The children had become bored with the meeting and had spent most of the time in the kitchen playing poker or checkers.

Erna sat closer than Cap thought safe, but he didn't complain.

She said, "When you went outside to put your mule away, Gustave asked me if he could call you papa, too. I told him that you were his papa now. Is that alright?"

He smiled as he replied, “I was surprised but very happy when Elsa called me papa.”

“They love you very much, Cap. As does their mother.”

“You know that I love them and you, Erna. I was also very happy to hear the doctor told you that you were doing well.”

She quietly said, “I asked him if I could be your wife tomorrow night and he said there was no reason for us not to be together.”

Cap knew she hadn’t invented the doctor’s response, but he wasn’t sure that she was ready yet. She’d only started walking this morning and even told him she wasn’t sure that she was ready for the big bed. She had surprised him with her quickly improving gait since he’d returned, but he still wasn’t convinced she her healing had progressed enough.

“We’ll see how you feel tomorrow.”

Erna nodded then slid her fingertips across the brocade as she said, “I still find this house to be far grander than I could ever have imagined. Maybe you can show me the giant bed tomorrow.”

Cap was surprised that she had already revisited the topic but replied, “We’ll see.”

The reason Erna had told him of Doctor Bloomberg’s answer was because she desperately wanted to be his wife in every way possible but when Cap had returned, she still wasn't sure. That changed when he kissed her fingers and she wanted to let him know.

Well beyond her need to give back what little she could to the man who had given her everything, she admitted to her swelling desire to experience true lovemaking. His few kisses had already inspired her, and she wanted to release her own flood of passion. She now honestly believed that she was strong enough already and was sure that Cap would still be gentle, despite his obvious desires for her. She would have asked him to show her the big bed tonight but thought it would be better to wait until after they were married. Cap was not another Franz Hartmann.

She finally smiled and asked, "Will you kiss me again now?"

He slid closer, lifted her chin with his left index finger and kissed her. Erna was expecting another jolt of desire when he did, but her recent thoughts of the promise of tomorrow night made the kiss even more thrilling. She didn't want it to end but knew it must.

When Cap leaned back, she whispered, "Please, Cap. Tomorrow, will you take me to the big bed?"

Cap may still have doubts, but the kiss had only allowed him to reply, "Yes, Erna."

Erna smiled as she said, "It will make me happy."

Their romantic moments were interrupted, as usual, by the children when Gustave shouted, "You won, Elsa!"

It was immediately followed by Elsa's high-pitched laugh before they heard the rush of her light footsteps coming down the hallway. She still had her doll hugged tightly when she burst into the parlor and hurried to the couch. Gustave entered the room just as his sister reached their mother and new father.

"I beat Goose in checkers!" she gushed as she bounced before them.

Erna smiled, then glanced at her older brother, suspecting that he may have let her win, but noticed he wasn't smiling. She must have actually beaten him.

She plucked Elsa from the floor and sat her on the couch on her right side because there wasn't enough room between her and Cap.

Elsa was grinning at her defeated brother as Cap said, "It's alright, Gustave. We all lose sometimes. I lost quite a few of those poker games but still left Deadwood with a lot of money."

Gustave didn't seem mollified, so Cap said, "Now that you're going to be my son and will be going to school next September, maybe I should call you Gus instead of Gustave."

Gustave glanced at his mother before he looked back at Cap and asked, "Why?"

"Well, I've known a few men named Gus, but never any named Gustave before. Gus sounds more American. So, if you go to school and say your name is Gus, the other boys will be more likely to accept you."

"They will?"

"Sure. You can even tell them that your father is the famous Mule Killer. When they hear that, they'll all want to be your friend just to hear the stories."

Gustave grinned and quickly asked, "Will you tell me all the stories, so I can repeat them? I know that I will be proud to be your son."

"I will tell you the stories with all their terrible details. But remember that you mustn't take pride in what I did. You must work hard in school and then when you become a man, you can be proud of your own accomplishments."

Gustave wasn't sure he understood, but knew he'd be spending a lot of time with his new father and would learn every day. He wanted to be a good man just like him.

He nodded then turned to Elsa and asked, "Do you want to play again, Elsa?"

Elsa nodded, then slid down from the couch took her brother's hand and said, "Okay. I should call you Gus now and not Goose."

Gustave smiled at Cap and his mother before he and Elsa left the parlor to return to the kitchen.

Erna said, "I've never seen them so happy, Cap. It's not just because of what you have given to them or because they are living in such a grand house. It is because they know that you love them as much as I do. You give them hugs and kisses and make them laugh. But you also give them a future that they could not have had before."

"I only will give them an opportunity to have a good future, Erna. What they make of that chance is still theirs as it is for each of us. You did all you could to give them that chance, but the world doesn't let women choose very much. Maybe it will one day."

Erna laughed lightly then said, "We are becoming too serious, Cap. We are getting married tomorrow. Perhaps we should just enjoy ourselves."

Cap smiled as he said, "We can do that, but before we start telling funny stories, I have to tell you that tomorrow morning, I still need to make my rounds on the east side. I'm sure it will be quiet, but I must be sure. After that, even John or Al can ride through the camps."

Erna briefly considered protesting, but immediately decided it would be pointless anyway. She had to accept that Cap would always try to protect people, or he wouldn't be himself.

"Alright. You won't be wearing a suit when you ride there; will you?"

Cap chuckled then replied, "No, ma'am. I don't even own one. I'm not about to buy one for our wedding, either. I'll be clean but that's all I can promise."

"That's alright. I'm just wearing one of the nice dresses that you bought for me. I just washed it before he ran away."

"Speaking of washing, I've been using the Chinese laundry on Third Street to get my clothes cleaned. We'll continue to use them now that you're here. I don't want to hear you say that it's a waste of money, either."

Erna's eyes grew into discs as she said, "I wouldn't dare to complain about such a blessing. I thought this house was beyond belief, but not having to do laundry is much more exotic."

Cap was smiling as she asked, "Is exotic a good word?"

"It is very good. Your English is improving very quickly. You still drop in a few German words now and then, but by springtime, you, Gus and Elsa will be speaking the language like a native."

"But I will still have an accent; won't I?"

"Yes, but it won't be as bad as some I've heard. I've met men from Boston and New York that had accents that were so bad that they may as well have come from the moon. Then there were the boys from the Deep South that used words I never could fathom."

Erna laughed at the idea that those born in one part of the United States spoke so differently than those who grew up in another locale. She thought that Cap was just joking to make her feel better. When she'd landed in Baltimore, she could barely speak English at all and hadn't noticed any variations as they headed west. It would be a while before she realized that he hadn't exaggerated at all.

He then said, "Let's return to the kitchen and I'll start cooking supper."

"I can do that," she protested.

"No, Erna. You must reserve your strength as much as possible for tomorrow."

She giggled as Cap stood then took her hand. She rose from the couch and they slowly left the parlor.

———

Cap was under his quilts in the same second-floor bedroom he used since he arrived. Erna and the children were both downstairs in their bedrooms and should already be asleep.

As he looked through the open door to the room across the hall, he wondered if he should really share the big four-poster with Erna tomorrow night. She certainly seemed eager, and her recovery had been nothing short of miraculous. But he harbored a deep suspicion that she was just putting on a show for his benefit. She had said often that she could never repay him for all he'd done for her and their children, and he hoped that her offer wasn't simply a form of payment in service of that debt. One that he never considered to exist.

He closed his eyes and thought he'd get a better idea tomorrow. She would be busy all morning. Of course, so would he. He had shopping to do after his rounds.

———

Not surprisingly, Charlotte arrived early the next morning while Cap was in the kitchen preparing breakfast. She ordered him away from the cookstove even as she was removing her hat.

An hour later, he was riding Jasper away from the house to make his morning rounds. Charlotte had passed along her husband's orders that he was not to show his face in the office for two days. She didn't object to his departure when he secretively explained why he needed to make his rounds.

When he reached the settler side of the east end, everyone seemed pleased to see him and those he spoke to said that everything had been very quiet.

He still had his Winchester in his hands as he crossed the road but hadn't cocked the hammer. As Jasper stepped along the path, Cap was astonished by some of the noticeable changes. Much of the trash was gone and what was almost shocking was that as he passed, most of the men nodded in his direction. Some even tipped their hats. No one smiled or greeted him warmly, but the simple nods were much appreciated. When he turned Jasper at the charred remains of the saloon, he slid his Winchester home.

On the return ride, he stopped at J.M Katz Confectionary and made several purchases that didn't require any artistry. He did need to buy a basket for the large order. After waving goodbye to Johann, he mounted Jasper to make the stop at Kitsch's Jewelry for the wedding bands.

He carried the basket with him when he entered the small shop rather than risk losing it to some sweet-toothed thief.

Ten minutes later, with the small box with the wedding rings in his heavy coat's pocket, he rode Jasper back to the house which was quickly becoming his home now that he had his family with him.

When he entered the kitchen with the basket, the newly christened Gus and Elsa bounced from their chairs and hurried towards him.

"What did you bring, Papa?" asked Elsa.

"I'll show you in a little while. You can have some now, but most will be saved until after your mama and I are married. Okay?"

The children both nodded vigorously as they stared at the mystery basket. Their small noses could already detect deliciousness inside.

Erna and Charlotte were in the parlor putting finishing touches on the room in preparation for the ceremony as Cap set the basket on the table then removed his hat and coat. He hung his Remingtons on their assigned hooks then looked at his expectant children.

"I want both of you to sit down at the table. I have to be careful when I take these out of the basket."

In concert, they exclaimed, "Okay, Papa!" then hurried back to the table where Gus helped Elsa onto her chair before taking his seat.

Their blue eyes were boring into the basket as Cap removed the covering red and white checkered cloth. He then lifted a long, flat butcher-wrapped item from the basket. After carefully laying it on the maple counter, he reached into the magic basket and removed another identical surprise. He did it twice more before he returned the covering cloth to the basket and set it aside.

Their focus lost none if its intensity as he peeled the butcher paper away from the first mystery treat.

Gus glanced at Elsa before he asked, “What is it, Papa?”

Cap grinned as he opened a drawer and pulled out a steak knife and a fork. He then sliced a piece off the end and cut it in half before setting the utensils down.

He picked up the two pieces and carried them to the table. Before he gave them to his anxious children, he showed them the pastry.

Then he said, “This is part of your heritage. It’s called a strudel. This one has cherries inside.”

Neither of the youngsters spoke as their small hands took possession of the strudel. Five seconds later, their fingers were empty, and their faces were full of childish joy.

It was Elsa who spoke first when she quickly asked, “Can we have more, Papa?”

“Just a little. We must save some for your mama and Aunt Charlotte. Okay?”

They both nodded as Cap pulled down two saucers and then sliced off two larger strips of the cherry strudel. He had another cherry and two apple strudels still under wraps. He also had more surprises in the basket.

As he set the plates before Gus and Elsa, Cap heard Erna and Charlotte's footsteps coming down the long hallway.

When they entered the kitchen, Erna looked at the children devouring the strudel then shifted her eyes to the counter and saw the others.

"You bought strudel!" she exclaimed.

Cap winked at Charlotte before replying, "Yes, ma'am. I bought two cherry strudels and two apple strudels. Most are for our guests after the wedding, but I knew that I couldn't avoid giving our children a taste."

"But you felt you could deny your future wife?"

Charlotte laughed as she stepped to the counter and began taking down more saucers.

Cap guided Erna to the table where he pulled back a chair and waited for her to sit down.

After she was sitting, he replied, "I suppose I could let you and Charlotte have a small piece."

Erna smiled as she looked up at him. There was cherry strudel sitting on the counter just a few feet away. She would have thanked God for a single cracker just a few days earlier.

Cap then turned and filled three cups with the reasonably fresh coffee then joined his family and Charlotte at the table. He had never had strudel before but when he'd stopped in the shop the first time, he knew he had to try it. When Johann Katz had explained its origin, he hoped that he'd be buying some to share with Erna, Gustave and Elsa exactly as he was doing now.

After she finished her strudel and coffee, Charlotte had to return to her boarding house to prepare for the afternoon's ceremony. She and Coop would be their witnesses, and the only guests would be the two youngsters at the table. Erna had asked her if it would be alright because she didn't want to stay on her feet too long, which would be more necessary if they had more guests. Charlotte had told her that it was perfectly understandable and hadn't even joked about not having to stay on her feet very long for a different reason. She knew that Erna wasn't quite as strong as she pretended to be.

———

But when the ceremony began in the middle of the afternoon, Erna looked as if she had never had any difficulties at all, much less the horror she'd faced in the past two and a half months.

As Cap stood beside her and faced Reverend Walther, he was prepared to catch her if she suddenly wobbled, but that never happened.

The big surprise was when he pulled the small box from his pocket and let her see the wedding rings. Erna was close to tears when he slid the small gold band over her finger and almost dropped his much larger ring as she tried to push it onto his. But she didn't and soon the minister pronounced them husband and wife and they shared a brief but memorable kiss.

After handshakes and kisses were exchanged, they adjourned to the dining room where they found the strudel and a large pot of coffee. Cap had placed another sweet surprise before each of the plates…a chocolate bar. But while most of the plates were empty, awaiting a slice of strudel, three of them already held a large peppermint stick.

Reverend Walther had no idea of their significance but didn't ask as he sat at the head of the table. Charlotte and Coop both understood, so there was no reason to mention them.

When Erna saw the peppermint sticks, she just smiled at Cap and squeezed his hand. It was a perfect wedding gift.

Gus and Elsa simply giggled as they hurried to their seats. But after everyone was sitting and Reverend Walther had said grace, Elsa looked at her new father.

"Papa, where is the angel?"

He smiled at his daughter then looked at Erna and replied, "You've lived with her all your life, Elsa."

That evening, after tucking Gustave and Elsa into the same bed they'd used since they arrived, Erna and then Cap kissed them on their foreheads before Cap blew out the lamp. They left the door open as they returned to the kitchen and sat at the table.

Cap took his bride's hands and said, "You don't have to come with me when I go upstairs, Erna. You must be exhausted after all you've done today."

She smiled as she replied, "I'll admit to being somewhat tired, Cap. But I want to come with you. I need this more than you could possibly understand."

"I don't understand at all, Erna. After all you've been through and when I found you just a few nights ago, I wasn't even sure if you'd live. I'll admit that I'm very surprised by how quickly you've recovered already, but are you sure that you're well enough?"

"The doctor told me it was up to me and I made my decision. I want to be your wife now. Tonight. In our big bed."

Cap felt as if he should have argued more, but his own desires were more than enough to end the discussion. He may not have understood why Erna seemed so adamant but discarded his earlier belief that she was just trying to assuage her feelings of indebtedness.

He stood, took her hand and after she rose, he blew out the lamp.

They slowly passed the children's bedroom, entered the parlor and soon started up the wide staircase. When they turned into the large bedroom, Erna had her first look at the enormous bed and almost giggled. But she was already growing anxious, and any hint of hilarity seemed wildly inappropriate.

She just allowed Cap to guide her to the edge of the bed before she turned and looked up at him.

He expected her to ask him to be gentle, but she didn't. Instead, she began unbuttoning his shirt as she continued to gaze up at him. He would still be gentle but was even more determined to make Erna happy.

Erna had experienced the truest form of lovemaking for the first time and had almost lost consciousness, but not because of her weakened condition. She had reached levels of ecstasy she had never thought possible as Cap had touched, kissed and caressed her much longer and with much more passion than she could have dreamt possible. It was why she wanted this so badly. She desperately wanted to know what it was like to be truly loved. Once she had agreed to return with him, Erna had wondered if she would have this experience, but even then, had been woefully short in her expectations.

As she curled up close to her husband with her blonde hair curled across his chest, she softly asked, “Did I make you as happy as you made me, Cap?”

Cap kissed her damp forehead before he replied, “You did more than just make me happy, Erna. You took my breath away.”

Erna smiled but didn’t say anything more as she listened to his heart beating. She still loved her children dearly but now she was Mrs. Cap Tyler, and her husband was already the new focus in her life.

EPILOGUE

September 2, 1878

Cap opened the back door and let Gus enter then followed and closed the door behind him. As he hung his hat, he smiled when he watched Elsa hurry from her room to see her older brother.

As Gus set his books on the table, Elsa asked, “How was it, Gus?”

He pulled his hat off and replied, “It was kind of scary at first, but then it got a lot better. The other boys knew who I was before Miss Jacobs even called roll because they had seen me with papa.”

As they chatted about Gus’ first day at school, Cap hung his coat on the rack then walked down the hallway. He soon reached the stairway and quickly trotted up the steps to the second floor.

He soon turned into the first bedroom on his right, the one he’d first used when he bought the place. It served a very different purpose now.

Erna was changing two-month-old Max’s diaper when he entered.

So, she only glanced at him and smiled before she asked, “Was Gus excited when you picked him up from school?”

“He practically ran me over when I was ready to put him onto Jasper. From what I was able to decipher from his excited chatter, he discovered that he was actually ahead of most of the other first years. Most of them couldn’t even read yet. He was even happier that the other boys were already very friendly toward him. He even found three boys who were newly arrived from Germany and promised to help them with their lessons.”

“He learned that from his father,” Erna said as she finished securing the diaper with one of the new safety pins

She laid Max in his cradle that they’d move to the large bedroom before they slipped into the big four-poster. After covering him with his soft cotton blanket, she turned and walked to her husband and took his hand.

“I assume Elsa was almost as excited when he returned. She missed having him around all the time.”

“That’s why I’ve been bringing him to the office more lately. I knew she’d be lonely, at least until Max starts running around and she can be the big sister.”

Erna laughed before they left the bedroom and headed back downstairs, so she could talk to Gus.

———

Aside from the noticeable changes in the Tyler family, there had been many more in Bismarck itself over the past year, and most had been good.

The Northern Pacific had begun shipping in equipment in February and even before the snow melted, they began the ground preparation on the other side of the Missouri River. By April, the tracks were already sixty miles west of Bismarck and marching across the Dakota Plains.

The two tent villages were gone, and new buildings were being erected in the location, taking advantage of the influx of more lumber and residents.

Mandan prospered and hired a town marshal, John Wilson. He was replaced by two new hires, Arthur Epstein and Joe Lennon. Neither had lawman experience, so it took a few months before they were settled into the job.

One of the frequent visitors to the town and to the Tyler home was Mac McDermott, who now sported an added chevron on his sleeve. Sergeant McDermott was the NCO in charge of a company now. The new regiment had arrived in April but soon was dispatched to the west where they were building a new fort to fill the gap between Fort Lincoln and Fort Bliss in Montana Territory. But more replacements had arrived to make up for the loss of Company C.

Charlotte had been giving more responsibilities to Angela as her pregnancy progressed and Coop's concerns multiplied.

Cap had even offered to sell the big house back to his boss, but Charlotte refused to give up her boarding house. What they did do was to buy a neighboring house in July when it became available just to give them some privacy.

With a fully staffed law office and a more settled environment, the earlier, tumultuous autumn days of 1877 faded into memory.

No one even remembered Hardy Newton, nor did anyone really care. He was simply never seen nor heard from again.

On the night of the eighth of December, with a nasty blizzard whistling through the town, Charlotte Donavan gave birth to a baby girl. They named her Mary Frances after Coop's mother.

They never returned to visit the Braun farm and let it return to the prairie. If someone wanted to take the land and sod house, then it could become their home. If someone did move in, they would be pleasantly surprised to find the furniture and stacks of canned food along the far wall. Cap hadn't bothered taking much of anything other than what he brought with him when he'd ridden to find Erna and the children that day.

Two of the few items he'd been sure to bring were now protected by a glass frame and hung over the big fireplace in the parlor. They were a pair of crumpled paper sacks. On one was a beautifully drawn image of an angel, while the second displayed what appeared to be a crudely formed raven. But to the family, it was just as meaningful.

CAP TYLER

34. Marsh's Valley 01/01/2018
35. Alex Paine 01/18/2018
36. Ben Gray 02/05/2018
37. War Adams 03/05/2018
38. Mac's Cabin 03/21/2018
39. Will Scott 04/13/2018
40. Sheriff Joe 04/22/2018
41. Chance 05/17/2018
42. Doc Holt 06/17/2018
43. Ted Shepard 07/13/2018
44. Haven 07/30/2018
45. Sam's County 08/15/2018
46. Matt Dunne 09/10/2018
47. Conn Jackson 10/05/2018
48. Gabe Owens 10/27/2018
49. Abandoned 11/19/2018
50. Retribution 12/21/2018
51. Inevitable 02/04/2019
52. Scandal in Topeka 03/18/2019
53. Return to Hardeman County 04/10/2019
54. Deception 06/02/2019
55. The Silver Widows 06/27/2019
56. Hitch 08/21/2019
57. Dylan's Journey 09/10/2019
58. Bryn's War 11/06/2019
59. Huw's Legacy 11/30/2019
60. Lynn's Search 12/22/2019
61. Bethan's Choice 02/10/2020
62. Rhody Jones 03/11/2020
63. Alwen's Dream 06/16/2020
64. The Nothing Man 06/30/2020
65. Cy Page: Western Union Man 07/19/2020
66. Tabby Hayes 08/02/2020

67. Letter for Gene	09/08/2020
68. Dylan's Memories	09/20/2020
69. Grip Taylor	10/07/2020
70. Garrett's Duty	11/09/2020
71. East of the Cascades	12/02/2020
72. The Iron Wolfe	12/23/2020
73. Wade Rivers	01/09/2021
74. Ghost Train	01/26/2021
75. The Inheritance	02/26/2021
76. Cap Tyler	03/29/2021

Made in the USA
Columbia, SC
06 April 2021